DRAGON BONES

RANDOM HOUSE

NEW YORK

DRAGON
BONES

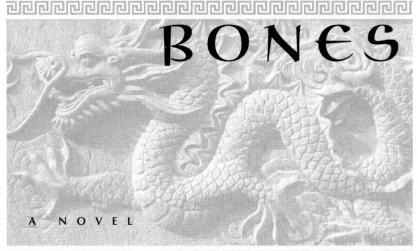

A NOVEL

LISA SEE

Copyright © 2003 by Lisa See

All rights reserved under International and Pan-American
Copyright Conventions. Published in the United States by
Random House, Inc., New York, and simultaneously in
Canada by Random House of Canada Limited, Toronto.

RANDOM HOUSE and colophon are registered trademarks of
Random House, Inc.

Library of Congress Cataloging-in-Publication Data
See, Lisa.
        Dragon bones : a novel / Lisa See.
            p.   cm.
        ISBN 0-679-46320-8
        1. San xia shui li shu niu (China)—Fiction.   2. Antiqui-
ties—Collection and preservation—Fiction.   3. Dams—
Design and construction—Fiction.   4. Yangtze River
(China)—Fiction.   5. China—Antiquities—Fiction.
6. Americans—China—Fiction.   7. Police—China—Fiction.
8. Married people—Fiction.   9. Policewomen—Fiction.
10. China—Fiction.   I. Title.
    PS3569.E3334 D73 2003
    813'.54—dc21   2002024871

Printed in the United States of America on acid-free paper
Random House website address: www.atrandom.com

9 8 7 6 5 4 3 2

First Edition

For my sisters
Ariana and Clara

The *Shu Ching: Book of History* is one of the three oldest books in the world. A collection of speeches, canons, proclamations, and dialogues dating from 2357 B.C. to 631 B.C., the *Shu Ching* is as fundamental to Eastern thought and culture as Plato and Aristotle are to Western. In 213 B.C., during the Qin (Ch'in) Dynasty, Emperor Qinshihuangdi ordered the *Shu Ching*—and all ancient manuscripts—burned. Han Dynasty scholars worked to save the words, seeking out fragments of text and re-creating history that had been lost. Although several sections of the *Shu Ching* have questionable authenticity and sometimes seem to fall more within the realm of myth than history, recent archaeological finds have begun to lend veracity to even the most unlikely claims. . . .

PROLOGUE

THE MAN WAS DEAD BY THE TIME HIS BODY HIT THE SWIRLING muddy waters of the Yangzi River just below the first of the Three Gorges. With no panicked attempts to reach for the safety of land or a protruding rock, with no last agonized breaths to endeavor, with no searing pain of water being gulped into lungs, the body was simply swept away by the fast-moving current. How quickly he cooled in the chilly pools. How swiftly he moved in these first few minutes with no obstacles in his way.

Each mile sent the man relentlessly forward past villages gray with age, factories that belched fetid smoke, and drainpipes that spewed loathsome refuse, chemicals, and raw sewage into the river. As he went, his skin wrinkled and began to peel. Internal gases formed, keeping him afloat. He often traveled as much as thirty feet per second, and the top of his head pounded into jagged rocks and rough cliff edges, tearing away tufts of hair and scalp. But other times the river widened and slowed, becoming shallow and treacherous to navigate. More than once the body was caught in the swirl of a whirlpool or on the edge of a sandbar before a shift in the current or the ripple of waves from a passing vessel freed him.

Did anyone see this *shui da bang*—water log—in its pitiless migration to the sea? The waters of this snake of a river had a drainage of more than 700,000 square miles, nearly one-fifth of China's total landmass. It divided the country into north and south in matters as basic as temperament, food, and religion. The Yangzi directly affected one-third of China's population, more than 400 million people—nearly one of every thirteen people on the face of the earth. So of course people saw the body. More than once a fisherman or a hand aboard a barge spotted the flash of ivory flesh bobbing in the murky waves. Ah, could it be a *baiji*—a white dolphin? Legend said white dolphins were girls who'd been transformed into water creatures. Today the *baiji* left on this river could be counted in the mere dozens, and some said that none had survived the pollution and the boat traffic. Could that flash of white possibly have been a *baiji*? A little miracle in this watery gash in the earth?

Soon the body entered the city limits of Wushan, where the startlingly green current of the Daning River poured into the muddy Yangzi. Sampans carried fishermen. Huge ferries bore men and women up and down the river to work, visit relatives, find better lives. Naked children played on inner tubes, laughing and teasing each other. One boy bumped into the corpse and for a moment mistook it for a friend pretending to be dead. Hadn't they all done the dead man's float at one time or another? The boy kicked at the body, and when he felt his toes sink in, then in some more into the rotting flesh, he drew away, swimming fast, not once mentioning to his friends his horror at what he'd encountered. He simply sidled alongside one of the small boats that carried tourists from their cruise ships on excursions up the Daning. If he smiled enough, if he waved heartily, if he called out "Welcome, welcome" as the fat foreigners snapped their photos, then he might just swim away with a few *yuan* before they chugged up the Daning to see the Lesser Three Gorges.

The body whooshed into the Wu Gorge, the second of the Three Gorges. The cliffs were so high that the sun barely penetrated down to the river. High, high up rose the Goddess Peak, which resembled a young woman kneeling before a pillar, with eleven peaks nearby. The local people believed this to be the embodiment of Yao Ji, the twenty-third daughter of the Queen Mother of the West, and her eleven handmaidens. Yao Ji had once occupied herself by wandering the mountains and riverbanks of the mortal world. While floating on a cloud one day, she'd discovered twelve dragons wreaking havoc on the river, causing hardship and death to mortal men and women. She called upon Yu the Great, endowed him with the power to control weather and move earth, then watched as he sliced open the gorges to lead the waters to the sea. Today the Goddess Peak was reputed to bring luck to those who glimpsed her in the shrouded mists, but there was no luck for the body, just the constant pull to the sea, as though Yu the Great himself had ordained it.

But wasn't that just a myth designed to explain this river, which remained an enigma not only to her people but to the outside world? In a country where legend, history, and politics were always woven together, most Chinese didn't even know the word *Yangzi*, which was the name for the last 200 miles of river, where it ran through the ancient fiefdom of Yang. As a nation, the Chinese called this waterway *Chang Jiang*, Long River, or *Da Jiang*, Great River, but those who lived on its banks had named every stretch of its 4,000 miles to reflect the nature of the water in that place—the Wild Yak River, the River of Golden Sand, Beautiful River, Ba River.

All this was beyond the comprehension of the rotting piece of flesh. Sometimes there were hours of gentle waters, of peaceful drift, of quiet shorelines and tranquil coves where a lone farmer worked a tiny patch, where a wife—her pants rolled above her knees—washed her family's clothes on the rocks, where an older sister minded her little brother. For hours everything was reduced to the sun, the sky, and the primeval push of water through rock. But there were cities too, where apartments hugged the river's edge and boats of all sizes vied for position. Superficially it may have seemed as though life were going on as usual—working, being with family, attending patriotic meetings, playing cards, strolling with a pretty girl, sitting with an ailing parent—but a sense of urgency hung over everything.

High on the cliffs, swatches of white paint at 177 meters above the riverbed proclaimed the future height of the reservoir behind the Three Gorges Dam. In seven years, when the reservoir finished forming, everything below those lines would be inundated. Between Yichang and Chongqing, well over a million people would be moved from their ancestral homes. The lucky few—those with good connections—would get residence certificates for cities. Others would be transplanted to new towns made up of high-rise after high-rise that stood out stark and white far above the future high-water mark. The unfortunate ones—the majority, in fact—would be sent to distant provinces. Promises had been made, but already some who'd been sent afar had returned with tales of hardship. What would become of them now? Could those people, who'd suffered so much in this tumultuous land, suffer any more?

And could the body, which continued on, suffer more, endure more? Caught in the propellers of passing boats, his skin shredded and tore. After his shirt disintegrated, birds swooped down and picked at the flesh on his back. As he traveled into the Xiling Gorge, the last of the Three Gorges, turtles and fish nibbled and ripped at the soft parts of his face—the eyelids, lips, and ears.

Suddenly he was at the dam site itself. This project, when completed, would be one of the greatest man-made edifices in the history of the world. The whole site was a mass of giant machines, concrete, and steel. Men and women worked round the clock, sending the dam higher and higher inch by inch toward its final height of 607 feet and over a mile in width. A sense of purpose imbued every boulder dynamited into gravel, every ton of earth moved, every mile of rebar tied down, every lock completed and opened for use. This would be China's greatest achievement—the completion of a dream for her people and a message to the world of her supremacy. And, not so incidentally, the dam would also generate electricity equivalent to eighteen nuclear power plants. This was not just nationalist power but power in its rawest, truest form.

A cofferdam diverted the river so that the work could go on. The body swept through those torrential waters in moments, then suddenly, amazingly, the land flattened. Fields stretched out for miles on either bank. There would be places now where the river would be more than two miles across, its torrents reduced to a gentle but implacable surge. The city of Shanghai still beckoned. Below that, the estuary spread out across fifty miles, with silt deposits projecting another mile of Chinese mainland every seventy years.

Along the river's course, shrines had been built as remembrances of terrible tragedies, pagodas rose to warn sailors of hidden navigational dangers, and temples reminded those who passed of the grandeur and risks of this place. But for every monument that cautioned passersby to *pay attention*—man was nothing, the river was all—other spots brought that message down to its most intimate human scale. For millennia a little spit of land protruded into the river just below the town of Anqing, where for the last three centuries the Jia clan had lived and worked the earth.

Every morning Jia Mingfu walked the banks to remove and sometimes salvage the trash that had come to rest. He'd seen trees that had journeyed all the way down from the headwaters high in Tibet, cans of string beans that had been sucked out of cottages, pieces of boats that had been ripped into splinters. He'd also seen more than his fair share of death. Flood season always brought down others like himself—farmers and their families who'd been washed off their land—while in winter he found the occasional young man or woman. The river wasn't that dangerous then, but the shortness of the days brought out a melancholy turn of mind, and broken love affairs were too much to bear.

Jia Mingfu knew by the smell that a body—perhaps human, perhaps animal—awaited him. He gripped the stick that he carried on these excursions a little more tightly as he hardened his heart for what he knew he would see—a corpse ravaged by exposure to water, rocks, the sun, wildlife, and the natural decomposition of flesh. As he'd done so many times before, he used his stick to brush away some of the trash that had accumulated on the body. Despite its journey, the dead thing was most definitely human, with its arms and legs still attached. But this creature with its red hair was no ordinary man. He was a *yang guizi,* a white devil, a foreigner.

DRAGON
BONES

THE IMPERIAL DOMAIN

(Dian fu)

The Imperial Domain extends 500 *li* in each direction from
the capital. This is the most populous domain, the seat
of power, and the heart of geography. The Central Nation
should truly be central.

THE SUN STILL HADN'T CRESTED OVER THE ROOFS OF THE STATELY
buildings on the eastern edge of Tiananmen Square when Inspector
Liu Hulan of the Ministry of Public Security gazed across a sea of
people gathered in the huge cement expanse for the first public as-
sembly of the All-Patriotic Society ever to be held in Beijing. Until
today, the All-Patriotic Society's clandestine meetings had taken
place mostly in the heart of the country, in towns and villages along
the Yellow River. Although the cult had recently gained a foothold in
the capital, no one had expected a show as brazen as this.

All religious cults were against the law in China, and it was part
of Hulan's job to do what she could to eradicate them, but she had
learned of this early-morning rally only fifteen hours ago from a man
she'd arrested for stealing from his work unit so that he might make
a more sizable donation to the Society. After several impromptu dis-
cussions at the ministry, it was decided to let the meeting go forward. If a high-ranking All-Patriotic Society member could be
drawn out and identified, then Hulan could make a very public arrest, which might prove fruitful in many ways.

Hulan had arrived here at three this morning and had super-
vised the stationing of policemen and soldiers around the perimeter
of the square. She had hoped that an official presence would serve
as a deterrent to converts and help keep the numbers down, but as

far as she could see no one had turned back. The adherents were orderly, polite, obedient, and simply paid no attention to the uniformed men and women with automatic rifles slung over their shoulders. If everyone remained peaceful during the promised *qi gong* exercises, chanting, and inspirational sermon, then there was no reason for anyone to get hurt. Sure, photos would be taken and a few people held for questioning, but the plain fact was that the Ministry of Public Security wasn't prepared on such short notice to detain more than a thousand people. There had been enough time, however, for the government to request that a camera crew from a state-run television station cover the event, and Hulan felt a certain amount of confusion about this.

Five years ago she had made a deal with some of the most powerful men in her country, who secretly guided China from a compound situated across the lake from where Hulan lived. She had been brought before them at the conclusion of the Knight International case, in which more than 150 women had lost their lives in a horrible fire in an American-owned toy factory operating deep in China's interior. The "men across the lake," as Hulan referred to them, told her they would let her marry the American attorney David Stark and give birth to her half-breed daughter—both of which were questionable actions under Chinese law and custom. They told her they would keep her name out of the media for good or bad. In exchange, Hulan had to promise she would follow the party line, obey orders without question, eliminate her eccentric methods, and keep the pact a secret among her, the men across the lake, and her mentor and superior, Vice Minister Zai. Hulan had agreed to the conditions, hoping they would allow her to have the private life she'd always longed for. But of course the game had changed. Her daughter had died and her marriage to David . . .

She forced herself not to think of that right now. Instead she turned her attention back to the television crew. They had a good vantage point on the steps of the Great Hall of the People, from which they could survey the entire square. Hulan recognized one of the reporters—a woman with a shrill voice who for many years had been the eager mouthpiece of the government. Her words carried on the humid air like rotting garbage, insisting that the government was not instigating a crackdown against the All-Patriotic Society but showing its tolerance by letting the group meet here today.

Hulan sighed. She would need to take extra care as she moved through the crowd, because she didn't want to be noticed by the camera crew. Still, Liu Hulan was easy to spot amid the other Beijingers here this morning. It wasn't that she dressed in a colorful way, for these days Beijing's residents embraced the most vibrant colors they could find. It wasn't that she wore designer clothes, although she certainly could afford to shop at any of the foreign-designer boutiques now in the city. Rather, she dressed in the most exquisite clothes of the finest silks, all of which had once belonged to her mother, her grandmother, or her other colorful ancestors. Hulan's outfits spoke to the people about her money, taste, social position, and culture; not only did she work for the Ministry of Public Security—perhaps the most feared of China's law enforcement agencies—but she also had to be a Red Princess, the wealthy daughter or granddaughter of someone who had gone on the Long March with Mao Zedong.

Hulan had been born in Beijing and had the happy and privileged upbringing befitting the child of two of China's most esteemed personages. At the outbreak of the Cultural Revolution, when Hulan was twelve, she'd been sent to the countryside to "learn from the peasants." She had been brought back to Beijing two years later to denounce her father as part of an ill-conceived effort to save her mother's life. Hulan's father had been sent to labor camp, and Hulan, at age fourteen, had been sent abroad to the United States. After boarding school, college, and law school, Hulan had become an associate at Phillips & MacKenzie, where she met David. They'd fallen in love, had lived together, and then twelve years ago she'd come back to China. Seven years later, Hulan and David had been brought together here in Beijing to work on two difficult and heartbreaking cases. In the first, Hulan's father—who had been fully rehabilitated and had become a high-ranking cadre—had died and the nation had held her responsible. The second was the Knight International case, which had begun as an investigation into suspicious working conditions and had ended in the deadly conflagration. Hulan herself had nearly died that day, and for a long time there was great concern for the well-being of her unborn child. The men across the lake successfully controlled the story of Hulan's role in that case. But although Hulan had been spared another round of public criticism, she'd blamed herself for the many deaths. She had been named for a martyr of the revolution, she told David at the time. She should have done more.

Now Hulan paced along the edges of the crowd, searching for the faces of known troublemakers who could be rounded up later. At one point she caught sight of Neighborhood Committee Director Zhang, the old woman who kept track of all the comings and goings in Hulan's *hutong* neighborhood. Madame Zhang had to know that this group was banned, but she was here now with her eyes closed and her wizened face rapt with spiritual feeling. Hulan should have suspected she might show up. Madame Zhang, who had been on the cutting edge of the *yang ge* dance craze a few years ago, would have to be up to the minute with the All-Patriotic Society and its appealingly accessible rituals.

In a country where aphorisms and slogans had forever been used to teach, influence, and coerce, the members of the All-Patriotic Society assembled here today were already well-versed in a variety of seemingly innocuous phrases, which they began chanting. "Be reverent," they intoned again and again before they switched to "The river brings us life." No one seemed frightened or anxious. Why should they be? They were not members of the Falun Gong, which was not permitted to use the square under any circumstances. They were reverent, and as such they felt righteous and safe.

Hulan circulated until she spotted a woman with a little girl about four years old. They looked poor—perhaps the woman had come from the countryside to the capital to look for work. If so, her presence in the city was against the law, which may have accounted for the anxious way she kept looking around. But there was something else about her that was troubling. Her hair was unkempt, and not only were her clothes dirty but the buttons on her blouse were all off by one. Still, the daughter was impeccably clean and beautifully turned out given their circumstances. The woman squatted on the ground so that she was eye-level with her daughter. Her hands worried over every inch of the girl, tweaking the neckline of her T-shirt, pulling at the hems of her shorts, and retying her red tennis shoes. All the while the little girl—her cheeks shiny and pink— chattered nonstop about nothing important, just Mama this and Mama that. A bag lay next to them. Hulan imagined what was inside—perhaps an orange for the girl, maybe another change of clothes, a toy if they had enough money. An ache began in Hulan's chest, and she looked away.

At 6:15, a man jumped up on a small wooden platform and held up his hands for silence. He looked to be about thirty, but he could have been much older. He was ruggedly handsome, and his hair was a bit longer than the custom. As the crowd quieted, he dropped one hand and held himself in a posture reminiscent of Mao as a young revolutionary. "I am Tang Wenting, a lieutenant of the All-Patriotic Society."

Hulan could have arrested him right then, but she wanted to hear what he had to say. She'd use his speech against him later, during interrogations.

"We meet in the light of Xiao Da's grace," Tang Wenting announced.

"Xiao Da, Xiao Da, Xiao Da," the followers murmured, and the sound echoed beautifully through the square.

As the lieutenant let the name wash over him, Hulan wondered not for the first time about the mysterious Xiao Da, the self-proclaimed leader of the All-Patriotic Society, who'd pulled off a semi-miracle in keeping his true identity a secret in a nation where there were no secrets. The fact that Xiao Da had been able to move through the countryside holding underground meetings for the last three years not only increased his legend but also exasperated the government. Numerous arrests had been made and many people sentenced to labor camp. On several occasions Hulan had tried to negotiate lesser sentences in exchange for the identity of Xiao Da, knowing that once he was gone the group would collapse. But either no one knew Xiao Da's identity or they weren't yet ready to give him up. It was all

very annoying. Even his name irritated Hulan. Xiao Da—Little Big—
what was that supposed to mean anyway?

Hulan's eyes sought out the little girl she'd seen before. The
mother was holding her daughter tightly by the waist, forcing her to
watch the lieutenant. The woman had her lips to one of the girl's
ears and was whispering intensely. The child's eyes were wide not
with excitement but with fear, though Hulan couldn't understand
why. The girl stayed quiet, refusing to say a word against the whispered barrage and remaining still within her mother's grip, which
seemed to tighten as the All-Patriotic Society lieutenant droned on.
It occurred to Hulan that maybe the woman wasn't a country bump-
kin or even a true Society follower at all, just a mother who had lost
her connection to the real world.

"Our political leaders tell us to give up the old ways," Tang
Wenting lectured. "They tell us, 'To get rich is glorious!' But Xiao Da
says we must say no to these new ways. We must repudiate technology and social progress, and go back to honoring old traditions and
old values. . . ."

Fifteen minutes later, the sun broke across the square and
Hulan could see its instantaneous effect on the religious adherents.
Beijing languished in the midst of *Fu Tian,* that debilitating period
of Give-Up Weather between July and August, when the heat and
humidity were at their most ominous and oppressive. Unprotected
as it was, Tiananmen was not a place to be during the heat of the
day. It was time to head home or to work.

The lieutenant caught the subtle change in the crowd. "Before
you go, I have a few words from Xiao Da's own lips that he asked me
to impart to you. Soon Xiao Da will step out of the darkness and into
the light. When he does, he will bring with him an object that will
unite all of the Chinese people. With it in his hand, evil will be punished. Those who are reverent will triumph. Together we will follow
Xiao Da."

This kind of rhetoric was exactly why the government perceived
the All-Patriotic Society to be a threat.

The young man bent his head piously as voices throughout the
square sang out, "Xiao Da, Xiao Da, Xiao Da."

He looked up and said, "Now is the time to remember our tributes. Nine Virtues, Nine Grades, Nine Tributes."

The All-Patriotic Society had grown quickly in three years. Although the group counted fewer members than the Falun Gong, the Ministry of Public Security had internal estimates of 20 million followers, nearly all of whom lived in the countryside. Once initiated, they donated their hard-earned salaries and sometimes their savings to the sect, based on a secret tithing scale involving nine grades. A lot of money was ending up in Xiao Da's pocket, and Hulan didn't want that custom to take hold in Beijing. She turned to signal to the policemen to round up anyone holding a collection basket.

Suddenly she heard a woman's voice scream, "For Xiao Da!"

Hulan spun around. The mother who moments before had been whispering into her daughter's ear now stood fully erect, her neck stretched so she could see above the crowd to the lieutenant. In one hand she held on to the back of her daughter's T-shirt; in the other she held a cleaver, which she must have brought with her in her bag. The blade was a good ten centimeters wide.

Everyone here was Chinese; all knew from experience when something bad was going to happen. People started to edge away and push each other to get out of there. For a moment Hulan lost sight of the mother and daughter altogether. She heard Tang Wenting's voice shout out: "Be calm! Xiao Da would want you all to be calm!"

Miraculously, the crowd responded to his words, slowing down, quieting.

"We need to help our sister," he went on. "Tell me, sister! What do you want to tell Xiao Da? Have you come to renounce alcohol, tobacco, and fornication? We are all with you!"

"I have come to punish this girl," the woman called back to him.

Hulan pulled out her weapon and held it lowered in front of her. "Put the knife down!" she yelled.

People scattered out of the way, then, like frightened animals, scrambled right back into her line of fire.

"All children are innocent." Tang Wenting maintained his facade of serenity. As much as Hulan distrusted the group and all it stood for, she was grateful that the lieutenant seemed to understand the gravity of the situation.

"This one is bad," the mother answered. "The evil needs to be cut out."

These words caught the interest of the crowd. Now they wanted to see what the ruckus was all about. Hulan shoved people aside, yet she still felt she was being pushed farther away.

"Only Xiao Da can pass judgment," the lieutenant countered. "And he believes in just punishments only."

A primal howl ripped out of the woman. "A mother can see evil too!"

She sank to her knees and pushed her daughter to the ground. She grabbed the girl's forearm and held it flat against the cement.

"Move out of my way!" Hulan screamed. But in a country where people witnessed executions as entertainment, no one moved. To the woman, she shouted, "Put the knife down or I'll shoot!"

"Mama! No! Mama!" These were the first words anyone had heard from the child. They floated out sweet and crisp.

Tang Wenting had come down off his box and managed to make his way to the mother. "You are suffering, sister," he consoled her. "We suffer with you, but we are not extremists. The river is life . . ."

These words did not offer solace. Instead the woman looked around wildly, searching the faces for understanding. Then her eyes dropped to her daughter's hand. When she raised the cleaver above her head, Hulan lifted her weapon and took careful aim at the woman's shoulder. The cleaver began to fall. The little girl struggled to free her arm. Her screams were unlike anything Hulan had ever heard before. Hulan fired.

Panic was instantaneous. People began running every which way. Hulan heard other shots being fired and hoped that bullets were only going over people's heads. She took a last few steps and reached the sad little tableau. The mother lay splayed on the ground, thrashing from side to side, blood everywhere. The little girl knelt beside her mother, sobbing. Tang Wenting was on his knees, trying to staunch the bleeding with his palms. Hulan dropped down beside them. "Move!" she ordered the lieutenant. He pulled his hands away, and blood squirted up, spraying the little girl's face.

"There shouldn't be so much blood," Hulan said to no one. She tore the woman's blouse. The entry wound was in the shoulder as it should have been, but the blood was not coming from there. Instead it gushed from a smaller wound at the neck, where a fragment of the bullet had embedded itself. It must have shattered when it hit the bone and either ricocheted or traveled internally to the neck, where it had shredded the carotid artery. Hulan turned the woman on her side and applied pressure to her neck. The little girl whimpered, "Mama, Mama," over and over again.

With all of the confusion in the square, no one came to help. The blood continued to pump out from beneath Hulan's hands until finally the woman stopped writhing. Tang Wenting was the first to move. He got to his feet, took two steps back, then stretched out his arm and pointed at Hulan. "Mother killer," he said in condemnation. Then he widened his arms as if to embrace those who still remained on the square. "Everyone! See this mother killer! She murdered one who was reverent!"

All of Hulan's senses were heightened. She could feel the blood already beginning to dry on her hands and face. She could hear commotion in the distance. She could see in her peripheral vision the television camera and could hear the excited tones of the female reporter, who certainly had the scoop of the day. Hulan was even aware of Tang Wenting as he pointed at her again and announced to the crowd, "This woman is our enemy! She has shown her true face! Xiao Da will make her pay!" But all Hulan really absorbed was the face of the little girl before her. Her eyes had a look that Hulan knew all too well. It was the empty stare of someone who had lost everything.

David Stark woke up alone in the bed that he'd once shared with his wife. He took a shower and dressed. On his way out to the kitchen, he stopped as he did every day to visit the room that had once been his daughter's. He lit incense, said a silent prayer, and touched her photograph. Then he left the room, put water on for tea, and turned on the television. He liked to catch the early-morning broadcasts because they helped him with his colloquial Mandarin. But when he glimpsed Hulan's face on the screen, he sat down and for the next hour watched in horror as events in the square spiraled out of control. As soon as he saw the little girl, he felt a pang of loss and grief that he was sure Hulan must have felt. After the mother died and Hulan picked up the crying child, David flipped off the television and went outside. Hulan would deliver the girl to the proper authorities, then she would need to return to the compound for a shower and change of clothes. He'd be waiting for her.

He made his way from the back pavilion—where he had lived alone these last months—past the other buildings that had once housed the acrobats, singers, and other performers who were Hulan's celebrated ancestors, past the building where Hulan's mother and her nurse resided, to the central courtyard. Hulan would have to come through here to get to her room.

David sat on a porcelain garden stool under the ginkgo tree and waited. This was the place where five years ago he had promised Hulan that they would be happy. That day he'd said that in a way they were both orphans, because they'd both been alone much of their lives. Hulan had lost her father, and her mother was just a shadow of a person; David's parents had been married just long enough for him to be born. Then his father, an international businessman, had gone back to his travels, while his mother, a concert pianist, had gone back to her recitals. If David and Hulan had each other, he'd said, they would not be alone. Once their daughter was born, they could create the kind of family that neither of them had ever had. David had promised Hulan that they would never be separated again, that they would be together forever, and that their child would be carefree, happy, and healthy too. He'd assured Hulan that all of her fears about loss were unfounded. He'd said he'd never leave. He'd been wrong about almost everything, and the guilt he felt about that every day was almost unbearable.

But David had made his promises, and she'd believed him. Vice

Minister Zai had taken Hulan off murder cases, and she'd never re-turned to them. David and Hulan had married in a small ceremony. Hulan's belly had swelled, and the doctor had repeatedly assured them that the pregnancy was normal. During periodic ultrasounds, David and Hulan could see that the baby—a girl—looked good, healthy and strong. To their eyes, she already had personality in the way she sucked her thumb and somersaulted in Hulan's womb. David and Hulan began to think like a family. They bought a crib and painted the alcove off the bedroom. Hulan searched through trunks and brought out embroidered baby hats decorated with gold good-luck charms.

Once Chaowen was born, their joy was complete. She was a beautiful child. In many ways she'd looked like a typical Chinese girl. Her face was round and perfectly pink. Her eyes were two lovely almonds. But Chaowen's hair was not a pure silky black, so anyone on the street could see that she was not one hundred per-cent Chinese. She enjoyed Christmas as much as Chinese New Year. (What child wouldn't?) In winter, she wore practical padded Chinese clothes; in summer, T-shirts and shorts. She spoke English to her father even on those occasions when he spoke to her in Chi-nese; she spoke Chinese to her mother even when she spoke to her daughter in English. In other words, Chaowen was headstrong and smart like both of her parents, which had often caused the neigh-bors to comment on the appropriateness of her name. *Chao* meant "to exceed." *Wen* meant "literary" or "cultural." Together they meant someone who was a scholar of culture.

Of course they'd disagreed about how to raise Chaowen. David had wanted her to be born in the States. He'd lost that one. He'd wanted to move back to Los Angeles so that his daughter would grow up exempt from political indoctrination. He'd wanted her to have access to great schools and good medical care. He'd wanted her to grow up knowing that she was absolutely free to make what-ever decisions and choices she wanted. But Hulan was adamant that they stay in Beijing. Her reasons were legitimate: she wanted Chaowen to know Chinese culture, Hulan's mother was too frail to leave, and they should all be a part of the New China. Because Hulan and Chaowen were happy, David reluctantly let his wishes be left behind.

For the three and a half years of Chaowen's life, Hulan had taken great joy in the simple things. To David's eyes, she seemed to relish the whack of the cleaver hitting the chopping block, the silly sounds Chaowen made when she tried to cajole something from her parents, the giggles and murmurs as the three of them cuddled together on the big bed, then the quiet period after Chaowen went to sleep. They had cocooned themselves in a wonderful life. They were young, they had money, and he, at least, had great faith that all of their troubles were behind them. But the Chinese have a saying that is all too true: Things always change to the opposite.

A year had passed since Chaowen's death, and David still could hardly bring himself to think about those last days. They'd started casually with a fever. Hulan had given Chaowen Tylenol and homemade popsicles to keep up her fluids. David had amused her with coloring books, fairy tales, and paper dolls. But when Chaowen's fever refused to drop and she became too listless to be entertained, they'd taken her to the emergency room. Bacterial meningitis—those two words changed his life forever. At first the doctors said she would be fine. Then she didn't respond to antibiotics. Her fever increased, and her burning body reacted with violent seizures. When her brain began to swell, the doctors started talking about long-term brain damage. David and Hulan would have accepted any challenge so long as Chaowen lived, but that wasn't to be. Her organs gradually shut down. When the medical team tried to resuscitate her that last time, David inwardly prayed for one more chance. Then it was over. The nurses removed all of the tubes, wrapped Chaowen in a blanket, and let Hulan hold her. Even with the ravages of her illness and death, Chaowen was beautiful—delicate hands, the softest skin, and silky hair that was a physical manifestation of the love between her Chinese mother and Caucasian father.

David's grief was deep and profound, but strangely enough he found comfort in Asian traditions of death and the afterlife. Hulan, however, was inconsolable. David had seen her overcome tragedy before. She'd vanquished the remorse she felt for the pain she'd inflicted on her parents during the Cultural Revolution, come back from that frightening night when her father had sought revenge against her, doggedly recovered from the physical and psychological harm stemming from the inferno at the Knight factory. He'd told himself that time—and one day another child—would heal her sorrow, but Hulan's last resources of resiliency had been sucked out of her in their daughter's final breath.

For the past year, Hulan had managed her emotions by covering them in the way she had since she was a child and by focusing her mind on something outside herself. When she began going out to the countryside on short trips to investigate the All-Patriotic Society, David didn't object, in the blind belief that she needed to work things through in her own way. But whereas once she had been flexible and empathetic in her job, she was now tenacious and unforgiving. The more obsessed she became with the All-Patriotic Society, the more he saw her pulling away from him. The more she became involved in her crusade, the more he distanced himself from her too. She couldn't talk to him about what she did in her work because he didn't condone it, and he couldn't talk to her about it because she didn't want to hear another explanation of his principles of freedom of speech and religion. She couldn't look at him because he brought back too many memories, and he couldn't look at her because he'd failed her.

After she'd moved out of their bedroom and into another building in the compound, he'd understood at last that, for all of Hulan's privilege and brilliance, nothing—not even David—could protect her from the punishment that she inflicted on herself. He suffered from self-recrimination too. What if they'd taken Chaowen to the hospital sooner? What if they'd been in the States? Would Chaowen have had better medical care? He'd kept these thoughts to himself, just as Hulan had hidden hers from him.

He knew it was a rare marriage that could survive the death of a child. He knew as well that Hulan might be happier if he went back to Los Angeles. His presence here was just a daily reminder of the family they had lost. But he couldn't leave Hulan, because he loved her and he knew she loved him still. He couldn't leave her, because he'd promised her that day in this courtyard that they'd always be together. He couldn't leave her, because he knew that somewhere in that shell lived the woman he'd fallen in love with. He saw himself as a brick, an anchor, a foundation. Her recovery was his job now, and he gave it everything that he'd once given to what others had called his "brilliant career." He believed that if he was steadfast, one day she would reach out for him again. He would be there, and she would return from the empty place where she'd imprisoned herself.

He heard her footsteps before he saw her. Her face was turned down, and when he softly called her name she stopped and looked up. She had a smear of blood across her left cheek, where she must have tried to push her hair out of the way. Her blouse was spattered with blood, while her skirt showed a large dark crust where she must have kneeled in it. Somewhere Hulan had managed to wipe off her hands, but he could see dried blood still caked between her fingers.

"Are you okay?" he asked.

"You know what happened?"

After he nodded, she looked up through the leaves of the ginkgo tree to the dull brown Beijing sky. After a moment, she said, "I had a good shot. That woman shouldn't have died. She was crazy. I should have recognized it earlier."

"I'm sorry," he said. Then, "But you saved the girl."

She looked at him as though she was trying to decipher the meaning of his words. For a single instant he saw a shadow of vulnerability, then she rearranged her features into a reassuring smile. He'd come to think of that look as her survival mask.

"I'm glad you're here," she said. "That means a lot to me." After a beat, she added, "But you should get to your office. Miss Quo will be worrying about you by now. And of course I need to clean up, then get to the MPS." A trace of uncertainty crept back into her voice, and she averted her eyes again. "There will be things I need to do. . . ."

"Is there any way I can help?"

Her determined smile gelled again, and he could see just how hard she was trying. "We could have dinner together. I'd like that." Then she held out her bloodstained hands for him to see. "I really need a shower." With that she walked past him and into the next courtyard.

They had managed to get through the conversation without mentioning the one thing that was on both of their minds. The little girl who'd lost her mother only an hour ago was the same age that David and Hulan's daughter would have been.

IT WAS STILL ONLY NINE IN THE MORNING WHEN HULAN LEFT HER room and walked to an adjacent building to pay a quick visit to her mother and her mother's nurse. Hulan's mother had been confined to a wheelchair since the Cultural Revolution. Her mind was "delicate," which meant that her rare moments of lucidity were often swamped by weeks or even months of no words, gestures, or acknowledgments of any sort. This morning, Hulan's mother stared into the distance, and the visit was short.

Hulan then left the compound and got into the backseat of a black Mercedes. Investigator Lo, her longtime driver, didn't speak— it had already been a long day for both of them—and he quickly drove her to the Ministry of Public Security compound on Chang An Boulevard. As soon as Hulan reached her office, a tea girl brought in a thermos and a porcelain cup, then quietly left the room. There would be an inquiry about the events this morning, and Hulan would need to write a full report, but before she started that she needed to finish up with her informant. Hulan opened his file and began making notations for the prosecutor. It was a simple case. Mr. Wong, a teller, had used his bank's official chop to move funds from several private accounts into one held by the All-Patriotic Society. Hulan had five other files with similar stories that had come across her desk in the last month. The difference between those and the case of Mr. Wong was that he was willing to trade what he knew so that he might not be sent to labor camp.

Unfortunately, stealing funds was not the only problem that Hulan had been able to link to the All-Patriotic Society. During the last few months, there'd been several cases of sabotage by workers who suddenly disapproved of the merchandise they produced in factories in the countryside and in Special Economic Zones. Equipment had been destroyed and defective parts inserted into products. There'd even been a couple of explosions in factories that manufactured high-tech components. The Chinese government took the position that the All-Patriotic Society was an extremist religious cult engaged in "domestic terrorism" and responded accordingly. Naturally, international human rights groups took a very dim view of China's zero-tolerance policy.

Having spent much of her life in the States, Hulan should have agreed, but she hated the All-Patriotic Society. She hated the way they preyed on the powerless, the old, and the poor. She hated the way people gave their money to Xiao Da. She knew from personal experience that fanaticism could be harmful to the state and to society as a whole. America might let religious cults gain power over the weak; China wouldn't. She told herself what others in the ministry told her: every time a file crossed her desk or she made another arrest she was protecting the masses and ensuring the stability of the government. Besides, she was grateful for the tasks assigned her. They kept her focused.

She knew that David didn't understand her obsession, but there was a lot she didn't understand about him anymore either. When he was at the U.S. Attorney's Office, he had labored to right terrible wrongs. He had followed a strict code of ethics and had a great belief in public service. He carried those ideals with him into private practice, where he'd had twenty or more other lawyers working on his matters, which often dealt with grave social or political issues. After David and Hulan reconnected, his law firm let him open a small office in Beijing. He was now a one-man show with a thriving practice. His days were busy and his clients paid him lots of money, but none of his cases was a great intellectual stretch for him or would make any real difference in the larger world. From her perspective, he now got through his straightforward business matters by occupying his mind with word puzzles and questions of culture. It was as if David were waiting for something to happen but it never came. The way things were between them now, she couldn't ask him about his choices, and she was grateful he didn't question her too much about hers.

When the tea girl returned after just a few minutes, Hulan looked up. "Yes?"

"Vice Minister Zai would like to see you, Inspector."

Hulan closed the folder and left the room. Hurrying down the hall and up the stairs, she felt confident that she could answer any questions he might have about this morning. When she stepped into the anteroom of Zai's office, his secretary stood, knocked gently on the office door, and opened it for Hulan.

"Good morning, Vice Minister," Hulan said as she entered.

"Good morning, Inspector Liu."

Their words were formal, but she was closer to this man than she'd been to her own father.

"Please sit," he said, motioning to the chair in front of his desk. She did as she was told and waited as he finished writing on a notepad. They were comfortable enough with each other that he could complete his task with her sitting across from him rather than have her wait in the anteroom as a way of showing his more powerful position. In these quiet minutes, Hulan looked around the room. It looked the same as when her father had held the job. Heavy crimson drapes covered the windows. Official seals and plaques decorated the walls. Nothing spoke of the personal nature of the man who sat behind the desk.

At last the vice minister looked up. She'd known him her entire life, so she could easily read the concern in his eyes.

"I am sorry about what happened today," she began.

"No need for apologies, Inspector. The woman's death was an accident, and the press will report it that way beginning now." He hesitated, then added, "It was a mistake to give the Central Broadcasting Bureau the ability to air the event live."

Yes, Hulan thought, we had an arrangement. Why had things

changed so suddenly and without any discussion? She had to approach the subject carefully. "A mistake or was it—"

He quickly cut her off. "There was no way to predict that a deranged woman would try to hurt her child."

"If she *was* crazy . . ."

He frowned. "The Falun Gong and the All-Patriotic Society are not the same."

What did he mean? That the self-immolations Falun Gong members had done were not the same as a woman trying to cut off her daughter's hand? That the accusations—mostly in the foreign press—that the Chinese government had hired people to set themselves on fire in public as a means to discredit the Falun Gong were true? That using "deranged" people for this end was unpredictable? What Hulan did know was that Zai had easily distracted her from her real concern. What was that camera crew doing there at all?

The vice minister looked at a sheet of paper. "I see that Tang Wenting was not arrested."

"He slipped away—"

"While you were tending to that child. This is not your job."

"You're absolutely right, Vice Minister."

Zai's voice softened. "Where is the girl now?"

"She was taken to the Number Five Home outside the Third Ring Road."

"Ah, then she may have a not so unhappy end." When Hulan looked at him questioningly, he added, "She might be adopted by an American family and have a much better life than the one she would have had." He leaned forward slightly. "You could adopt too, Hulan, perhaps an infant. It would not be so bad for you to find happiness again."

He was trying to be thoughtful, but his words hurt, reminding her of sympathizers like Neighborhood Committee Director Zhang, who'd told Hulan she should "try again."

Zai cleared his throat, letting her know that this personal conversation was over, but what he said next had nothing to do with this morning's events in Tiananmen Square. "A new case has come to our office. It is an unidentified body found in the Yangzi River."

Hulan was so taken aback by the abrupt change in subject that she responded without thinking. "Surely this is a common occurrence. Why should the Ministry of Public Security be involved?"

"Because the body is that of a foreigner." He spoke evenly, but she noticed the involuntary way he glanced at the walls. Did the government still listen to every conversation that went on in this room?

"Has anyone reported a missing foreigner?" Hulan asked, going along with Zai for now. "If the person fell off a cruise ship, the whole country would have been searching for this . . . man? Woman?"

"Man. As you point out, he could not have fallen from a cruise ship. But let us not discuss the possibilities. I am assigning you the case. We need to know who he is and how he came to be found in the waters of our great river."

"You know I'm busy today. I have to write a report on everything that happened this morning."

"That can wait. More important, it might be better for you to delay. You may want to work on your facts—"

"I don't need to think about what happened. I did what was necessary in the moment. Beyond that, I don't do murder cases anymore." A solution popped into her mind, but she had to offer it with the proper contrition. She looked down at her hands folded in her lap and said, "I am out of practice with the dead. Give the body to Luo or Cui." These inspectors had risen quickly in the ranks the last two years. As a reward, they'd gone to the United States as part of an exchange program and had spent two weeks at the FBI's training facility at Quantico.

"I'm not asking them. I'm assigning you. You have no choice."

Hulan caught something in his tone and looked up. He *was* nervous, and it was exactly because someone might be listening. She held his eyes until he nodded almost imperceptibly. People were listening. The men across the lake . . . Without being given a chance to explain fully her actions this morning, she was going to be punished, and Zai couldn't or wouldn't help her.

"Who is the dead man?" she inquired, keeping her voice steady.

"That is for you to discover."

"But you must have an idea—"

Vice Minister Zai scowled. "Identification is all that is needed at this time," he said. "You're dismissed."

It had been nearly five years since Hulan had gone down to the basement of the Ministry of Public Security building to Pathologist Fong's domain. Back then she'd been known as someone who could look at any crime scene or decomposing cadaver with an analytical eye. She'd developed a technique of stepping back and back again from a body to take in the whole scene. Her colleagues had always thought her hard-hearted in this regard, and in retrospect maybe she was. But, she told herself, her heart wasn't hard by nature. She just couldn't allow herself to acknowledge what was before her as human. A body was merely a question to be answered. Step away and step away again . . .

She paused before the swinging doors leading into the forensics lab. She tried to prepare herself for what she would see and smell, but what was the point? Water deaths were particularly unpleasant, and she was hopelessly out of practice. But she would deal with it, accept her punishment, then get back to her real work. She pushed through the doors and was assailed by the odors of formaldehyde, bleach, antiseptic, and lurking just below that the unmistakable smell of human death. The outer offices were empty, and she passed through two more sets of doors before she found Pathologist Fong. He peered up at her, regarding her critically. He was a small man, and it had always bothered him that he was shorter than she. At last he said, "You've come to see our"—and here he switched to barely discernible English—"John Doe?"

Before she could respond, he scurried down the hall. He pulled out a set of keys, opened a door, and motioned her in ahead of him. In the center of the room was a stainless-steel table. To the right was a sink; to the left a counter with a scale, other equipment, and numerous jars and bottles filled with liquid and specimens. The refrigeration unit for corpses was on the far wall. Hulan didn't know how many bodies were in there, but even from behind steel doors the smell of decay began to clog the back of her throat.

Fong's movements slowed. She remembered this about him. His caustic sense of humor would still be present, but his actions would be deliberate and careful. He had more respect for those who entered this room on a gurney than for those who could walk in of their own volition. He slipped on latex gloves, leaving the drawer open for Hulan to get a pair. As she pulled on the gloves, he dabbed a bit of mentholated ointment under his nostrils, then handed the jar to Hulan. She swiped her finger through the ointment, ran it under her nostrils, and felt the rush of menthol into her sinuses.

Pathologist Fong transferred the body bag onto the lab table. Hulan slowly exhaled to steady herself, then crossed to stand next to the pathologist. In one long, swift movement, Fong unzipped the bag, revealing the body from head to toe. The mentholated ointment didn't begin to disguise the horrible stench that assaulted her.

"We always save the most beautiful ones for you, Inspector," he recited as though it had been only a few days since he'd last spoken those words to her. He took two discreet steps back to give her time to examine the body alone.

The autopsy had already been performed and the y-incision sewn up with crude stitches, but this was the only thing about the body that could be said to be normal. Stretched out, the bloated corpse seemed like some grotesquely huge monster. The algae-covered flesh had shriveled into what was known as washerwoman's skin as a result of prolonged submersion in water and had burst here and there both from trauma and to let out gases. The eyes and nose were gone. The mouth was agape, and she could see the shredded remains of the tongue. The genitals were still complete. The fish had not snacked there. In fact, compared with the torso, the bottom half of the body was in relatively good shape.

"A trip down the Yangzi is no picnic," Fong commented dryly. "It is one of Chairman Mao's more obscure sayings, but true nevertheless."

Hulan ignored the joke. She ran the tip of her finger along the flesh of the man's arm. "He lost his shirt . . ."

"That's my inspector. You disappear but you don't forget how to

26 ...

look. They should send you out to teach the young ones who come in here. Stupid as water buffalo—"

"Pathologist Fong . . ."

"Yes, of course he lost his shirt. If he'd been wearing a T-shirt maybe it would have lasted, but a dress shirt would not have held up in those conditions. He was wearing jeans. Levi's 501s. Very strong material."

She leaned in to get a closer look. All the river muck couldn't disguise the red color of his hair. She asked, "You're positive he's a foreigner?"

"I can guarantee you that he's not Han Chinese."

In Sichuan Province alone there were more than forty ethnic minorities, but red hair was highly unlikely.

"I'm sure you've also noticed his size," Fong went on as he picked up a chart. "Once you allow for bloating and such, I figure he stood 182.8 centimeters tall and weighed 77.2 kilos. Since he's a foreigner, I put that into American measurements. It may make identification easier. He was a little over six feet and about 170 pounds. He may have been young. You know those foreigners and how fat they get. No"—he broke into his unintelligible English—"beer belly, no extra tire around the gut." He put down the chart and waited.

"What else?"

"He had some papers in his pockets."

"How could they have stayed with him?"

"You ever get your jeans wet, Inspector?" When she nodded, he went on. "First the water swelled the fabric. Once the body began to bloat, what was in the pockets became fully trapped."

"Anything more you can tell me?"

"You mean was there foul play?" Fong asked.

"You're watching too many American TV shows."

He beamed as though this had been a compliment and once again spoke in English. "Foul play, John Doe, perp, jacket . . ." He switched back to Mandarin. "It's important to learn these terms as part of globalization."

She stared at him until he finally answered her question. "You see this body. You see the damage to the head and face especially. How am I supposed to know if someone or something hit him on the head *before* he entered the river? He was hit on the head many times *after* he was in the river. On this I would testify in court. I ran a toxics screen, but it was inconclusive for poison, alcohol, or drugs. A better question might be, did he commit suicide?"

"And?"

"He was dead before he entered the water."

"No water in the lungs?"

"The presence of water in the lungs and even the stomach would not be a surprise given the duration of submersion. However, the lack of hemorrhages in the lung tissue indicate he did not die from drowning."

"Murder?"

"Too much postmortem damage to determine how he died," Fong answered, "but you can definitely rule out suicide. A corpse can't dispose of itself after all."

"Can you tell how long he's been dead?"

"Ten days, maybe more. If we get the rate that the river travels, I might be able to pinpoint a location for you."

"That won't be necessary. Once we have identification, I'm sure we'll know where he died."

"We have many new ways to work on identification . . ."

"Don't tell me you're another of our compatriots to travel abroad."

He smiled crookedly. "I go to pathology conventions wherever I can. Between those and *CSI* on my satellite, I've learned a lot. I call my method Chinese Forensics with Capitalist Tendencies." He paused and looked down at the body with an expression that seemed almost sympathetic. Had the pathologist softened over the years? "We have other tests we can run—"

"Hold off on that for now." Seeing Fong's deflation, she added, "But I'd like to see the papers you found."

Once out of the lab, Fong was all brisk business again, and he hustled down the hallway. Although his lab was orderly, his office was a mess, with piles of journals on the floor, files in haphazard stacks around the room, and books jammed into shelves. Fong flung himself into the chair behind his desk. The only other chair in the room was filled with papers. Hulan stood, remembering not to touch anything. Pathologist Fong was funny that way.

He opened a drawer, pulled out a large plastic bag, and dropped its contents on the desk. Each piece had been wrapped in its own plastic sleeve.

"Why aren't these materials in the evidence locker?"

Fong grimaced, then leaned forward as if to tell her something in confidence. "He's a foreigner. Special care, Inspector, special care."

Did he know something she didn't? Probably. Undoubtedly.

She quickly sorted through the artifacts. A driver's license would have made her job easy, but she didn't see one. Various other papers—probably discount cards, old receipts, and business cards—had come through the arduous and wet journey, but whatever information had been on them was now illegible. She picked up another plastic sleeve. Inside was a piece of lined paper about twelve by eighteen centimeters that had been torn from a notebook.

"You found this in the wallet?"

"Wedged in his back pocket."

"What is it?"

"Notebook paper obviously. Judging from the quality, I'd say foreign. It might be easier to trace than if it were Chinese, but what are the odds?"

She turned it over in her hand, then held it under the light on Fong's desk. She could see something still on the paper. She looked at Fong, who said, "I checked under a microscope, and it looks like symbols of some sort."

She examined the paper more closely. Could it be shorthand? Fong wouldn't be familiar with those squiggles, but she'd seen enough of them when she'd worked at Phillips & MacKenzie to recognize them. But this definitely wasn't shorthand. She put the paper back on the desk. Fong waited for her to speak, then when she didn't he gestured to the plastic sleeves. "Just because you don't see the words doesn't mean they aren't there. I have tests I can do to see what I can pull up."

For a moment she seemed lost in thought, then she said, "Let me make a couple of calls first."

Anyone in the building could have done what Hulan did next, which was call the American Embassy—a logical step because Americans outnumbered all other foreigners who entered China on tourist or work visas. Although Hulan hadn't been in contact with anyone at the embassy for a long time, she felt no awkwardness in making the call. Those who'd been there during her last encounter were now dead, in jail, or long gone.

The receptionist patched her through to a junior staffer, Charlie Freer, who seemed personable, informative, and tactful, which made him altogether perfect for his job. "Car accidents, heart attacks, that's what I usually deal with," Freer explained by way of introduction. "We always get information on those cases quickly, and it's my job to make arrangements to get the deceased back home. But I haven't had many missing persons cases per se. Actually this is my first. I mean, what American goes missing in China?"

What he said was true. Most tourists traveled the country in tours and on set routes, while the people who worked here were watched in much the way the Chinese themselves were watched.

"But to answer your question," Freer continued, "I do have a report of a missing archaeologist. It took a couple days to get it. The phone lines are iffy where this guy was working, but you know how that is."

Hulan did. If Freer's missing person worked on the Yangzi, that could explain a lot. The phone lines weren't bad in the major cities along the river, but there were few phones in small towns and villages, and cell connections were notoriously bad because of the height of the gorges.

"We did our usual bit," Freer conceded. "We have a system that we use wherever Americans travel. We notify expats living in the region by fax and e-mail. We send out notices to tourist hotels and restaurants. I like to think that I can find anyone here in China by nightfall."

"I thought you didn't get missing persons," Hulan said.

"Well, there are missing persons and *missing persons*, Inspector. I had a situation just last week where I got a call from a family in California. A man back home had had a stroke and was officially brain-dead. They needed someone to pull the plug, but the brother, who had medical power of attorney, happened to be here on vacation. The sister-in-law made it clear that we weren't going to find this guy in the usual places. In my job you can tell when you're going down a certain path. You know how I deal with problems like that?"

Hulan admitted she didn't.

"I ask, Would your brother—sister, father, aunt, fill in the blank—be what you might call a free spirit? These are people who travel under the radar, if you know what I mean. I wouldn't want the local Public Security Bureau turning up and finding our Joe mellowing out and smoking a joint or, worse, being a Goody Two-shoes and working with some human rights group. That would be a real diplomatic fiasco."

"So where was the brother?"

"Tibet."

Enough said. Both sides had their watchers. Both sides had their policies. Both sides had their own reasons to track people down and spirit them away.

"About your missing person—"

"Brian McCarthy, a graduate student from Seattle," Freer said. "He was reported missing on July twentieth, but I wasn't called until Monday the twenty-second. I called his sister in the States to let her know but only got her answering machine. Next thing I heard she was on her way to the Three Gorges. And of course I informed your ministry of the details, since McCarthy was here as an expert."

Why hadn't Vice Minister Zai just given Hulan McCarthy's name? She shifted uncomfortably in her chair. She knew she was being used, but she didn't know why.

"McCarthy was working near a town called Bashan on the Yangzi as part of a cooperative archaeological program between

China and other nations," Freer continued. "From what I could tell in my conversations with Dr. Ma—he's the supervisor down on the site who called me—this Brian seemed very reliable. Not the sort who'd go off without notifying his superiors."

"Do you have a physical description?" she asked.

Over the phone line she heard Freer shuffle paper.

"He was six feet two inches and one hundred and seventy-five pounds. It says here that he had blue eyes and red hair. Is that a help?"

The body in Fong's lab had to be that of Brian McCarthy. Over the next few minutes, Hulan provided Freer with the closely matched physical description of the body and explained how and where it had been found. They exchanged further information and made a deal of sorts. Charlie Freer would contact the sister in Bashan and help her get her brother's body home; Hulan would tie up loose ends on the Chinese side by speaking with Dr. Ma at the archaeological site, and with the various governmental entities, which would include the Ministry of Public Security, the State Cultural Relics Bureau, and the China Travel and Tourism Administration Bureau. Freer gave her Ma's phone number at the dig but again noted that the line was unreliable. "They have a hard line, but it's temperamental, and I've never gotten through on the cell. You might try sending an e-mail."

Hulan gave Freer the information about whom to contact at the MPS to get the body released when the time came, then said goodbye. Next she tried phoning the supervisor at the archaeological site, but all she got was an electronic whine. She booted up her computer, accessed the Internet, and typed her message:

Dear Dr. Ma,

We have found and identified Mr. McCarthy's body. Please inform me of the circumstances by which he might have come to be in the Yangzi.

After sending the message, she quickly checked her other e-mail. She was just about to log out when the computer informed her that she had new mail. It was from Ma:

Inspector Liu,

I am sorry to hear about Brian. We believe he accidentally fell in the river. The current is swift and dangerous here, but we've been lucky until now.

The reply was terse, but Hulan assumed that Ma probably didn't want to deal with the Ministry of Public Security. The less said, the less likely that something might be misconstrued. It was a policy Hulan herself used on many occasions.

She logged out and went back upstairs to Zai's office.

"I've made the identification," she announced. "Brian McCarthy, your foreigner, was working at an archaeological site on the Yangzi River. The local Public Security Bureau ought to be able to take it from here."

"Perhaps," the vice minister said, then added, "Let's walk."

They went outside and stood in the shade of the porte cochere. As always, a few men—investigators of the third rank—played half-court basketball. They were strong men, tough in their jobs, but not particularly good athletes.

"Why didn't you tell me before what you knew?" Hulan asked Zai.

"What was there to tell? Like the Americans, we sent out notices and made the usual inquiries when we were first informed McCarthy was missing, but really there was nothing to be done and no one to be assigned until he turned up."

"That's not what I meant." She didn't like hearing the agitation in her voice. "Am I being punished for what happened this morning?"

Against all rules regarding interactions with subordinates, Zai answered her honestly. "They don't see your assignment to this case as a punishment. You're a valuable asset to them."

"Then let me do my real job! The All-Patriotic Society—"

"Are you forgetting that a threat has been made against your life?"

"I didn't believe it for an instant."

"Nor I. We have seen no violence from the Society's leadership. Nevertheless, you killed one of their followers—"

"If she actually was—"

"You are now the 'mother killer,'" he reasoned patiently. "Retribution may come not from the top but from someone who saw what happened this morning on his television screen."

"That might not have happened if they hadn't sent the television crew!"

"You wouldn't have been seen if you hadn't shot that woman," he countered. "Your actions caused you to be noticed. You will be safer if you leave town for a while, and it will be easier to protect you if the foreign press picks up the story." He held up a hand to prevent her from interrupting him. "But you must try to look beyond the mistakes of this morning. This is an opportunity for you to come back to the types of cases you do so well. Life and death, this is what you know. This is what you're able to read better than anyone in the building. I want to see you do what you do best. I want you to remember your job."

"How can I ever forget my job? I've done everything they ever asked of me, and this is how they show their gratitude?"

"What happened to you, Hulan? There was a time when you would have asked for this case."

"You know better than anyone in the world what happened to me," she shot back. Zai was the one who'd brought her back to Beijing during the Cultural Revolution to denounce her father. Zai was the one who'd sent her into exile to America. He'd been by her side for every catastrophe in her life, including the death of her child.

"You can't keep blaming yourself," he said. He lowered his voice and added, "You have to start living your life again."

"I can't," she admitted.

"We all have walls around our lives. Some are imposed on us. Some we impose on ourselves." He edged closer to her and squeezed her upper arm. "You and I both know that the trick to survival is how we choose to live within those constraints. Do we sit passively or do we push against them? Do we rise above what's been handed to us or do we give up? This case is a gift. Remember who you are."

She turned and headed back to the building.

Zai raised his voice. "Do not go far, Inspector. I will need you back in my office at three o'clock."

Hulan stopped and turned to stare at her mentor. She didn't see the usual kindness in his eyes. He was now only her superior.

"Why?"

"At three o'clock, Inspector. Be on time."

She watched him walk past her and into the building. The heat shimmered off the asphalt. The scuffle and squeak of sneakers eased the basketball's erratic dribble. Hulan didn't know what lay ahead, but standing there in the open courtyard she felt confused, scared, and angry. She had known these feelings many times in her life, and her bitterness about that was bottomless.

WHEN DAVID GOT TO HIS OFFICE, MISS QUO, HIS ASSISTANT, offered a few consoling remarks about Hulan, then dropped the subject. That's how it was sometimes in China. Who among the general populace had not been a target at some time or other? Who among the billion people who inhabited this country had not done something they'd regretted at least once? David, who'd come from a culture where people were expected to share their feelings, had never fully accepted the way the Chinese—even those you were close to—wouldn't talk about personal matters. Nor did he under-stand the fatalistic approach the Chinese sometimes took toward the worst possible disasters and inequities. As a practical matter, what that meant to David today was that he was expected to table his worries and get to work.

For the last five years, David had been the sole presence in the city, and indeed in all of Asia, for the legal firm of Phillips & MacKenzie. Usually at this time of year he paid social calls to his Chinese clients around the capital before they left for the comforts of the shore or the bright coolness of a mountain resort. Most of his American clients abandoned the country entirely, choosing this sea-son to go home to the States, visit their families, take the kids to Disneyland or Disney World. Others—those without spouses or children—might head below the equator to Australia or even New

Zealand. Sure, it was the dead of winter down there, but what a relief from the weeks of days over one hundred degrees, eye-stinging and lung-choking smog, and humidity so thick that after one minute on the street your flesh was a clammy muck of sweat.

David could see the enervating effects of the climate in the face of the man sitting across from him. Director Ho Youmei of the State Cultural Relics Bureau looked like he wanted to fly out of his skin. He was dressed impeccably in a suit obviously made abroad, but the poor man was wilting all over. But maybe it wasn't the heat that was getting to the director. Today he had broken with so many traditions that David thought Ho either was a man with a serious problem or had become far too westernized for his own good.

Ho had called this morning to make an appointment for 1:30. He'd refused to reveal on the phone why he needed an American attorney's services, why a meeting was required on such short notice, and—most surprising—why he wanted to come to David's office, which automatically put the director in the weaker position.

They'd had tea and exchanged the usual pleasantries. Ho's English was near perfect, but he was hesitant to delve into his problem. This was understandable. All across China—from the Special Economic Zones along the coast and the major cities to the most remote villages deep in the interior—average people, companies, the army, and government ministries all wanted a piece of the economic pie. To get rich is glorious! Private companies and government bureaus alike were bound to get into trouble.

"I've heard good things about you, Attorney Stark," Ho said at last. "You're well-known in Beijing for your discretion in sensitive matters."

So this was to be a job interview.

"I'm one man with a small practice."

"Ah, Chinese modesty. I've heard you are an expert."

"Many people say many things, but are they reliable character witnesses?"

"I'm sure Minister Li at the Ministry of Justice would be amused to hear you question his reliability. He says you are a *Zhongguo-tong*—an honorary Chinese."

"The minister and I are well-acquainted, but we both know he is given to exaggeration."

Ho laughed. "Old Li said you would say this as well."

"I'm happy to be predictable then."

The irony, if such a thing could be said of David's career, was that the Chinese government often hired him, a foreigner, because he adhered to American legal ethics. He honored attorney-client privilege in all of its manifestations, including work product. This was especially important to bureaus and ministries. What was common in the United States—hiring an attorney to conduct an internal investigation of malfeasance and then quietly negotiate restitution and punishment—was a rarity in China, but word had circulated that David could get results without necessarily bringing in the police. Furthermore, he was fluent in spoken Mandarin, even though he was still basically illiterate. He'd gotten pretty far with his tutor in the written language until he'd reached the word *yang*. The word meant different things when pronounced in each of the four tones: *disaster, sheep, raise one's head,* and *sample.* He'd mastered the distinctions but had finally balked when he learned that *yang* in the second rising tone could also mean *pretend, ocean, melt,* or *beetle,* depending on the intricacies of the written character. But he'd stuck with the spoken language, which was why he knew gutter curses and wasn't shy about using them if a case required it.

He was also well-respected in the foreign business community. If he accepted a matter, it was because he knew he could deliver. And deliver he did, for in these last five years David had developed that quintessential prerequisite for good business dealings in China—*guanxi,* connections. No matter which side of the cultural fence a client was on, David had impeccable connections. He worked hard to maintain his contacts back in the States with the FBI and the U.S. Attorney's Office, but the people he had private access to in China were even more impressive. He often consulted with the Ministry of Public Security. Beyond this, it was a well-known fact that his wife was a Red Princess, very rich, very well connected in her own right.

For these reasons, David's practice thrived. He'd conducted numerous internal investigations of corruption for a variety of Chinese governmental entities and had handled several politically awkward matters that required someone intimately familiar with U.S. law. He'd litigated on behalf of the Ministry of Culture in a dispute with an American film company over a proposed theme park. He'd worked as a liaison between U.S. and Chinese Customs departments in numerous matters involving smuggled artifacts. These cases rarely made the papers in either country but were common knowledge in some circles.

"It is your absence of predictability that has made you a friend to China," Ho continued. "My old friend Nixon Chen said this about you as well."

No one had better *guanxi* than Nixon Chen. Nixon was a childhood friend of Hulan's, a former associate at Phillips & MacKenzie, a Red Prince, and probably the most important private lawyer in Beijing.

"Again you embarrass me, but let me say that it's an honor to meet with the director. I too have knowledge of your reputation . . ." Unlike Hulan, David couldn't pull a *dangan,* a secret personal file, but he'd chatted just enough with Nixon and a few others this morning to be able to flatter the director.

They could go on this way for hours. David used to chafe at these formalities, but now he enjoyed the exchange of compliments and the constant deferring that were part of the delicate dance leading first to business, then to deeper relationships. But Director Ho glanced at his watch, settled further into his chair, and stared at David. The message was clear: he wanted to move on.

"How may I help you, Director?"

"Minister Li said you are familiar with my field."

"Yes," David said. "On behalf of the ministry, I just negotiated the return to China of a sculpture stolen during the Boxer Rebellion and taken to England."

Every case required that an attorney become an overnight expert, and in recent years David had learned a lot about how artifacts moved. Ho would already know this, but he still delayed saying what he wanted by giving David background information. Another common custom . . .

"When China closed to outsiders," Ho began, "Chairman Mao decreed that we had no use for the ancient past. Few excavations were conducted. Then, during the Cultural Revolution, the Red Guard were ordered to destroy any artifacts that could be read as symbols of a decadent or imperial past. Today we have a new mandate. We are to prove that China has had five thousand years of uninterrupted history. Although every schoolchild can recite that fact, we have no physical proof of the first two thousand years. So now we are trying to unite history, chronology, and newly discovered artifacts to validate our claim to the rest of the world. Unfortunately, we still know very little. For years we believed that the cradle of Chinese civilization was on the Yellow River, but we've discovered sites in other parts of the country that may suggest otherwise." He smiled wanly. "As you know, China is backward in many respects."

David knew the buildup. He'd heard it several times before. Now Ho would begin to talk about his problem, and it would probably involve foreigners—Americans most likely. Would it be an unfair exchange of information? Would it be something as simple as fraternizing between the races on a remote dig in the interior? None of this, David knew, was one-sided; each contingent liked to blame the other. That was the given.

As was the tenuous relationship between China and the United States that percolated above and below the surface of all that transpired between the two countries. Which country was more powerful? Which culture was more important? Most Chinese saw the United States as the most unfriendly nation to China, as the country they most resented, and as the one that would eventually pay the price for its bad manners. This last covered a broad range of indignities—from the perceived persecution of Overseas Chinese like Wen Ho Lee to the constant nagging by the West on issues such as human rights, the one-child policy, and sovereignty over Hong Kong, Taiwan, and Tibet, that the average Chinese thought were none of America's business. So, could the United States bomb the Chinese embassy and get away with it? Yes, though the fury that this act had brought to the surface had shocked the world. Could China shoot down an American spy plane and get away with it? Yes, though the righteous indignation with which David's government responded was disingenuous to say the least. To David, it was all part of the cosmic Jell-O that made up his universe. Push a little on this side of the world, and a shudder rippled across the Pacific. Shove a little on that side of the Rim, and set off tremors here. David's job then was to maneuver through these shifting tides without anyone questioning his integrity, his loyalty, or his demeanor.

"China has embarked on the greatest construction project in the world," Ho continued. "But once the Three Gorges Dam is completed, the reservoir will cover over two thousand archaeological sites. What we call Site 518 lies two hundred and eighty of your miles downstream from Chongqing, just east of the Qutang Gorge. I have come here today because we've suffered the loss of several artifacts from this excavation."

"You've been in contact with the local authorities . . ."

"We've worked with the Security Bureau in Bashan, the town closest to the site, but what do a few policemen in a small village understand about thefts of this sort?"

And couldn't it be possible, even probable, that those policemen were somehow involved? David mused.

"What specifically is missing?" he asked.

An odd stillness came over Ho.

"I've relied on the leader of the dig to keep me informed of what's been stolen, but I am a long way from the Three Gorges and don't receive as much information as I'd like."

"Are you saying you don't know?" David was skeptical of the idea.

"I am aware of the identity of certain pieces, but the team is pulling out artifacts faster than they can be cataloged, and we cannot begin a search until we file an international report detailing each missing item."

The vagueness of the sentence mixed with Ho's body language contained a lot of possibilities. Could the Cultural Relics Bureau be so disorganized as not to know what it was finding? Maybe the bureau wouldn't know, but certainly they'd have to know at the site, wouldn't they? There had to be something more . . .

Ho pulled on an earlobe and confided, "Even in the year 2002, archaeology is still a largely unmechanized profession. We work with shovels, spades, scrapers, and brushes. As a result, we see cuts, bruises, and sometimes broken bones. But Site 518 has had more than the usual number of problems."

Ho gazed away as he said this last bit. David understood. You could tackle something head-on or pretend that you really weren't saying it.

"I've handled several cases involving work-related accidents," he prompted. The only good that had come out of the terrible events at the Knight toy factory was that they had opened a new practice area for David in workplace safety. These past few years, he had been hired not only by the Chinese but also by American and European companies to help avoid or correct abuses.

"I'm aware of your expertise in these matters. I've been told you bring to the table a unique set of abilities. Our entire country is grateful for what you did at the Knight factory." Ho followed this piece of flattery with a new disclosure. "So far this summer we have had five accidental deaths."

"All at Site 518?"

"All in the vicinity."

"From what you've said, fatal accidents should be rare."

"Correct."

"So then what are these 'accidents'?"

"A worker fell from a ladder. A bridge collapsed and three men died. And there was a drowning."

"Except for the man who fell from the ladder, these don't seem necessarily work related."

Director Ho jutted his chin. It was the Chinese equivalent of a shrug, but what exactly did that shrug mean?

"Is there any way these deaths are connected?"

"They were all local day workers."

This didn't seem like much to go on. After all, most of China's vast population could be categorized as local day workers, whether in fields or in factories.

"Has anything been done to improve safety or to investigate these deaths more closely? Again, what does the local Public Security Bureau have to say?" David asked.

"How do we improve safety when we have phantom accidents?" Ho came back silkily. "How do you get the Public Security Bureau to do something when nothing seems wrong?"

"Phantom?"

"We have nothing to pinpoint and no one to accuse."

"Be grateful," David reassured the director. "It probably means no one's to blame. The Public Security Bureau would investigate if there were something to worry about."

"That's what I was told."

Sometimes David's job was closer to that of a psychiatrist or priest than that of an attorney. People wanted to tell him something, but he had to wait until they were ready.

"We are a country of more than a billion," Ho said, still circling his problem. "We cannot worry about the death of every peasant. A foreigner's death, however, brings us unwanted attention."

Again Ho fell silent, but this time David wouldn't allow the director to skirt the issue. "Tell me exactly what happened."

"A young man named Brian McCarthy worked at Site 518 as a foreign expert. He was recently found dead. Today I was informed that it was not an accident. This makes me question the other deaths."

But what Ho said next showed that he was less concerned with the loss of life than with the bureau's reputation in the international community. "Our difficulties make their presence known at an inopportune time," he went on. "The world's eyes are focused on the Three Gorges Dam . . ."

Actually, David thought, the dam had transfixed environmentalists, politicians, and investors in great debates about pollution, safety, and money, but most people around the world had not even heard of it.

"Not everyone wants to see the dam finished," Ho explained. "Even in our own government there are factions against it . . ."

This was also true. Premier Zhu Rongji had startled the country recently when he made public comments critical of the quality of construction, as well as of the graft and corruption connected to the project.

"Everyone is looking for someone to blame," Ho complained. "The tiger will continue to roar and the phoenix will rise again, but an ant is insignificant."

The implication was clear: China was losing face on the world stage and Ho was worried that he might be set up to take a fall to divert bad publicity about the dam.

"Our situation is complicated by the fact that the team at Site 518 is international," Ho continued. "Suppose one of them is involved in either the thefts or the deaths?"

"Then you would want to work with the Ministry of Public Security."

"Exactly, and yet we both know that this may not be the best thing for foreign relations."

True again. The MPS was deeply feared. Its agents were notoriously aggressive, and they didn't follow rules that might be considered commonplace by someone from England, France, or the United States.

"What do you want me to do?" David asked.

"I want to hire you to look into the disappearance of our artifacts. Find them and whoever is taking them. If you discover something internal to our bureau, I'd like you to keep it that way."

"Absolutely," David answered. "I consider all matters that I take on to be sensitive and private."

"I also need someone who can shepherd us through whatever may come up with the investigation into Brian McCarthy's death."

"I have a lot of experience dealing with local security bureaus."

But this wasn't quite what Ho had in mind. "I understand that you have special *guanxi* with the MPS."

"That my wife is employed by the ministry is no secret," David responded, though he was a little surprised by the segue from his general experience with local police to his very particular connection with Hulan at China's equivalent of the FBI.

"Vice Minister Zai assures me that you and your wife have

worked well together in the past on matters sensitive to the state," Ho stated evenly.

David hadn't expected Zai's name to come up either. It seemed that Ho had gone to considerable lengths to check out David's credentials.

Then Ho dropped his final bombshell. "Your wife has been assigned to investigate Brian McCarthy's death. So, in addition to looking into the thefts, I'd like you to represent the bureau's interests if it's discovered that his or any of the workers' deaths are connected to Site 518."

Ho pushed his chair back and stood. "We have an appointment at the Ministry of Public Security at three o'clock. You can inform me of your decision to take the case after you've heard what the vice minister has to say."

When David and Director Ho were ushered into Vice Minister Zai's office, Hulan was already there. David remembered back with incredible clarity to the day five years ago when he had first entered this room. He recalled the total shock he experienced at seeing Hulan, the woman who had disappeared from his life seven years previously. From that moment of supreme confusion, they had reconnected and fallen in love again.

Now he felt conflicted. It seemed they were being brought together for an investigation, but this whole setup was suspicious. Why throw them together again after so many years? What was it about this case that required the two of them? Just what was Ho after? Not to mention Zai. Hulan wouldn't like being pulled away from her All-Patriotic Society campaign, David knew that much. Their eyes met briefly, and he read profound wariness in hers. It put him at ease to know that she picked up on his caution too. David had heard enough Chinese bureaucrats obfuscate or lie or try to paint something in rosy hues when the colors of the situation were as dark as mud that he never believed every word that was spoken. Only speak one-third of the truth. Hulan had taught him that.

True to personal form and social custom, Zai had retreated beneath a veneer of bureaucratic authority, which was exactly what David expected. Familiarity didn't mean that this meeting would be anything less than formal. In the center of the room, four over-stuffed chairs had been placed facing each other with a little table between them. Tea was poured. Watermelon seeds were set out in a dish. Cigarettes were offered. Compliments were exchanged. David watched Hulan through all of this. Whatever emotions she'd felt this morning were now deeply hidden, but he wondered if she too was thinking of that day five years ago when he'd walked into this office. What did she see when she looked at him now?

Zai smoothly led them into the purpose for the meeting. "Attorney Stark, Inspector Liu," he began, falling back on formal titles befitting the situation, "we have brought the two of you together in hopes that you can once again help China by using your special skills. In the past, Inspector Liu has not let political correctness influence her reasoning, while Attorney Stark has always understood the importance of keeping secrets. Inspector Liu carries with her a badge of government authority, while you, Attorney Stark, can sometimes get people to answer your questions for the very reason that you do not carry a badge. You have not crossed any politically difficult lines in the past. As a result, no one has lost face."

"Keeping things to ourselves is what American lawyers are trained to do," David said.

"Which may be particularly important in this situation." Zai shifted his attention to Ho. "Director, have you told Attorney Stark about McCarthy's death?"

When the director nodded, Zai said, "Good. Now I hope you will explain to Inspector Liu a little bit about your other problems."

After Ho repeated much of what he'd told David earlier about the missing artifacts, Hulan asked, "But why are you so interested in what happened at Site 518? Haven't several sites along the river been looted?"

"Looted and vandalized," Ho admitted ruefully. "Most of the people who do this are not sophisticated. We call them 'mound-digging rats.' They don't know what they're finding, and in many cases they've broken more than they've stolen. Some of these hooligans have been arrested. They've been sent to prison or labor camp for terms of one to fifteen years."

"What about the artifacts that aren't broken?" Hulan asked.

The director cleared his throat of Beijing grime, then said, "Sadly, many of them leave the country and are put up for auction. Sometimes they disappear into private collections or even into unwitting— or unethical—museums." Ho leaned forward and spoke directly to Vice Minister Zai. "At least a million of our relics are being held captive in private and public collections in other countries!"

"Until very recently almost anyone could walk into a country and take whatever they wanted," David explained, "but then some of the most famous museums in the world would not be so famous if not for this practice. I think of the Elgin Marbles in the British Museum or the Egyptian artifacts in the Louvre. Often relics of this sort can be repatriated. Countries that wish to keep their friendship with China are most willing to negotiate returns."

"Attorney Stark is right," Ho agreed. "But we must know where they are in order to retrieve them."

"What about the Poly Group bronzes?" Hulan asked. "You knew where they were."

David had always admired the way Hulan refused to succumb to the strictures of female decorum in her investigations, although Director Ho was not so appreciative of her impertinence.

"Those bronzes were ransacked from the Summer Palace by British and French troops one hundred and forty years ago," Ho said plaintively. "When Christie's and Sotheby's put them up for sale two years ago, we asked that they be returned to Beijing."

David remembered this case clearly. At the time, Hulan had said that the government should have hired him to deal with the auction houses. Instead the PRC issued a proclamation to the effect that there would no longer be a policy of looking the other way while the nation's treasures were sold off in a city that once again belonged to China. The Hong Kong courts thought otherwise. One country, two systems. Mainland China's laws protecting national treasures did not apply in Hong Kong, where stolen antiquities were openly displayed for sale in shops along Hollywood Road. So the bronzes had gone on the block, with the Poly Group, a commercial arm of the People's Liberation Army, making the winning bids to the tune of $6 million U.S. The Poly Group said they'd made the purchase as a matter of patriotic pride. But instead of donating the bronzes to a museum, the group had used them as a marketing tool, sending them on a tour around the country to attract new customers.

"We would all like to prevent a repeat of that embarrassment," Zai confided to David, "which is why you are here. From the ministry's perspective, prosecution is less important than retrieval and repatriation, if indeed the artifacts have left the country."

David thought about what Director Ho had said in their earlier meeting. All kinds of diplomatic problems could arise if the thieves turned out to be foreigners. It would be easier in the long run to settle things quietly . . .

"Of course, if Chinese nationals are involved," Zai went on, staying a step ahead of David, "Inspector Liu should make arrests."

"Explain something to me, Vice Minister," Hulan cut in. "What is the real concern here? Brian McCarthy's death or these missing relics?"

"The young man's death is a tragedy, no? We can all agree on that. And of course I'm concerned about the others . . ."

"Others?" Hulan asked, and David could tell by her voice that she couldn't help being intrigued by the facts.

Over the next few minutes Zai recounted what David had learned about the deaths of the peasants.

Hulan inquired, "Why was I not informed of this before?"

"It was better that we all hear this together," Zai responded evenly.

"Is there any proof that the thefts and the deaths are connected?" she asked.

"None," Zai answered, "but you should assume they are. Again let me clarify, you are to investigate Brian McCarthy's murder. If these other deaths also turn out to be murders, then you know your duty. Attorney Stark is to look into the thefts and—"

Perhaps finally understanding how closely she and David would need to work together, Hulan said to Zai, "It is not my place to make suggestions to the vice minister, but I still believe this case would be better served by someone else. Perhaps someone who is not so visible."

Vice Minister Zai laughed good-naturedly. "One reason to send you to the Three Gorges is that there is no television reception there. They may be the only place in the country where today no one has seen your face."

"Well, then," Hulan backpedaled, "perhaps I should go alone. As you pointed out earlier, a threat has been made against me. Assign Investigator Lo to accompany me. There is no reason to put David in danger—"

"Investigator Lo will remain here to handle any requests for information you may need from the capital." Zai turned to David. "Yes, there could be danger, but that is true in everything we do, isn't that correct, Attorney Stark?" To Hulan, he said, "If you need additional help, you will find it in Bashan's Public Security Bureau."

He regarded David closely. "We await your decision and hope that you, too, will see the importance for your country in taking on this matter. Our two nations have had too many aggravations in recent years. Fortunately everything has returned to business as usual. But we don't know what could happen the next time. It's very important that you two prevent anything that could be humiliating to either of our countries." Zai paused, then asked, "Attorney Stark?"

"I'd be honored to represent the bureau's interests in this matter," David said, though from the look on Hulan's face he knew this was not the response she wanted to hear.

"Very well," the vice minister said as he stood up. "Inspector Liu, I suggest you escort Director Ho to his car."

Zai was once again asserting his position over Hulan, and she obeyed without question, leaving David and the vice minister alone. Zai took a sip of tea, then sat back in his chair and openly scrutinized David. At last he said, "When Director Ho asked for help, I thought of you for all of the reasons we have just discussed, but I have other considerations as well. You know I would not knowingly send you into jeopardy. Although I cannot anticipate what you will encounter, I trust that you will employ abilities that I did not mention to Director Ho. Our Hulan thinks and acts intuitively. She has a compulsion to put her physical body between herself and evil."

This was true, David thought. It was as though she dared the guilty to punish her instead of the intended victim.

"We both know this method has not always worked well for her in the past," Zai went on. "You, David, are so different. Physically you are much better equipped to handle danger than Hulan, yet you use your mind to deal with trouble. I don't mean this as a criticism. You simply use logic and linear thinking to solve problems."

This was true as well. David believed that civilization and culture rest on the conviction that logic will always win. Besides, lawyers are supposed to use their brains, not their fists, to deal with difficult and painful situations.

"She puts herself into danger. You think yourself through it. Together you have found a way to solve the most convoluted cases. But this is not why I am sending you." The vice minister's formality was replaced by the friendly tone of the person Hulan and David had dined with once a week until just a few months ago. "This is a good way for you and Hulan to be together—alone! This could be the last chance for the two of you."

"Vice Minister, I don't know—"

"Don't speak, David. Just listen. The Three Gorges are one of the most beautiful places on earth. Enjoy the sights. Talk to each other. Have dinner by candlelight." He clasped his hands together with something that approached conspiratorial glee. "To help things along, I had the two of you booked together in one cabin on a slow ferry." He laughed then, truly pleased with himself. "You'll know how to handle things from there."

If Zai had been anyone else, David would have been infuriated by the intrusion into his private life. Still . . .

"Hulan may not appreciate what you have done—"

Zai's laughter faded. "This is not just for Hulan. You have suffered too. She needs to understand that."

David didn't know how to respond.

After a moment, Zai said, "She loves you. She's just forgotten how to show it."

THE ENFEOFFED DOMAIN

(Hou fu)

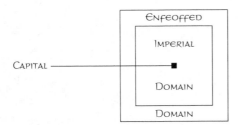

The domain of nobles extends 500 *li* from the Imperial Domain. This is home to high ministers, great officers, barons, and princes.

CHAPTER

4

ALTHOUGH HULAN KNEW SHE WAS BEING MANIPULATED FOR reasons she didn't fully understand, she could rationalize Zai's motives for sending her and David to Bashan. David was perfect for the job. No one in China knew how to handle a situation like this more discreetly than he did. He'd be able to find the missing artifacts and protect the national and international reputation of the Cultural Relics Bureau if charges of corruption, theft, or bad labor practices came up. And Hulan had experience in dealing with both murder and foreigners. But why had Zai sent her deliberately out of the room to speak with David alone? When David got back to Hulan's office, she asked what that conversation had been about, suspecting there was another political thread running through this situation that Zai hadn't wanted to discuss with her.

A bemused look came over David's face. He rubbed his forehead as he searched for an answer. She assumed it had to be bad. He tried to smile reassuringly, but it came across as an embarrassed grimace. "I'm not going to lie to you. Zai sees this as a romantic interlude for us," he admitted at last. "A kind of second honeymoon."

Hulan felt herself blush, and she suddenly didn't know where to look. "I—"

"Don't worry, Hulan." David laughed, and she knew he was trying to defuse the awkwardness of the situation. She joined in his laughter, shaking her head. But when he added, "Nothing will happen unless you want it to," she colored again.

The next several hours were crazy. She gathered some things from her office and made a few calls to wrap up her other cases, then Investigator Lo drove her and David back to the compound. While David threw some clothes in a bag, Hulan visited her mother and wrote out instructions for the nurse. When it came time for Hulan to pack, she found herself thinking again of Zai's plan. There was such unease between her and David now, but the possibilities of this trip kindled the first sexual thoughts she'd had in a long time. She was embarrassed that Zai had even discussed her marriage with David and unsure whether David would be at all interested in her anymore, but there was something about the whole situation that made her feel . . . She struggled to find the right definition for her state of mind. Finally, she told herself that she didn't want anything to happen—how could it after everything that had passed between her and David?—but she owed it to Zai to try. When it didn't work out, she would be able to tell him she'd done her best out of respect for him.

At 9:00 P.M., Investigator Lo picked up David and Hulan to take them to the airport. On the way, Hulan asked Lo to tell Pathologist Fong to go ahead and do further tests on the notebook paper found in Brian McCarthy's pocket. Lo should also begin gathering data on all the foreigners and Chinese officials at the site. It wouldn't hurt if he took a look at Director Ho's *dangan* too, for he seemed overly concerned about his own position. Once Hulan got to Bashan, she would obtain a copy of the police report on Brian's death from the local Public Security Bureau.

When she concluded, Lo glanced at her in the rearview mirror and said, "I still don't understand why Vice Minister Zai has ordered me to stay behind. I should go with you."

She sensed rather than saw David's amused smile.

"It's not our place to question the vice minister's orders," Hulan answered steadily.

Zai's plans didn't quite work out the way he'd envisioned. After landing in Chongqing at 1:30 in the morning, Hulan and David shared a double bed at the Holiday Inn. They both kept to their sides of the bed and managed not to speak of anything of consequence either then or a couple of hours later, when they got up to go to the Chaotianmen Docks to board the ancient-looking ferry that would take them downriver to Bashan. Their room was private and mercifully equipped with bunk beds. But as they slowly floated down the Yangzi, Hulan found herself thinking about her husband, and about Zai's plan.

Around noon, Hulan and David went to the dining room and were lucky enough to get a window table. They'd left the city behind and were once again deep in the vastness of China's interior. After lunch they stayed where they were, nibbling peanuts, sipping tea, and watching the world unfurl before them. They hadn't spent this much time together in months. Hulan was nervous, but as David chatted idly about the river she found herself noticing how relaxed he seemed. He had always been a handsome man and easy to talk to. His brown hair showed just a trace of gray at the temples, and his blue eyes still looked at her lovingly. Here, away from Beijing and their sad memories, she caught glimpses of the person she'd fallen in love with.

Later, after dinner, they spent a little time on deck. The air was still warm, and the humidity settled on their skin in a soft sheen. When David took her hand, she didn't pull away. But when they'd gone back to their cabin, he had undressed, gotten into the top bunk, and gone to sleep. She lay awake for a long while, feeling the gentle movement of the ferry on the water, listening to David's breathing above her, and wondering if there truly was a way to cross the gulf that had formed between them.

But there was another thing to think about. She was afraid of this murder case. Seeing Brian McCarthy's body had brought back memories of burning flesh, of screaming women, of lost lives. Did the events at the Knight factory have to end the way they had? Could she have done anything differently? These thoughts inevitably led her to Chaowen. Could Hulan have done something differently when Chaowen first fell ill? Wasn't there *something* that could have been done? Hulan had failed as a daughter and failed as an investigator, but wasn't it too cruel that she had failed as a mother too? These questions had tormented her for so long, and the feelings they stirred in her pushed her out of bed. As she took out her Luger, cleaned it, then repacked it, the recriminations and self-doubt seemed overwhelming. She didn't know if she'd learned from her mistakes—any of them.

Just before dawn they were roused by a shipwide announcement that they were about to enter the Qutang Gorge, the first of the Three Gorges. David and Hulan hurried out onto the deck and stood at the prow looking downriver. The air felt as thick as a swamp. David's shirt stuck to his skin, and dark, wet spots began to blotch the cotton. Hulan dabbed at her forehead and the back of her neck with a handkerchief. But this was a new day, and she took David's hand. He was cautious enough not to risk looking at her, but he squeezed her hand to acknowledge her gesture. Each of them was making tentative steps. If they were at Zai's suggestion, so be it.

The deck hummed with excitement. Even those for whom this trip was a daily or weekly occurrence pressed against the railings to watch as the ferry entered the gorge. Two large mountains flanked the river, forming the Kuimen Gate, its giant peaks hidden in mist. The water churned turbulent clouds of yellow silt as the ferry fought its way through the dramatic entrance. Precipices hung out high overhead. Rain and time had caused crevasses to form, and the limestone walls had been pitted into great spongy forms.

The voice on the loudspeaker recited, "The Qutang Gorge is eight kilometers long. It is the shortest but most majestic of the Three Gorges. The widest point is just one hundred and fifty meters and can be just as deep, making this part of the river one of the deepest in the world. The river has been known to rise from fifty to seventy-five meters during monsoon season."

Two elderly women with thick Sichuan accents elbowed their way to the railing next to Hulan.

"Please note the old towpath," the voice on the loudspeaker continued. "In olden days our countrymen pulled boats up the river by using ropes." Static rendered the next part of the message unintelligible, but one of the women next to Hulan pointed up the cliff on the southern bank and jabbered animatedly. Toward the top were coffins that the Ba people had attached to the sheer rock face thousands of years ago. The static cleared, and the announcer directed passengers to observe other highlights. The ferry came around a bend in the river, and Hulan saw a painted line marking the future water level. The uppermost reaches of this gorge would still be here, but its grandeur would disappear.

"'A bridge will fly to span the north and south,'" Hulan murmured.

"What did you say?" David asked.

"It's a line from a poem by Mao. He envisioned the dam back in the fifties." She looked at David and smiled. "Don't expect any more poetry. You've just heard all I know."

Although most Chinese of her social class were well-versed in both the classics and contemporary works, Hulan had great holes in her knowledge. Having been sent as a child first to the countryside, then to the States, she'd forgotten most of the folktales of her childhood and had missed the university courses in Chinese history and literature that others of her generation took.

A few minutes later, the ferry docked at Bashan Village—Bashan meant Ba Mountain—which lay about 130 meters above the waterline on the north shore. Boats—from small two-man fishing vessels to a bright white modern hydrofoil—bobbed in the waters along the pier, where passengers greeted family and friends. Bearers shouted out their best prices, then carried baggage, gifts, and goods like television sets and refrigerators bought in Chongqing up the steep stairs that led to the town itself. On the edges of the stairs the usual food and water vendors crowded together with women and children who sold homemade items—knit booties, fans, sandals, and woven straw hats.

Dr. Ma Zhongyan, the leader of the Site 518 excavation, was easy to find in the pushing, shouting, waving throng. He was dressed in khaki pants, a white linen shirt that had wrinkled in the humidity, and a Yankees' baseball cap. His feet were planted apart, and his arms hung loosely at his sides. Ma's English was as perfect and American as Hulan's, showing not only that he'd been educated abroad but that he'd spent a great deal of time in the United States from an early age. Maybe he was a Red Prince, but if so, Hulan would have known who he was, and she definitely didn't.

They climbed into Ma's Jeep, and he beeped the horn to alert the crowds milling about at the top of the stairs that he was coming through, but the action was hardly necessary. The Jeep apparently had no muffler, and the engine itself rattled and groaned. Ma ground the Jeep into gear and, after a series of jerks, eased into traffic.

Bashan was a relatively small town by Chinese standards. The buildings by the dock were practical, with corrugated roofs and electrical lines hung in a jury-rigged jumble overhead. This town wasn't large enough to merit a New Immigrant City, so everyone here would be moved and everything left behind would be inundated. A large placard on the central plaza declared the fact in huge red countdown numbers—423 days left. In the meantime, life in the old town continued as usual. They drove past open-air meat shops, vegetable stands, and kiosks for cosmetics, tires, hair cutting, tooth pulling, fortune-telling, and herbal remedies. The farther they got into the town, the older the buildings, which were constructed of homemade brick with old-style sloping tile roofs. Though this place was far off the tourist track, signs in Chinese and English welcomed all visitors and proclaimed Bashan's hospitality.

"Our group has practically taken over the town," Ma shouted above the roar of the engine. "It hasn't been very developed or influenced by the outside, but we do have a good hotel for our foreign experts. The headman thinks our business is so important that he's allotted electricity all day to the quadrant of Bashan that includes the Panda Guesthouse. Of course, promising electricity and providing it are two different things. Still, I think you'll find the Panda Guesthouse quite nice."

The words *guesthouse* and *quite nice* rarely found themselves paired together in China.

"Don't worry," Ma said. "The Panda Guesthouse was originally a courtyard home for a very wealthy family. All of our VIPers stay there. We can swing by now if you'd like."

They didn't, and Ma continued on. Billboards and posters advertised regional products—pickled mustard tuber, Magnificent Sound cigarettes, and canned lichee. There were also the usual one-child admonitions, as well as other government slogans promoting New Immigrant Cities in the Three Gorges. But here and there were crudely painted characters slapped onto rough walls: BE REVERENT, FOLLOW THE NINE VIRTUES, and BE CAREFUL FOR THE END AT THE BEGINNING. Hulan had never before seen such a blatant display of All-Patriotic Society slogans. The phrases contained nothing inflammatory—they were the usual exhortations for righteous living interspersed with meeting times—but practice of the religion was illegal nonetheless. Why hadn't the local Public Security Bureau painted out these signs? Why hadn't they made arrests during the advertised meetings? Once she'd dealt with Brian McCarthy's murder, she'd investigate the local All-Patriotic Society's movements.

The Jeep slowed as it approached a narrow bridge that crossed the river. There was considerable foot traffic here, and Ma explained that this old bridge connected the village to the countryside and served as the main artery for transporting produce and other materials in and out of Bashan. A few children hung over the guardrails, throwing rocks into the Bashan Stream, which ran below the pylons. The Jeep crossed the bridge and continued east along a dirt road that cut over the hills and followed the course of the Yangzi. Hulan saw no other cars, trucks, or bicycles. Cultivated terraces planted with corn rose above her as far as she could see and extended down to the river's edge.

They traveled east another kilometer. The hillsides became steeper until finally they were no longer arable. Green gave way to dust and rocks. Every few meters they passed electric poles that teetered precariously on the side of the road. No wonder electricity and phone service were iffy at the site. A strong wind or a slight bump from a passing pedestrian could easily topple one or more of the poles.

Ma braked at a barrier made up of a two-by-four propped on two piles of stones and held in place by large rocks. He jumped out, moved the two-by-four, drove the Jeep through the gate, and jumped out again to replace the board. This security gate wouldn't have been much of a deterrent for thieves whether from inside or outside the camp.

Ma drove down to a cluster of work tents about three meters above the river. He had Hulan and David wait by the Jeep, then jogged over to one of the larger tents. When he returned, he had cold-water bottles and hats for each of them. Now that they didn't have the breeze from the open Jeep, the heat was crushing. There were a few trees, all of which were dwarfed and deformed as if from some disease, so the camp had no relief from the sun except under the tarpaulins. And while it seemed unbelievably dry with all of the dirt and rocks, the air itself was thick with the humidity that rose off the river, exacerbating the worst aspects of this Give-Up Weather season.

After handing off the water bottles, Ma said, "It seems I have a double audience and a double duty here. Attorney Stark, you've been sent by my boss to check on me and my missing artifacts."

No one disagreed with this assessment.

"And you, Inspector Liu, have come from that most worrisome of places—the Ministry of Public Security—to investigate what happened to a young man who was my responsibility. That's the kind of checking I really don't like. But it seems that, in either case, I have no choice. So, before I show you what I think happened to Brian and what I know about the thefts, I want to explain a little about what we're doing out here. I think it will help Attorney Stark and at the same time give you, Inspector, a sense of the people we're working with and our goals."

Ma pointed up the hill to where most of the work seemed to be happening. "We're standing about a fifth of the way up from the river to the top of the site. Most archaeological sites in the Three Gorges are classified as 'second tier,' which means they're located between one hundred twenty-five and one hundred fifty-five meters above river level. Even today, towns and villages in this area are found well above the reach of floodwaters. Time has left behind layer upon layer of history in these platforms. The dam, when completed, will reach—"

"One hundred and seventy-seven meters," David finished.

"Exactly, which means that most towns and nearly all archaeological sites along the river, this one included, will be inundated. These last three years—with help from our foreign friends—we've excavated not just in areas that are exposed to the elements but in the caves as well."

"Caves?" David asked.

Ma again pointed up the hill to several dark openings in the earth. "This whole hillside is honeycombed with caves."

The pattern was set. David asked questions; Hulan listened and looked around. He was direct; she preferred the indirect.

"Come, let's walk." Ma set a vigorous pace up the trail. Hulan felt sweat trickle down the backs of her legs, and she took a drink from her water bottle. But if Ma expected his visitors to show any signs of physical weakness, he was mistaken. David was in great shape. He ran every day, even in the heat of the Beijing summer, and Hulan had the toughness of having spent her youth at the Red Soil Farm in the harsh countryside. Hard physical activity in relentless heat ranked as only a slight inconvenience.

"Our main interest is the Ba civilization," Ma resumed. "We believe one of the reasons the Ba people settled here was that the caves offered protection from the elements. They were also good places to hide in times of danger. You may not know this, but China has more caves than any other country in the world. You came down from Chongqing, right? During the war with the Japanese, the people of Chongqing hid in caves during air raids. Today many of those caves are shops. Actually, about forty million people live in caves throughout China. Do Americans use their natural resources so well, Attorney Stark?"

"Can't say we do." David responded to the challenge with equanimity.

"And of course nearly every province in China has caves renowned for the beauty of their stalactites and stalagmites. We also have caves filled with Buddhist carvings . . ." Ma paused just long enough for them to catch it, then added, "But I guess you know that."

So Ma knew a bit about David and Hulan, which meant, if nothing else, that he'd read the newspaper coverage of the Knight factory debacle five years ago. Hulan gave him a cool look.

"As an archaeologist, I've been in many caves in many countries," Ma continued easily. "I'm always touched by the idea that once people used those dark holes in the earth not only as means of artistic or religious expression but also to record their daily lives—the animals brought down in a hunt or the battles won. People were leaving history on those walls even before written language was invented. Unfortunately, although we continue to look, we have yet to find any artifacts in the Site 518 caves. Primarily we scrape at the ground in the pits, looking for artifacts, looking for the past, looking for civilization, looking for the *lives* of the people who came before us."

"What exactly are you looking for?" David asked.

Ma sighed, then said, "Thanks to your Indiana Jones, many people think that archaeologists are treasure hunters. We aren't. Our group—archaeologists interested specifically in the Yangzi watershed—has four questions that fascinate and perplex us. We call them the Four Mysteries, and I'm sure you'll hear about them at lunch, although you never know. The people on our team have many interests." He quirked his head. "How much do you know about archaeology, Attorney Stark?"

"Your mandate is to prove five thousand years of continuous culture."

"Real culture, as opposed to a few people huddled around a fire carving crude weapons from stone," Ma said, then motioned for them to sit on some large boulders. "For years scholars suspected that people may have lived in the gorges during the Stone Age, but it wasn't until this final push before inundation that Paleolithic sites dating from 50,000 to 12,000 B.C. were located. We've also found Neolithic sites, one of which is right here beneath our Ba excavations. The ceramics that we've uncovered are stylistically different from those found outside the gorges. We think this means that the Qutang Gorge must have been some sort of cultural divide. So Mystery One is why did societies in the Three Gorges area—and the Qutang Gorge in particular—develop so independently? Mystery Two: the Chu Mausoleum . . ."

Hulan tuned out his words and tried to imagine Brian McCarthy in this landscape. Site 518 was far larger than she'd imagined, extending up and down the hillside. The land was terraced, but whatever cultivation had occurred here was long gone, leaving only dirt and rocks. Peasants crisscrossed the dusty terrain with wheelbarrows, while others—Chinese students and foreigners—squatted in pits sheltered by tarpaulin canopies.

The longer Hulan sat here, the more she could catch snippets of conversations drifting down the hill to them. The day workers spoke only Chinese, while the students and foreigners spoke the international language of science—English. From across the way she heard an older man—American—say to a young woman with long bare legs, "You're running out of time. If you want that to happen, then you've got to . . ." Then the young woman nodded toward Hulan. When the man turned and saw her too, the rest of his sentence evaporated. He waved, said something more to the young woman that Hulan didn't catch, then the two of them walked over to the boulders to meet Ma's visitors.

Ma interrupted his recitation of the Four Mysteries and introduced David and Hulan to Stuart Miller and his daughter, Catherine. Hulan didn't need to hear Ma's flowery praise to know Stuart's accomplishments. He owned Miller Enterprises, a conglomerate with multiple subsidiaries, including Miller Engineering. The state-run Chinese press called Miller "a good friend to China," who had shown his friendship in many ways. Most recently he'd signed a billion-dollar contract to provide crews, expertise, and machinery for the building of turbines for the Three Gorges Dam. He was a distinguished-looking man, in his early fifties. His daughter had gotten her good looks from her father. Catherine's hair hung in long, lustrous brown curls. Heavy mascara and eyeliner outlined mesmerizing deep brown eyes. Voluptuous young breasts pushed against the fabric of her T-shirt. Her lips were full, and for a second Hulan wondered if she'd had silicone injections. But no, her lips matched too perfectly the rest of Catherine's face to be anything other than natural.

"Is our leader boring you to death with his Four Mysteries?" she asked, then, to take the sting out of her words, playfully jabbed Ma's arm.

"Maybe you can do a better job," Ma dared her back in the same spirit. "I was on the last two."

Catherine let her eyes rest on David, took a breath, and said, "Since we've found remains here from nearly every culture, time period, and dynasty, Mystery Three is: Did each era and its relics influence subsequent cultures in the gorges? Which brings us to Mystery Four: What happened to the Ba civilization? We think it originated as far back as five thousand years ago. But who were the Ba and what happened to them? We want to find the answers before the dam is completed."

It still didn't seem terribly interesting to Hulan, but she noticed that David looked captivated. Perhaps it was the change in narrator.

"I don't believe," Stuart Miller said into the silence, "that you're here for archaeology." Hulan turned and saw him appraising her. "Why have you come to Site 518?"

"I'm investigating Brian McCarthy's death," she answered. "My husband has been hired to look into the theft of relics from this site."

Dr. Ma winced. Apparently this was not how he wanted to transmit this information to the Millers. However, they showed neither concern nor shock, which seemed very strange to Hulan.

"Brian was one of my students," Stuart informed them. "Did you know that? I sponsor graduate students to do archaeological work in China."

"Why?" Hulan asked.

"He's a rapacious collector," his daughter boasted. "Absolutely rapacious."

"I like fine things." Stuart's smile didn't break for an instant, but then he hadn't become a billionaire by telegraphing his thoughts or emotions.

Catherine's laugh floated out like bubbles.

"Cat," her father warned.

"You can't take antiquities out of the country," David pointed out.

Stuart rubbed his forearm. "I know that. But as you'll see, every-one here expects the worst of me because I'm a capitalist. The truth is, I support a lot of the archaeological work that's being done on the river. We've got to save as much as we can before it disappears for-ever."

"That's pretty altruistic—"

"If it's true, you mean?" Stuart finished. David shrugged, and the businessman laughed good-naturedly. "Look, I can help get things out of the ground, but I can't get them out of the country. However, if they get out some other way and are put up for sale at public auction, what can I do? I'm a collector. If the documentation is in place, I'd be a fool not to buy something I like."

A loud bell sounded, followed by the clank of shovels and picks being dropped. The day workers walked down the hill. The people who'd been crouching under the canopies stretched their legs, brushed the dirt off their clothes, and also began wandering down the hill.

"Lunch," Ma explained, eager to break up the conversation. "Come, Mr. Miller. You and your daughter should be first in line." Ma led his two guests toward an open-sided tent down by the river.

"He seems knowledgeable but awfully territorial," David said after the threesome set off.

"He's very clever," Hulan agreed, "but he's worried." She stood and rubbed her hands together. Somewhere along the way she'd picked up something sticky. "I'll wait for Investigator Lo's report on the people down here, but I don't have to read Ma's *dangan* to know that he's probably hiding something. As for Stuart and Catherine Miller—"

"They should be interviewed separately," David said.

Hulan looked up at him and smiled. He took some loose strands of her hair and gently tucked them behind her ear. "Let's go down," he said. "I'm starved."

And though it broke all rules of professional decorum, they walked down to the eating tent hand in hand.

CHAPTER

5

THE DAY WORKERS GATHERED TOGETHER IN A THIN SLICE OF shade formed by the shadow of the mountain, eating their lunches from tin containers. The official site workers—the Chinese students and the foreigners—sat at long tables under a canopy. A buffet of rice, noodles, and a bland-looking concoction of chicken and vegetables had been set up.

After making sure that Hulan and David had served themselves, Dr. Ma led them farther under the tent. Even here people separated themselves into little hierarchical bands. Ma passed the student tables as too lowly. He stopped at the last table, where Catherine and Stuart Miller were eating. People scooted down the bench to make room for David and Hulan, who sat together, with their backs to the mountain, the river coursing before them. Yet the appearance of two strangers didn't seem to matter to those at the table, who didn't pause for even a moment in their heated conversation.

"Are you crazy?" a man with steel-rimmed glasses asked, his German accent heavy. "The Nine Tripods? There's no way—"

"Why *couldn't* they exist? Why couldn't they be *right here*?" This came from a blond woman with an English accent.

"How about because eight of them disappeared in a fire over two thousand years ago?" the German shot back. "And by that time one had already been lost on the Sie River, which is *not* the Yangzi."

In just these few moments, Hulan realized that the lunch conversation would be sprinkled with specialized interests discussed in professional jargon. She and David would need to listen carefully, discarding what was unimportant and homing in on what was vital to their respective cases.

Catherine seemed to sense this, and she addressed David. "They're talking about the bronze vessels that Yu the Great made to create a visual map of his empire," she explained. "Each tripod looked like a bowl standing on three legs. Together they passed from dynasty to dynasty as emblems of power. What happened to the Nine Tripods is intriguing to archaeologists like us, but most people have never heard of them."

The Englishwoman picked up again as though Catherine hadn't spoken. "Artifacts have disappeared throughout history. That doesn't mean that they don't exist or that they can't be found or even that they're where we think they should be. Think of King Tut's tomb or the terra-cotta warriors—"

Dr. Ma put his hand over the woman's hand and asked, "Lily, can we put aside Yu the Great and your lost tripods for a few minutes so I can introduce all of you to our newcomers?"

Ma began with team members at the far end of the table. Professor Franz Schmidt, the German, was a heavyset semiologist from the University of Heidelberg. Next to him sat Dr. Annabel Quinby, a dour-looking archaeologist from Harvard. Across from her was a much older man with a bad sunburn and a peeling bald head. Dr. Paul Strong had retired long ago from Cambridge, where his specialty was linguistic anthropology. Six Chinese sat at the table, one of whom was Chinese American. Dr. Michael Quon, Ma explained, had many fields of expertise, and they were honored to have him visiting the site from his home in California. The other five Chinese were representatives from different provincial museums. "We call them the five vultures, isn't that right, gentlemen?" Ma asked.

The five nodded wearily. Apparently they'd heard this opening many times before and knew where it was going. So had the foreigners, who listened with only moderate interest.

"They sit in their cave day after day, waiting for us to open a tomb with spectacular finds"—Ma lowered his voice confidentially—"and hoping that the relics will go to *their* museums. But do you hear how I say the word *hoping*, Inspector? Hope is all our vultures have, because if we ever find anything significant, then I'll decide what goes where."

Hulan searched the faces of the Chinese men for a raised eyebrow or an unconscious flinch when Ma called her "Inspector" but saw only bland indifference.

"You should see the gifts they bring me thinking they can curry favor!" Ma went on. "A roast pig. A bottle of VSOP cognac. A carton of cigarettes."

"Bribes?" Hulan asked.

"Of course," Ma answered cheerfully.

Hulan followed up with "And you accept them?"

"Someone has to take them."

Were things so corrupt down here?

"But enough of this. Let me introduce you to the rest," Ma said. "To your left, Inspector, is our favorite little hothead, Lily Sinclair."

The phrasing was demeaning, and Lily reddened. She looked to be about thirty. Although her blond hair was short, the cut was expensive. She wore a gold ring on her right hand, a diamond bracelet, and a gold chain around her neck. Her outfit superficially looked like everyone else's—shorts, T-shirt, and work boots—except she'd probably purchased hers at a Hong Kong boutique. Again, everything simple and very expensive.

"Lily's from London but works at Cosgrove's in Hong Kong," Ma continued. "Do you know Cosgrove's?"

"It's an auction house," Hulan replied. She felt David's thigh resting alongside her own. He put his hand under the table and gently squeezed the flesh just above her knee. The warmth of his hand penetrated through her clothes.

"I wouldn't expect an inspector from the Ministry of Public Security to know about the international art market," Ma commented, "but you aren't the usual, are you, Inspector?" He didn't wait for an answer but went on a bit longer about Cosgrove's and how it had made its reputation almost two hundred years ago by selling works that were a cut above the more commercial objets d'art that were part of the China trade.

Dr. Ma now circled back to his earlier confession. "Inspector, things aren't as bad as I make them sound," he confided. "If I accept the gifts, then I have some control over what happens on my site. Those bribes have gone a long way in boosting morale in the camp. How many day workers get to experience the Red Prince life by drinking a shot of brandy? I think our method—though dishonest on the surface—keeps everyone more honest down deep."

"Honest?" Stuart asked, his voice high and mocking. "Who at this table is here for honest reasons? Certainly not Miss Sinclair."

"Oh, Stuart, are we going to do this again?" Lily asked dolefully.

Ma sighed theatrically, then explained to David and Hulan. "Every day and at every meal these two have the same conversation—"

"That's because she's trying to get her hands on your artifacts so she can sell them at Cosgrove's." Stuart's accusation was light-hearted, teasing.

"You know perfectly well that I could never get an artifact out of the country even if I wanted to, which I don't," Lily admonished, clearly taking Stuart seriously. "I for one don't plan on ever spending a night, let alone an hour, in a Chinese prison. I'm just here to increase my knowledge of Asian art."

Stuart and a few of the others laughed. He leaned forward across the table and asked, "Then how do you explain the sale of the *zun* last spring at Cosgrove's?"

"That was perfectly legitimate and you know it!" Lily's cheeks flushed pink, and she held her back straight.

Stuart glanced over at David and grinned. "She's cute when she's upset."

"What's a *zun*?" David asked.

"A ritual wine container," Lily answered huffily.

The others at the table laughed again. They enjoyed razzing Lily, and apparently she took the bait every time.

Annabel Quinby explained: "It so happens, Mr. Stark, that last summer we found a very beautiful bronze *zun*, but it disappeared before measurements or photographs could be taken. Two months later Cosgrove's auctioned it."

"That *zun* came from a private collector!" Lily exclaimed. "Cosgrove's had all of the proper documentation to prove it!"

"And it was sold to a private collector," Annabel added. "Isn't that right, Mr. Miller?"

"It's made a wonderful addition to my collection!" Stuart growled, acting out the part of a ravaging barbarian to the great amusement of the others.

"See what I mean?" Ma said, addressing Hulan and David again. "They go on this way every time they get together—"

"I don't see why it's so funny," Lily said. Her comment brought on a few more hoots. "Well, I don't."

"Forget about them, Lily," Catherine soothed. "They're just picking on you because you're a girl. Believe me, they don't want you for your antiquities . . ."

The men, right down to the elderly Cambridge professor with the peeling scalp, suddenly found the food on their plates very interesting.

Catherine purred to David sotto voce, "They're a bunch of boys . . ."

There probably wasn't another woman within a thousand square miles built like Catherine, and every man at this table knew it. But Catherine had singled out David, and Hulan understood why. People wanted to connect with him. They wanted to engage him, touch him.

Catherine modulated her pitch once again to include the others. "But I don't know why we can't consider Lily's idea about the Nine Tripods. Could there be a find anywhere that would be more significant to the history of China?"

"The terra-cotta warriors," Professor Schmidt suggested.

"A great tourist site certainly," Catherine agreed, "but what do they really say about power?"

"Qinshihuangdi had enough power to unify the country," the professor replied. "He had enough power to build the Great Wall."

"No one really knows the true origin of the Great Wall," Ma cautioned. "Qinshihuangdi receives credit for it, but we all know that much of that is myth, not reality."

"Myth and reality are connected," Catherine said, "especially where Yu the Great is concerned." Again she focused her attention on David, leaning close enough to him that her breasts brushed against his forearm, which, Hulan noticed, he didn't move. "Do you know who we're talking about?"

David shook his head.

"But you do, right?" Catherine said to Hulan. "'If not for Yu, we all would be fishes,'" she recited.

Hulan was accustomed to the deficiencies of her education, but these scholars were appalled when she confessed her ignorance.

Catherine explained that Da Yu—Yu the Great—was the first emperor of China to found a hereditary dynasty. His reign began in 2205 B.C. after he controlled the floods. These deeds were recorded in the *Shu Ching*, China's first historical text. Qinshihuangdi was the great unifier, though his reign lasted only from 221 to 206 B.C. China got its name from him and his dynasty—Qin, China. As Professor Schmidt had already pointed out, eight of the nine tripods that Da Yu made were believed to have been lost in a fire that marked the overthrow of Qinshihuangdi's reign. One was lost in a river.

"Lily thinks it could be *our* river," Catherine concluded. "I think she should keep on with her search, don't you? To have a direct tie to Yu—"

"You have to understand, Attorney Stark," Ma interrupted, "China has no great epics like Gilgamesh, the Mahabharata, or the Iliad. Yu's story is the closest, although it isn't about creation or the spirit world. It's about the relationship between man and the physical universe. This approach is uniquely Chinese and something we still see in Chinese culture today. Even now our rulers are considered responsible for natural phenomena. Losing control over nature marks the end of their Mandate of Heaven. All that began with Yu, a real man who took on mythical aspects."

"Such as?"

"Using a winged dragon to help cut rivers to drain the land of floods, marrying a fox spirit with tiny hoofed feet, creating nine provinces, which he then memorialized in the tripods." Catherine put her elbows on the table and rested her chin on one of her palms so she could face David at a pretty angle. Hulan had no doubt that Catherine's thigh was now resting against his, and she found this thought strangely titillating. "Lily will do anything to find that submerged tripod." Then, without shifting her gaze from David, she asked the Englishwoman, "Who are you going to send to a watery grave this time, Lily? Professor Schmidt or Dr. Strong?"

"That's not funny!" Lily practically yelped.

The others laughed uproariously.

"It always comes down to power and the symbols we use to portray it," Professor Schmidt said. "You heard Dr. Ma. In China power is granted to those who hold the Mandate of Heaven."

"That was a feudal idea," Hulan corrected. "Only emperors were believed to be sons of Heaven."

"Only emperors? What about Mao?" Stuart challenged. "You have to admit that Mao was in the game for the power. And what about that fellow from the All-Patriotic Society? He clearly cares about power."

"The All-Patriotic Society is a cult—"

"And you've never heard of the Cult of Mao?" Stuart inquired. "But Mao was mortal, and I presume Xiao Da is too. Still, they're both very much about power. How do you show your power to your people and to the world? With a sword? A nuclear arsenal? A scepter in the West or a *ruyi* or *gui* in ancient China? All of these are symbols of power."

"You should see his collection," Lily said in obvious admiration, but Stuart was on a roll.

"Power can be found in something as mundane as bricks and mortar if they're put together the right way," he continued. "Consider your Great Wall and Three Gorges Dam. Wouldn't you say they're both international symbols of China's power?"

Hulan cut him off suddenly, her tone brittle. "All of this is very interesting, but I'm not here to talk about symbols. I'm here to investigate the murder of Brian McCarthy."

"What do you mean *murder*?" Hearing the tremor in her voice, Lily put a hand to her throat. "Brian's death was an accident." She turned to Ma. "That's what you told us. You said it was an accident."

Ma spoke reassuringly. "Of course it was. Our foreign friends must remember that our ways are sometimes different." He paused, then added, "And very crude. You must think of our legal system as you might a jar of stinking tofu. Best to keep a lid on it."

In another time, in another place, these might have been the last words that the director of the dig would have spoken in public. Hulan needed to see his *dangan* to understand who he was and why his words ran so freely.

A representative from one of the provincial museums was the first to speak. In Chinese he said, "I thought you were here to investigate corruption."

"Often where there's murder there's also corruption," Hulan crackled back in Mandarin.

The other museum representatives shifted in their seats. The foreigners—all apparently fluent in Mandarin—picked up on their colleagues' sudden nervousness.

"I'm interested in whatever will lead me to a murderer," Hulan continued in English. "If this Yu will lead me to Brian's killer, then I'll follow that path."

"Are we in any danger?" Annabel Quinby asked.

Before Hulan could respond, Dr. Ma jumped in. "You are all perfectly safe." He next addressed Hulan. "Almost everyone at this table helped search for Brian when he disappeared. We've come to accept that he fell in the river and drowned, and we've all taken extra precautions to be careful whenever we're near the shore. As soon as we're done here, I'll show you what I think happened."

"I wouldn't be here, Dr. Ma, if the facts supported whatever accidental theory you might have." Hulan scanned the faces at the table. "I think everyone should be careful until we've figured out exactly what happened."

An uncomfortable silence settled over the group as this warning sank in. Then Stuart Miller swung his legs out and over the bench. "Come on, Cat, let's visit awhile before I head back to the dam.

You'll give the old man that, won't you? And don't worry, Inspector, we'll protect each other."

His cavalier manner trumped everything Hulan had just said. Catherine gracefully rose out of her seat. Michael Quon also got up, and the others waved him off, teasing him about his afternoon walks and how hard it was to get a dilettante to do any real work. Then the scholars carried on among themselves about the Four Mysteries just as Ma had predicted, while the men from the Chinese museums talked about the tastelessness of the dishes at the annual Cultural Relics banquet last spring.

All of this was out of Hulan's realm of experience. Usually when the word *murder* came up, people wanted to hear the facts of the case; they wanted to know if there were suspects and who they might be; and they weren't so easily convinced that they were safe themselves. Were the scholars so buried in their academic world that they didn't care about what had happened to Brian? Were the museum scouts—the vultures—so sure of their positions that they weren't even a little afraid of having someone from the MPS in their midst? Only Lily had shown any emotion about Brian's death, but then she was the only person at the table who'd been accused of theft, smuggling, and murder.

6

AFTER LUNCH, DR. MA, DAVID, AND HULAN SET OUT TO WHERE IT was believed Brian had gone into the river. The late afternoon humidity felt as heavy and thick as porridge. The sky was a white blanket, and it looked as if it was about to rain, but for now dust billowed up with each of their footsteps and clung to the sweat on their arms, legs, and faces.

Hulan's mind wandered in the heat. It was odd, she thought, how barren this area was. Coming down the river on the ferry, the hillsides had been lush and green, with vines cascading over rocks and ferns thriving in the moisture. Trees and bamboo had twisted into spidery forms as they reached for sunlight. Orchids and other tropical flowers had bloomed in shady spots. But here there were no trees or ferns or flowers. Instead Hulan saw only rocks and dirt and the occasional scraggly plant, while below them the murky waters of the Yangzi flowed past. Was it common for an archaeological site to be so desolate? Did the work that took place here require that the land be cleared of all flora?

Once they reached the upper path, Ba Mountain rose above them on their left. They passed a house—a hovel was more like it—that had been built into the cliff. The exposed portions, such as they were, had been constructed from bricks, cardboard, and corrugated metal sheeting. A woman in threadbare clothes sat on the front step, comforting a crying infant. This family would eventually be moved out of the inundation zone, but in the meantime, where was their kitchen garden? What did they eat?

The path narrowed, and now the cliff rose so high and steep next to Hulan that her shoulder and arm brushed along jagged outcroppings. To her right, the path fell away precipitously perhaps a hundred meters to the water. If Brian had fallen here and bashed his head on the rocks on his way down, he would have been dead when he hit the water, making his death an accident after all.

After climbing for half an hour, they reached a small crest, then began heading down the cramped walkway. Dr. Ma nimbly hopped from rock to rock, easily transferring his weight when the stones shifted under his boots. Hulan and David were more cautious, very aware that a false step could, at the very least, get them cut, scraped, or gouged.

They reached a small cove with a sliver of beach. Ma turned to them, hands on his hips, a light sheen of sweat on his forehead. "We found Brian's daypack on a rock out there," he said, gesturing with his chin toward the river. "He had a container of noodles, chopsticks, and a bottle of water sitting next to it."

"Where?" Hulan didn't see any boulders protruding from the water.

"You can't see it now. With the rain the last few nights, the river's been rising. It's probably two meters higher than when Brian last came out here for lunch."

"You think Brian walked all the way out here for a meal?" Hulan asked. "Why would he do that?"

"You just ate with us," Ma answered. "Imagine having variations of that same conversation three times a day for several months, then coming back here a year later and having them all over again. Even I like to get away sometimes."

Hulan edged down the bank. The rocks were wet, and with her shoe she tested to see how slippery they were. Plenty slippery. The river was narrow here too, so the current was fast. Brian's body would have been carried away very quickly.

"Who found his things?"

"I did," came Ma's quick reply.

"And what brought you here?"

"Inspector, we're a small group in a small area. We all have our little sanctuaries to get away from the others. Some of our people have places where they like to get away together, if you know what I mean. Men and women working side by side, the heat, the isolation . . ."

"Was Brian seeing anyone?" she asked.

"In particular?" Ma seemed to consider the possibilities. "I don't think so."

Hulan felt a few drops of rain and looked around for shelter.

"What about the other deaths?" David asked as the drops became heavier.

Ma's lips curled disapprovingly. "I've discussed these accidents with the Public Security Bureau. If they are of no concern to our local officials, why should they be of concern to a foreigner?"

"Because I was hired by your boss to inquire about them."

Ma nodded curtly, then said, "You have to forgive me. In our country innocent people are often blamed for crimes or misdeeds where none have occurred."

The sky finally opened up, and it began to pour. Ma grabbed Hulan's arm and hastily pulled her away from the river's edge. David scrambled after them. At the base of the cliff was an opening to a cave. The three ducked inside.

Ma shook the water off his hat and wiped his face. "It's monsoon season, and we've been getting rain every afternoon, but this is supposed to be a big storm. It shouldn't affect us too much up here, where the river will rise many meters but stay within its banks. Bad flooding is predicted below the dam site however. The land flattens down there, and the floodwaters sometimes spread out miles beyond the riverbanks."

The day was so hot that the rain should have been a relief, but the heat had not subsided. Yet a cool breeze coming from the deep darkness of the cave began to envelop them, bringing with it an awful smell like mold or rotting fruit. Hulan thought for a moment she heard a baby's cry, but then the sound was swallowed by the cave's echoing silence. This place was creepy, but the two men didn't seem to mind.

"It's a long walk back to camp. Let's stay here a bit and see if it lets up," Ma suggested. He squatted peasant-style, his knees drawn up to his chest. He looked out at the rain and began answering David's earlier question. "We've had other deaths out here. I can't deny it, but I can't take full responsibility for them either."

He looked around, reached for a stick, and began to trace in the soft earth of the cave floor the route they'd taken from Bashan dock all the way to this little cove. "We've come about a kilometer east of Site 518, walking parallel to what's known as the Unlocked Gates Gorge—two peaks on the other side of the river. That's here," he said, jabbing an *x* just across from where they were now. "It's not one of the official Three Gorges because it doesn't straddle the river and isn't very long or dramatic, but technically it still qualifies as a gorge. On one side of the gorge about midway up the mountain is what's known as the Beheading Dragon Platform. On the other side is the Binding Dragon Pillar. You can see them from the river."

He drew another line extending north from the town. "Bashan sits on the banks of a stream that feeds into the Yangzi. We crossed the bridge over that stream today. By the end of next year, that bridge will be submerged in phase one of inundation, so a new one was built on higher ground but not very well, apparently. Peng, Dang, and Sun were day workers who lived in the hills. They were crossing the new bridge when it collapsed."

Ma's words seemed distant as he conjured up the accident. "Inspector, I'm sure you've heard Premier Zhu Rongji talk about the dangers of 'tofu construction.' And I'm sure I don't need to tell you about the corruption that's happening along the river in regard to the dam. Money's been pocketed, and new roads, bridges, and buildings have failed. What I don't understand, though, is your interest in the collapse of our bridge when there have been others with greater fatalities." He lengthened the line for the Yangzi, then marked another spot much farther east. "A bridge gave way downstream from here, killing eleven people. And what about the collapse in Chongqing? Forty people dead. Eighteen of them police—*your* colleagues, Inspector. Who's concerned about them?"

He cocked his head as if something had just occurred to him. "And our three workers weren't the only ones to die on that bridge. Did you know that? Peng was walking with his wife, mother-in-law, and five-year-old son. There were also a couple of farmers from this side of the stream who were crossing into Bashan to sell their produce at the town market."

"I assume the Public Security Bureau investigated the collapse," Hulan said.

Ma jutted his chin dismissively. "Captain Hom is the contractor's brother-in-law."

David and Hulan exchanged looks. Village politics and connections were not so different from those in the capital.

"And the other accidents?" David inquired.

"A young man fell from a ladder and broke his neck. It could have happened to anyone, but it happened to another day worker, named Yun Re."

"How? Where? When?" David asked.

"It happened during *xiuxi* about a month ago. Naps are especially important on a site like this, because the heat can be so oppressive in the afternoons. The caves give everyone a break. You feel it, don't you? The coolness? We're near the entrance, but if we went in farther, it would get even colder because a cave maintains its temperature based on the annual average between the internal and external temperatures. The average temperature in these caves is about sixteen degrees Centigrade." Then he added for David's benefit, "Or about sixty of your degrees. We've got tents, but who wants to sleep in them when you can escape the heat in the caves?"

"I don't see where the ladder comes in," Hulan said.

"We've got bunks. They've got ladders."

"And this is just for your day workers," Hulan clarified.

"I never said that. The vultures and students each have their own dormitory caves. Mine is private," Ma confessed. After a moment, he went on. "The last death wasn't at the dig. One of our workers drowned."

Again David asked the obvious questions, and Ma answered

them. "On June twenty-eighth, Wu Huadong didn't show up for work. Two days later, his body was found in a whirlpool about a *li* from here. That's about a third of one of your miles." Ma used his stick to mark the spot.

"How was the body found?" David asked.

"Someone on a ferry spotted it and reported it to the captain, who radioed to Captain Hom's office. Hom must have sent someone out in a boat to retrieve the body." After a moment, Ma added, "We think Wu Huadong fell in the river somewhere near here, probably from the path we came down."

Again David and Hulan glanced at each other. It would be easy to slip off that path, even if you'd traversed it hundreds of times.

"Was Wu also from Bashan?" Hulan asked.

"We passed his house walking out here," Ma answered. "That was his widow and child."

So Wu would have been very familiar with this terrain, Hulan thought.

"Could the Englishwoman have had anything to do with either Brian McCarthy's or Wu Huadong's death?" she asked.

Ma spat on the ground. "Not possible."

"Dr. Ma, did you hear the way your group went after her? Accusations of murder and theft are hardly the usual conversation among friends."

"You may have noticed Lily's a bit high-strung," Ma said. "Usually we only have to deal with her for a few days at a time. After two weeks, I think the team would do anything to get her to leave."

"If she's that difficult, then why let her visit at all?"

"Lily brought us Miller. If not for his funds, this site would have been worked with bulldozers."

"How does Director Ho feel about this?" David asked.

"The fish would die if the ocean were too clean," Ma observed. He looked out into the rain. His shoulders slumped, and he seemed suddenly fatigued. David and Hulan waited.

"You also want to know about objects that have disappeared," he said into the silence. "Of the things that I know are missing, most are relatively minor pieces—some bone, stone, and jade artifacts."

"That you *know* are missing?" David pressed.

"You have to understand, Attorney Stark, that we're under tremendous pressure down here. We don't have time to follow the usual protocol by cataloging every piece right as we find it. Some artifacts have disappeared from our storage tent before cataloging and condition reports were completed, but I've also had workers show me artifacts that never even made it to the tent."

"So you were never able to take measurements—"

"Which is why I can't put them on the international list of stolen artifacts," Ma finished for David. "That's not to say I don't know *some* of what's missing. For example, Brian showed me some jade *bis* he'd found. They're perforated jade disks believed to embody the powers of Heaven and convey to the emperor the ability to commune and consult with the gods. But each one is unique. They come in different sizes and types of jade, while the decorative work can be plain or quite elaborate."

"Valuable?"

"On the open market, I'd put them at three to six thousand dollars U.S. apiece."

More money was at stake than Hulan had first realized, and that was just for the *bis*.

"Unfortunately," Ma continued, "without exact measurements and details about the carving on them, I can't prove they came from this site."

"So they aren't on the list," David verified.

"That's right, and I'm sorry to say neither is the one object that I consider to be truly significant. It was a *ruyi*."

"That's what Miller was talking about at lunch."

Ma sighed. "Miller's got the best collection of *guis* and *ruyis* in the world."

"What are they exactly?" David asked.

"In the most simple terms, a *gui* is a kind of tablet that was given as an imperial gift either at the start of a mission or at the completion of a particular task," Ma explained. "A *ruyi* was also an imperial gift—but it was more personal in nature." He wiped away the map with his hand, then drew two objects in the dirt. The *gui* was long and flat with a triangular top. The *ruyi* looked like a scepter with a long handle and a head, which widened at the top into a circle with wavy edges about six inches in diameter. "A *ruyi* can be made from jade, bone, even bronze, but the one Brian found was formed from a fungus. The stem was knobby and very dark. The head, if it had been of jade, would have had carving—an insignia, characters denoting a name, or a simple geometric decoration. Obviously this one had no carving. It unfurled in a natural form."

"A fungus?"

"Probably a *lingzhi* mushroom."

"Would you consider this *ruyi* to be valuable?" David asked.

"Depends on how you measure value, but it might be, considering its provenance."

"Could someone like Stuart Miller smuggle your *ruyi* out of China?"

David was asking the archaeologist to rat out his benefactor, but Ma's verdict seemed measured yet truthful. "He could, but if he had, I don't think he'd be hanging around the site." After a pause, he added, "It doesn't look like this rain is going to let up. Do you want to stay here and explore the cave for a while?"

The idea of going deeper into the darkness sent a shiver through Hulan.

"I'd rather speak with the families of the other victims," David said.

Ma shook his head. "I can't help you there. In light of the deaths, the families were given extra money to move before the deadline."

"To Beijing?"

"Their stories are doubly tragic. They were sent to the Xinjiang Autonomous Region."

That was a remote and desolate area, and about as far west as you could go and still be in China. While it was true that the government was trying to colonize the region with displaced families from the inundation zone, it was also a great place to send someone you never wanted to hear from again.

"But the Wu family is still here," David said.

"Yes, and you can visit them if you want," Ma responded. "But do you think your visit will be a comfort to Wu's wife or father?" He glanced at David, then Hulan, but neither of them said a word. Since there seemed to be nothing more to say, he stood and said, "We should get back."

The walk back up the cliff was arduous and wet. The rocks were slick and, with little greenery, there wasn't much to grab on to. Once they reached the main path, the threesome picked up their pace. When they arrived at the Wu house, David knocked on the door and called, "Wu Taitai. Wu Taitai." No one answered.

CHAPTER

7

DR. MA DROVE DAVID AND HULAN BACK TO BASHAN AND DROPPED them at the entrance to the Panda Guesthouse. They were sopping wet from the hike back to the dig and the Jeep ride into town. They entered the lobby, checked in, and set out for their room, which was located in the fourth courtyard. The Panda Guesthouse was a traditional Chinese compound—slightly larger than Hulan's family home and far smaller than Beijing's imperial Forbidden City. In typical fashion, the guesthouse had been built on a north-south axis with a series of connecting courtyards, buildings, and pavilions, all surrounded by a high protective wall. As David and Hulan walked, painted landscapes portraying subjects from the Chinese classics unfurled on the eaves above them. Carved wooden screens covered the windows they passed. The third courtyard housed a traditional Chinese garden with three huge scholar's rocks serving as the centerpiece. David and Hulan reached the fourth courtyard, and he opened the door to their room. It was lovely in the sense that it had one double bed and no television.

David knew that if anyone was going to make the first move, it had to be Hulan. Still, he was completely unprepared that it happened so soon or so effortlessly. Hulan didn't say a word as she came toward him. She gently put her hands on his cheeks and brought his face down to hers. Her lips were soft and yielding. She pulled back, and he looked into her eyes. She couldn't hide what was in them from him, and he realized that all this was happening just a little too easily. But as soon as she undid the first button on his shirt, he reached for her as though it had been years and not months since the last time they had made love. He wanted to believe—if only for the time that they were here in the Three Gorges—that they still could have a life together.

Their wet clothes clung tenaciously to their skin, but every inch revealed was reclaimed and reconquered. They didn't hurry as they touched and tasted each other. For these minutes they forgot everything except the needs of the flesh. When he finally entered her, she moaned in pleasure as she lifted her hips to meet him. They moved together across tides of sensation and emotion, until neither of them could endure another moment. *This* was why he'd wanted to get her out of Beijing, away from the MPS, away from their own bed, away from memories of Chaowen.

By the time they were sated, they were both as damp as when they'd walked into the room. The sheets lay in a rumpled pile at the foot of the bed. The air from the overhead fan slowly cooled their sweaty bodies. They had so much to talk about. Even if this encounter had been staged by Zai, even if Hulan had forced herself in the early moments, couldn't this be a new beginning? But David couldn't and wouldn't push Hulan. She wasn't yet willing to reveal her mind's deepest intimacies, but she was ready to talk about the case that had brought them here. For David, it was a start, and his heart welled with cautious happiness.

"How can I prove Brian was murdered?" She rolled onto her side and put a hand on David's chest. "By the time I saw his body, whatever evidence might have been there had long washed away."

"Witnesses—"

"What witnesses? If someone saw Brian getting tossed in the river, don't you think it would have been reported?"

"People don't always want to come forward—"

"Maybe in America, but this is China, David. 'Leniency to those who confess . . .'"

"A witness is not a criminal who has to confess."

"Of course not, but the idea could apply to witnesses, too, in terms of the common good for society."

"What about the day workers?" he asked.

"Pretty convenient that their families have been moved," she responded. "On the other hand, it's common knowledge that the poorest of the poor are being sent to faraway lands. But the Wus are still here, and we should talk to them."

Finding out what had happened to the site workers was David's assignment, but he and Hulan had been sent down here together. It was only natural that lines would blur.

"There's always circumstantial evidence," he offered.

"Yes, lawyers love that, but what circumstantial evidence do you see?"

"The contractor and the police captain are brothers-in-law."

"That's not circumstantial! That's dead-on proof of corruption as far as I'm concerned, but we're not here to investigate local corruption."

"What do you make of Lily?"

"The others don't like her, but I don't see her as a murderer. Do you?"

"No," David said, then after a beat added, "I find it interesting what people *don't* talk about. We're at a famous Ba site, but have you heard anyone talk about the Ba?"

"Only in the context of the Four Mysteries."

"Right. These people are choosing to spend all of their waking hours in difficult living conditions absolutely removed from the rest of the world because, we must assume, they're passionate about the Ba, but the way they were discussed was in the philosophical context of those four archaeological mysteries. No one seemed particularly concerned about the artifacts missing from the site."

"They talked about the *ruyi*."

"Not exactly. Everyone went on about Miller's *ruyi* collection. Only Dr. Ma mentioned that a *ruyi* was missing and that it didn't have much value. I mean, it sounded like a mushroom on a stick. What's the value in that?"

"I don't know. Maybe it fills a hole in Miller's collection."

"Which is why his daughter is out here?"

As soon as the words were out of David's mouth, Hulan let her hand trail down his torso. She put her head on his shoulder. "I was wondering how long it would take you to get to her."

"I just find it hard to believe that a girl like that would want to spend the summer in a place like this."

"Just because she's beautiful doesn't mean she doesn't have her interests."

Hulan's voice had a teasing quality about it, which he hadn't heard in over a year, and it had an immediate effect on him. She sighed deeply, and her warm breath traveled downward, doing little to relieve his suddenly heightened state.

"You said we were here about Brian, and yet we heard almost nothing about him," David said, trying to change the subject.

"He was one of Miller's protégés."

"Yes, we learned that, and I have to tell you I'm concerned about Stuart Miller," David said.

"Because he's a businessman?"

"He's not just *any* businessman, Hulan. He's Miller Enterprises!"

She pulled away and got up. She picked the wet clothes up off the floor and draped them over a couple of chairs. He watched as she opened her bag, pulled out a dress, shook it loose, and put it on a hanger. She was naked and unabashed as she went about her mundane tasks.

"We'll stay awhile longer," she said, "talk to Lily and the Wus, and see if one of those pieces of circumstantial evidence shifts and becomes tangible." She turned to him again, put a hand on her hip, and asked, "Do you think they have hot water in this place?"

His voice was gruff as he said, "Come here."

A little after seven, David and Hulan emerged from their room. The rain still came down in sheets, and they strolled under the covered corridors that edged the linked courtyards back toward the main entrance. The restaurant was in the largest pavilion in the compound. It had a veranda—dotted with potted plants and wicker furniture—

which overlooked a lotus pond. Faded vermilion brocade covered the restaurant's walls. The tables and chairs dated from the Ming Dynasty, and had all the scuffs and dings of four hundred years of use. David and Hulan sat at a table for two. Little dishes of lotus root, string beans with chilies, and salted cashews were already set out as appetizers.

Only two other tables in the vast room were occupied, but instead of clustering guests together, each party had been isolated, which was just fine with David. He'd done his work for the day and didn't want to make small talk either with Lily, who sat alone reading a book, or with the archaeological team—minus the Millers—who'd gathered at a large round table. With them was a young woman with cropped hair whom David didn't recognize from the dig. Aside from the occasional bouts of drunken laughter from that table, the only sound came from the comforting sough of rain through the stand of bamboo outside the window. Beijing's horns, smog, and crowded streets seemed very far away.

David took a quick look at the English menu, then set it aside. He'd let Hulan read the Chinese menu and question the waitress about local specialties. He felt incredibly and surprisingly happy. Hulan appeared peaceful and relaxed. She should be, he thought, his mouth spreading into an unself-conscious grin. Her inhibitions, reserve, walls, or whatever you wanted to call them had fallen from her this afternoon in layers. He'd done that for her—again and again.

The young woman at the archaeologists' table got up and crossed over to David and Hulan. She wore a sleeveless black top and trim khaki pants. Her arms were strong and tan, and she was pretty in an athletic sort of way.

"They tell me you've come to look into my brother's death," she said to Hulan. "My name is Angela McCarthy. May I talk to you for a minute?" Without waiting for an answer, Angela pulled over a chair and sat down. "I'd like to know what you can tell me about Brian."

"Not much, I'm afraid," Hulan answered. She glanced at David. This was not the way either of them had planned on spending the evening.

Angela bit her bottom lip and confided, "I knew something was wrong when I didn't hear from my brother." She smiled sadly and explained. "Our parents died in a car accident ten years ago. Because of that we had a rule that we had to make contact every two days. We kept in touch on the Internet. He was able to send or receive e-mail at least once a day. Anyway, when I heard he'd disappeared, I suspected the worst and decided to come here." Her eyes reddened as she fought back tears. "Our family has not been lucky."

The waitress arrived with notepad in hand. Hulan said a few words in Chinese, but when the waitress turned away, Angela said, "Oh, please, don't let me interrupt you."

She made a move to leave, but David grabbed her wrist. "Stay." Then, "Hulan, why don't you go ahead and order? Angela, have you eaten?"

She had, but she readily agreed to have a glass of wine. Hulan placed the order, and the waitress left. Hulan said, "I have to admit, I'm surprised to see you here when your brother's still in Beijing."

Angela looked back and forth between David and Hulan despondently. "I need to know about Brian."

"We may never know exactly what happened," Hulan said, not without some sympathy in her voice. "You should prepare yourself for that."

"Dr. Ma already told me what happened to my brother. He fell in the river and drowned. There are risks in everything we do. I *know* that. My brother knew that too. There's nothing I can do about how he died, and a few more days in Beijing won't hurt him now. But I *need* to understand his last days. How did he spend them? Who did he talk to? What was he interested in?"

"For what purpose?"

Hulan was so matter-of-fact in her question that Angela answered in the same pragmatic way. "Do you know what it means to lose someone?"

Hulan kept her face expressionless, but David knew the impact the question would have on her, for he felt it too.

Angela didn't wait for a response. "Grief counselors would probably say I'm looking for closure. If I can piece together . . ."

At last Angela's toughness cracked and the tears flowed.

The waitress returned with a bottle of wine and three glasses. By the time the wine was poured, Angela had regained her composure. David suggested she tell them about her brother. As she spoke, he saw in her face that same forlorn look of grief that he'd seen so many times this past year when he'd looked in the mirror or at Hulan.

"Brian always loved dirt," she began. "I'm two years older, but some of my earliest memories were when we were—gosh, I must have been about four, so he would have been two. He'd play in the dirt all day if our mother let him. I know it sounds hokey, but *dirt* was one of his first words. He was entranced by it. So I guess it was only natural that he'd end up digging in it for a career."

She faltered again, and David said, "I understand you're from Washington."

"We grew up in Seattle. We were both doing graduate work at the University of Washington, but these last couple of years we hadn't seen much of each other. I've been out in the field myself working on my dissertation. He was over here last summer as a Miller fellow. This year he was going to stay until October, then come home and write his master's thesis."

"He must have been smart," David said.

"He was book smart." Angela did nothing to hide the sisterly impatience in her voice. "But he was dumber than a toad's butt when it came to just about everything else."

David restrained himself from looking in Hulan's direction.

"He was ambitious too," Angela continued, still irritated. "He wanted a lot more than a Ph.D. and tenure. Out here he made great new contacts, but what does he do? He fucks them."

"He couldn't or wouldn't follow through?" David tried to clarify.

"No, I mean he *fucked* them." Angela looked at each of them, saw their confusion, and spelled it out. "Sex. Women. Every time he had an opportunity put in front of him, he literally screwed it up. He gets the Miller Fellowship, then sleeps with the daughter. He gets some freelance work with Cosgrove's, then sleeps with the woman who hired him. You've met Lily Sinclair, haven't you? She's sitting over there."

Although it was a large room, Lily heard her name and looked up. When Angela smiled and lifted a couple of fingers in salutation, Lily put her book down, got up, and began walking toward them.

"She's really quite nice," Angela said under her breath. "We've talked a lot since I got here. I can see why my brother liked her."

When Lily reached the table, Angela said, "I've just been telling them about you and Brian and what a dumb ass he was . . ."

Just then the waitress arrived with dinner. Hulan had ordered well, selecting dishes that utilized local ingredients—pan-fried dumplings in hot chili oil, a river fish steamed with ginger and scallions, and braised pork with pickled mustard tuber. Neither Lily nor Angela made any move to leave.

"Are you sure you won't join us?" Hulan asked. "I can order more."

Both women said they'd eaten already.

"Well, then, let's talk." Hulan asked the waitress to bring another wineglass. Lily, sensing David and Hulan's hesitation, encouraged them to eat. It was all terribly rude by Chinese mores, but Hulan didn't waver for a second and with her chopsticks began pulling the delicate flesh from the bones of the fish.

"So now you know about Brian and me," Lily said. Her English accent made it seem more sophisticated than it probably was. "I didn't bring it up before. How could I in front of the others?" She leaned forward and lowered her voice. "The men. They're real gossips, and you can imagine what it would mean if it got out that I'd slept with Brian. They'd think *they'd* have a chance."

David suspected Stuart Miller already knew, which was why he'd needled her so mercilessly at lunch.

"I can tell you it wasn't true love or anything like that," Lily conceded. "It was just a way to spend the evenings in this place. And the boy was talented. Brilliant."

Was she referring to Brian's sexual prowess or his brain?

"I told them that already," Angela confirmed. "He *was* brilliant."

"Angela told us he did work for you," Hulan addressed Lily.

"Freelance work. Research mostly. It wasn't related to the Ba or this site, but he could do a lot of it on the Internet after hours, so it suited him. He could *find* anything."

"What kind of research exactly?"

A shadow fell over Lily's face. "If you're asking if it had anything to do with his accident, I can guarantee you that it didn't."

"My brother was into all kinds of stuff," Angela said with studied candor. "And Lily's right. He loved the Internet. He loved technology of all sorts. He had one of those digital cameras, and he used to put snapshots on a website so all of his friends back home could see them." Angela took another sip of wine. "That's how I knew about Lily and Catherine. I recognized them as soon as I got here." She caught herself. "They weren't dirty pictures or anything like that! Just—oh, I don't know—the hillsides, the dig, the people he was hanging out with."

"Actually, I felt he put up rather barren landscapes," Lily said. She thought for a moment, then added, "Those shots must have been taken in the area around Site 518. He probably posted them so his friends wouldn't be envious."

Angela concurred. "What better way to divert attention from his good luck than to show his friends and colleagues that he was living on a mound of dirt in the middle of nowhere? There's nothing worse than academic jealousy. Believe me, I know."

Lily's responses to further questions about Brian were vague, perhaps out of consideration for Angela. So he faded from the conversation, and Lily regaled them with tales of the Panda Guesthouse, which for hundreds of years had been the compound for the Wangs, an extremely wealthy and very corrupt family that had once controlled all of the salt in the region.

"In addition to his salt wells," Lily explained, "Wang was a smuggler of some note. Until Mao took over, Wang had his own troops and a fleet that plied the river from Wuhan to Chongqing. But his businesses aren't what make him memorable. He was reputed to be quite insatiable in his appetites. He had close to fifty concubines and apparently took them in a variety of combinations. You've seen the decoration in this place. It's beautiful and tasteful, but I've been in rooms in the more interior courtyards with truly stunning pornographic scenes."

"What happened to the family?" Hulan asked.

"During the revolution—Liberation, as you call it—most of the Wangs were wiped out." Her slim fingers gestured delicately toward the veranda. "All of the women were decapitated in the third courtyard, where I'm staying. The blood was ten centimeters deep. At least that's the legend."

"And Wang?"

"He got to see his women killed one by one. They say that by the end of the massacre he'd completely lost his mind."

David watched Hulan through all of this. The similarities between the Wang and Liu families—though in different provinces and different times—were striking.

"So Wang was assassinated," Hulan prompted.

"Not at all!" Lily exclaimed. "In his madness, he wrestled away from the guards and *poof*—disappeared. To hear people around here tell the story, it's as though he had supernatural powers. One minute he was in the courtyard, the next he'd vanished from sight. It's said he 'rode the current out to sea,' meaning that no one knows exactly how he got out, except that he showed up three years later in Hong Kong. He was only sixty-seven. He married again, outlived that wife by a couple of decades, and married again just before he died. The last Madame Wang lives in great opulence in Hong Kong."

"How do you know all this?" Hulan asked.

Lily looked at them in surprise. "I thought you knew. Cosgrove's has represented the family since Wang arrived in Hong Kong. Mr. Wang didn't have much cash, but with the profits from the sale of the family heirlooms he'd smuggled out with him, he was able to start an import-export business. He became quite the Hong Kong tycoon." She shook her head in admiration. "It's amazing, isn't it, how the rich always get richer even when they 'lose' everything?"

"Did he ever explain how he got his treasures out of the compound and to Hong Kong?" David asked.

"Of course not! A family's got to keep its secrets! But Wang did capitalize on the mythical elements of those stories, which only added to the mystique—and value—of his artworks. Anyway, that's why Cosgrove's is tied to this godforsaken place. We still do business for the family. I have lunch with Madame Wang once a month."

"She owns the property now?"

"Mr. Wang lived just long enough to get his properties back during the PRC's campaign to bring in capital from Overseas Chinese in the early eighties. Madame Wang has even relaunched the salt business."

"Are the salt wells near the Ba dig?" Hulan asked. "Is that why that area is so barren?"

Lily smiled. "There are other reasons for that—"

"If the family's so wealthy," David cut in, "why would they turn their compound into a hotel?"

"Money," Lily answered, rubbing her thumb and forefinger together. "The family wanted to restore it for themselves, then the government decided to build the dam. When Madame Wang learned that the compound would be inundated, she abandoned further renovations and decided to open a guesthouse to recoup her initial investment. The Panda Guesthouse, no less! How many Panda Guesthouses do you think there are in this country? Thank God for the discovery of Site 518, otherwise she would have gotten none of her money back."

And on it went. Lily's tales made for lighthearted conversation, and even Angela seemed to brighten. After dinner, David and the three women walked out into the night. The rain still came down in a warm rush, and the air smelled of wet bamboo. They walked under the covered corridor to the next courtyard. When they reached a door marked Room 5, Lily said, "This is me. I'm going straight to bed. I'm exhausted." Then she asked if David and Hulan would be going back out to the dig tomorrow. "There's a bus that takes the team out there at eight, but I'd be delighted if I could avoid riding with that lot."

They agreed to meet her downstairs at 7:30 and take her with them in Ma's Jeep. Lily gave a slight wave, and her cheeks had that heightened color that made her appear younger than her age. As she slowly closed her door, David thought that Brian McCarthy must have been an interesting young man to have attracted two women as different as Lily Sinclair and Catherine Miller.

THE PACIFIED DOMAIN

(Sui fu)

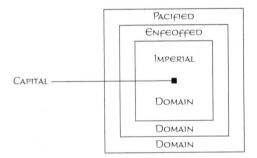

CAPITAL

PACIFIED

ENFEOFFED

IMPERIAL

DOMAIN

DOMAIN

DOMAIN

Beyond. Within the first 300 *li*, the people cultivate lessons of learning and moral duty. In the second 200, they are exhorted to devote themselves to war and defense.

MORNING SLITHERED IN DARK AND WET. THE OVERHEAD FAN swirled thick air, and a smell of mildew permeated the room. David took a shower and dressed but felt little refreshed. Hulan, who didn't own a pair of shorts, let alone a T-shirt, dressed for the humid weather as a peasant might, in loose cotton pants that came to just above her ankles and a short-sleeved blouse with hand-tied frog buttons, all soft and faded from washings and age.

They were the first to arrive in the dining room. A radio blared news about the storm. Some evacuations had been ordered in the middle reaches of the Yangzi, and the People's Liberation Army had been sent downstream to Hubei and Anhui Provinces to shore up levees, dikes, and embankments. As they listened, David and Hulan helped themselves to a breakfast buffet that included watery scrambled eggs, canned ham, fresh deep-fried crullers, and *congee* with pickled turnip, salted fish, and ginkgo seeds for garnishes.

Once they sat down, David stirred a little soy sauce into his *congee* and said, "Dr. Ma's done a good job convincing the people out here that Brian's death was accidental, but I don't get Angela going along with it so easily."

"Sometimes it's hard to understand the emotions and actions of survivors." Hulan blew into her tea, sipped, then said, "She's suffering . . ."

David set his spoon down. "See, that's what bothers me. She didn't ask us for information and she didn't share much either, except for making sure we knew who Brian slept with. I would have expected her to ask more questions. Wouldn't you be curious if an investigator showed up? Wouldn't you want to walk the site with someone from the police?"

A few of the scholars straggled in, but there was no sign of Angela or Lily.

"Maybe she already has with the locals," Hulan said.

They ate quietly for a few minutes, then Hulan said she was far more concerned with Ma. "He hasn't been forthright. He doesn't want you here, and he wants me here even less. The innocent explanation is that running this dig is a big opportunity for him and he doesn't want you to make him look bad to his superiors back in Beijing."

"A not-so-innocent explanation," David added, "is that he's somehow involved with the thefts. But to me this all seems like a lot of trouble for some miscellaneous objects that have so little importance Ma didn't bother to catalog them properly."

Hulan disagreed. "If these artifacts have no value, then why are you here?"

"Director Ho may have arbitrarily picked this site as a lesson to others."

"'Beat one monkey to frighten the whole pack,'" Hulan recited. "That could be, but I doubt it."

David signed the check, and they left the restaurant just as Stuart and Catherine entered. David and Hulan stopped back at their room so he could pick up a notebook and water bottle, which he put in his satchel, then they met Ma at the Jeep a little after 7:30.

"Lily's coming with us," David said, holding the front seat forward so Hulan could climb in the back. Then they waited. After fifteen minutes, Hulan volunteered to go in and call Lily's room, but David jumped out because he was in the front seat. The desk clerk—an older man in a gold-braided uniform—called the room but reported no answer. David followed the main corridor back to

Room 5 and knocked on the door. Lily didn't respond. He looked around the courtyard, then walked quickly to the dining room. The others were grouped together. Lily wasn't with them or even sitting alone, as she'd been the night before. He retraced his steps to the lobby, said a few words to the clerk, and went outside to get Hulan. Once they were back inside, he said, "I think something's happened."

"Lily?"

He nodded and watched Hulan's features harden. They hurried back through the corridors to Lily's room. David waited there while Hulan went to get her weapon. She kept it aimed down at her side as she returned to Room 5, where the elderly desk clerk now stood with David. At first the clerk tried to allay their fears, explaining that foreigners didn't always spend the night in their own rooms. But when Hulan showed him her credentials, he turned the key in the lock. Hulan lifted her weapon. The clerk's eyes widened, and he moved aside.

Hulan slowly pushed the door open with her foot. The shutters were closed and the lights off, making it hard to see anything in the dimness other than the shape of the bed illuminated by the hint of light that emanated from around the edges of the window. The smell of death oozed from the room.

David reached out and held Hulan's arm to prevent her from entering.

"There's no danger now," she blurted staccato. "No one's alive in there. Send the clerk to call the police."

Hearing the cold detachment in Hulan's voice, David felt a sense of dread that extended far beyond what awaited them in the room.

"Try the light," Hulan ordered as the desk clerk scurried away.

David reached around the doorjamb and flipped the switch. He wasn't sure if the *whoosh* of breath he heard came from himself or his wife.

Lily lay atop the bedcovers. Her naked body was in calm repose, her hands folded delicately over her heart, her eyes and mouth closed. This peaceful tableau was covered in what looked like a layer of rust-colored paint, but the dried blood was only on the body and nowhere else—not on the bed linens or the floor.

Hulan stepped into the room, and David followed in her tracks to a couple of feet inside the door. From where they were standing, they could see that Lily's feet were gone. Her stumps rested in two small puddles of coagulated blood. She had to have been killed and drained elsewhere. Even the smearing—the careful coating of blood over Lily's body—had to have been done somewhere else, then her body posed in its peaceful aspect.

Otherwise the room appeared tidy. Lily's clothes were put away and the drawers shut. A pile of papers sat in a neat stack on the left side of the desk. The phone was on the hook. The room had the same furnishings as David and Hulan's, right down to the thermos for hot water that stood on the nightstand. Nothing was askew; nothing seemed out of order. Again, at least to the unassisted eye, there were no pools or even spatters of blood.

"Are you okay?" Hulan asked at last.

"Yes. And you?"

She nodded.

"Have you seen anything like this before?"

"Other mutilations, yes. But this coating? Never." She stood still in deep concentration. Finally she shook her head and said, "Let's work quickly before the others arrive."

"What do you want me to do?"

"I want to take a closer look. Go around to the other side of the bed . . ."

"What about my footprints?"

"It's a wood floor. There's no blood. We may pick up microscopics later, but there's nothing obvious that we'll be corrupting. I think it's fine. Don't touch the bed."

As though he'd want to . . .

He went right as Hulan went left.

"Start at her head," Hulan directed. She leaned forward, putting her hands on her knees for balance. He did the same. "Tell me everything you see, no matter how insignificant."

What could possibly be classified as insignificant here? he wondered.

He forced himself to focus on Lily's head. Seeing how her blood-coated hair lay in a thick, rusty helmet against her skull, David felt a wave of nausea sweep through him. He tried to use the same clinical tone that Hulan had adopted and found it helpful.

"Her hair looks like it's been combed," he said.

"I think so too. It's like the blood was poured over her hair and combed through to get every hair exactly in place." She added, "I'm assuming it's blood. It smells like it."

David's nausea worsened. Then, as his eyes traveled down, his stomach rolled again. "Her nose—"

"Cut off. What would do that so cleanly?" Hulan leaned in even closer until she was just inches from Lily's face. "No jagged edges, no ripping. Whatever was used was very sharp. And, David, what do you make of this on her forehead?"

At first he saw only blood, and the truth was he didn't want to look much closer. But as he made himself focus on that few square inches, he did begin to see something.

"Is it a clot?"

"I don't think so. The blood is spread so evenly everywhere else. Why make a mistake here on her face? No, it's something *under* the blood. It looks like a pattern of some sort. The pathologist will need to be careful with that."

Hulan fanned out her hand a few inches above the body and used it as a guide as she traveled down from the neck.

"She's naked," David observed.

"Is that because the killer wanted to paint blood over the entire corpse? Painted in some way, don't you think, not dunked?"

"She wasn't dunked. You can see the smearing. A cloth, a brush, maybe even hands."

"Let's hope it was hands. We might be able to pick up prints."

They'd almost reached Lily's ankles when they heard the footsteps of several people running down the hallway. The sound was a tremendous relief to David. Lily's sawed off stumps were well out of his league.

Hulan swiftly moved to the door and let David out ahead of her. Then she pulled the door shut, stood with her back against it, and waited for the clerk and three other men—presumably from the local Public Security Bureau—to come to her. She introduced herself, speaking more slowly than usual and clipping her Beijing accent to account for any misinterpretations that might be caused by differences in dialect.

"I'm here on special assignment for Vice Minister Zai of the Ministry of Public Security. This is my husband, Attorney Stark. He is a foreigner, but he's here on official business from the State Cultural Relics Bureau. You must pay him the highest respect, as though he were a black-haired person." Her tone was authoritative and offered no room for argument. "I will be handling this case."

She extended her hand. The eldest of the men shook it and responded in heavily accented English. "I am Captain Hom," he said, a Magnificent Sound cigarette dangling from his lips. "These are my officers, Su Zhangqing and Ge Fei. We handle our own cases in Bashan, even those dealing with foreigners."

Now Hulan switched to English. "Not this time. However, I welcome your advice."

This was the alleged corrupt police captain they'd heard about. David had expected a typical "fat rat," someone who would be heavier from living the good life. Perhaps Hom had been fat at one time, but his jaundiced skin now hung on his bones like a deflated balloon. In a pathetically obvious gesture, Hom swelled his chest in an attempt to gain the upper hand. "A foreigner and an inspector from Beijing may not know what constitutes a crime in our town," he coughed out.

"I can assure you, Captain, that a crime *has* taken place in that room. If you've had others of this sort, I'd be most interested in hearing about them."

"Let us see then."

Hom's tone managed to be both confrontational and dismissive. Hulan's eyes narrowed, and David almost felt sorry for the man.

"Have you agreed to my conditions?"

Hom grunted noncommittally.

"I need to hear the words," Hulan pushed.

"Inspector Liu, you are in charge," Hom conceded at last. He threw his cigarette on the ground and stubbed it out with his boot. "For now."

Hulan's eyes moved to the other two officers—young men dressed in rain-spotted uniforms. "No one touches anything. Understand?"

"Yes, Inspector," one of the young men mumbled, while the other stared mutely at the floor.

"One last thing," Hulan said. "I can see you two are inexperienced. No one will think less of you if you decide not to see this."

"My men," Hom declared indignantly, "are professionals! They are also men. Perhaps a woman such as yourself—"

Hulan didn't wait for the rest but opened the door and gave it a solid push. Hom marched past her, with his two minions right behind him. The one who hadn't had the nerve to address Hulan before came reeling back out the door and vomited. A moment later the other young man came running out of the room with his hand over his mouth. He looked frantically from left to right, then ran down the hall and around the corner. The sound of heaving cut through the air. David's stomach churned, the added smells doing nothing to help his own unsteady state. Hulan let out a deep breath and met his gaze. Her wordlessness was eloquent, filled as it was with a combination of sadness, resolve, and duty. Then she stepped back into the room with David and the desk clerk right behind her.

Hom stood by the side of the bed. His Adam's apple bobbed up and down as he swallowed. The desk clerk mewled but held his ground.

"I think we can agree that something unique has happened here," Hulan said gently. "I'd like to have our pathologist come to Bashan. I hope this won't complicate your procedures."

"We have no procedures to deal with something like this. Is she a foreigner?"

"I'm afraid so."

Hom groaned.

"Do you have a lab?" Hulan asked.

"There's a morgue in the town. Not an official morgue, do you understand? Our quarter of town has electricity for only a few hours a day. If someone dies, the body is turned over to the family very quickly."

"Even for murder?"

"We've had murders, of course, but we know very soon who the killer is. A husband, a jealous boyfriend. We get a lot of help from the Neighborhood Committee."

"And for foreigners?"

"They are new to Bashan Village. We are not a stop for cruises, and the people who are here for Site 518 are few and quiet."

David listened carefully. Hom, despite his incongruous wasted appearance, may indeed have been corrupt in letting his brother-in-law get away with the fatalities caused by the collapse of the bridge, assuming those accusations were true, but he was also either stupid or inept, because he wasn't seeing the overall situation very clearly.

"This is not the first time a foreigner has died in Bashan," Hulan pointed out.

"If a foreigner is stupid and falls in the river," Hom retorted, "this is not grounds for investigation, but it does cause me a lot of paperwork."

"I'd like to see your file on that case," Hulan said, "as well as the files for the other accidents that have occurred in Bashan recently. But first, let's deal with immediate problems. Miss Sinclair's body will decompose very quickly in this heat. I suggest we find some-place cool, and soon." She paused, considering. "No, on second thought, leave her here. Maybe the pathologist will be able to tell us something—"

"This room will be a stinky mess . . ."

Hulan ignored Hom's observation. "I'm hoping you can call in a couple of other men to secure the building."

"You think the killer's still here?" Hom asked.

She didn't answer his question directly. "Several guests in the hotel should be finishing their breakfasts right about now. They all knew Miss Sinclair. I want them held in the dining room. I want everyone else in the hotel brought there too. No one leaves without my approval." She held up her palm in caution. "No one is to mention what he's seen in this room. Is that understood?"

The men nodded. Hulan turned to the desk clerk.

"How many exits do you have?"

"Four, one at each of the four compass points in our exterior wall," he answered. "We use only two of them. The east and west gates on the sides are always locked. The back gate is for employees and deliveries. Guests always have to pass by the front desk to come or go."

This was typical procedure for keeping track of people in China. Even Charlie Freer at the American Embassy relied on watchers like this desk clerk to find Americans on occasion.

"Then, Captain Hom, I suggest you post officers at the front and back gates," Hulan said. "Again, no one may leave, and everyone must be brought to the dining hall. Also, send some men to search the hotel. I want to know if she was killed here or if her body was brought in. Make sure they check the perimeter, including all windows and doors, for traces of blood. Do you have enough men to cover all of that?"

"Not in the bureau, but there are some others I can call."

"Let me make this very clear, Captain. You will be held one hundred percent responsible for those men."

Hom fumed but said nothing.

Hulan went on. "I also need to make some phone calls. Do you have a secure line down here?"

Hom shook his head.

"Maybe with the headman?"

Hom again shook his head. He looked increasingly glum.

"We can't worry about what we don't have," Hulan said. "David, can you guard the door until we find someone to relieve you? Captain, let me say that this can be your most aggressive man. Do you understand what I'm saying? I don't want *anyone* entering this room. Are we set then?"

"What about Dr. Ma?" David asked.

Hulan frowned. "Yes, where is he?" Then, "I'll stop downstairs and bring him in. David, I have to call Lo and Zai. I need Lo to get me some additional files, and I want to see if we can get Pathologist Fong down here. As soon as Hom sends someone to guard the door, join us in the dining room."

The others departed, leaving David to stand watch. But it wasn't long before he relinquished his post to a heavyset man who looked like he'd done a fair amount of arm-twisting in his day. David threaded his way back toward the second courtyard. Except for the constant beating of rain, an eerie stillness had settled over the hotel.

By now everyone had been pulled together in the dining room. What had been a peaceful oasis last night was filled with the jabbering of different languages and dialects. The foreigners sat together. The hotel employees stood in a large cluster, and—between the maids, bellmen, kitchen workers, laundry workers, and waitresses—they outnumbered the guests about ten to one. Policemen were stationed along the walls.

Hulan addressed the crowd in Chinese first. "I am Inspector Liu Hulan. I come from Beijing, so I hope you will forgive my accent." Though her tones were pure, David suspected that many of these people could barely understand her. "One of your foreign guests has been found dead."

A low murmur rose from the employees, and David saw the foreigners exchange glances.

"I don't need to remind you of the laws of our country," Hulan cautioned. "'Leniency to those who confess, severity to those who hide.' But I want to make myself very clear. I do not suspect any of you. However, because you work here you have special information. Together you are the eyes and ears of the guesthouse. If you have seen or heard something, I need to know what that is so I can help our foreign friends. In this way we can show our superiority to the outside world."

Hulan always knew the right times to haul out nationalism, and this was one of them, which became even clearer as she continued.

"You are Chinese. You are responsible for the welfare of our foreign guests. For this reason I must ask of you a profound favor. I hope you will let me speak to our foreign guests first." Naturally no one protested. "I would like you all to wait here. The men from the

Public Security Bureau will begin interviewing you. You will be co-operative. I will return later, and we will speak together again."

Hulan switched to English. "Miss Sinclair has been murdered. Although Dr. Ma has told you that Brian's death was an accident, I hope you will now believe me when I tell you that these are not random acts." If they had any remaining doubts, she added, "The deaths of two foreigners from one small hotel cannot be a coincidence. I hope you will listen to me this time when I tell you to be careful. I am also asking for your help. I want to speak with each of you individually. In the meantime, you're not to discuss this among yourselves. David, Captain Hom, please come with me."

Together they left the room and stood in the corridor.

"Captain, I want to get through the foreigners this morning," Hulan said. "It'll be superficial the first go-around, but I'd like to hear what they have to say, even if it's brief. Do you have people to interview the staff?"

"I'll take care of those myself," he said.

"I can't prevent you from doing that," she replied. "But I'd prefer it if you'd come with me. The foreigners will answer questions more honestly if they see your uniform. I want you there, but I'd appreciate it if you'd let me do the questioning. I have a lot of experience with outsiders. This is why Vice Minister Zai sent me here. It is our duty to respect the central government, is it not?" She didn't wait for a response but added, "I'd like you to listen and give me your input later."

"This is not how we do things in Bashan, but I won't interfere."

"Good! David, who do you think I should talk to first?" Hulan asked.

David was startled to realize that she planned on doing the interviews without him. He answered, "Angela was the last person to see Lily alive."

"Besides us."

He heard the recrimination in her voice, but there was nothing that they could or would have done differently.

"You should go out to the site," she said.

He raised his eyebrows. "While you're still here?"

They'd always done these things together. She was not only cutting him out of what was happening in the hotel but getting him out of the way entirely.

"I wish you could hear what these people have to say," she hastily explained, "but it wouldn't be appropriate for you to be here." Then, "But you could track down Dr. Ma for me."

"He wasn't outside?" David asked, though he smarted at being relegated to such an insignificant chore.

Hulan lifted her hands in puzzlement. "The Jeep was gone when I went to check."

"I don't think we should split up."

"As I said, it wouldn't be appropriate for you to stay." She didn't give him a chance to argue. Instead, she turned to Hom. "I'd like you to provide Attorney Stark with a car and a driver."

Hom nodded morosely, his disapproval strong on his features.

"Arrange it now," Hulan ordered, and Hom left them.

Hulan turned back to David. "You have the right to question whomever you want to out there."

"Hulan—"

She put a hand on his sleeve. "I have some ideas about all this, but we'll have to talk about them later."

They walked to the lobby. David pulled a couple of chairs together around a low table, delaying in the hope that Hulan would change her mind, but she evaded any further discussion by disappearing behind the front desk to search for paper and pens. Hom came back inside. His jacket and hat were dripping wet. He took them off and offered them to David. "You'll need these."

David thanked Hom, then Hulan said, "I'll come out to the site later, because we should still see the Wus. Will you wait for me?" She left no room for dissent, and he reluctantly agreed. She kissed his cheek. "Be careful."

"You too." Then David stepped out into the rain.

9

A FEW MINUTES LATER HOM RETURNED WITH SU ZHANGQING AND Ge Fei, the two officers who'd first arrived on the scene. They were pale, and Ge still reeked of vomit. Hulan thought their inexperience, as well as the horror of the crime, which only they had seen, might work in their favor when they interviewed the hotel's employees. She didn't want the officers pumped up. She didn't want them intimidating anyone—as if they could, the poor kids. She handed them each a pad and a pen.

"Write this down exactly and ask only these questions," she instructed. "What is your name? What are your hours in the hotel? If you were here last night, did you see or hear anything near Room 5? If you were not in the hotel, did you see the deceased in town? Did you see *any* of the foreigners in town? Have you ever seen the deceased in an argument? Are you a member of the All-Patriotic Society?" Both young men simultaneously raised their eyebrows at this last question, but she didn't want to explain to them her reason for it yet. "This is the information I want. Nothing more. Nothing less. You will interview everyone. Each interview will get a separate piece of paper. Do you have any questions?"

The shy boy cleared his throat. "How will they know who we're talking about?"

"Su, are you Su?"

The boy looked at the floor and nodded.

"You've asked a good question," she said. The praise brought back a little color to the boy's cheeks. "There were four foreign women in the guesthouse. Three of them are in the dining room. When you go back, have the workers look at the foreign women. The one who's missing is dead. Any other questions? No? In that case, you're dismissed. Captain Hom, please bring me Angela McCarthy."

Once alone, Hulan tried to collect her thoughts. Yesterday she'd told these people to be careful, and now one of them was dead. Lily could now be added to the list of those Hulan had failed.

Angela and Hom stepped into the lobby. He motioned her to a chair opposite Hulan, then took a position against the wall. The young woman, who last night had been rather casual about her brother's death, seemed devastated now, her eyes swollen and red from crying. "How could this happen?" she sobbed. "We were with her . . ."

She buried her face in her hands and wept, but it wasn't Hulan's job to offer comfort.

"Did you see Lily again after we all said good night?" Hulan asked.

Angela shook her head and blew her nose into a tissue.

"Did you talk to her on the phone?"

Again Angela shook her head.

"Did you hear anything after you went to bed?"

Angela wiped her eyes with her palms. Her lips trembled as she exhaled and said, "My room's in the fifth courtyard. I wouldn't have heard anything coming from her room."

"The killer had access to the hotel," Hulan informed her. "He put Lily's body in her room. So I want to ask you again, did you hear anything? Someone talking, footsteps . . ."

Angela shook her head, then searched her pockets for another tissue. "Was she raped? Did she suffer?"

Hulan ignored these inquiries. "Do you remember anything from last night that could relate to what happened to Lily?"

Angela shook her head again, still weeping quietly. The American was useless in this state.

"You may go. But, Miss McCarthy, I'm going to want to talk with you again. I'd like to know more about what you and Lily talked about before last night. Will you think about that?"

Angela stood up, looked around uncertainly, and said, "Thank you."

Hom next brought in Stuart Miller, who bounded into the room as though he owned it. "I don't mean to be unsympathetic, truly I don't, but I have to get down to the dam today. We've had some glitches—a delivery of defective components and possible sabotage. People are counting on me."

Hulan motioned to the chair opposite her. "Please sit down."

"I prefer to stand, because we're going to have to make this quick."

"Mr. Miller, this is a murder investigation and you're in China," she explained patiently. "Don't be stupid."

Stuart sat down, crossed his legs, and—still trying to control the situation—hurriedly began. "I've known Lily Sinclair for five years in her capacity at the Cosgrove's branch in Hong Kong. She's—she *was*—a fine young woman."

"Did you see or speak to her last night?"

"No."

"I noticed that you and your daughter weren't in the dining room last night. Where did you have dinner?"

"I have a boat tied up at the dock. I have my own chef."

"Is that your hydrofoil?"

"It belongs to my company, yes."

"Was your daughter on board with you last night?"

"My daughter and I can't help you, because we don't know anything."

"You may not know what you know—"

"Don't try to trick me, Inspector. I have very powerful friends."

"No one's trying to trick you." She waited for that to sink in, then added, "You should know I was educated abroad as an attorney. I will respect your rights as though we were in America."

"Am I supposed to believe that?"

"Either you can believe it or we can do this in the manner of your worst nightmare. Don't forget"—she leaned forward and tapped a finger on his knee—"we are far from any of your powerful friends."

Stuart stared at her finger, and she withdrew it. She wondered if she'd pushed him too far, but then he responded in the way she'd anticipated. He laughed long, hard, and appreciatively. As David might have said, Stuart Miller was a successful businessman. He knew how to play his hand.

"Ask away, Inspector, ask away."

But after all that, he had little to offer. He'd last seen Lily the previous afternoon at the dig. Yes, he had a teasing relationship with her, but he felt she'd understood it in the spirit he intended. He couldn't imagine that Lily had any enemies, certainly none that would be here as part of the archaeological team.

"Did you know that she represented the family that owns this hotel?" Hulan asked.

"The Wangs, yes. I enjoy Madame Wang's company myself when I'm in Hong Kong. She'll be sorry to hear what happened."

"Did you spend the night on board your boat?" Hulan inquired, shifting her focus.

"Of course. My daughter did too."

Hulan thought about asking him about the conversation she'd overheard him having with Catherine yesterday but decided against it. Hulan had been the headstrong daughter of a headstrong man. Her only hope for a remotely honest answer was from Catherine.

"At lunch yesterday you mentioned the All-Patriotic Society. Do you know if Lily was a member?"

If he was surprised by the question, he didn't show it.

"That would be very hard to imagine."

"You're sure she wasn't a follower?"

"Let me put it this way, Inspector," Stuart answered adroitly. "Lily was about as secular as you can get. If she practiced a religion, it would have to have been free enterprise."

"Do you know of anyone else in the hotel or affiliated with the dig who could be a member?"

"It's good manners not to talk politics or religion—" Seeing the look on Hulan's face, he added, "No, not that I know of."

"How about you or your daughter?"

"Of course not."

"Thank you. Now I have just one last question and you can be on your way. Why did you come to the guesthouse for breakfast?"

"I didn't. Like I said, I'm going down to the dam, but Catherine's going to stay here. I came up to say good-bye to everyone." Hulan waited until Stuart explained sheepishly, "I was trying to be polite."

Hulan smiled again. "You see, Mr. Miller, that wasn't so bad. You can go, but I'd like you to leave contact information so I can reach you if need be."

"No problem," he said as he stood. "And I want to apologize for my earlier outburst."

"No apology needed. Have a good trip, and don't—"

"Leave the country?" Stuart grinned, shook his head in amusement, then ducked out the front door and into the rain.

While Hom went for another foreigner, Hulan jotted down some notes. Stuart Miller probably thought the world revolved around him, and to some extent it probably did, but that didn't mean he had anything to do with Lily's murder. At least Hulan hoped it didn't, because she liked him. He was charming in the way he tried to dominate through humor. On the other hand, lots of killers were charismatic, loved to take control, and were—like Stuart—chauvinists.

She interviewed Professor Schmidt and Dr. Quinby, who had nothing to add, except that they felt terrible about Lily's death. Then Hom brought in Michael Quon. It was interesting how each of these people responded to the situation—with acute sadness, mild belligerence, musty indifference, or a desire for control in an uncontrollable situation. Michael Quon managed to work in all of these emotions.

He'd seen Lily in the dining room last night, but he hadn't spoken to her then or later. He liked her as a person, but he didn't have much respect for her profession. "It's not personal," he said. "I just don't like the idea of artifacts falling into non-Chinese hands."

"Do you mean foreign hands or non-Chinese hands?"

He regarded her quizzically. "I'm not sure I understand your question."

"Well, you're Chinese but you're a foreigner."

"I'm Chinese American."

"And?"

"I'm of the belief that artifacts should be repatriated no matter what country they're from."

His manner was frank and his body language relaxed. His dark eyes never left hers. It was unusual for a Chinese to be so insinuatingly direct.

"Mr. Quon—"

"Dr. Quon," he corrected.

"*Dr.* Quon, are you an archaeologist?"

"Do I look like one?"

Of course he didn't. That was why she'd asked. He was completely unlike any of the others she'd spoken to this morning, and she included Stuart Miller in that assessment. Michael Quon wore slacks, which had kept their creases even in the heat and humidity. The top two buttons of his silk shirt were unbuttoned, and she could see his pulse throb in the hollow of his neck. None of those stiff hiking boots for him. Instead he wore soft leather shoes. His fingernails were clean and trimmed. His hands were smooth and callus free. And, she realized, not only did he acquiesce to her scrutiny but he seemed to savor it. No, he wasn't like the others at all.

"I have an interest in archaeology," he said at last, "but I'm not one by training."

"Then what is your field?"

He considered the question. "I guess you could say my specialty is mathematics."

"If that's so, then why are you here?"

"It is so, and I'm here because the reservoir will begin filling next year. I wanted to see this while I could—"

Hulan interrupted him, hoping to disrupt his rhythm. "Let's get back to what happened to Miss Sinclair. Where is your room in relation to hers?"

"I'm in the fourth courtyard, the same as you and your husband," he responded.

"Did you hear anything last night?"

"Just the rain."

That was all David and Hulan had heard too.

"And you were in your room—"

"Until this morning, yes."

"Alone?"

"Yes."

"How well did you know Brian McCarthy?"

"I met him last year when I came through. We did some caving together."

"Caving?"

"Spelunking, if you prefer. We explored caves." He hesitated, then said, "When I arrived this year, he was already missing." He rose. "If there's any other way I can help . . ."

"That's everything for now . . ."

"But?"

He was smooth, this one.

"But nothing," she said abruptly. "You're dismissed."

She'd wanted to ask him other questions. Had he planned to go to the dig today? If so, why was he wearing those particular clothes? What kind of a mathematician was he? Did he teach? Where? And what was he really doing here? Had he been invited? By whom? Had he heard of the All-Patriotic Society? But her desire to have Michael Quon out of her sight had outweighed her desire for answers.

Dr. Strong was next. His sunburn hadn't improved, and he was in quite a muddle about everything. He rambled on about his work with oracle bones and their importance to the history of the Chinese language. He talked about how throughout history the Chinese people had had a love of numbers: the Nine Provinces, the Five Punishments, the Three Obediences. He told her that, although he was eighty-seven years old, he got along well with the younger generation. Brian had been a particular favorite. They'd carried on an e-mail correspondence all of last year. He was old, Dr. Strong admitted, but he wasn't so old that he couldn't learn how to do e-mail! Could Hulan see that correspondence? What a hilarious idea! His computer was in Cambridge, and all of the old e-mail disappeared eventually anyway. Didn't she know anything?

Yes, he knew Lily, although he preferred talking with Catherine. (He was old, he confessed again, but he wasn't so old that he couldn't appreciate a beautiful woman when he saw one!) His room was in the same courtyard as Lily's. He'd heard noises, but he always heard noises in this place. In fact, he could say that he hadn't had a decent night's sleep since he'd arrived this June. But then, he was an old man and given to insomnia no matter where he was.

The rain had gotten much worse, and the road to Site 518 far more treacherous than it had been yesterday. As a result, David's driver concentrated on keeping the car on the slippery track and out of the largest mud holes. But David paid little attention to the dangerous conditions. He was totally wrapped up in the events of this morning, playing out each piece. His first concern, of course, was Hulan. Just when things were beginning to go well, the universe revealed itself to her as cruel and capricious yet again. He was very worried about how she would handle this, and the fact that she was shutting him out of her investigation bothered him deeply. Then there was the murder itself. As it always was with death, it came as a total shock. What had been done to Lily Sinclair made him sick. Obviously he didn't know her well, but from what he had seen she had been smart and funny. She was too young and too beautiful to be taken so soon and so viciously.

His mind spun back to Hulan. She didn't want him with her, and she didn't want to share her earliest suspicions with him. She preferred that he continue with his own investigation of the thefts, but because he was a former prosecutor, it was David's nature to look for patterns and make links. Whether or not Hulan liked it, he was already formulating his own ideas about Lily's murder, how it could be related to Brian's, and how both of them could be connected to the thefts from Site 518.

The car bumped into the camp, and David stepped out into the warm rain. Since last night the river's level had risen to within a few feet of the lowest tents, and some day workers were moving them up the slope. David didn't see Dr. Ma down there, so he trudged up the hill until he found the director squatting under a canopy brushing at a shard. The archaeologist, aware of David's presence, didn't look up. "We work on a schedule out here," Ma remarked. "I'm not a chauffeur, and I can't wait around for VIPers, no matter who they are."

"Lily's dead."

Ma lifted his head, but his face was impossible to read. He set down his brush and stood.

"What happened?" Ma asked.

"She was murdered."

"How?"

"I think you'd better take that up with Inspector Liu. She'll be coming later."

Ma nodded thoughtfully, then: "And you're here because—"

"I was sent to do a job. As a courtesy I'm telling you that I'll be interviewing some others about the missing artifacts."

Ma held David's gaze. "Do as you please." Then Ma dropped back to his haunches, picked up his tool, and went back to his work.

David hesitated, half wanting to put Ma in his place, half wanting to ask what his problem was. Instead he went in search of the museum representatives. He found them in one of the caves, sitting around a table on upturned crates, smoking cigarettes and playing cards. They motioned for him to sit, and he did. Though he couldn't be sure that all of the caves were like this one, it did match the description Ma had given yesterday. Three-tiered bunks rested against the walls deeper in the cave. Lanterns hung in rocky recesses, though most of the light came in through the cave's mouth.

David had a difficult time with their Sichuan accents, but between his Mandarin and their English they were able to communicate. He'd let Hulan decide how she wanted to handle Lily's death and kept his inquiries specific to the thefts.

Li Guo, a representative from the Three Gorges Museum, upriver in Wanxian, turned out to be the most loquacious of the group. "Look no further than the foreigners," he recommended as he pushed his horn-rims firmly onto the bridge of his nose. "They all want to steal from us."

"I'm a foreigner," David reminded them. "I don't want to steal from you."

The men nodded vigorously. A couple of them knocked on the table with their knuckles, signaling their approval.

"Yes," Li agreed cheerfully, "you're a foreigner and our government sends you to salvage our heritage. Our leaders tell us our country is changing. When we see you here, we know that this is so. But then," he added philosophically, "we would rather speak with you than with the inspector. She's a tough one."

After a pregnant pause, David asked somberly, "Have you forgotten she's my wife?"

The men stared at him dumbly for what seemed a full minute, then gave themselves over to raucous laughter. Li called for a bottle of *mao tai,* and one of the other men rummaged around until he found one. David reached into his satchel and pulled out a bag of pressed radish seeds to contribute to the impromptu party. The liquor was poured, shots thrown back, and aphorisms traded on the nature of wives. After the way the day had begun, David was grateful for the strong drink and the jokes. Still, he had to come back to the thefts, and the group was ready for him when he did.

"Ask Dr. Ma. He's in charge," the man from the Chongqing Municipal Museum suggested.

"Ma would not give a straight answer even if our Supreme Leader came back from the grave and asked the question himself," Li scoffed. His glasses had steamed up, and he wiped them on his shirt.

"Why not?" David asked.

"Dr. Ma looks young, and he is on the outside, but inside he's an old man. Understand?"

"Old in his political philosophy . . ."

"He is political, yes," Li said as he poured another round of drinks.

"Is he a Party member?"

The men jutted their chins. Who could know? Maybe.

"But he was educated abroad," David went on.

"He shows one face to the outside world," Li answered, "but his inner face is very outdated."

David tried to read between the lines. Did Li mean that Ma was old-line politically, or did it have to do with social class?

"His manners are not classic Chinese—"

"Attorney Stark, Ma has his place. We have ours. Or didn't you hear what he calls us?"

"Vultures—"

"A rude accusation in any language," the man from Chongqing observed.

"And he makes others," Li went on. "As you know, bribery and corruption are serious offenses in my country."

"But you've given gifts," David prodded carefully.

"I can tell from your Mandarin that you've been in our country for some time," Li noted. "You are familiar with our customs, no? Is it not correct to bring a gift to your host?"

Absolutely. Cigarettes, Danish sugar cookies, VSOP cognac were all acceptable, even expected.

"Is Ma removing artifacts from here?"

But the men weren't ready to go that far.

"Let me answer this way, Attorney Stark," Li began. "We five are here every day. We sleep here. We have our meals here. Our work units pay us to sit and watch and wait. As you can see, this is exactly what we do."

Indeed, this table at the mouth of the cave offered a good view of the goings-on below.

"We are not archaeologists," Li continued. "We are simple work-ers who were lucky to find good work units. Yes, we compete for which museum will get an object, but I think we've been fair with one another." The others unanimously agreed. "We represent museums with different interests, so we cooperate." He waved his hand knowingly. "This is not how it's usually done, but if I let Hu have something today, he'll let the Three Gorges Museum have something tomorrow."

"Then Ma is—"

"A liar," Li finished, then took another sip from his glass. The others could have countered this assessment, but they all nodded pensively.

"Who's stealing the artifacts?"

"You ask the wrong question, Attorney Stark."

"What's the right one?"

"Focus on the *ruyi*. Who has it?"

"Stuart Miller?"

"If he had the *ruyi,* he wouldn't be coming here."

"Ma said the same thing."

Li spat on the ground. "Even if Dr. Ma and I agree on this, you still need to think more broadly."

"Okay then, who does have it?" David asked. Li waited for him to delve further. He did his best to oblige. "Where is the *ruyi* now? How did it get there? And who's going to be the ultimate owner?"

"The *ruyi*'s in Hong Kong. Ask Lily Sinclair how it got there. Then ask her how it can be going up for auction at Cosgrove's tomorrow night."

David felt foolish and a little miffed, for neither Ho nor Ma had told him any of this, yet it seemed to be common knowledge.

"I don't see Lily here," David went on evenly. "Why don't you tell me?"

Suddenly Li Guo stepped out of his guise of a vulture who'd been fortunate in his work unit. "Once artifacts are out of the country, false papers of provenance are easily created," he said. "Auction houses, dealers, collectors, and museums all choose to accept these implausible claims, even as our superiors expect us to find our missing objects. Meanwhile, we're still trying to figure out who has jurisdiction."

David had encountered this before. Was it the responsibility of the State Cultural Relics Bureau, the Provincial Relics Bureaus,

Customs, or people from museums to track down stolen artifacts? It always seemed like bureaucratic buck-passing to him. After all, how could a small museum in a poor, isolated region—or the men in this cave—have the ability to find where artifacts had appeared abroad or, if located, negotiate for their return?

Hulan had deliberately left Catherine for last. The young American was dressed in an outfit nearly identical to the one she'd worn yesterday. Full makeup highlighted her eyes and lips. Her posture was perfect, to accentuate her most notable physical attributes, but Hulan was not impressed by Catherine's beauty or intimidated by her sexuality. If anything, they were off-putting.

"I didn't see Lily last night," Catherine recounted. "I had dinner with my father, then I went for a walk."

"Alone?"

"I'm not afraid, if that's what you mean. China's very safe."

It would be very safe for a woman of Catherine's race, especially in a small town such as this; however, it obviously hadn't been safe for Lily.

Hulan tried to reconcile the rather dim young woman who sat before her now with the young woman who yesterday knew more ancient Chinese history than anyone else at the table. She was deliberately acting dumb, which Hulan took to mean that Catherine was hiding something.

"Catherine—do you mind if I call you that?" When Catherine nodded and her posture loosened, Hulan confided, "People always think it's a mistake to get involved in a murder investigation; however, the person who killed Lily needs to be caught and punished before he does it again. Now please answer my questions truthfully."

So they began again at the top. Catherine had eaten dinner with her father on the hydrofoil at eight o'clock. After dinner, Stuart had gone to his stateroom to handle some business. She'd returned to the hotel around eleven to get a couple of things from her room. She hadn't seen anyone except the desk clerk. While walking back to the boat she'd spotted Lily in one of the alleyways that led off Bashan's main road. They'd walked together for a while until Catherine realized that they were heading out of town. She'd said good night at the bridge that crossed Bashan Stream, then gone back down to the dock.

"What did you talk about?"

"Nothing in particular. We didn't like each other very much—"

"I noticed that at lunch—"

Catherine's eyes widened as she remembered the conversation from yesterday.

"Do you really think she sent the day worker to 'a watery grave'?" Hulan asked.

"That was a joke! We picked on Lily because she was such an easy target. All she cared about was her career—"

"And the others don't?"

"Inspector, Site 518 isn't exactly the path to fame and fortune."

Unless you stole from the site, Hulan thought. But Catherine was already wealthy, and if she wanted fame, all she had to do was slip on some Versace and return to the social whirl of her economic class. "Okay, I accept that," Hulan said. "So let's go back to last night. You're walking together through town. You must have talked about something."

"Lily was fishing for what my father was going to bid on at the next round of auctions, but the truth is, he doesn't share that information with me. I'm only his daughter, not his curator."

"He's old-fashioned, you mean."

"He believes women have their place. Look, he's wealthy, he's a widower, and the kinds of women he meets . . . Well . . ."

"It's hard to get his attention."

Catherine nodded. Hulan thought about Catherine in a new light. How could she compete with the other women who must flow through her father's life? Hulan didn't think that Catherine's dressing and acting like Electra would have much appeal to Stuart, or would it?

"Still," she resumed, "he values your opinion."

Catherine cocked her head questioningly.

"I heard the two of you talking yesterday," Hulan explained.

"At lunch," Catherine remembered brightly, "of course."

Hulan acknowledged that this was so, but Catherine had also given her an opening. "I heard you before that too. Your father said something about you running out of time . . ."

Catherine winced. Hulan waited.

"My father . . ." The words closed in on themselves, and the young woman tried again. "My father wants the best for me. For him that means a good marriage."

"Another old-fashioned view—"

"But still as common as air," Catherine finished bitterly. "I've told him that his views are so antiquated they belong in one of the Site 518 pits." After a moment, she added, "My father is very hard to please." Another beat, followed by "All men are when you think about it."

"Is that why you're here? To prove something to him?"

"Maybe to myself. How pathetic is that?"

They talked for a few more minutes. Catherine had no idea where Lily had been going. She regretted now that she hadn't asked, but at the time she honestly hadn't thought about it. They simply weren't that close.

"How about your father and Lily? Were they close?"

"Do you mean did they"—Catherine searched for the appropriate words until she settled on—"have sex?" When Hulan nodded, Catherine laughed and her whole face changed. She appeared for a moment as she truly was behind the facade—young, open, and naturally beautiful. "Probably, although Lily *definitely* wasn't his type." Still smiling at the idea of it, she added, "Don't get me wrong. He had a lot of respect for her. She helped him a lot with his collection."

"But she wasn't as knowledgeable as you."

"I know more history and art. She knew more about the business of art—museums, auctions, private collections, and financial transactions above and below the table."

"Was Lily the person responsible for artifacts disappearing from Site 518?"

"Probably."

"Do you have any knowledge of her taking artifacts out of the country, whether from Site 518 or elsewhere?"

Catherine answered with determined frankness. "Over the years Lily obtained amazing pieces for Cosgrove's to put up at auction. Where she got them, *how* she got them, I don't know, but if she did it illegally, it wouldn't surprise me. If my father bought some of those pieces, well, that wouldn't surprise me either. He's a man of many passions, and he doesn't take no for an answer."

Hulan thought about that, then asked, "Will you be going down to the dam site with him?"

"My father? Oh, I'm sure he's halfway there by now," Catherine answered, her lightness returned. "But, no, I wasn't going with him. I'm part of the Site 518 crew. I'll be here all summer."

Hulan had gone about as far as she could with these preliminary interviews, and she still had other people she wanted to see. She and Hom walked with Catherine as far as the lotus pool, then said good-bye. Then Hulan and the captain went to the restaurant's veranda, where a couple of Hom's men reported that the search of the interior and exterior of the compound had been completed. No murder site or blood trail had been located. Someone had gone to considerable lengths to make this element of Lily's murder an enigma. Hulan would come back to this, but for now she and Hom went on to the dining room, where Officers Su and Ge sat at small tables interviewing employees one on one. Everyone else sat at the larger banquet tables, smoking cigarettes and drinking tea. A hush settled over the room while Hulan spoke quietly to Su and Ge. Hom took a chair between his men, lit a cigarette, and exhaled the smoke through his nose.

With the limited scope of questions on which Hulan had insisted, the two officers had been able to get through twenty employees, most of whom were on the day shift and hadn't arrived until this morning. None of this first group had ever observed Lily Sinclair in an argument. None of them had seen or heard anything near her room. Three people had caught sight of her in town last night. No one admitted to being an All-Patriotic Society convert, but then, Hulan hadn't expected that anyone would at this point.

"We've had a good beginning together," she announced to the room. "If Officer Su or Officer Ge has already spoken to you, you may go. I may still call on some of you individually."

Hom leapt to his feet. Before he could voice his objections, Hulan continued, "Captain Hom will preside over the rest of the interviews. You must be as honest with him and Officer Ge as you would be with me in Beijing." The thinly veiled threat was met by sullen silence. "Officer Su, please come with me." With that she and Su left the room.

Hom was right behind her, though. "You can't dismiss those people!"

She turned to face him, trying to keep hold of her temper. "*You* will not tell me what to do. *You* will not tell me how to run an investigation. If *you* do, you will become the subject of *my* interest. Do you understand?"

Hom's face bloated in ill-disguised anger.

"I'm going to Site 518," she went on. "Officer Su will drive me. You will stay here and arrange round-the-clock guards for the guesthouse and Site 518. We will *not* have a repeat of what happened to Miss Sinclair."

David left the vultures' cave and approached a group of day workers, who told him that they came to the dig in the morning, left in the evening, and got paid once a week.

What happened if someone unearthed an artifact?

"We are told to call for Dr. Ma, and he comes." The man who spoke was so thin that his belt was wrapped twice around his waist. "Then the others arrive, and they all work together."

Was anyone ever alone with objects that were found in the ground?

"This is a big place, but there are many people and eyes everywhere."

What about at night?

"Everyone goes home."

A man with a shorn head added, "Except for Dr. Ma."

"And the vultures," someone else called out from within the gathering. "They also sleep here, but they are good men."

This was met with murmurs of agreement.

David backtracked. "You're treated well?"

Someone else in the crowd spoke up. "We are peasants. We move dirt here, we move dirt on our farms, no difference."

"Do any of you remember Brian McCarthy, the American?"

"He drowned."

"We tell the foreigners to be careful of the river."

"Did he steal things from Site 518?" David asked. He felt a subtle shift from curiosity to wariness. "What was he interested in, can anyone tell me?" The workers began drifting away. David called out after the retreating backs, "What about the other accidents? Your friends Wu, Yun, Sun, and the others?" But by now he stood alone in the mud and rain of Site 518.

The difference between the day workers and the Chinese graduate students was that the latter were smart enough not to answer any of his questions, so David marched back up to the museum representatives' cave, where he was greeted with more shots of *mao tai*. The vultures' tongues loosened, and they began to gossip about Michael Quon, the wealthy American. He'd traveled to many important sites—to the Xia palace at Erlitou, to the Neolithic settlement of Banpo, to Xi'an for the terra-cotta warriors, and to Zhoukoudian, where Peking Man was found. But the question on all of the vultures' minds was, Were all Americans as rich as Michael Quon? Were they all able to travel freely like some modern-day Da Yu? They agreed they must be, because Miller and his daughter were also rich.

"But Miss Miller works here," Li Guo pointed out to his companions.

"And we're grateful for it!" Hu practically hooted.

"Hu misses his wife," Li explained. "We tell him you can look, but we need to care for Miss Miller, because she's the smartest of all of the foreigners."

"Smartest?" David asked.

The vultures nodded enthusiastically but said they admired Dr. Strong more than anyone else on the site. "He once knew more about our ancient cultures than anyone alive. Even now you can hear him say important things if you have patience."

They'd liked Brian too. At the beginning of last summer, he'd talked to the vultures a lot, then he'd gotten into hiking with Michael Quon. The two of them explored caves, and the vultures remembered Brian coming back one day and announcing that the caves were "like a mother," although they had no idea what he was talking about.

"But he was different when he returned this year," said Hu. "Don't you agree?"

"Yes, he only wanted to talk to Dr. Strong or Professor Schmidt," Li admitted.

"What about?" David asked.

"Dragon bones—ancient oracle bones used for divination," Li answered, again revealing his hidden expertise. "For hundreds of years during the Qing Dynasty, the farmers along the Yellow River who dug them up believed them to be the bones of dragons and sold them to doctors who ground them up for traditional Chinese medicine. Then about a hundred years ago scholars realized that the markings on them were actually ancient writing, dating back thousands of years. Many people—including Dr. Strong—spent years trying to decipher the meaning."

Since that time, five thousand characters had been identified on oracle bones, of which half had been deciphered, with half of those proving to be directly connected to contemporary language. This was the first step in demonstrating that China had the oldest continuously used language in the world while establishing that the lists of the Shang emperors found in ancient texts were accurate. Those emperors were not mythical. They were actual men.

So what had sparked Brian's interest in dragon bones?

"The boy had become interested in symbols and language, which is why he wanted to talk to only Schmidt and Strong," Li answered. "He was particularly curious about the Xia culture of the Yellow River."

Why?

"Because in draining the world of floods, Da Yu created arable land. He taught the people how to farm and raise animals. He taught them rituals of divination and sacrifice. We believe Yu was the beginning of what today we would call civilization."

"But why was Brian so curious about the Xia if they lived on the Yellow River?" David asked.

The vultures didn't know.

By the time Hulan arrived at the site, David was more than a little drunk. The vultures were his comrades now, and they patted him on the back and shook his hand and made a few more off-color remarks before sending him away with Hulan with the admonition that "strong branches tremble when the petals shake."

David's wife was not amused.

CHAPTER

10

DAVID AND HULAN WALKED THROUGH THE RAIN ALONG THE TRAIL toward the Wu house. "I've been thinking about Lily's mutilations," David said, "and wondering if they're purely unique to this killer or have some specific reason behind them—say punishment for Wu Huadong's drowning."

"Ma said Lily couldn't have been involved in Wu's death." Hulan dodged a puddle, then edged back next to David.

"But what if the scholars' teasing accusations that Lily sent Wu to look for the tripod in the whirlpool turned out to be true?" David adjusted the satchel strap on his shoulder. "What if Brian and Lily were *both* responsible? Someone out there could be sending a very potent message, only no one's understanding it."

"Actually, David, I understand it quite well. The All-Patriotic Society lieutenant said the group would make me pay for killing that woman in Tiananmen Square. The best punishment would be to discredit me by proving that I'm incompetent."

He was astounded by the leap her mind had made. "Why? And how?"

"Lily died on my watch."

He stopped. "Are you serious?"

"Absolutely."

"Hulan, honey"—he tried to sound reasonable—"I don't think anyone around here knows that happened."

"Because they don't have television? They do have an All-Patriotic Society chapter. You've seen the signs in town, haven't you? Word travels."

"But you said yourself that what was done to Lily was completely unlike anything you'd seen before. That blood coating—"

"Exactly! The mother in the square was going to cut off her daughter's hand. Now Lily's feet are amputated. The smearing of the blood is a literal message to me—that the cult is holding me responsible for the bloodshed."

"If that's so, then what about Brian? The modus operandi appears completely different—from the way Brian and Lily were killed to the way their bodies were disposed of—but as you told everyone in the guesthouse, their deaths were not random acts. Do you really think there could be more than one murderer in Bashan killing foreigners?"

She slogged through another puddle, listening.

"If you accept that fact, then Lily's death can't have anything to do with what happened in Beijing," David continued, "because Brian was killed long before you ever knew about that rally, probably before it was even planned. What ties Brian and Lily together is Site 518. When we find their killer, you'll see that this will boil down to greed—the theft of artifacts, not some larger conspiracy involving you and the All-Patriotic Society."

He had hoped his analysis would convince her, but she said, "I still think the link is the cult." She could be so stubborn.

"Can we both keep open minds until we get more facts?" he asked. "We'll know a lot more after Pathologist Fong does his autopsy. When will he get here?"

"Soon. I have him flying in by helicopter. I'll meet with him when we get back to the guesthouse."

There she was again purposefully pushing David away from her inquiries. Maybe if he got her more involved with his, she'd be more open to accepting his help. They didn't have much time before they reached the Wu property, so he quickly filled her in on what he'd learned at the dig. When he finished, Hulan asked the question that had been gnawing at David. "But why didn't Ma or Ho tell you this before? Surely they knew about the auction."

"They had to know," he agreed. They talked a little longer but came no closer to an explanation; then David said, "I think I should go to Hong Kong tomorrow and try to block the auction of the *ruyi* and whatever other Site 518 artifacts are set to go on the block."

"Fong ought to be done with his examination by then. You could fly down to Wuhan in the helicopter with him, then catch a plane to Hong Kong," Hulan offered helpfully. It seemed a logical and simple plan.

They arrived at the clearing where the Wu house stood. If anything, it looked more desolate than yesterday. Rain poured off the roof and ran across the barren land and over the precipice to the river below. A rocky outcropping hung out over the house; just under the ledge a giant boulder seemed ready to dislodge itself and crush everything below it. On either side of the house were natural stone formations that resembled Grecian columns, only where the friezes and cornices might have been were two large stones smoothed by aeons of wind and rain.

Hulan knocked on the door and called out, "Wu Xiansheng, Wu Taitai." They heard movement inside and a grating sound. The door opened slightly, and a thin-faced woman peeked out.

"*Wei?*"

"*Wo jiao Liu Hulan. Zhe shi Stark Lushi,*" Hulan explained, pointing first to herself and then to David. "We want to talk to you about your husband."

The door closed, and David and Hulan waited in the rain. Low, agitated voices, then the door opened again, revealing an older man, his eyes filmy white with blindness.

"I'm from the Ministry of Public Security," Hulan said. "I've brought a foreigner with me. We've come from Beijing to speak with you."

The man waved them inside, closed the door behind them, and felt his way to setting a rough-hewn piece of wood horizontally into two brackets that sat on either side of the frame. The young woman—the widow of the man who'd drowned—stood barefoot in the center of the room, her sleeping baby wrapped in a sling against her chest. Hulan edged forward to get a look at the infant, but the widow covered her baby's face and backed away. Superstition and suspicion went hand in hand in the countryside.

The man barked at the woman to bring tea. She stared at him dully. These people didn't have enough money for tea leaves.

"On a day such as this, a cup of hot water would be nice," Hulan commented, keeping both sympathy and condescension from her voice. Without a word the woman picked up a thermos, poured hot water into three grimy jars, and handed them around. Then she backed away and stood against the wall. Her feet and arms were filthy; her clothes were heavily mended rags.

"Wu Huadong was my son," the blind man spoke out into the room. "I am Wu Peng."

Wu's Sichuan accent was so thick that David could barely understand the words, so he surreptitiously tried to take in the surroundings. The room was larger than it looked from the outside because the back wall and part of the sides of the room were carved out of limestone rock faces. Two low sleeping platforms lay against the walls. A hutch had been constructed from three scavenged crates that were tucked into an alcove, which had also been chiseled out of the mountain. A piece of dingy cloth hung from the top crate down to the hard-packed earth floor, hiding what was inside. A homemade table sat against the wall. A clothesline had been strung kitty-corner across the room, and the baby's clothes were drying, contributing greatly to the eye-stinging odor that combined urine, spit-up, and mildew. Lack of air circulation caused by no windows and the locked door exacerbated the stench.

David had been in other peasant homes, but he'd never seen anything like this. Even if the poor couldn't afford glass windows, they left an open space for ventilation, which was sealed in the winter by newspapers. In the middle of summer, he would have expected to see the door open at the very least. Yet not only was it closed but a substantial barrier had been laid across it to prevent entry. Looking around, though, David saw nothing that could be of any value—no mementos, decorations, or personal belongings other than one eight-by-ten-inch piece of paper with Chinese characters that had been jabbed onto a nail. There wasn't even a simple altar to commemorate the dead husband and son.

"People say your son's death was an accident," Hulan said as David began to follow the conversation.

"How can it be an accident?" Wu was wiry, and his face was as cragged and worn as the cliffs outside. "Our family has lived on this ground for many centuries. My son was born here and knew every rock of the land. How could he fall into the river?"

"If not an accident, what do you think happened?"

"There are evils to be guarded against," Wu stated.

Hulan stiffened. David understood the words but was unsure of his wife's reaction.

"Lust comes in many forms," Wu went on. "For a woman. For money. For power. My son worked for a greater good, but he was deceived."

"By Xiao Da?" Hulan asked.

Little Big, the leader of the All-Patriotic Society, the man whom Hulan held in such contempt. After the conversation David and Hulan had just had, he tried to listen more closely.

"Not by Xiao Da," Wu corrected. "By others who wish to rip our country from our hands."

"Such as?"

Wu sneered. "The *yang guizi.*"

David had no trouble understanding those words. He'd heard them shouted at him on the street many times. *Foreign devil.* Hulan didn't even look his way but addressed Wu in the same tone that provoked confession even from the innocent.

"You are loose-tongued, yet you say nothing. You make general accusations, yet you tell me nothing to help me with your son." She stood. "I shall report to Beijing that there is nothing to learn here."

David had been alarmed by a lot of things Hulan had said and done today, but he was unprepared for the cold way she was suddenly treating the old man.

Wu Huadong's widow crept forward and whispered shyly,

"Please, Miss, don't go. Excuse my father-in-law. His heart is clouded by sorrow. Please."

The woman eased back against the wall and lowered her head. When Wu said nothing, Hulan took a step. Hearing her, the old man held out a sinewy arm to block her path.

"My son worked at Site 518," he said.

"This is common knowledge," Hulan replied sternly. "Say something meaningful or get out of my way."

"He did special work for someone there. I don't know who, but it was a foreigner."

Hulan sat down. "A man or a woman? American? English?"

Wu's milky eyes blinked. He turned his head from side to side, trying to find her through sound. "A foreigner is trouble no matter what it has between its legs or from what corrupt soil it emerges. Huadong often went to meet this person. That last morning he held his hand out to me. 'From the fist of the past to my fist to the fist of the future.'"

"What did he mean?"

"He said he wanted to bring something from the earth and give it back to our country. It would show the world our strength."

"Your family's?"

Wu drank from his jar, then said, "Family pride, country pride, same thing."

"Pride brings loss, humility receives blessings," Hulan recited in response.

"We are humble, but we are not so blessed," Wu countered.

"You speak then of our homeland."

"For centuries our China has been invaded by the foreign element. They have come up our great river. They have stolen from us. Now, even outside our borders, they insult and betray us. The bombing of the embassy—"

"Uncle Wu," she interrupted him, "you know much, yet you are far removed from the course of the world."

"The river's course is all that matters."

Hulan suddenly shifted direction. "Where will you move when the dam is finished?"

"We have been given instructions to move to Xinjiang. They have offered us extra money, but we will not leave."

"Your son felt this too?"

"Huadong said we would not have to go. He would stop the dam."

"Your son was educated?"

Wu cleared his throat and spit on the floor. "We are peasants for countless generations. Our blood has been part of this land since Da Yu's dragons cleared the river."

"As we are speaking frankly," Hulan said, though to David the whole conversation seemed to be spoken in riddles, "I must ask why you stay."

"It is our home."

"But your land is no good," Hulan stated the obvious.

"This has been so since before my grandfather's time, but I have heard stories of great crops that once grew outside our door. This is what Da Yu created for us when he drained the flood. The land is the treasure. That does not change."

"You contradict yourself."

"The land is the treasure," Wu repeated. "It is *shi tu*."

David thought about those words. *Living earth?* That was hardly what lay outside the door. *Scorched, desolate, barren,* were the words that came to mind when David thought about the land from here to the dig.

"My grandfather's grandfather told him this," Wu went on. "My grandfather told me, and now I tell my grandson."

"Let's go back to your son. If he was not educated, how did he plan to stop the dam?"

"I don't know."

"You don't know or you won't say?" Hulan pressed.

"He went away sometimes. When he returned he would say that outside corruption would be turned to justice."

"Did he go to the dam?"

"Maybe to Shanghai—"

"How could he afford that?"

Wu didn't answer the question. Instead he repeated, "From the fist of the past to my fist to the fist of the future." Then, "My son is dead, and he was murdered by foreigners." It was a brash but sadly empty accusation.

Hulan gestured to the piece of paper on the wall even though the old man couldn't see it. "You're a disciple of the All-Patriotic Society."

"We aspire to be reverent," Wu admitted.

"You know this cult has been implicated in domestic terrorism," she stated.

"These are false accusations."

David admired the man's bravery in acknowledging publicly that he was a follower of an illegal group. Or was it stupidity?

"Do you have explosives here?" Hulan demanded.

Wu looked shocked, then shook his head.

"I think your son was a troublemaker." Her voice was cruel in its accusation. Father and widow wordlessly accepted the denunciation as Hulan walked to the wooden crates and lifted the cloth to examine the contents. "Did your son have a special hiding place?"

"No," Wu answered without hesitation.

Hulan gazed about for other potential hiding places, then suddenly addressed Huadong's widow. "*Ni!* You! What do you know about your husband's activities?"

The poor woman visibly trembled in fear. Sensing this, the infant whimpered. The woman shook her head in vehement denial.

"The two of you must have had a special place to meet. This is just one room . . ."

David understood Hulan's implication. There was no privacy here, but that word didn't exist in the Chinese language, so Hulan finally had to spell it out.

"You have a baby. Where did you and your husband go to be alone?"

But before the woman could respond, her father-in-law said, "I am an old man, but I still remember the ways of a husband and wife. I sat outside."

"I'm going to say some names," Hulan said. "I want you to tell me if you ever heard your son speak of them. Brian McCarthy . . ."

"The foreigner who drowned," Wu answered.

"Like your son," Hulan pointed out.

"The river takes the careless. My son was not careless." It seemed Wu wasn't going to budge from this position, but David had seen this stubbornness before. No parent wants to accept a child's faults.

Hulan continued listing the names of the foreigners at the dig, but neither Old Wu nor the widow professed to having ever heard of them.

"Ask if they ever spoke to Brian," David said. "If Brian went to that spot down by the river often, then they must have seen him on their land."

Hulan asked the question. Huadong's widow shifted her weight. Her father-in-law answered, "He crossed our land every day. We did not speak to him."

"Are you sure?" David asked in Mandarin. Wu's eyes widened. He hadn't expected the foreigner to speak the mother tongue, even if it was the northern dialect.

"I don't speak English," Wu responded.

"But Brian spoke Chinese," David revealed.

An awkward silence hung in the room. The widow stood motionless against the wall. David glanced at Hulan. Anything else? his expression asked. These inquiries are going nowhere.

David kept his eyes steady on Hulan as he asked the old man one last question. "Were there any marks on your son's body when he was pulled from the river?"

"I felt him with my own hands," Wu answered. "He was as perfect as the day he came into the world."

Prosecutors never asked a question unless they knew the answer, but David had been pretty sure what Wu would say. Hulan's line of questioning had been fruitless. The Wus' situation was unfortunate, but they were a dead end nevertheless.

On their way out, Hulan stopped to examine the All-Patriotic Society flyer more closely. "Bashan Village is foolish to advertise nightly meetings so boldly."

"Xiao Da says we should not be afraid of our beliefs," Wu said.

"You have heard him say this?"

"When he speaks, I listen." The old man felt for the paper, pulled it off the nail, and handed it to Hulan. "Go to the meeting tonight. Open your heart."

Hulan took the flyer and stuffed it in her pocket, then she pulled the hood of her poncho over her hair and stepped out into the rain. Once outside, David turned to take one last look at the widow and her cradled baby. Underneath all that dirt and sorrow was a very pretty young woman.

"*Zai jian*," he said.

"Be reverent," the old man answered, then shut and barred the door.

A HALF HOUR LATER THEY WERE BACK AT THE HOTEL. IT WAS close to six, still raining, still hot, and Hom's guards still manned the front entrance. David and Hulan wandered back to their room in the fourth courtyard. They were wet and muddy. Hulan took the first shower, and by the time David was out of his she'd made tea from the hot water in the thermos. He sat down and took a sip. The closeness he'd felt to Hulan just yesterday seemed very distant now.

"I have to ask you something, Hulan. Why were you so hard on that old man?"

"Sometimes you have to be tough if you want a straight answer. You know that."

"He lost his son. That woman lost her husband—"

"And they're both cult members."

Suddenly her obsession with the group became clear to him. She used it as a barrier against her feelings—against facing her grief over Chaowen's death, against connecting to him because she knew he was opposed to China's religious policies, against dealing with Lily's murder or even that old man's anguish. That wall may have protected her emotions, but it was blinding her to the facts of the case.

"I'm sorry we came out here," he said.

"There's nothing to be sorry about."

"Of course there is . . ."

She sighed. "I don't see that we have time for you to feel guilty or for us to have some heartfelt discussion about my weaknesses, okay?"

He sat back stunned. This day had been a far bigger trigger for her than he'd realized. "Don't shut me out, Hulan. We came here to-gether—"

"Things have changed. You're an American civilian. You can't help me with a murder investigation."

"When has that ever stopped us? Besides, this is dangerous—"

"Can we just forget I'm your wife? Let me do my job, then we can go home."

He scraped his chair away from the table and walked to the win-dow. He knew she didn't understand how her words hurt him. He knew as well that she had no idea of the depth of his frustration. But that had become their pattern since Chaowen's death. He worried; she ignored him. He tried to protect her; she shut him out. He tried to engage her; she avoided him.

He had a choice. He could come right back at her or he could control his feelings.

He stared out the window as he spoke. "We're on a train—"

"A train?" He heard the apprehension in her voice. It seemed to ask, Am I to get some metaphor about my life now?

"Things are moving quickly. That always happens in a case. Today . . ." His solar plexus ached and he realized he was bone-tired from the effort of always having to be *up* for her, yet here he was doing it again. "You feel it, don't you, Hulan, the way we're now just along for the ride and we have to go where that ride takes us. And the day's not over."

"No, it's not," she agreed briskly. "While you were in the shower, I learned that Fong's here. He's with the body. I need to see him. And I'd also like to check in with the men who did the interviews with the staff."

"And then you're going to go to that All-Patriotic Society meet-ing," he finished for her.

Hulan held up Wu's flyer. "This cannot be a coincidence. I think it's why Zai sent me. That, and the dam."

But that wasn't at all why Zai sent her. He'd given David and Hulan the gift of a second chance. That Hulan was blowing it off wounded David more than he could absorb.

"I'm suspicious of Stuart Miller's presence here and his connection to the dam," she continued, oblivious to his silence, "as well as Wu Huadong's claim that he could stop it. And—"

She stopped speaking. The silence that weighted the room was much louder than the one they'd experienced back at the Wus' hovel.

He picked up his satchel and went to the door. "Let's find Fong."

It was a test to see just how much she wanted to exclude him from her activities. But maybe she wasn't ready for a full confrontation, because she glided past him and through the door as though nothing had happened.

He followed her down the hallway to Lily's room. A couple of Hom's men stood outside. Pathologist Fong stepped into the hall. He had quite a bit to say about the way he'd been brought to this backwater in a military helicopter that, according to him, should have been decommissioned forty years ago, the nature of the facilities, and the conditions under which he had to work. As per Hulan's request, Lily's body had not been moved or anything else in her room disturbed. This meant that, when Fong arrived, Lily had been dead for some time in hot weather. The first thing he'd done was open the window. All of this was beyond the pale as far as the pathologist was concerned.

"Come inside, Inspector," Fong said in English. "I'll show you what little respect you have for my position."

"I have the greatest respect for you, Pathologist Fong. That's why I requested you. Only you—"

Fong snorted in mock disgust, then opened the door to Lily's room. Two long tables had been brought in. Fong had set up his equipment on one and Lily on the other. Flies buzzed over the dark, bloody outline on the bed where her body had been. Vats of water occupied a corner, and extra lights exposed Lily's body with clinical harshness. She lay naked on the table. With her veins emptied and her skin washed clean, she appeared desiccated, wrinkled, and tinged blue.

"You moved her," Hulan observed.

"I saw what I needed to see on the bed, but I can tell you right now you should have just sent her to Beijing."

"You can take her tomorrow," Hulan said. "I wanted you to see her here. Every crime scene is a message, and I wanted to know what you thought."

"Stop trying to flatter me. It doesn't become you."

David watched in grim fascination as Hulan reached into her bag, then slid a pack of Marlboros across the table. She didn't smoke but had thought ahead to have the bribe handy. Fong took a cigarette, lit it, and slipped the pack into his shirt pocket. Temporarily placated, he described what he'd discovered.

"You can see I haven't cut her open. What's the point, unless you want to know what she had for dinner?"

"She ate here in the guesthouse," Hulan informed him.

"See? Why do extra work when I can get the answers I need from you?"

Fong peered up at Hulan, and it struck David that although the pathologist was speaking in English, they'd tuned him out completely.

"What killed her?" Hulan asked.

Fong rubbed his chin in feigned concentration. "My guess would be she bled to death."

"Pathologist . . ."

"Ha! You're so serious, Inspector!" Fong approached the body. "Her feet were cut off and she bled out. But think about that. I understand you said good night to her around nine. You found her at eight. So eleven hours passed."

"One of the foreigners saw her about midnight," Hulan said.

"So perhaps eight hours from the time that the last witness saw her to when you found her. During that time she was drained of her blood and positioned back in her room before rigor mortis could set in. That process begins immediately at death and usually becomes manifest within two to four hours, then advances until approximately twelve hours. In hot weather, such as you have here, it can disappear as soon as nine hours after death."

"Which means what?"

"The questions I keep asking myself are: How long did it take for her blood to drain, and at what point did she die?" He squinted at Hulan. "I'm trying to establish a time of death."

"And?"

"Hard to do, because I can't use the usual methods. Livor mortis, the purple discoloration of the skin that we usually find, is determined by how the blood settles, but most of her blood is gone. Body temperature is usually reliable, but readings are difficult in this situation, because her temperature would have dropped very quickly as the blood drained. But then maybe I have to compensate for that because the air temperature in this room is so warm. When I get her back to Beijing, I'll run a few tests."

David was appalled at the matter-of-factness of the conversation, but Fong wasn't done.

"But I know I'm not answering *your* question. How did she sit still for it is what you want to know. There are no signs of struggle— no skin under her fingernails, ligature marks on her wrists, or bruising to show she put up a fight." His fingers rested lightly on Lily's pale skin. "She was a beautiful woman for a foreigner."

"Beauty doesn't matter when you're dead, Pathologist."

Fong chuckled. "No one is colder than you."

David moved to Lily's desk, which had already been dusted for fingerprints. He stood with his back against the wall in the same way Huadong's widow had earlier.

"Any evidence of sexual assault?"

"None."

"What was the weapon?"

Fong scratched his head. "Not a saw because there's nothing on the bones or the surrounding tissue to suggest serration, and a knife wouldn't have made it through the bones. I think the amputation was done in one motion."

"What else?"

"As you know, she was killed somewhere else and brought here. The blood that coated her body looked like a smooth layer, but on closer inspection I discovered that more had been applied once she was placed on the bed. This suggests that someone came here with a container filled with her blood."

"You're sure it was hers?"

"Why go looking for other blood when hers was available?" Fong asked. "I wish it was applied by hand, but it wasn't. The blood was blotted on. Maybe a sponge. Anyway, I picked up particulate matter on her skin—man-made, natural, I'm not sure yet. I also found slight abrasions and traces of what looks like the same material in her mouth. I'll analyze it later."

Lily had kept her room very neat, David thought as he listened to Fong and Hulan. Lily had a Filofax, some loose papers, and a couple of notebooks in a neat stack. A Mont Blanc pen rested just so to the right.

"Although the room looks clean, it isn't," Fong continued. "I found drops of blood from the door to here and traces in the bathroom, where someone washed his or her or their hands. I also picked up a few drops in the hallway going to the left. Nothing in the alleyways. A bit of blood in the drain, a couple of drops in the hall, and nothing else. The killers were clean."

"Killers?"

"Although she was drained," Fong explained, "she still would have leaked. How do you prevent her feet from leaking unless you keep them above her head? How does one person carry that much dead weight and keep those feet up? And who carries the bucket of extra blood? You are looking for three conspirators."

"What about fingerprints?"

"We've picked up some in the room, but the body had the first priority. I'd like to move her somewhere. Do they have a walk-in refrigerator here?"

"It's a guesthouse, not the Sheraton Great Wall," Hulan observed dryly.

"Very well, some ice will do."

"Fingerprints?" Hulan repeated.

"I did the desk. I thought you might want the papers."

"Can you gather those up for me?" Hulan asked, and David was momentarily surprised that she was addressing him.

As David put the papers in the side pocket of his bag and zipped it closed, Fong went on. "You haven't asked me about the most important clue. Attorney Stark," he called out, "you will like this." He motioned David to Lily's side. "Look at the mark on her forehead."

"We noticed it earlier," David admitted.

"But it was covered in blood and not so clean as now." Again Fong's finger touched Lily, this time ever so softly against the mark on her forehead. "It's a burn. What do you call it in English? It's something your cowboys do."

"A brand."

"Yes, a brand! She was branded!" Fong beamed, pleased by the new word. "Now look closely. Look! It's a symbol. You see it? Three lines like . . ." Fong's hands rippled through the air.

"Like waves," David said.

"No, same direction," Fong corrected himself.

"A current?"

"Waves of a current, exactly. *Chuan*. It is the character for *river*."

"No, it isn't," Hulan objected. "The strokes should be straighter."

Fong poked an elbow into David's side. "As a child, our inspector spent too many years abroad. This is why she knows only the polite customs of our country. She asks you to dinner, she puts you in the seat of honor at the north side of the table. But you ask her about our culture and she is as stupid as a water buffalo. I can say this because I've known the inspector for many years."

Hulan gave the pathologist a disapproving grimace.

"Three lines all *waving in a current*," Fong continued, giving an indebted nod to David. "This is the ancient character for *river*. We are in the province of four rivers, no? *Sichuan* means 'Four Rivers.'"

"Thank you for the education, Pathologist Fong," Hulan said tartly. "I shall report your helpful attitude to the vice minister."

"*Hao, hao,* good, good," Fong replied, absolutely unabashed. "Because this is not the only mark I have seen like this. Your other foreigner, the one named Brian McCarthy, had this same *chuan.*"

"Are you sure? His face was a mess, and you said yourself that his flesh was torn on river rocks."

Hulan usually did such a good job of hiding her feelings from her colleagues, but Fong's information was putting chinks in her wall. Once again, David felt deep pain—for himself, for his wife, and for all of the tragedies that had brought them to this room.

"Yes, I have spent more time with your other foreigner," Fong continued in the most cheerful tones, "looking at the wounds you speak of for research before he goes back to his homeland. He is in such bad shape, I thought, Who would know what I do to his body now? It is good for our country to study the effects of the river, and here is an opportunity to study them. Perhaps I will write a paper and send it abroad."

"You're telling me that you know for certain that Brian McCarthy was killed by the same person who killed Lily Sinclair?" Hulan queried. "You have hard proof?"

"Hard proof? Ha! How can I possibly have that after the journey he took? I only know that when he was branded the burning went past his flesh and into the bone, and that this woman here has the same brand on her forehead. It's up to you, Inspector, to determine if the same person did it!" Fong rubbed his hands together and looked about. "Investigator Lo promised that if I came down here I would be given a tour of the Three Gorges. I have always wanted to see our special heritage."

12

BEFORE THEY LEFT, FONG GAVE HULAN A MANILA ENVELOPE, which she took without opening. Then, while David dropped his satchel in their room, Hulan exchanged a few words with Su Zhangqing and Ge Fei, the policemen who'd interrogated the employees. By the time David returned, the young men had given her their notes and a synopsis of what they'd ascertained.

"You worked hard today," she commended them.

The young men beamed. It wasn't every day that someone from the Ministry of Public Security praised them, but their pleasure turned out to be short-lived.

"I hope you'll go home and have a good meal, but then I'd like you to come back—"

"To interview the night staff," Su, the bright one, guessed.

"It's a much smaller group," she explained, "but it may take longer. They were here last night. If you find an eyewitness or suspect that someone knows more than he's telling, please find me. I'll be out of the hotel for an hour or so, but I'll be back."

She and David left the officers and went to the dining room. The scholars were grouped together at their customary table, though neither Angela nor Catherine was with them. Hulan ordered a simple meal, telling the waitress to hurry. The food came and they began to eat.

"Do you think you'll find anything pertinent?" David asked, pointing with his chopsticks to the stack of employee interviews that lay atop the manila envelope next to Hulan's plate.

"I'll take a look later. You never know."

"And Lo's files?"

"I haven't opened them either," she said, "but they can wait. I don't think there'll be any surprises."

After dinner, they swung by their room one more time, then stopped at the front desk to speak with the night clerk, who reported that he'd seen Miss Sinclair leave the hotel around 11:30 last night. He also remembered that Miss Miller had gone down to the dock to have dinner with her father. Later she'd come back to the hotel to pick up a few things and had gone out again a few minutes after Miss Sinclair left the hotel.

"Did Miss Sinclair say where she was going?" Hulan asked.

"No, but she went for a walk almost every night after the temperature cooled," the night clerk said. "She didn't care if it was raining. I think she liked it. Sometimes she would stay out until one or two in the morning."

Hulan made a few more inquiries. The clerk hadn't left his post all night. He hadn't seen any other foreigners leave or enter the hotel. He hadn't heard or seen anything that struck him as suspicious. Since this was his primary job—watching over the foreigners and reporting their behavior to the Public Security Bureau—he wanted to emphasize that she could trust his account.

It would be about a twenty-minute walk to the All-Patriotic Society meeting. David and Hulan put on borrowed plastic jackets, accepted a flashlight and a couple of umbrellas from the night clerk, then stepped outside. It was still light, and families who'd finished their dinners sat in front of their homes under the eaves enjoying the relative coolness of the early evening drizzle. But despite the peaceful domesticity about him, David walked with the same sense of foreboding that he'd felt going into Lily's room this morning. This wasn't a good idea. Hulan wouldn't handle the meeting well, and he wasn't sure he was up to dealing with the consequences.

Following the map on the bottom of the flyer Wu had given

them, David and Hulan crossed the Bashan Stream bridge and headed out of town toward Site 518. This was the same direction that Lily had walked last night, Hulan told David. They continued for another quarter of a mile before stepping off the road and onto a slippery path which led down to a rocky platform that rested about fifty feet above the Yangzi. They weren't familiar with the vicissitudes of the river and didn't know how much higher than usual it was running, but even so they could hear and see its fury. The water swirled and foamed, waves crested and splashed, and pebbles and broken tree branches rolled and collided along this rocky shoulder.

They followed the path east until they came to a secluded inlet. Like the cove where Brian had gone into the river, this one had a little beach and a cave. But surely this was a false beach, since the true water level was several feet lower. Even above the roar of the river they could hear the sound of chanting emanating from the cave.

They entered the dark maw. Lanterns lit the way deeper into the earth. With every step the sounds grew louder. They saw no one— no guards, no malingerers, no mothers taking their children back outside for making noise. The deeper they went, the cooler it got. Light from the oil lamps danced on the walls. A dank, musty odor filled their nostrils.

Suddenly the tunnel opened into a large cavern, where immense stalactites hung down from the ceiling. Close to a hundred people stood together, swaying and chanting, "Subdue the wild tribes in our hearts. Practice the abstinence of alcohol, tobacco, and fornication." The words were in Chinese, and the tones in which they were chanted sounded beautiful and mesmerizing.

Perched above the people on a rocky ledge before an alcove stood a man in common peasant clothes. It was Tang Wenting, the All-Patriotic Society lieutenant who had been in Tiananmen Square three days ago.

"Do you see who that is?" Hulan whispered excitedly. "Do you believe me now that there's a connection?"

Tang Wenting led the chanting, which changed to "Give up material possessions. Cherish the sanctity of life. Advocate peace and peaceful means."

"I won't let him get away tonight," Hulan said. Her eyes scoured the cave, looking for possible escape routes.

Tang Wenting held his hands up for silence. "We meet in the dark," he said, "but we live in the light of Xiao Da's blessings. Where Xiao Da sends me, I go. I am his sword."

Then he moved aside, leaving the alcove completely unobstructed. A strange, melodious voice emanated from the shadows. "You all remember me. I am Xiao Da."

"Can it really be him?" Hulan exclaimed over the crowd's murmurs of "Xiao Da, Xiao Da, Xiao Da."

"To the outside world, Xiao Da remains faceless," Tang Wenting said. "In this way he can represent all the faceless people of China."

Hulan whispered in English to David so that those around them wouldn't understand. "Is that a recording, or is someone actually in that alcove?"

"I am a part of you and a part of China," the voice proclaimed. "I see a world where the faceless will become the true voice of China."

The voice didn't sound electronic or distorted by any means other than the natural acoustics of the cave, but it didn't sound of this world either.

"If that's truly Xiao Da," Hulan whispered again, "I'm going to arrest him."

But as David looked around, an arrest seemed impossible. He saw no way to get up to the ledge other than scaling the cliff below it. This had to mean that the man wasn't in an alcove but in another cave with its own separate exit. Xiao Da and Tang Wenting might not have anticipated that Liu Hulan would show up, but they had planned an escape route nevertheless. Putting that fact aside, the cave was also filled with All-Patriotic Society followers. They weren't going to allow Hulan up to that higher cave even if she could master the cliff. Finally, and not insignificantly from David's perspective, Hulan had not brought her weapon. It was tucked in a bag on the top shelf of the closet back at the Panda Guesthouse. There weren't going to be any arrests tonight no matter how much Hulan wanted to make them. She must have realized this too, because her urgency had been replaced by a calculating stillness.

"One day—and I tell you it's coming soon—China will be the dominant power in the world," Tang Wenting announced. "Xiao Da is leading us to that time. He sees in us the future of our country. We are patriots."

As soon as he left off, the voice from the alcove took up a more soothing refrain. "We don't practice rituals that take advantage of the gullible. Our only ritual is to honor the spirit within. We are pure of heart. We are reverent."

Then it was back to Tang Wenting. "Wherever Xiao Da leads us, we will be at his side. We will show the world our faces. We will show the world China's strength."

David understood the sentiment to a degree. Patriotism was a natural outgrowth of China's newfound prosperity and its emergence after decades of isolation. Nothing was more "patriotic" in China these days than the dam, and nothing was more universally appealing to the downtrodden than the idea of a savior. So it came as little surprise that the men above began to combine these twin concepts, although their take was unique to say the least.

"They've told us to leave our ancestral homes to make way for the dam and its lake," Tang Wenting declared. "They've told us to move *up* our mountainsides, but how can we do this when Premier Zhu puts a ban on any form of habitation on land steeper than twenty-five degrees?"

"What he says is true," someone called out. "All the good land is already occupied."

"And what about the fishermen who trawl the river for their livelihoods?" Tang Wenting asked. "What will they do in a city so removed from the life force of the river?"

"The river brings us life," Xiao Da sang.

"The river brings us life," his followers droned in reply.

"Nothing can change the great river."

"Nothing can change the great river," the followers repeated.

"They've told us to move to a New Immigrant City or one of the other big cities," Tang Wenting continued, "but has anyone here received an urban residency permit?"

Cries of "No" echoed through the cavern.

"They tell us to leave our land to take jobs in factories, but how can we when they've all been shut down for inefficiency, corruption, and pollution?"

The crowd was right with the lieutenant.

"These things are an illusion the government uses to trick and entice us. They offer us money to move to other provinces, but what will we find when we get there? When the mud sinks to the bottom, the river becomes clear."

"They promised me three thousand *yuan* a head for me to take my family to Xinjiang," a man in the audience crackled indignantly. "But when I got there I was told I'd have to drill one hundred meters to get water. I don't have a drill, and water is abundant here. I came home and I won't leave again."

"They talk about the good life that awaits us somewhere else, but why should we leave when this is our ancestral home?" Tang inquired.

The voice from the alcove thrummed forth. "Forbearance does not mean tolerating evil beings that no longer have human nature or righteous thoughts."

"The fat rats will have to pay for their sins," Tang interpreted.

"See how they smoke their expensive cigarettes, how they drive fast cars, how they drink foreign liquor," Xiao Da intoned. "All of these things are an abomination to those who are reverent."

This last caused a break in the sermonizing as the adherents took up the chant of "Be reverent, be reverent, be reverent." The lieutenant joined in, letting his strong tenor reverberate through the cave. When his voice lowered, so did those of the followers, until finally there was quiet again.

"We have all heard of the corruption that spoils the purity of our river and its people," Tang said. "What about the local officials who have added the names of *their* relatives to the lists of relocatees, making *their* families eligible for relocation funds? What about the exaggerated reports filed by fat rats to the government about arable land that is being lost? Bashan officials have inflated the size of the town by twenty-five percent. They've filled their pockets with the difference between the real value of the land and the reported value of the land. These atrocities are common in all towns to be inundated. The fat rats lie and steal from the government . . . *and from you.*"

"Why don't we petition the central government to make amends?" a man brayed out. "Let's demonstrate so the government will remedy the situation."

"What is a piece of paper but a way for the government to hunt you down?" the lieutenant asked. "What is a demonstration but a way for the government to say that you're causing civil unrest? We all know what happens to troublemakers in our country."

"Then what can we do?" For the first time the speaker was a woman.

Xiao Da answered, "Combine docility with boldness. It is the fifth of the Nine Virtues."

"They've told us that the dam will be a monument to show the world China's importance," Tang Wenting picked up, "but we know it is only a way for a *yang guizi* with a hydrofoil to get rich and steal our heritage."

So far the sermon had been about governmental corruption, but now Tang was bringing Stuart Miller into the equation. The people here may not have known his name, but who in Bashan didn't know by sight the person who owned the gleaming white hydrofoil tied up at the dock?

"We do not care for concrete and steel when our hearts and souls are at stake," Tang Wenting went on. "The fat rats hurt the river people. May we not throw rectitude at them? Should we not inquire about our leaders who show a pious face to the people but in private enjoy the rotten fruits of foreign decadence? And what about men like Stuart Miller who invade our land like so many ants—greedy, insistent, an army of nuisance that nibbles away at our pride?"

The crowd grumbled its reaction. The mood had shifted from spiritual to questioning to belligerent.

"I see tonight that we have visitors," the lieutenant announced to the crowd. "You!" he called out, pointing to Hulan. "Tell them who you are."

"Liu Hulan," she answered.

"Inspector Liu Hulan of the Ministry of Public Security, who comes here to frighten us away from our beliefs," Tang Wenting clarified for the followers.

The cave suddenly seemed far smaller, and David realized just how precarious a situation they were in.

"You bring a foreigner, I see."

"This is David Stark," came Hulan's calm reply.

David felt a low, simmering hostility push in around him. He smelled human sweat and saw petulant faces staring at him.

The lieutenant tossed his head in disgust, but from within the darkness the enshrouded voice spoke tranquilly. "His name is of no concern to us. We need to know what kind of man he is. Is he reverent?"

"He's a *yang guizi*," the lieutenant said. "He's a big-nose foreigner who has no right to be on our Chinese soil."

"You're wrong." Hulan matched the even tone of the hidden voice. "Attorney Stark is a *Zhongguotong,* a friend to China."

"Who says this?"

"Our leaders."

"Waaa!"

An even louder "Waaa" from the crowd echoed the lieutenant's response.

"You and I don't share the same leaders," the lieutenant said. "We follow Xiao Da."

"Xiao Da, Xiao Da, Xiao Da." The worshipful susurration reverberated through the cave.

"When a true leader gives repose to the people," the hidden voice pronounced, "his kindness is felt and the black-haired race cherish him in their hearts."

The construction of the sentence had an archaic sound that reminded David of the heightened language of the classical dramas sometimes shown on state television. Could this be a Confucian saying or perhaps a snippet of classical poetry?

Tang Wenting bowed his head piously, absorbing the sound. Then he raised his eyes and asked David in brittle Chinese, "What do you have hidden behind your smile?" Again the crowd parroted this two or three times before the man repeated it himself. "What do you have hidden behind your smile?"

This was the same question that had been posed to President Clinton when he'd come to China. Clinton didn't know how to respond, and neither did David.

Hulan stepped forward and demanded, "If Xiao Da is so special, why does he not show *his* face?"

David wasn't so sure that her question was a good idea, although it did divert attention away from him.

"And why don't you ask Stuart Miller to show his true face?" Tang Wenting asked in response. "Is your government so greedy for this dam that they will look the other way while he steals China's soul?"

"You are afraid to answer my questions!" she fired back. "Why doesn't Xiao Da tell the people who follow him who he is? Why is he hiding behind you? Is he that afraid?"

The lieutenant put his hands on his hips and shouted back staunchly, "Xiao Da afraid? Not of you!"

"Is he afraid because he instructs his followers to kill and maim?"

"Waaa! You dare to speak this profanity? Only Xiao Da can punish the wicked!"

"So he hides because he kills and mutilates," Hulan pressed.

Now David was convinced that this definitely wasn't the right attitude to be taking in the midst of a crowd of worshipers in an isolated cave far from anything resembling police backup.

Then Tang Wenting pointed his finger at Hulan as he had that day on the square. "There is only one killer here, and that is you, Liu Hulan! Mother killer!"

Hulan recoiled from the impact of the denunciation. The followers, who were insulated in the Three Gorges not only from the outside world but from events in their own capital, did not know how to respond. The lieutenant proceeded to inflame them. "Mother killer! Mother killer! Mother killer!" The adherents picked up the chant even though they didn't know the reasons behind it. "Mother killer! Mother killer! Mother killer!"

David felt hands on him, shoving, pushing. He couldn't see beyond the faces twisted in loathing. Then he was tossed out of the cavern and back into the tunnel with the oil lamps. A moment later Hulan was thrown into his arms. The angry mob retreated. Hulan regained her balance and headed back to the room. "Hulan!" he called sharply. She didn't even look his way but marched steadily forward. What could he do but follow? They edged to the opening into the large cavern. The lieutenant was on his hands and knees, touching his forehead to the stone floor of the ledge on which he perched, then lifting it again with an enraptured look on his face, then back down to the floor. The followers mimicked the obeisance in devout silence.

"As we go forward," the disembodied voice lulled, still the epitome of harmony, still unfazed by the near violence of moments before, "we must all remember, if not for Yu, we all would be fishes, and if not for Xiao Da, we would become fishes."

These words held the crowd in worshipful thrall until the lieutenant finally stood and spoke once again. "Now is the time to remember our tributes."

About a dozen men emerged from the shadows holding baskets. "Remember the Nine Virtues, remember your grade, remember your tribute." The voice floated out over the heads of the worshipers. "Nine Virtues, Nine Grades, Nine Tributes."

People pulled out money and dropped it into the baskets as the low murmur of "Be reverent, be reverent" resounded off the limestone walls.

They left before the meeting concluded and hurried through driving rain up the pathway to the road that led back to town.

"My God, Hulan! What were you doing back there?"

"Trying to get Xiao Da to reveal himself!" Her delivery was fast, her words angry.

"We could have gotten hurt!" he volleyed back.

"So you finally admit that the group is dangerous!"

"Those people were dangerous because you provoked them!"

"What about the threat against Stuart?"

"What threat?"

"It was implied! First Brian, then Lily. Stuart's next!"

"Stop!" When she didn't, he grabbed her. "Stop! What are you talking about? What are you doing? Where are you going?"

She fought against his grip. "I'm going to the Public Security Bureau to get Captain Hom. He's got to come back here and arrest these people."

"By the time you get to Hom's office, everyone in that cave will be gone."

The truth of that sank in, and she stopped struggling. They were standing on a deserted road in a storm in the dark at the end of what had already been an emotionally grueling day. They still had a twenty-minute walk back into town. Maybe he could calm her down and get her to think clearly.

"You once trained as a lawyer. Try to look at this logically." He attempted a smile. "Come on, let's walk." He took a couple of steps, and when she started walking beside him, he said, "We'll take it one accusation at a time. First, the All-Patriotic Society—"

"It's why I'm here. I know it! Zai didn't send me here to protect me from the media or from internal MPS scrutiny. He sent me here to find Xiao Da."

"Honey, if he'd known Xiao Da was here," he reasoned evenly, "why didn't he just have the man arrested?"

"What if he sent me here because he knew that foreigners were joining the group? It would be a huge embarrassment if the All-Patriotic Society spread abroad as the Falun Gong has."

"That's a valid point, but you have no evidence whatsoever that any of the foreigners here are members."

"Stuart Miller—"

"Is clearly *not* a member."

"He's the next target—"

"I don't think so. I think this Tang Wenting may want the followers to believe something about Miller. But I'm suspicious of that too. Was he talking about Stuart Miller for their benefit or ours? He let the meeting go on for a long time before he acknowledged us, even though he had to know we were there. He used that time to try to convince us—"

"That Miller's the one stealing China's heritage," Hulan finished. "Still, one of the foreigners from Site 518 could be a member of the group."

"I doubt it. They're all academics. They're too cerebral for that mumbo jumbo."

"Since when? Americans are always getting caught up in that stuff. Madonna with Cabala. That kid who joined the Taliban. Every housewife who ever took a yoga class . . ."

"That's simplistic and condescending. And besides, not everyone at the site is American."

Hulan shrugged, and rain poured off her clothes.

David could be obdurate too, if that was what she wanted. "All right then, could the All-Patriotic Society be involved in either the thefts or the murders? Most crimes are motivated by greed, but those people back there say they don't care for material things, and I never heard them advocate stealing. And I certainly didn't hear anything to suggest that they were interested in killing people. Just the opposite. They talked about the sanctity of life."

"The hidden voice talked about the sanctity of life—"

"Brian's and Lily's murders were ritualistic in nature," David continued right over her. "They were *branded*. Didn't you hear what they said? They don't practice rituals."

"Everything they did was a ritual—"

"That takes advantage of the gullible. Their only rituals had to do with 'honoring the spirit within,' or something along those lines. Besides, you just saw those people. Do they really seem like they'd get together to torture and brand someone? A good part of the residents of Bashan Village would have to be aiders and abettors."

"This country is made up of aiders and abettors. The Cultural

Revolution . . ." Hulan's voice trailed off. When she next spoke it was with renewed indignation. "Time and again human history has shown that fervent nationalism can lead to domestic instability, international conflicts, even war."

"This isn't the Cultural Revolution," he reminded her, "and Xiao Da hardly has the power of the Gang of Four."

They walked in silence for a few minutes as the rain pelted them.

She tried another tack. "Captain Hom is getting rich off of the people who live here."

"Five minutes ago you wanted his help." Knowing that had to sting, he added, "But we aren't here to investigate local corruption."

"I have larger obligations that you can't possibly understand—"

"Like finding and arresting Xiao Da? I'm married to you, Hulan. I know what it would mean to you to shut down his operation."

"Could that really have been Xiao Da back there?" she asked, and for the first time he thought he heard doubt in her voice.

"Why would he come here to meet with a hundred supporters when he could have gone to Beijing and addressed thousands?" David asked. "The All-Patriotic Society probably uses this system to make people believe they're 'seeing' the real Xiao Da. It's very clever and would explain how the group has grown so quickly, because everyone has a personal experience to share. Not only is it good advertising but it allows the Society to link politics and spirituality by presenting two faces: the first and more practical in the form of a real man, the other and more ethereal in the form of a disembodied voice."

Hulan listened, and David pressed his advantage. "I'm not going to tell you it isn't strange that Tang Wenting is here, because it is. I'm not going to tell you that the group is completely harmless, because the hostility in the cave was scary, but it had to do with all of the terrible things these people are dealing with—moving, uncertainty, feeling powerless. And I'm certainly not going to tell you that I support everything the Society advocates, but you know as well as I do that people ought to have the right to practice their religion."

"Even if that means making threats against the dam? Wu Peng said his son was going to stop it."

"Wu Huadong was a peasant living in abject poverty. How exactly was he going to stop the dam?"

"I don't know, but I'm going to the dam tomorrow to find out."

"You're way off track. We never should have gone to that meeting—"

"Why can't you respect my opinion?" she asked. "You said we should see what other facts came in. Now that they have, you're choosing to ignore their implications."

"That's not true," he said in exasperation. "I'm trying to keep us focused on our assignments. You're investigating what are now two deaths. I'm supposed to be looking into these thefts—"

"To me, those things are minor compared with seeing Tang Wenting in that cave! He said he'd make me pay for what happened in Beijing, and now he's here!"

"His presence in Bashan doesn't necessarily make him vengeful or dangerous. Yes, he threatened you in the heat of a terrible and emotional moment, but he may just be making his regular rounds to chapters in the countryside. And remember, he tried to stop the woman in the square from cutting off her daughter's hand . . ." He held back the rest—that Hulan's solution had resulted in death.

This argument was moving into perilous territory. He took a deep breath and started over. "Two people have died here in Bashan. You need to table your campaign against this religion for now and solve Brian's and Lily's murders."

"It's not a religion. It's a cult," she muttered.

"Call it whatever you want, Hulan," he said, his frustration rising again, "but we both know you're using it as a barrier—"

"Xiao Da is using religion to control the group in a political way. He's teaching people to mutilate—"

"Where do you get that?"

"The mother on the square," she answered. In response to his look, she added defensively, "Well, you brought it up."

"You said yourself she was crazy."

"Then what about Brian and Lily?"

"They were branded. *That's* what you should be looking at. What does that brand mean to the killer?"

"You don't understand!"

"Then help me."

They had stopped again. They were wet, muddy, and standing on one of the most barren tracts of land David had ever seen.

"I killed that woman." Hulan's voice was tired. "In the square. I'm the mother killer. If I'd followed my instincts then, she'd still be alive."

"Oh, honey, that has nothing to do with this."

"And if I'd followed my instincts when we got here, then Lily would still be alive too."

"You can't blame yourself."

"Of course I can."

Even in the dark he could see she was trembling. This wasn't about Xiao Da, Tang Wenting, or the All-Patriotic Society anymore, nor was it about Lily or the woman in the square. It was about Chaowen. David had longed for this conversation for months, but he had never anticipated that it would come in the middle of an argument.

"There was nothing we could do," he said softly, trying to rein in his anger of moments before.

"I was her mother!"

"You've got to stop punishing yourself."

"I can't."

She wanted to say something more, and he gently coaxed her. "What is it?"

"You should have done something," she said at last.

"What, Hulan?" he asked in anguish. "What could I have done?"

"You should have made us move to the States. She might never have gotten sick, and if she had, she would have gotten proper medical care . . ."

He heard what she said as an unfair, cruel, and false accusation. He was the one who had wanted Chaowen to be born in the United States; he'd wanted her to grow up there. It was Hulan who had refused to leave China—over many years and many requests. It was she who had insisted they not take Chaowen to the hospital "just yet." Some Tylenol would do, Hulan had claimed. And then it was she who had emotionally deserted David, leaving him to mourn his bright and beautiful daughter alone.

"If going to Los Angeles would have saved our daughter's life, then you are to blame," he retorted without thinking. "Just as you're to blame for not wanting to go to the hospital sooner."

Finally she'd gotten him to say what they'd both been censoring all these months. Hulan didn't say a word. She just turned away from him and began walking toward Bashan.

They were soaked to the skin by the time they got back to town. David took a hot shower and got into bed, then watched as Hulan, wearing a white silk wrap that was sheer enough to hint at her nakedness underneath, called Beijing and left a voice message for Vice Minister Zai outlining their travel plans as well as what she'd discovered about the cult: the group appeared to be advocating violence, a high-ranking All-Patriotic Society lieutenant was in Bashan, Xiao Da himself might be here too, and the MPS should send a team to make arrests at one of the nightly meetings in the cave as soon as possible. After hanging up, she gathered a few things to take with her tomorrow. Then she opened the window to its widest. Warm, moist air followed her to the bed. She sat on the edge of the mattress and looked at him squarely.

They were way past apologies, and she spoke with chilling matter-of-factness. "Tomorrow you and Pathologist Fong will drop me at the dam so I can ask Stuart Miller about what we heard tonight and find out more about his relationships with Brian and Lily. You and Fong can continue on to Wuhan airport. He'll catch his flight to Beijing, and you can fly to Hong Kong for the auction."

She turned off the light and curled on her side away from him. He lay there listening to the whirring of the overhead fan. Once he thought she was asleep, he got up, dressed, slipped out into the corridor, and walked to the veranda outside the restaurant. He sat in a wicker chair and watched as the downpour tapered off to heavy mist.

David was in deep despair. He'd loved Hulan for so many years, even those when she'd been lost to him. He'd believed theirs was a true love, but tonight—after everything that had happened today—

when he heard her self-reproach for what seemed the millionth time, he'd let down his guard and lost his patience. He'd personally given up much to have a family life in China. He'd abandoned his love of the great issues of law and justice, settling instead for small cases of little significance. (Looking for a few stolen artifacts in a small town in China's interior was a far cry from the international disputes he'd handled before.) It was a choice he'd willingly made so that the three of them could be happy.

David didn't hate Hulan for what had happened to Chaowen. Hulan had done what any mother would have done in the same circumstances. An hour or a day wouldn't have made any difference; the meningitis strain was too virulent, and Chaowen could have contracted it anywhere. But when David heard Hulan blame him for Chaowen's death, he'd cracked. In that moment he'd finally faced what had been before him these past months. Hulan might never get past the what-ifs. She might look at him forever with eyes as empty as if a curtain had fallen over her soul. He'd thought she was lost and he could save her. What he hadn't understood was that that same blanket had covered him. He was lost, too—in his career, in his spirit, and in his marriage. He loved Hulan with all of his heart, but if there was to be redemption for either of them, she would have to reach out to him.

THE SWORN DOMAIN

(Yao fu)

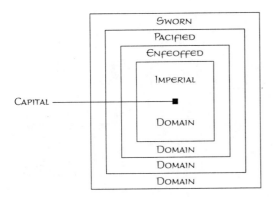

Sworn
Pacified
Enfeoffed

Imperial

Capital ——————

Domain

Domain
Domain
Domain

Remoter still. Within the first 300 *li* are allied barbarians and people of restraint. The last 200 *li* are saved for criminals undergoing lesser banishment.

13

THE HELICOPTER SWOOPED DOWN FOR A CLOSER VIEW OF A particularly dramatic outcropping of rocks and verdant foliage in the Xiling Gorge. David sat up front with the pilot, Hulan was in the backseat with Fong, and Lily's body was shrouded on one of the helicopter's pontoons. Pregnant clouds hung heavily over the lofty, pine-covered summits. Down below, the swollen river swaggered past villages and towns, terraced fields and honeycombed rocks.

The rotors made a sickly racket as the pilot tried his best to maintain altitude. When the helicopter took a particularly nasty dip in an air current, Pathologist Fong, who yesterday had minced no words in his description of his trip in this same antiquated bird, looked over at Hulan with an expression that said, I told you so. Fong turned his attention back to the river below. The pilot had only two pairs of earphones, so he was giving the pathologist his promised tour. This left David and Hulan to experience the deafening sounds of the rotors and motor, which was probably a good thing. At least they had an excuse not to speak to each other.

She'd heard him leave their room last night. She'd heard him come back just before dawn. They'd grabbed a quick bite in the dining room with Fong, and at seven the three of them had met the helicopter in a little clearing just west of Bashan. David hadn't said ten words to her in that time.

Ahead of them lay the dam site. What had once been the sleepy fishing village of Sandouping was now a vast blight on the landscape. Huge chunks of land had been bitten out of the earth so that part of the site looked like a strip mine. The other part was the massive wall of the dam itself. The river looked wide here, at least two kilometers across. A cofferdam funneled the waters so that the work could continue, but today the river was so high and furious from the accumulation of rain from Tibet to here that no ship could safely pass. So large freighters, open-sided ferries, and gaily painted cruise ships had come to a standstill, while small fishing boats bobbed about them in the turbulent yellow waters.

The pilot landed in an open space in the far corner of a parking lot jammed with buses. Hulan glanced at Fong. "Ten minutes, okay, Pathologist?"

"I was promised a scenic tour of the Three Gorges," he complained. "Now all I get is the visitors' center?"

"You've also had a helicopter tour. How many people in Beijing can claim that?"

Everyone got out, and together they entered the visitors' center—a large room with white lace curtains and numerous display cases. The pathologist, hoping to make the most of his ten minutes, hustled across the room to the introductory display.

The place was chockablock with baggage and cranky Chinese, Japanese, and American tourists whose boats had been unable to pass through the narrow open channel. Now they would board buses and either go downstream to Wuhan, thus ending what had been advertised as a memorable experience but had concluded as a series of sights unseen, or go to a little port farther west and head upstream against the increasingly difficult current.

Hulan gave her name to a woman in a bright kelly green uniform who sat behind the front desk. The woman called to the site and said someone would be down for the inspector in a few minutes. Hulan then found David, Fong, and the pilot staring into one of the exhibit cases. She wanted a minute alone with David, but she wouldn't ask for it and give the pathologist more to gossip about in the MPS hallways other than that she and David hadn't spoken during breakfast. Hulan stared at David, trying to get his attention, but he deliberately avoided her eyes.

"I guess we should get going then," he said.

Hulan walked them to the exit. When the pilot and Fong went on ahead, she grabbed hold of David's arm. "I think this is right," she said, when what she meant was she wished she could relive last night, the past year, the day Chaowen first fell ill. She would do them all differently.

The hurt on his face lacerated her.

"You'll be back tomorrow," she said, when what she meant was that he hadn't let her finish her confession last night. She had been ready to acknowledge fully her failure as a mother, not his as a husband and father.

He stared out to the parking lot. Fong was standing next to the helicopter, apparently waiting for David to take the backseat.

"Take my cell phone," she said quietly, when what she meant was that she understood that he could never forgive her. She could never forgive herself either. "It doesn't work in the gorges, but you might be able to reach me in the hotel."

And with that he pushed through the swinging doors.

"Tell the pilot to come right back after he drops you off," she called out, when what she wanted to say was that she loved him.

The chopper revved noisily to life, wobbled uncertainly into the air, hovered for a moment, then swung away downriver and out of view.

During these last few days Hulan had unraveled in many ways. Coming out here, she'd been skeptical of Vice Minister Zai's secret romantic plan, but then she'd found herself being drawn in and drawn out by David. It was wonderful to be held again by him, to talk to him, to make love to him, but she saw now that those fleeting moments had weakened her defenses. Last night in the cave, she'd been pushed even further, which aroused a terrifying set of memories going back many years. During the Cultural Revolution she'd experienced what zealotry could do to people. She'd also seen the damage and death that her actions and inactions had caused. She'd accepted responsibility for her mindless obedience and the tragedies that had come as a result. She lived with it every day in the person of her mother. She felt guilty every time she chatted with Neighborhood Committee Director Zhang or saw Vice Minister Zai. She let her day-to-day life become a penance, and she'd become an inspector at the Ministry of Public Security so she could right her past wrongs. But how many times had she failed in that? Her father's death, more than 150 women at the Knight factory, Lily yesterday . . .

None of those came close to the way she had failed her daughter. Last night when she'd tried to confess—after all these months of holding her guilt inside—she heard the words come out of her mouth and magically transform into syllables with very different meanings as they'd reached David's ears. She hadn't meant to accuse David; she'd hoped to tell him that she'd made terrible mistakes— hanging on to China and refusing to give up the past—which led ultimately to Chaowen's death. Even though she had wanted finally to accept responsibility for her failings, she was unprepared for his complete condemnation.

The pain of that and the knowledge that her punishment could never end forced her to focus her mind just as she had these past months. She collapsed her grief, her loss, her suffering, her guilt, until it was a tiny, manageable speck. Then she tucked it into her heart and opened her brain, letting the All-Patriotic Society's chants, sermons, exercises, and donations fill it. This coping mechanism didn't inhibit her ability to intellectualize; she understood that one disturbed Chinese woman didn't represent everyone in the All-Patriotic Society, just as she knew that a few pedophiles didn't represent all Catholic priests or that Osama bin Laden didn't represent all Muslims. She could look at the group from David's perspective and see that it might even be beneficial to some people.

Hulan would question Stuart Miller about what she'd heard in the cave last night and warn him that the group was making threatening noises about him. Then she would do something that was nearly unbearable for her to contemplate. She would give up the group as her buttress against her internal torment, dedicate herself to solving this case, and go home. Chaowen would not be waiting for her, and David might eventually leave, but Hulan would finally try to accept the consequences of her life. She felt a wave of doubt, then forcibly shook it from her mind.

Where was Stuart's car? She looked up toward the dam site and saw no vehicles on the highway. She turned away and walked to a model of the dam, where she began reading:

> Begun in 1994, the dam is the most ambitious engineering project in the history of the world. The Three Gorges Dam will be the only man-made edifice other than the Great Wall of China to be seen from space.

That the Great Wall could be seen from space was an exaggeration, but there'd be no getting around national pride here.

> The Three Gorges Dam will be the largest hydroelectric plant in the world, providing one-tenth of the country's electricity needs. Twenty-six generator sets of turbines will have an installed capability of 18,200 megawatts of electricity . . .

She moved to another display, which listed the dam's vital statistics in Western measurements for the benefit of tourists: 20,000 workers, 953 million cubic feet of concrete, 354,000 tons of rebar, 281,000 tons of other metal. The dam, when completed, would be five times wider than the Hoover Dam. The "Lake Within the Gorges" would be 370 miles long—placid, beautiful, and useful. Gigantic cargo ships and ocean liners—which were now barred above Wuhan because of the Three Gorges' shallow depths and narrow passages—would be able to navigate up 1,500 miles from the Pacific Ocean, making Chongqing the largest inland seaport in the world.

The receptionist found Hulan and told her that the car had arrived. She went outside, introduced herself to the driver, and got into a muddy Mercedes. They followed the river back west along a brand-new four-lane highway, stopping occasionally at booths manned by heavily armed guards so that the driver could show his stamped certification documents. Up on the hillsides, she saw military bunkers.

They passed through one more security checkpoint, then drove onto the sprawling site itself. Huge billboards appealed to the workers' patriotic duty in large red characters: ASPIRE TO BUILD THE THREE GORGES DAM FOR OUR CHINA and FIRST-CLASS MANAGEMENT, HIGH-QUALITY WORKMANSHIP, FIRST-RATE CONSTRUCTION. Colossal red cranes towered over giant yellow earthmovers. Bulldozers and dump trucks rumbled over the earth down to the water, where they dropped their loads of rocks and boulders into the channel. Workers dressed in blue coveralls and rattan hard hats did much of the labor by hand, chipping at the earth with hammers and shovels. Reddish dust billowed up everywhere and dissipated into the gray sky.

The driver wended his way past trucks, bamboo scaffolding, and groups of men and women taking breaks. He stopped next to the massive pit and motioned for Hulan to get out. Once she was outside, the noise was deafening and the heat truly astounding. The driver handed her a hard hat and shouted directions in her ear.

She threaded her way down into the pit until she found Stuart Miller, shirtsleeves rolled up, dripping with sweat and giving instructions to a group of workers. He acknowledged his visitor with a wave, gave a few more directives, patted one of the men on the back, then came up to Hulan with his hand outstretched and his face spread in a proud smile. Only after shaking hands did he glance down, see how dirty his were, grin naughtily, then brush them off on his very dusty pants.

"Amazing, isn't it?" he shouted. He didn't wait for an answer but took hold of her elbow and pulled her along the path. He exhibited an almost adolescent delight in showing Hulan this very male accomplishment. He expanded on many of the facts that she'd just read in the visitors' center, pointing out that his company's generators would be the first to become operational. Miller Enterprises was providing the first eight, another foreign company was providing the second eight, then the two companies would form a joint venture with a Chinese consortium to teach the Mainlanders how to build, install, and maintain the final ten.

"We're just a year away from electrical output," he boasted. "People talk about how some of the turbines will produce up to eight hundred megawatts. Do you want to know what that means in real terms? By 2009, when the dam is fully operational, the electricity produced will displace the burning of about fifty million tons of raw coal each year. Put another way, each of these turbines will generate electricity equal to one nuclear power station. Personally, I'd take a single dam built to the best specifications in the world over the possibility of twenty-four Chernobyls."

When Hulan said something about wanting to talk privately, Stuart's enthusiasm ebbed. He nodded, gestured back up the hill, and set a brisk pace. He waved to people as he went, and Hulan saw just how many non-Chinese were here.

"You hear a lot of negatives about the dam, especially from the tree huggers back home," Stuart yelled over the din. "But those fuckers are talking out of their asses. What's the loss of a dolphin compared with the health issues that will be helped once the dam is completed? Pulmonary disease is the number-one cause of death in China. Did you know that, Inspector? China's also the second highest producer of regional acid rain and transglobal greenhouse gases."

Neither of these facts surprised Hulan given the quantity of cigarettes that people smoked along with the coal that was used as the primary energy source for the entire country.

"So you see," Stuart said, pausing for a moment to stress his point, "the dam will significantly reduce China's reliance on fossil fuels, help the country move to a low-carbon economy, and give the nation a way to live up to its global obligations to reduce harmful emissions."

Men were such strange creatures, Hulan thought. She'd arrived unannounced on Stuart's doorstep, so to speak, and all he could talk about was the dam in pseudotechnical jargon. On the other hand, what was he supposed to talk about? Brian? Lily? The thefts? They were standing at the site of the "most ambitious engineering project in the history of the world." Why wouldn't Stuart brag? And why wouldn't he do it in the technical language he knew best?

She needed to look beyond her preconceived notions. She'd lumped Stuart Miller in the same category as David's father—an international entrepreneur and astute businessman. Yet Stuart, who by all rights should have been behind an executive-size desk in the penthouse suite of a skyscraper somewhere, was literally down in the trenches here at Sandouping. At the same time, the man had money and wasn't shy about using it for creature comforts. He had his hydrofoil. He had his art collection. Here on the site, he had a luxury far more plebeian: a fleet of nine trailers, each with the Miller Enterprises logo emblazoned on the side, lined up in three rows.

Stuart took her into his office trailer. The interior was outfitted in the sumptuous materials of a private jet. Nothing could completely block the construction noise, but soundproofing had buffered it down to a dull throb, and an air conditioner had cooled the air by at least thirty degrees to a refreshing seventy-five.

"I thought you collected *guis* and *ruyis*," Hulan said, tipping her head in the direction of a Ming Dynasty teak étagère filled with exquisite museum-quality porcelains.

"They're my special interest, but I have others." Stuart moved behind his desk and gazed at his collection. "Back home I have some amazing Shang Dynasty bronzes—mostly ritual vessels."

"Bronzes? Like Lily's tripods?"

"Not Lily's. Da Yu's. It's said he made them with his own hands. If that's so and if they were bronze, then China's Bronze Age would have to be pushed back quite a ways." Seeing her incomprehension, he explained, "The introduction of bronze is by definition the beginning of culture."

He turned back to his artifacts. "But why limit yourself to dates and medium when there's so much beauty to be found? I collect widely myself—jade, ceramics, and some, though not a lot, of Ming Dynasty Buddhist figures. Those kinds of things are very popular right now. I recently let Lily put up one of my Buddhist sculptures for auction. I didn't love the piece, so I sold it and used the hundred and twenty-five thousand dollars to buy some other things that I'll probably keep forever."

She noticed that his voice had dropped to a hoarse whisper. It struck her that this must be what he sounded like when he made love. These bits of bronze and porcelain and stone had laid claim to his heart.

"Do you go to a lot of auctions? Are you going to the one tonight at Cosgrove's?"

Stuart ignored the question, and she let it pass for now. It was important to let a man like Stuart believe he was leading the discussion. The more in control he felt, the more he would reveal.

"You have to surround yourself with things you love," he said. His hand gently caressed a blue-and-white plate with a stylized white melon pattern. "Of course I'll have to sell these when the dam is finished and I leave China for good. But as long as I have this trailer as my home base, I get to enjoy them, maybe even more than if I had them back in L.A. or my place in Hong Kong. Outside everything is raw and rough and mechanical. But in here, I just see the quiet simplicity of the pieces."

He clapped his hands, signaling he was done with this. His voice jumped a register as he told her to take a seat. He sank down into a chair covered in soft beige suede, hit the intercom button, and ordered tea. Then he turned his full attention to Hulan. "So why the visit?"

"Have you or your daughter had any contact with the All-Patriotic Society?"

"You asked me that yesterday."

"And I'm asking again." She told him how vehemently the All-Patriotic Society opposed the dam and what it would mean to the Three Gorges' cultural heritage, and that he seemed to embody everything the group despised. Stuart, however, didn't seem surprised by either the animosity or the fact that he'd been named.

"My position here at the dam has been publicized across the country. I'm a presence on the river, and my hydrofoil makes me even more so."

"Nevertheless," she said, "I'm concerned for your safety."

"Look where I am, Inspector. This place has security up the ying-yang."

"Maybe this isn't about the dam but is about something more personal. Yesterday I learned some new information about how Brian and Lily were killed. It seems likely the same person murdered them. You might be the connection."

"Do you think I'm next?" The idea amused him. "Like some murder-on-the-Yangzi Agatha Christie novel?"

"You financed Brian's work at Site 518," Hulan went on, "and you did business with Lily. You could say that they were both at the dig because of you."

His chuckling abruptly stopped. "Wait a minute. Are you making me for the next victim or the killer?"

She gazed at him steadily, curious where he'd go next.

"Look, Brian could have gotten his fellowship from any number of sources, and you wouldn't have to look very far to learn that I do business with many auction houses and dealers." He foundered. "Yes . . . Well . . . Do I need a lawyer?"

"If you feel you need one."

Stuart thought about it, then said, "Go ahead. I have nothing to hide."

"Were you in China when Brian died?"

"I was visiting Cat at the site when they found his things. We used my hydrofoil to look for him."

Why had no one mentioned this?

"Tell me more about Brian and Lily. I understand they were lovers."

"More than lovers. They were business associates."

"He did research for her—"

"Research! That's funny! He was her courier." Stuart rubbed the nap of the suede on his armrest, turning it a darker color. "She's dead now, so I guess it doesn't matter, but she wasn't exactly on the up-and-up."

"Meaning what?"

"She got stuff out of China, then doctored the records so that an artifact would have untraceable provenance. She hired people like

Brian to work for her. I give fellowships to kids like him, but it doesn't surprise me when they do a little extra work on the side."

Three knocks on the door announced the arrival of the tea girl. Stuart cleared a spot on his side of the desk and told Hulan to move whatever was in her way.

Once the tea girl left, Hulan said, "You still haven't explained how Lily could get artifacts out of China or how she sold them."

"I don't know how she did it exactly. People don't usually tell you the ins and outs of their criminal activity even if you both know it's happening."

"But you've given some thought to it," she prompted.

"Sure," he said. "Who wouldn't? I figure Lily used kids like Brian and other archaeologists who're working on sites in China and need extra cash—I guess that would cover the lot of them—to find things. After all, they're on a site. It would be very easy to find yourself alone with your brush and sieve, uncover something, pocket it, and keep working. No one would know."

"Which would explain why Dr. Ma doesn't know all of what's missing," Hulan prodded.

Stuart disagreed. "Brian brought Ma pieces for identification, but I don't think they came from Site 518."

"If not Site 518, where?"

Stuart shrugged. "I don't know, except that the pieces I saw last year weren't consistent with Site 518 artifacts."

"What were they consistent with?"

"I'd say the Erlitou site on the Yellow River."

"But Brian wasn't up there, was he?"

"Not to my knowledge." He paused, then said, "As for getting pieces out, just look at the river. If it were me, I'd put my contraband in a bag of fruit or tuck it inside a duck basket, then get on one of those ferries or barges. Who's going to stop one of those?"

"Who else knew what Brian and Lily were doing?"

"The scholars literally have their heads in the sand," Stuart answered. "And Cat's as naïve as the rest of them. Dr. Ma knew, but all he cared about was *where*."

"Where?"

"If Brian wasn't going to Erlitou, then where did he find those artifacts?"

Hulan tucked that thought away, then said, "I get the impression you were one of Lily's biggest customers."

"Only at Cosgrove's." He hesitated, then explained, "I love beautiful things, but I can't do anything to jeopardize my position here at the dam."

"Are you sure she put Site 518 artifacts up for auction at Cosgrove's?"

"Absolutely. I bought a couple of pieces myself—"

"That you knew were stolen relics."

"If they were at Cosgrove's and supported by proper authenticity papers, I considered my purchases clean and legal transactions." He smiled. "Lily let me know what was coming up for auction. She took me on private tours even before the public previews. She made a lot of money off of me, but you have to understand that Cosgrove's was just her day job. She made real money—I'm talking serious cash, and it was *all cash*—dealing on the side. It's totally illegal and unprofessional. That's why I never went to her directly, because it always seemed too risky. I guess I was right."

"Can you talk a little more about your relationship with Lily?" Hulan asked. "Just how intimate was it?"

CHAPTER

14

THE PILOT CONTINUED HIS SIGHTSEEING MONOLOGUE FOR
Pathologist Fong's benefit, but the trip down to Wuhan was hardly
as grand as it had been in the Three Gorges. The floodwaters that
had been confined within the high, narrow walls of the gorges now
spilled over low, wide banks, inundating fields and farm buildings.
David could see people sitting on rooftops, whether waiting to be
rescued or waiting for the waters to recede he didn't know. Bridges
and roads disappeared into water. What had seemed like just high
water back at Bashan now looked hugely destructive, but David felt
numb to all of the misery below. He was exhausted and trying to
hoard his resources to deal with the day ahead.

The government helicopter touched down at the Wuhan airport,
and two vans pulled up. Under Fong's watchful eye, a couple of men
put Lily's body in the back of one of the vans. David said good-bye
and got into the other one. He passed through the terminal without
incident, and the flight down to Hong Kong was uneventful. He
landed at the new airport, where a Rolls-Royce was waiting to take
him to the Mandarin Oriental Hotel. Tourism had been down ever
since the handover, so he was given a spectacular room overlooking
the harbor. He dropped off his bag, then immediately went to the
mezzanine, crossed over into the Prince's Building through an enclosed pedestrian bridge—thus avoiding Hong Kong's murderous

··· 179

humidity, not to mention the torrential rain pounding the gray streets below—and entered his favorite tailor shop in the city.

When he'd left Beijing, he thought he was going only to an archaeological dig, but his khakis and short-sleeved polo shirts wouldn't do in Hong Kong. He didn't have the three days necessary to have a suit made, so he selected a Zegna suit of fine dark wool. The tailor promised to have the alterations done by three. David then continued on through the passageways and over another pedestrian bridge into the Landmark Building, where he bought some ties, a couple of dress shirts, a pair of shoes, socks, and a lightweight linen sports jacket to make himself moderately presentable when he went to Cosgrove's.

The Hong Kong headquarters for the auction house was on the fifteenth floor of the Swire House, again just a short walk over yet another pedestrian bridge. The elevator opened onto a lobby paneled in rosewood. On the left, a Plexiglas case held a Tang horse; on the right, a carving of a seated Guan Yin. Framed posters of past auctions decorated the walls. Commerce may have been bustling outside and the weather abysmal, but in here it was utter quiet and sublime elegance.

David gave a business card to the receptionist and said, "I don't have an appointment, but I'd like to see the person in charge. I have some information regarding Lily Sinclair."

A few minutes later, the door to the inner offices opened, and a tall, dapper gentleman with silver hair and severe wire-rimmed glasses stepped through. He introduced himself as Angus Fitzwilliams, executive director of Cosgrove's Hong Kong branch. Fitzwilliams led the way back to his office, and they sat down. The desk was as neat as the man. Although a big event would be happening later today, there were no papers or files strewn about. The only items on the desk were a phone and a photograph of a middle-aged woman sitting on a couch upholstered in chintz. Behind the desk was a credenza, also totally free from papers. The lack of a computer terminal added to the conceit that no work went on in this room.

"I see from your card that you're a lawyer," Fitzwilliams said in clipped tones, "so I suppose I should deduce that Lily has gotten into some sort of trouble over on the Mainland. I have to say it was only a matter of time, but if she thinks she's going to get any help from us, you should report back to your client that she's sadly mistaken."

"I'm afraid that isn't it, although I wish it were." There was never an easy way to break this sort of news. "I'm sorry to inform you that Miss Sinclair is dead."

Fitzwilliams visibly struggled to control his emotions, then managed, "I always worried about her traveling alone so far off the beaten track. And, well, I don't know if you're aware of just how bad those drivers can be on the Mainland."

"It wasn't a car accident. Miss Sinclair was murdered. Her body was found yesterday."

Fitzwilliams's fist clenched, and he brought it down on the desk with a dull thud. He stared at his hand in wonder and slowly released the tension.

David didn't speak, curious about what Fitzwilliams would say next.

"When will her things be returned to us?"

Not the usual first question in such a moment.

"The Chinese government will return her personal effects to her family," David answered.

"Lily considered Cosgrove's her family," Fitzwilliams assured David. "Her things should be sent here as soon as possible."

No questions about how she was murdered or by whom. No questions about when her body might be returned.

"I'm not with the Chinese police," David said, "so I'm the wrong person to speak to about that."

Fitzwilliams's eyes narrowed as he registered this. "Yes, of course you aren't with the native police. Then what are you doing here?"

"I represent China's State Cultural Relics Bureau. It was in this capacity that I met Lily."

"Cosgrove's cannot take responsibility for activities our employees do outside these walls."

"But I think you can and must," David said. "Lily was out in the field looking for artifacts and collections to bring to you. She also wooed clients for you. What she did clearly has a direct connection to Cosgrove's, and I think any court would agree with me. What concerns me, however, is that it sounds as though not only did you know Lily was into things that she shouldn't have been but you're eager to acquire whatever she had in her possession at the time of her death."

"I'm not accustomed to this sort of situation," Fitzwilliams admitted. "I don't know the proper responses you're looking for."

Again David waited, using the old prosecutor's trick. Again Fitzwilliams came through, filling the void just as he was supposed to.

"Lily always said she was lucky, and who was I to deny it? She would browse the antiques shops up on Hollywood Road until she found some treasure or other, then she'd persuade the dealer to put it up for auction. It's a lot easier to sell through us than to wait for a connoisseur to come through the door. Or she'd bring in a piece of porcelain saying that she'd picked it up in a pawnshop on the Mainland. Since the porcelain wasn't marked as an antique, she'd bring it out simply as a curio. We'd come away with something that Lily said she'd bought for one hundred *yuan* suddenly worth twenty-five thousand Hong Kong dollars. She had a good eye."

David could always come back to Lily as a person and who might hold a grudge against her, but once you let a witness start filling the void, you had to be willing to listen, even if it sounded like an unnecessary detour. You also had to know when to reel your witness back in if he got too far afield. For now David was willing to go where Fitzwilliams took him.

"Tonight, for example," Fitzwilliams went on, "we have about twenty artworks that Lily found at Cathay Antiquities. It's an old and reputable company run by the Leong family, but now that the old man's dead his son Roger is running the place. Lily got him to put up six jade pieces, which are estimated to sell for about two hundred thousand Hong Kong—twenty-five thousand dollars U.S."

Those could be the jade artifacts that Dr. Ma had told David about.

"What was Lily's role in all this?" he asked, hoping to draw Fitzwilliams out without being too obvious.

"You have to understand," Fitzwilliams said, "this is Hong Kong—the great global shopping mall—where every merchant thinks about inventory and supply. There are only so many Chinese antiques in the world. Roger didn't know the value of what he had, and he was also selling to customers who didn't know what they were getting. Lily identified what was genuine, potentially profitable, and aesthetically pleasing."

"What about provenance?" David asked.

Light refracted off Fitzwilliams's glasses as he answered. "Lily always validated Cathay's claims of provenance. I was skeptical of several of those documents, but wrongdoing in the art market is hard to prove even for us here at Cosgrove's. We can't and don't condone criminal activity. What I'm trying to tell you is that I had no proof and I couldn't very well fire Lily without it."

"People have been fired for less than what you're telling me now."

"Unfortunately that wasn't possible. Lily was a strong-willed woman."

Fitzwilliams was an English gentleman of the old school. And although his debonair manner must have served him well in the art business, he was as readable as any other man. Beneath the smooth answers David heard fear, and he'd caught Fitzwilliams's unconscious glance at his wife's framed photo as he'd spoken about Lily's disposition.

"You had an affair with Lily," he surmised.

Fitzwilliams took a deep breath and let it out slowly. "Actually no, but how could I prove otherwise? It would have been her word against mine, and Lily could be very persuasive. She was an excellent saleswoman."

"So you were concerned about personal embarrassment."

"Wouldn't you be in the same situation? I love my wife very deeply, and I saw no reason to cause her needless pain. I hope and believe that she would have known the truth, but gossip can do a lot of harm to a marriage. I was worried about Cosgrove's reputation as well. Our industry has suffered in recent years from scandals of various sorts. Fortunately Cosgrove's has remained out of the press."

Which, David noted, did not mean that Fitzwilliams was denying any wrongdoing on Cosgrove's part—only that any whiff of indiscretion had not yet found its way to the media. In fact, from where David sat, Cosgrove's was a lot closer to a sophisticated artifact-laundering operation than an art purveyor. Objects came in with dubious credentials and came out with the legitimate provenance of having been sold at Cosgrove's.

"When was the last time you saw Lily?"

"I didn't kill her, if that's what you're implying. I can prove that I haven't left Hong Kong for several months."

The image of this prim man draining the blood from Lily's body flashed through David's mind. No, he didn't see Fitzwilliams as the killer.

"When did you last see her?"

"Lily was here about a month ago. She brought in several artworks, which we'll be selling tonight. I was quite aggravated with her frankly, because we'd missed the deadline for the catalog. She'd given us descriptions, of course, but we didn't have photos. The prices we realize are very dependent on catalog photos, because they attract interest from people who can't bid in person. But Lily assured me that these pieces would bring in record prices even without the photos." Fitzwilliams lifted his shoulders, suddenly at a loss for words. "Did you ever meet her?"

"Briefly, and I know that she was not the person she pretended to be."

Fitzwilliams sighed regretfully, but the English accent, the elegant surroundings, and his pseudo-pious demeanor didn't change the fact that Lily had probably been selling illegally obtained artifacts through Cosgrove's. David knew, though, getting the man before him to admit that would be difficult. "I believe there are some items to be auctioned tonight that came from an archaeological dig on the Mainland," he said.

Fitzwilliams looked at David in stark indignation. "We don't have anything like that!"

"The jade pieces you mentioned earlier are probably from Site 518. I've also heard that you have a *ruyi* going on the block tonight. Unfortunately, Lily Sinclair is the prime suspect in the smuggling of several artifacts matching these descriptions, if not the thefts themselves."

"Well," Fitzwilliams responded hesitantly, "I'd need to see documentation with those objects properly identified."

Knowing that wasn't possible, David offered another option. "I was hoping *you'd* show me the documentation for the pieces that go on sale tonight."

"All of them?" Fitzwilliams inquired with false sincerity. "We have one hundred artworks on the block this evening."

"Just the pieces that Lily brought in," David amended, realizing full well that Fitzwilliams had known exactly what he was asking for.

Fitzwilliams shook his head in abrupt little jerks. "That won't be possible. Our files contain privileged information. However, I think what you're looking for is readily available in the auction catalog, which provides a thorough description according to our standards. I'll make sure that you're given a complimentary copy before you leave. This will also serve as your ticket into the preview, if you'd care to see the items before the auction begins."

"I appreciate that," David said, "but why not pull the questionable pieces from the auction until they can be properly authenticated?"

"It's too late for that."

"I could get an interlocutory injunction."

Fitzwilliams's supercilious smile told David just how complicit the director had been in Lily's illicit activities. The man practically gloated as he said, "It's Saturday afternoon. By the time you get one, the auction will be over."

Which would mean David would have to retrieve the pieces from their new owners. It would be a difficult, time-consuming, but not insurmountable job.

In the most civilized and pleasant manner, Fitzwilliams gave David the catalog for tonight's auction, then very definitely gave him the boot. David stopped for lunch, then went to the tailor to pick up his suit. Once back in his room he turned on the TV to a BBC news broadcast and began leafing through the Cosgrove's catalog *Fine Chinese Ceramics, Works of Art, and Jade Carvings.* On nearly every page was a spectacular four-color photo of a sculpture, ceramic, or bronze accompanied by a description written in the most academic verbiage that incorporated dimensions, stylistic components, historical information, and from which collection the piece was being sold.

Interspersed among the big color layouts were pages with simpler descriptions of pieces along with prices that Cosgrove's estimated they would sell for. These would have to be the artworks for which Lily had not provided photographs. As David read the descriptions, he saw that most of them—including the jade—had come from Cathay Antiquities. If these had truly been in Cathay's possession here in Hong Kong, photographs could have been taken in time to be featured in the catalog. Three *ruyis*—none with a photograph—were also listed. The description of one of them sounded like Dr. Ma's missing artifact—a fungus with a long shaft. It had also come from Cathay Antiquities.

David closed the catalog and stared out across the harbor. Hulan often said if you knew the victim, then you'd know the killer, but variations of that axiom were true for almost any crime. Know the source of narcotics and the way in which they are moved to find the traffickers. But, unlike drugs, Chinese antiquities presented spoils that were very narrow in scope, with an even more limited supply of end users willing to spend half a million U.S. dollars on a Chinese plate, and an almost minute pool of thieves who could pull off the initial theft, smuggling, and getting the pieces to a final buyer. Although he still had no hard evidence, Lily was the only person at Site 518 with the three essential ingredients to make the scheme work: opportunity, a method or methods for moving the contraband, and a distribution source.

David turned away from the view as the voice of the BBC anchor filtered into his consciousness. Flooding on the Yangzi below the Three Gorges had resulted in 780 deaths in the last two days. The rising river and turbulent waters had caused traffic on the river to stop. Sixty thousand tourists—including fifteen thousand foreigners—on 350 boats had been off-loaded either above or below the Three Gorges Dam site. Seventeen hundred vehicles had been mobilized to evacuate tourists and residents alike, although many roads were closed.

David had watched the river rise dramatically in Bashan, had encountered the disgruntled tourists at the visitors' center, and had seen the boats bunched on either side of the dam site. Below the dam where the river had breached its banks, he'd seen dead animals floating in sodden fields, people waiting on their roofs for rescue, and water spread all the way to the horizon, but he hadn't registered just how bad the situation was, which became apparent as the report continued.

All schools below the dam site had been closed and production at sixteen hundred factories temporarily suspended. Telephone lines were down in many places. There'd been periodic power outages, and the government was recommending that people boil their water. More than five hundred dikes along the middle and lower reaches of the river had minor ruptures, and close to a million people had been mobilized to make repairs. In Hunan Province below the dam site, the Minzu Yuan dike was in danger of total failure. Preparations were being made to move three-quarters of a million people.

The anchor turned the report over to a weather analyst, who said that the monsoon system was moving east, where it would meet a typhoon brewing in the Pacific. Torrential rains were expected over the next few days, and the river would continue to rise as the runoff collected and continued its eastward push. A high death toll was anticipated in the provinces below the Three Gorges. Meanwhile, Hong Kong residents should prepare for typhoon conditions.

15

"WAS I INTIMATE WITH LILY? JESUS!"

"Mr. Miller, after what you've just told me, I see even more of a connection between the three of you. Brian worked for you, but in a sense he also cheated you. Lily brought to your attention objects that you could buy legally, but at the same time she denied you many things that you would have liked to have added to your collection. They're both dead . . ."

"But the link isn't me. The link is what they were smuggling."

"Perhaps, but I hope you see how that still brings me back to you. You're the only major collector who's on the scene and has a vested interest in Brian's and Lily's activities. So I'll ask you again, how close was your relationship with Lily?"

"As I told you before, I liked her a lot. We did business together. We often dined together. And, yes, we slept together on occasion. But it wasn't personal, if you know what I mean."

"How is sleeping together not personal?"

Stuart tilted his head down and looked up at her in a manner that could almost be considered coy. "I can see that you're what we might call a woman of a certain age. Haven't you had the occasion to have sex with someone just because it was convenient or the moment was right or a situation presented itself or you just wanted to have a little fun with no strings attached?"

"Which one was it with you and Lily?"

"For her or for me?"

"Let's start with you."

"It usually happened up at Bashan. So I guess you could say it was convenient, but it was also fun and there were no strings attached. Lily was good company. She loved to tell stories, and it was wonderful to watch how she embellished and elaborated on the truth. Did she tell you the one about the pornography that decorates the walls of the guesthouse?"

Hulan nodded.

"A total fabrication, but those stories were part of what made her such a great salesperson. Her fanciful tales of hidden treasures and concubine ghosts gave romance to material objects. It was malarkey, but entertaining malarkey. Without being too crude, it was that aspect of her that made her amusing in bed. I hope I'm not embarrassing you."

"And for Lily? How did she see view your relationship?"

"Business, pure and simple. She and her company made a considerable amount of money off of me."

"You said earlier that you like to be hands-on."

He nodded cautiously as he followed her abrupt segue.

"Would you say you're hands-on enough to have cut off Lily's feet?"

Stuart's cheeks flushed and his head jerked back as though the words themselves had hit him in the face. "Lily! I . . ." He put a hand to his brow and rubbed. "I apologize. I hadn't thought about what might have been done to her." He dropped his hand and took a deep breath. "She must have suffered terribly."

Hulan watched him closely. Lying about committing a murder was to be expected, and people tended to do it pretty well, given the stakes. Grief, by contrast, was hard to imitate, but she'd met experts at the game. A lot would depend on how he answered her other questions.

Hulan veered back again to the dam. "You mentioned you've had some problems here in the construction zone."

Stuart looked puzzled. "I don't remember any problems."

"Faulty components . . ."

"Oh, *those* problems." He laughed sadly and shook his head. "I just wanted to avoid your interrogation."

Hulan prompted: "Work being sabotaged . . ."

"Inspector," his voice sounded world-weary, "have you been on a construction site before? Construction—whether it's a simple home remodel or a project like this—is always plagued with problems. So yeah, we've had problems, but I don't see what they could possibly have to do with your investigation."

"Still, I'd like you to take me through some of your difficulties as you see them."

"We've had delays in the delivery of materials, because your Customs people held them up down in Shanghai."

"What else?"

"We've ordered materials here in your country, but each time they arrive we seem to get defective batches."

"Another outside problem, correct?"

"Another problem caused by your country, if that's what you mean," he replied irritably.

"And you say these complications are to be expected?"

"Like I said, every project has headaches. This one has had them for what? Eight years?" He hesitated, then asked, "Do you know anything about the dam?"

Avoidance, she knew that route well herself.

"I just saw the displays down at the visitors' center."

"I mean the history of the thing." Stuart pushed away his teacup, then leaned back in his chair. "It's been one obstacle after another since day one. Sun Yatsen first proposed a dam in 1918 as part of his Grand Plan for National Construction. Forty years later, Mao commanded that a dam be built that would show man's supremacy over nature, the Party's supremacy over the masses, and Mao's supremacy over both—"

"I know this—"

"But it was beyond China's capabilities," Stuart continued, "so Mao ordered boulders blasted and the course dredged, effectively taming the wildness of the river and eliminating the need for trackers. You know what they are, right?"

"The men who pulled boats upriver."

"Brava, Inspector."

She didn't like the way he was testing her, but she decided to let it go for now, because of course he'd want to reestablish the upper hand. This tactic was more common among men than women. Men didn't like others to see their pain.

"Different people had different ideas all the way up until two months before the events at Tiananmen," he went on, "when the State Council rejected yet another dam proposal. But how do you divert a country—and the world—from the disgrace of what happened on that square? Li Peng, prime minister back then, pushed for the project to go forward as a monument to national pride. He claimed that China would need no outside help. Of course, it did. So here I am. But so are a lot of outside contractors and suppliers. And yes, we've all had problems, not just in dealing with the bureaucracy of your system but with work being unintentionally sabotaged. But I want to assure you that we're vigilant, and we've got a foolproof safety system of redundancy upon redundancy—from the smallest moving part to my turbines to the computers that will run the whole thing to the best software in the world that will scan for viruses and any other problem 24/7 from now till eternity."

"You're still speaking in generalities. Tell me more about sabotage."

Stuart thought for a moment. "I'll lay out two scenarios for you. Let's say you find that someone's dumped a load of concrete over your equipment by accident. It doesn't harm the dam per se. It's just a nuisance. You with me so far?"

She nodded and he went on.

"Scenario two: We install a piece of equipment. Everything is checked and approved, then checked and approved again. Redundancy upon redundancy even before you become operational to make sure everything is as safe as it can possibly be. You go back the next day and two screws are gone. Would that cause a problem today? No. Will it ever cause a problem? Probably not. But consider the size of the dam. Now subtract a couple of screws here and there throughout the dam. Now you have to worry about overall integrity. As they say in your country, the collapse of the dam begins with an ant hole."

"You said before that security here is tight enough for you to feel safe. If that's so, then how do these saboteurs get in?"

"I don't think they do. I truly believe that our difficulties have had less to do with malicious intent or 'saboteurs' than with ineptitude and inexperience. I fault paying people, who've never done this kind of work before, a hundred and twenty-two dollars a month for very hard labor. At the same time, I fault *us* for not realizing that those workers might want to pick up whatever they can find here and sell it for whatever price they can get."

"Could the All-Patriotic Society be involved?" She circled back just to satisfy herself.

"Look, Xiao Da is a nutcase, but that doesn't mean his group has anything to do with our problems. The real danger to the dam is large-scale terrorism."

Stuart, who came from a country that prided itself on religious freedom, wouldn't understand that China considered the cult a domestic threat. On the other hand . . .

"Sadly, your country has already learned that religious fanaticism can lead to horrible acts of terrorism," she reminded him. "What would be the biggest threat here?"

"A bomb. Dams are often targeted during wars for defensive or offensive purposes. If this one ever went, millions of people would die. Which is why the dam is protected by two divisions of soldiers, as well as missile batteries."

"Have you ever met a man named Wu Huadong?"

"I don't believe so."

"Did he ever work here?"

"I don't know," Stuart answered in frustration. "I don't recognize the name, but that doesn't mean he hasn't worked on the project."

"Do you have people here who are members of the All-Patriotic Society?" Hulan asked.

"I don't personally hire the people who work on my crews. As for the others, well, there are about seventy thousand people working here—"

"At the visitors' center, I read it was twenty thousand," she said.

"They said it would be twenty thousand when they started. It's closer to seventy thousand today. They said it would cost ten billion dollars U.S. to build. Later that figure was revised to twenty-four billion, but it will probably be closer to seventy billion by the time it's done."

"Let's get back to the All-Patriotic Society," she suggested, returning to her original subject.

"You tell me, Inspector. Wouldn't it be against the law to work here if you were a member of that group?"

"People don't always tell the truth," she observed.

Stuart tipped his head in agreement.

"What about foreigners?" Hulan asked. "Is there anyone who might want to stop the project?"

"Where shall I start? Greenpeace? The Sierra Club? International Rivers Network? The National Wildlife Fund? They're all in an uproar over environmental issues—the species that will be lost, the silting that will eventually clog the dam, and the cesspool that the reservoir will create. Who else? Hell, my government's National Security Council said that the U.S.—and by extension industrial companies like mine—should steer clear of the project. And what about the bastards over at the U.S. Export-Import Bank who decided they wouldn't guarantee loans to U.S. companies seeking contracts here? Yeah, there are a lot of people and organizations that don't want to see the dam completed."

"But you can still guarantee that it's safe."

"Let me put it this way," Stuart blurted, finally losing his cool, "I don't think that anything that's happened with my turbines will put the integrity of the dam in question, but you don't have to take my word for it. Go ask one of the foreign inspectors." Sensing a momentary advantage, he pressed on. "Don't you watch your television news? Haven't you heard your premier speak of the problems of 'tofu construction'? He isn't just talking about those new rattraps along the river they're moving people to; he's been talking about the dam. 'Quality means the life of the Three Gorges Project. The responsibility on your shoulders is heavier than Mount Tai.' Are you telling me you haven't heard that?"

"I've heard it," she allowed, "but I'm not so naïve as to think that those workers that you spoke so highly of just a moment ago or even the so-called technically advanced outsiders like yourself can bear the weight of Premier Zhu's mountain."

"Do I hear sarcasm, Inspector?" Stuart shot back. "Just who do you think the Chinese will blame if something does happen to the dam? Themselves? Not likely. You've got to hand it to Zhu, going against the political tide and speaking out on quality. People listen to him, which is why your government has hired a French company to oversee quality control. They're outsiders who won't be as susceptible to bribes as others are within your country."

"You're making a lot of money—"

"You bet your ass I am," he admitted freely, "but that's not why I'm here."

"If it's not the money, then why?"

Stuart looked genuinely surprised by the question, and Hulan realized that all thoughts of Lily had faded from his mind. "It's the project! My God, woman, don't you see its magnificence?"

"It's big . . ."

Comprehension suddenly flashed over Stuart's features. "You think this is some male thing—some giant phallic symbol or whatever you women think when you don't understand something. You're way off base, Inspector. It's not about the money, although don't get me wrong, it's great. It's not even about the size, although it's awesome and I'm honored to have my company be a part of it." He stood, went to the window, pulled open the blinds, and looked out. "Look at it, Inspector. Think about what it will mean to your country. China's future depends on power. The dam will help provide that."

He turned back to her. "Am I upset about what will be lost along the river? Yeah, I care about that a lot, so I'm funding environmental and archaeological projects. And yes, I'm preserving artifacts by buying them through proper channels when they become available on the outside market."

"Does saving a few relics make you feel better about the lives of the people who'll be affected by this project?"

"You want to talk about displacing people now?" He threw her a reproving glance, then hurried on. "Take a city like Wanxian. Two-thirds of it will be lost under the reservoir, but a new city is being built to replace it. There'll be indoor plumbing and electricity for everyone. The New Immigrant City of Wanxian will get its first ever railway connection and an airport capable of handling jumbo jets. Suddenly the people of Wanxian—a place with abundant natural resources but virtually unknown to outsiders—will have the whole world open to them. *That's* exciting to me."

He motioned out the window. "At its heart this is a simple construction job involving concrete and steel, but think about what it *means*. Hundreds of thousands have died in floods along the Yangzi in the twentieth century alone. And I have to tell you that China's record on building dams isn't very good, so the death toll from collapses is truly mind-boggling. But these things aren't all in the distant past. Five years ago, four thousand died in what was just another ordinary rainy season. And are you aware of the current situation? What you've experienced as a bad storm up in Bashan is causing severe flooding downstream from here. Do you know how many people have died or how many have been evacuated in the last few days?"

She shook her head.

"We don't know how bad it's going to get, but I'll lay out a possibility for you." He still had his face to the window, but she could see how his features had hardened. He'd punish her now for her accusations. "The mother of all storms whipped through China in 1975. The rains came in three successive waves, each lasting at least twelve hours, each with the intensity of a fireman's hose. Birds fell from the sky, killed by raindrops that had the force of arrows. Two days later, two of this country's largest dams downstream from here collapsed. Sixty dams below them fell like dominoes. Overnight. The revered river dragon had escaped with such demonic force that tidal waves wiped out entire towns." His voice was bitter and accusatory. "Somewhere between eighty-six thousand and two hundred thirty thousand people died. But you know how your government manipulates statistics. Were there five or five thousand deaths at Tiananmen? Li Peng might know, but instead of saying, he diverted attention to the dam, right? So, let's be conservative and say that it was only eighty-six thousand who died overnight. Two million people were trapped for weeks by the high waters. Another eleven million were stricken by disease and famine. I'm talking now about typhoid, hepatitis, malaria, and starvation. That's the thing about China. The variety of scourges and the numbers of victims are always daunting."

His fingers toyed with the string from the blinds. "For the Three Gorges Dam, your government is moving over a million people *upstream* so that millions of people *downstream* will benefit for decades, maybe even centuries, to come. Can't a Communist like you see the good in the sacrifices of the few for the good of the many?"

He turned to face her once again. "You want to know why I'm here. It's *all* of it." His arms opened to embrace his worldview. "It's the money. It's saving people's lives and livelihoods. It's making sure this dam is built right. It's getting my hands"—and here he gripped them into tight fists—"dirty, but not in the filthy way that you've suggested. It's knowing that this pile of concrete and steel will be a monument to human achievement that will make a direct impact on people's lives. Can you say the same for anything you do?"

16

WHEN STUART'S DRIVER DELIVERED HULAN BACK TO THE VISITORS'
center, the helicopter still had not returned from Wuhan. The winds
had picked up, and the rain was falling so heavily that she couldn't
see the river from the building. The stranded tourists hadn't
budged, and wives complained in a variety of languages that their
husbands should *do something.* The receptionist in the kelly green
outfit was no match for those husbands, who banged on the
counter, complained loudly, and generally acted like the spoiled foreigners that they were. Hulan found a spot against one of the walls
as far from the tourists as she could get, sat on the floor, tucked her
knees up under her chin, folded her arms across her knees, buried
her head, and waited.

Finally, the chopper returned from Wuhan. The pilot said he
didn't recommend flying in this weather, but Hulan climbed in beside him nevertheless and was back at the Panda Guesthouse by
one. The desk clerk gave her two thick envelopes that had been
dropped off by one of Hom's men, then she went straight to her
room. The rain was worse than yesterday, and the ungodly racket it
made as it pounded the building exaggerated the empty silence in
the room. She sat on the bed and tried to call David, wanting to find
out if he'd made it to Hong Kong safely, but the phone wouldn't dial
out. She padded back out to the lobby and was informed that all

phone lines were down because of the storm. "But we still have electricity, Inspector," the day clerk said brightly. She walked back to her room, feeling low.

She shook out her shoulders, then went through the room, pulling together all of the notes and files she'd gathered. David had been right yesterday when he'd said they were on a train. They'd jumped from interview to interview, heading out far from the scenes of both Brian's and Lily's deaths. Hulan especially had gone far afield, trying to make connections to the All-Patriotic Society and the dam where none apparently existed. Now it was time to put those dead ends aside, hole up, and try to couple what she'd actually learned with what the paper trail had recorded.

She worked chronologically from Brian's disappearance, looking for inconsistencies. Hom's report stated that on the morning of Saturday, July 20, Dr. Ma arrived at Bashan's Security Bureau to announce that one of his foreign experts had gone missing and was feared drowned. A house-to-house search was conducted along the river in the hope that Brian had washed ashore alive but injured. No mention was made of Stuart Miller's hydrofoil. However, Hom noted that he'd phoned the provincial government on Monday morning at 9:00 A.M. to file an official report on the missing foreigner. At that time, Dr. Ma placed calls to the American Embassy, the Cultural Relics Bureau, and Angela McCarthy in Seattle. An inventory of Brian's belongings—from his backpack and from his room—made up the rest of the file. These effects were kept locked either in Hom's office or in Brian's room at the guesthouse until Angela arrived from America on Wednesday, July 24.

The timing of that puzzled Hulan. If Ma had called Angela at 9:00 China time Monday morning, it would have been 6:00 on Sunday night in Seattle. Hulan didn't know if China had a consulate in Seattle. If it did, then Angela could have been there first thing Monday morning to apply for a visa, which could have been processed within an hour or so given the emergency situation. Angela would have had one of two choices to get across the Pacific: Seattle–Tokyo–Hong Kong or Seattle–San Francisco–Shanghai. The earliest she could have arrived in China would have been

Wednesday evening, because she would have lost a day crossing the international date line. From either Hong Kong or Shanghai, she would have needed to fly to either Wuhan or Chongqing, then taken public transportation—a bus, ferry, or hydrofoil—to Bashan. The absolute earliest that she could have arrived here would have been sometime Thursday evening or Friday morning. Yet Angela had signed the release for her brother's belongings on Wednesday, which meant that she had already been on her way to Bashan before she knew what had happened to her brother.

Why hadn't anyone, Angela especially, mentioned this? In fact, at dinner the other night she'd specifically said that she'd come out *after* she'd gotten word that her brother was missing, because the two of them had such a close relationship that she knew he'd never go anywhere without telling her first. She'd lied. For the first time, Hulan had found an anomaly in the written record, and she felt a sense of urgency as she opened the material Investigator Lo had sent.

China kept track of foreigners through entry documents, mandatory hotel registration forms, as well as the ubiquitous watchers who monitored not only Chinese citizens but foreign visitors as well. Hulan began with the entry forms, which provided dates of visas, where they'd been obtained, ports of entry into China, dates of arrival, in-country movements if known, and anticipated departure dates. These forms also furnished standard information on date and place of birth, home address, profession, and the like.

Angela's entry form confirmed what Hulan had already deduced. The American had arrived in Hong Kong on July 20, the day her brother's absence was first noticed by Annabel Quinby. Hulan set this page aside for now and quickly scanned the information on the other foreigners. Doctors Quinby and Strong planned to stay for the summer, while Professor Schmidt was in China on a year's sabbatical. Stuart Miller traveled in and out of the country regularly. Catherine Miller had been in China for three years, having studied at Beijing University before coming to Bashan. Nothing in these records seemed out of the ordinary.

Dr. Quon, the mathematician, had arrived in Bashan a week

after Brian's disappearance. Hulan figured that Quon was a Chinese American of a certain type. Now that he'd found his roots—having already visited his home village and seen the usual tourist sights—he was finding adventures farther afield as China's ecotourism industry expanded. He'd visited several archaeological sites over the last three years. Last summer he'd spent three days in Bashan in July, then had circled back for another week at the end of August. Although he'd planned to leave China on this trip on August 1, he was still here.

Hulan turned her attention to Brian and Lily. The two of them had been in Hong Kong at the same time on at least a dozen occasions in the last two years. Lily's most recent entry form, dated July 16, stated that she'd be leaving China on July 21—two days after Brian's disappearance and three days before Angela's arrival in Bashan. But, like Michael, she'd stayed. This was not a criminal act. People had the right to change their travel plans and extend trips, but Lily had stayed an additional two weeks in Bashan. Not only was that a long time in a small town in a remote area in the middle of the hottest and rainiest season, it was also longer by a week than any other visit that Lily had made here since the site opened. She had stayed for a reason. Maybe the answer would be in her papers.

But Hulan didn't have them on the bed. She got up and looked through the room again but didn't find them. Then she remembered telling David to gather them up during their meeting with Pathologist Fong. Something of vital importance could be in those papers, but Hulan had no way to reach David.

There was nothing she could do but pick up another of Lo's files. Inside she found a one-page synopsis for each of what Dr. Ma had called the five vultures. Lo had not found a single blemish in any of their *dangans*, nor were any found in those of the Chinese students who worked on the site. However, he hadn't been able to obtain any information on Dr. Ma. This didn't surprise Hulan. Still, she'd put off meeting with him long enough.

Hulan saw nothing in the files Lo had sent to suggest that the day workers' deaths—even that of Wu Huadong—could possibly have been connected to that of Brian McCarthy or that of Lily Sinclair. These were just five male peasants in a country of 900 million peasants. Still, she would have liked to have matched this information with Hom's Public Security files on those cases. But he hadn't provided them, though she had asked for them several times. She had to wonder why.

She had two packages from Hom's officers. She looked through the interviews with the hotel's day staff and found that the maid who cleaned Lily's room reported that the sheets showed the foreigner had not had sexual relations in three days. (The maid had never seen a man in Lily's room.) On the night of Lily's death, several of the day employees spotted Lily and Catherine walking through town between 11:00 and 12:00. Su Zhangqing, the smarter and shyer of Hom's men, had had the presence of mind to make a simple map of the town showing the guesthouse, the main road out of town, and the dock. He'd placed little *x*'s everywhere someone reported seeing the two women either together or separately. This map corroborated Catherine's story that the two had split up and gone in different directions.

Hulan next glanced through the interviews with the night staff. The waitresses recounted what she already knew—that after dinner Lily and Angela had left the dining room with the inspector and her foreign husband. The chambermaids on the night shift followed a schedule that took the foreigners' routines into account. Beds were turned down, new towels brought in, and thermoses restocked with hot water between 7:00 and 9:00, when the foreigners were sure to be in the dining room. No one had seen anything suspicious in any of the guest rooms.

The night maid serviced Lily's room at the usual time of 7:15 P.M. Looking at the cleaning schedule, Hulan saw that the day maid wouldn't have hit Lily's room until around 10:00 A.M. Had the killer counted on the discovery of her body not occurring until then? Certainly everyone who worked at Site 518 would have been out of the hotel. But then, would they have left on the bus knowing that Lily wasn't with them? Hulan and David had made a plan to take Lily to the site with them at 7:30, but as far as Hulan knew only Angela was aware of this change.

Later today Hulan would find and interview Dr. Ma, Captain Hom, and Angela McCarthy, but first she needed to revisit Lily's death. She was convinced that if she knew *how* Lily's body had gotten back to her room, everything would fall into place.

Moving Lily's body had to have been a hugely difficult job, between the dead weight, concerns over seepage, and fear of discovery. Hom's men had searched the guesthouse for ways that the body could have been brought in. Sure that they'd missed something, Hulan decided to search the grounds herself. She walked to Lily's room, which was in the third courtyard, turned, and stood with her back against the door. All of the courtyards had guest rooms, but only Lily and Dr. Strong had rooms on this one, which held a traditional Chinese garden, albeit with larger than usual scholar's rocks set in a dramatic tableau. If the murderers had walked stealthily— which Hulan had to assume given the gravity of the crime—Strong might not have heard anything other than the usual night noises he reported.

To Hulan's right—south—were the restaurant and the lobby. To her left was the courtyard that housed her and David's room. The few blood drops that had been found were in that direction, so she went left, stopping to check the east and west gates that were set in the compound's protective wall. Spiderwebs clung to the corners, and thick rust corroded the hardware. These gates had not been moved or tampered with in any way for many years. She continued north into the courtyard where her room was, then into the fifth courtyard, which had originally been for the concubines. Just as Stuart had said, Lily's description of the deeper courtyards had been an exaggeration. The painted decoration and the architectural elements were grand, true, but this was to be expected the further into any traditional compound you went.

Hulan almost had to laugh when she got to the sixth and last courtyard. Here Old Man Wang would have had his private apartments, which would have been decorated in opulent and lavish fashion. These would have been flanked by equally well appointed rooms for his sons and sumptuous rooms for his wives. Today, more than fifty years after Liberation, these rooms farthest from the lobby had been transformed into the working guts of the hotel. In the center area were employee bicycles, tables set up for communal staff meals, and laundry lines strung with the clothes of the workers who lived here. She peeked into windows and in through dark doorways, finding a toolshed, linen storage, a locker room for the staff to change into their uniforms, and living quarters for a few of the higher-level staff and their families. She threaded her way past these last rooms until she found the back wall to the compound. An old guardhouse enclosed the back gate. Hulan pushed on the door and stepped inside.

A tiny old woman dressed in loose black cotton pants and a white cotton shirt perched on the edge of a cot, destringing China peas. Her face was as wrinkled as a dried plum and her teeth were few. Seeing Hulan, the old woman jumped to her feet. "*Huanying, huanying!* Welcome, welcome! Have you eaten yet?"

"I have, Auntie," Hulan said, using the polite honorific.

"Tea then, you must have tea." The old woman shuffled across the room to prepare the brew. Hulan stood quietly while the woman did her tasks, knowing that good manners required them to go through this little ritual.

Once the tea was steeping, the old woman turned to Hulan and clasped her hands together. "Inspector, you are as beautiful as my grandson says."

"Who's your grandson?"

"You've met him. He works in the lobby at night."

The old woman poured some tea into a dirty cup, swirled the liquid, and dumped it on the floor. Then she poured fresh tea into the cup and handed it to Hulan. The cup was still dirty, but Hulan took a politely noisy sip. "*Xiexie.*"

The old woman motioned to the cot. "Sit."

Hulan did as she was told, and the old woman sat so close that their thighs touched. The top of the woman's head came to Hulan's shoulder.

"I've been waiting for you to come see me," the old woman explained. "I am Wang Meiling."

"You are related to the owners of the guesthouse?"

"Landlord Wang and my father were third cousins."

Poor third cousins was what the old woman meant. Poor third cousins who'd been used as servants ever since Wang had made his fortune, which probably accounted for why this old woman was still alive. During Liberation, the lives of servants, even if they were related to the worst landlords, were spared, unlike those of wives, children, and concubines.

"Do you live here?"

"My room and my job are together. No one goes through this gate unless they pass by me. Good for me at my age."

"And your grandson?"

"All the Wang descendants live here. My son is the day manager. His wife runs the laundry. If I live long enough, maybe I'll see my great-grandson in the great house."

"It's good for family to be together," Hulan observed.

"Good today. Not so good during the Cultural Revolution," the old woman sang out hotly in a quavering voice. "The villagers got mad like it was 1949, not 1969. They thought *we* were the landowners. They killed my husband in the courtyard." The woman nodded, remembering. "So much blood in this house, but we stay. Where else would we go, hey?"

"You'll have to move when the lake begins to form."

"How are they going to make me move when I see so much death in this place? I lose four babies here—two girls, two boys. Only one son lives. The rest, all dead. You hear about the concubines? I was here that day. I was here the day they killed my husband—same way too. Cut off his head. Your name is Liu Hulan. You understand what I'm talking about. Some people they call a martyr, some people are bad elements."

"You know why I'm here?"

An amused cackle filled the little room. "Is there anyone in Bashan who does not know why you're here? Drink your tea. I'll tell you what you want to know. You want to ask me if I can be trusted to watch the gate. You wouldn't use those words! You'd be more polite."

"Is that so?"

The old woman nodded somberly. "Everyone says you respect workers, not like Captain Hom. He is as corrupt and corrupting as phlegm-filled spit in a bottle of baby milk."

"I guess you know everything, Auntie."

"I know who comes in and out of here!"

"Does anyone else watch this entrance?"

"Not necessary!" When Hulan didn't say anything, the caretaker asked, "You think maybe I fall asleep on the job? Not possible!" She didn't appear insulted, just adamant.

"What about the gate to the outside?"

"Let me show you." The woman hobbled a few steps to the door, stopped, and looked back at Hulan. "Come!" Hulan joined her. "Go ahead. You open it."

Hulan tried the handle. The sound was awful, but the door didn't open.

"You hear that noise? Terrible! My grandson says he will oil it for me. I tell him he's a stupid turtle." She said this with pride and obvious affection. "You can't open the door without my key, which I keep in my pocket."

"And you watch this gate all day and all night," Hulan verified.

"We have a changeover between five-fifty and six every morning and every evening. Once that time is past, I lock the gate. If we have a delivery, they knock and I let them in."

"Are there any other circumstances that someone could enter or leave through here?"

The caretaker thought before answering. "Maybe a worker gets sick. Maybe a worker's child gets sick. But otherwise no. You want to work here, you follow the rules. If you are late, I don't let you in. You lose a day's pay. If you try to enter through the lobby, you're fired on the spot."

"Tough rules."

"Tough life. Not my fault."

"Could you open the door for me?"

"For you, yes." She pulled out her key and put it in the lock. The hinges creaked and groaned even worse than the handle.

Hulan stepped through and looked both ways down the alley.

She opened her umbrella and turned back to the woman. "I'll walk back around to the front."

"Just don't come back here. I won't let you in!" The old woman cackled again, enjoying herself immensely, then she closed and locked the door.

No one could get past that old woman unless she let them.

Hulan turned right, walked to the intersection of another alley, and saw dead ends in both directions. Still, she went right and followed the wall of the compound to the east gate. She examined the rusted keyhole and determined that no one had tried to tamper with this side either. As she retraced her steps, she looked up and saw glass shards embedded on top of the compound's protective wall. She also studied the places where the interior buildings intersected with the wall. The steep roofs were composed of porcelain tiles glazed to a shiny green finish. Only an expert martial arts practitioner would have been able to scale the wall and the roofs. Three men carrying a dead body and a bucket of blood would have had an impossible time of it.

Hulan went back to the north gate, continued on to the corner, and turned left to go back around to the front of the hotel. While not a large thoroughfare, this was a busy enough street that Hulan doubted even under cover of darkness three men with their gruesome burdens could have passed unnoticed. And even if they had somehow escaped the eye of a wakeful villager, how could they have come through the alley without leaving behind some forensic evidence? Hulan was back to the question that had prompted her to go on this quest: How did a trio of what she presumed to be men get Lily back into her room without being seen either inside or outside the compound and leaving only the most minimal traces behind?

17

DR. MA WAS NEXT ON HULAN'S TO-DO LIST, BUT WHEN SHE ASKED the day clerk to arrange transportation to Site 518, he answered that he'd be honored to find a car and driver, but she wouldn't find the archaeologist because he'd gone to Hong Kong. Again Hulan cursed herself for being sloppy—first Lily's papers, now Ma. Hulan had her suspicions about him, but it hadn't remotely occurred to her that he'd go to Hong Kong.

She asked for and received directions to the Public Security Bureau. Hulan went back outside and opened her umbrella. It was Saturday afternoon and pouring rain, but people were out and about. On one corner a woman sold fresh bean curd. Nearby a man was having a tooth pulled. On the square above the dock a free market bustled. From its second-floor location, the Public Security Bureau kept an eye on all these activities.

The bureau was small—a single room with a counter and four desks flanked by two offices set off by glass partitions. The usual posters promoting the one-child policy had been pinned to a bulletin board, while a population resettlement schedule for Bashan covered another wall and was accompanied by encouraging slogans: DEVELOP LAND TO RESETTLE RELOCATEES and GAINING BENEFITS FROM INUNDATION.

Captain Hom sat behind a desk in one of the private offices.

Hulan lifted a section of the counter and made her way to his office. Opening the door, she was engulfed by the blue haze of cigarette smoke.

"You've returned from the dam, I see," he said.

"Everyone seems to know everyone's comings and goings in Bashan."

"For VIPers."

She put a hand on the back of a chair. "May I?"

His face visibly fell. She sat down, and he leaned back in his chair with a deep, rattling sigh.

"I read your report on Brian McCarthy's death," she began. "It was very thorough, but I have a couple of questions if you don't mind."

When he said, "Whatever I can do to help," she knew he was putting a smiling face on a bad situation.

"I'd like you to go back to the day Dr. Ma contacted you about Brian. What happened exactly?"

"He came in like you did just now. He said that one of his foreign guests had gone missing." Hom used the end of his cigarette to light another one, then stubbed out his first in an ashtray overflowing with butts. "I wasn't worried. We'd gotten numerous reports from peasants back in the hills about McCarthy. Was it all right for him to be there? Would they get in trouble if he slept on their land? All natural concerns because not many foreigners get very far from the river. Tourist boats have never stopped here, so we simply didn't have foreigners until the Cultural Relics Bureau designated Site 518 as one of the most important digs along the river."

"Is it really one of the most important?"

Hom grunted. "Why do you think people have come here from all over the world and not gone to one of the other digs in the gorges? I go there and I see little pieces of nothing being pulled from the ground. I see my world about to be destroyed, but they see only that patch of barren land and the answers to the Four Mysteries that they think are hidden there."

"You speak frankly."

"Inspector, I have tried to speak frankly with you before. Perhaps you have not heard me."

No, she hadn't, and even though he seemed to be speaking honestly now, she didn't trust him. After all, allegations of corruption didn't spring from nowhere. She would listen to him, but she would remain aware that he was the most powerful man in a remote town operating completely unchecked until now.

"Dr. Ma and I drove out as far as we could, then walked down to the river," Hom said, his cigarette bobbing in his lips as he mouthed the words. "Once I saw the boy's things, I knew something bad had happened. No one—not even a foreigner—would leave a laptop computer sitting on a rock with his lunch. So we hiked back up to the car and I radioed for additional help. Some of my men went up into the hills, but the logical conclusion was that the boy had gone into the river. I came back here to notify the river authorities to alert ship captains. At about that time, Stuart Miller came in and offered the use of his hydrofoil in the search."

"You didn't note this in your report."

"Dr. Ma said I shouldn't. I had to obey, because he outranks me."

"Ministry of State Security," Hulan said, finally giving voice to what she'd suspected about Ma from the first day she'd met him.

Hom nodded almost imperceptibly.

"What's he doing here?"

Hom's lips turned down at the corners, and he lifted his shoulders slightly. He didn't know and knew better than to ask.

He reached into his pocket for his keys, unlocked a drawer, pulled out a folder, and pushed it across the table. "This is the accurate record of what happened that day."

Hulan opened the folder and began to read. The events had unraveled as Hom had just told her. "I assume Angela McCarthy came to you to pick up her brother's things," she said.

Hom blew smoke through his nose. "I brought his belongings back from the river and kept them here until she retrieved them."

"Tell me about her."

The girl was upset, but then what did the inspector expect? She had lost her last remaining relative.

"At the time no one suspected any criminal activity," Hom explained, "but even if I had I still would have turned over his belongings. We'd found a backpack with his lunch, a bottle of water, some pencils, a notebook, and a couple of paperback books—nothing of real value beyond the computer." Hom frowned. "Did I make a mistake, Inspector?"

She chose not to respond. Instead she asked, "Did you inquire how Miss McCarthy arrived here so quickly from the U.S.?"

"She's a foreigner. She must be rich. People like that can do whatever they want."

It was a simple explanation for someone who had probably never been on a plane.

Hom looked at her as though he hoped she'd be leaving now. When she didn't move, another series of emotions played out on his face—recognition, a flash of anger, then defeat—and she thought how odd it was for someone in their shared profession to be so transparent. Unless, of course, he was doing it on purpose.

"I suppose you will you be putting a black mark in my *dangan*." He sighed in resignation.

As he spoke, Hulan thought of the old saying that the fish was the last to know he lived in the water, meaning that you were a creature of the pond until someone pulled you out. Hom knew she could expose his inadequacies by pulling him out of his little pond.

"I'm not like that," she said at last.

"You aren't?" He sounded skeptical. "You've been looking into other business . . ."

"It's true I'd still like to see the files on the other cases that I've asked you for."

"I'll tell you anything you'd like to know."

"I'd prefer to read the files," she insisted.

Hom took another drag on his cigarette and stared at the ceiling. After a long pause he said, "I never created files for those cases."

His confession left her speechless.

"I'll tell you what I know about them so that they'll no longer be questions in your mind," he continued evenly. "The Wu boy drowned. We may live on the river, but that doesn't prevent accidents from happening. Still, I have my suspicions about what Wu Huadong was up to. A boy like that does not usually travel up and down the river, but if I pursue it, what will I accomplish? The boy is dead, and whatever his misdeeds might have been died with him. I can tell you, however, that Stuart Miller did not volunteer his hydrofoil on that occasion."

He glanced at her to see if she had any questions. When she didn't, he forged ahead. "I don't know what I can tell you about Yun Re, except that he fell from a ladder and broke his neck. I could blame the Cultural Relics Bureau for having a bad ladder, but again, what would it accomplish?" He hesitated for just a fraction of a second, then said matter-of-factly, "You already know my brother-in-law built the bridge that collapsed."

She nodded.

"Have you ever had to protect a family member or a friend?" he asked.

In another place this question might have seemed strange, but this was China and who, including herself, had not either protected or turned in a family member sometime in the last fifty years?

"It doesn't matter what I say or do," Hom went on. "People in Bashan believe what they want. If it makes them feel better to believe I'm corrupt, so be it. It may be better than the alternative—"

"Going after your brother-in-law—"

"He would deserve his punishment, although I'd feel sorry for my sister and my niece. No, I was thinking of the others—the victims in all of the cases that you've asked about. I felt if I didn't make reports, then the families would never wonder if something wrong had happened. If they had no one to blame, then they wouldn't seek retribution. I don't want to see anyone get in trouble. I want to protect the families in case of unrest and a crackdown." After a pause, he added, "But then that goes for everyone in Bashan."

All this confirmed her worst fears about the captain, but before she could speak, he asked, "Do you know what my main job is?"

"It's the same as for any captain in the countryside," she answered staunchly. "Protect the populace, weed out political trouble-makers, arrest those who are corrupt or commit criminal acts."

"Actually, for the last few years my job has been to supervise the removal of people from our village. Premier Zhu wants a half a million river people moved by next year. All of the Public Security Bureaus along the river will have to enforce the rules to meet the quotas. I'm afraid—and so are my colleagues up and down the river—of the resistance that we are facing. Corruption is terrible and affects all of us. Everyone is taking a cut from the monies allocated for resettlement, so little is left for the people who must move. Meanwhile, people like my brother-in-law are getting rich building roads, apartment towers, and bridges with inferior materials. Peasants are mad and rightly so, but we're no longer living in the past when the masses do just as the Politburo orders."

He leaned forward through the smoke that lingered about his face and added for emphasis, "I don't want anyone to get hurt. I don't want anyone to leave Bashan with a black mark in his *dangan*. So I look the other way and let people do things perhaps they shouldn't."

"Like letting them go to All-Patriotic Society meetings. You are aware that this group is against the law and that attending its gatherings is grounds for detention."

"Yes, of course."

"The higher-ups would be more concerned with this lapse than your looking the other way for your brother-in-law."

"I know, and I'll accept my punishment, but I hope you'll hear me out first."

"Go ahead."

"The All-Patriotic Society is a peaceful group—"

"They don't seem peaceful to me. They were quite antagonistic toward us last night."

"I heard you went to a meeting." He rubbed a nicotine stain on his middle finger. "I think the people saw you and your foreigner as intruders in the one place they've considered safe. Instead of showing their fear, they revealed anger. This reaction is common, is it not, whether in our personal relationships or as a community?"

Hom was overtly breaking the law by allowing the cult to operate in Bashan—and confessing his crime to her—for reasons she had yet to comprehend.

"Usually the All-Patriotic Society promotes harmony," he continued, "which is what I'll need in the coming months to control the emotions of the masses. You and I have seen the opposite of that, correct? We're both old enough to have lived through the Cultural Revolution. We both know what can happen when hate is stirred up."

"You take on a heavy and dangerous responsibility."

Hom looked away. "I am one generation away from the land. I know what it is to eat bitterness."

"But do you know what it means to be a martyr?" she asked.

"Yes," he answered evenly.

Hulan doubted that he did. It was one thing to have a noble cause and quite another to spend ten years in a labor camp.

"Do you recognize my name?" she asked.

"You were named for Liu Hulan, martyr for the revolution."

"I've lived my whole life with the burden of that name," she confided, "but I've been like her in name only. I was given opportunities to save others which I didn't take, and I saved myself at the expense of people I loved. But I want to tell you something. The real Liu Hulan revealed herself to be a Communist and had her head cut off by the Kuomintang so that others in her village could live. It was a moment of immense bravery for a foolish teenager, and she paid with her life."

"Why are you telling me this?"

"Because the real Liu Hulan never got a second chance or even a chance to change her mind. She was fifteen. A year earlier, a year later, she might have made a very different choice. You have a chance now to change your position. Follow the rules and you could still save yourself."

"Inspector, unlike that poor girl, I am a grown man who's had several years to think about my decision."

"Do you know what will happen to you?"

"Not much." He held up his cigarette. "One in every eight male deaths in China is caused by smoking. It seems I'm to be added to those statistics, but I hope I live long enough to see my people safely moved and Bashan underwater."

He pushed back his chair and stood. The conversational tone he'd just used was replaced by bureaucratic formality. "Thank you for coming by. If there's anything else I can do to assist you, please let me know."

Hulan stood for several minutes at the top of the steps leading to the dock, noting that there were far fewer stairs visible than there'd been when she and David arrived three days ago. The water had risen at least six meters, and the floating dock had been repositioned to accommodate the higher level. She took all this in, but her mind was occupied by thoughts of Captain Hom. The people of Bashan believed he was corrupt, but he was one of the most honorable men she'd ever met. She looked up to Hom's office window and caught him staring down at her. He was a man swimming against the tide. His honesty and his convictions would bring him to a no-good end. She turned and began walking through the rain back up the hill toward the Panda Guesthouse.

She thought about what Hom had said about the people of Bashan and realized that from the moment she'd stepped off the ferry she'd sensed something unsettled about this place. On the surface it seemed like any other little town in the interior of China, with its cafés, dry goods shops, and vegetable stands, but there was an energy that percolated just under the surface. She had initially thought it had to do with the dam—the spirit of the great project infecting the populace with civic pride.

She realized now that this strange vitality boiled out of something far more intimate—fear, anger, and the uncertainty of the unknown. Everything these people had known would be gone soon. Longtime neighbors would be dispersed. All of the alliances, all of the petty arguments, all of the secrets traded, would disappear into the ether as though they'd never existed. Strange sights would replace street corners that had been as familiar as the back of one's hand. Houses that had been homes for generations would be lost under the lake, and that thought would have to be terribly unsettling because of the joys and sorrows that would be drowned and gone forever. And all the past generations, who'd been laid to rest in places selected for their good *feng shui*, would never again be visited, their graves never again cleaned for Spring Festival, offerings never again brought.

Hulan was jolted out of these ruminations by a voice repeating her name. She turned and saw Michael Quon. He held a hand over his chest, panting, then he smiled and said, "I've been running after you, calling you. You obviously were very lost in thought, something I'm afraid I'm always accused of."

"Dr. Quon."

"Michael is fine." He dropped his hand and smiled again.

"Can I help you?"

"Ha!"

It seemed to Hulan that the light and airy syllable reached into the deepest darkness of her heart.

"I was out for a walk. I saw you and you looked"—his forehead knit as he searched for the right word—"pensive. Are you all right?"

"I was thinking."

"As I said, that's what I'm always accused of doing. That's when it's best to get some fresh air, take a walk, clear the mind. Want to join me?"

He didn't wait for an answer, but when he started up the hill she found herself keeping pace with him.

"Have you walked the Qutang Gorge yet?" he asked, his voice buoyant. When Hulan said she hadn't, he said, "Take an hour, Inspector, and come with me."

"I can't."

"Take it from a fellow brooder, you'll think better."

After everything that had happened today—the tense exchanges with David, the parries with Stuart Miller, the hours with the paperwork, the retracing of what might have happened to Lily, the interview with the gatekeeper, and this last meeting with Hom—she was weary in spirit. She had only one person left on her list, but Angela McCarthy could wait an hour. So Hulan walked with Michael Quon.

They left the main road and joined a path that continued west. The land here was completely different from the scorched earth near Site 518. Pine groves clung to the hills. Waterfalls cascaded from high precipices into deep gullies. Then suddenly she and Quon were on the old towpath cut right into the cliff she'd seen that first day from the ferry. She closed her umbrella, because the path was little more than a meter wide and she could touch the rocky ceiling above her. Below, the swollen river raged past. If the rain continued another day or two, this path would be submerged.

Without speaking, they walked single file until up ahead Hulan could see the two imposing mountains that formed the Kuimen Gate at the entrance to the gorge. For the first time in days the sun broke through the clouds, and Quon abruptly stopped.

"Look!" Rays of sunlight caught on wet outcroppings of rock even as high above them mists still hid the peaks. "When you see something like this," he said, his voice a respectful whisper, "you know why the landscape painters were inspired to reflect on the insignificance of man in the face of nature."

"It's beautiful," she agreed.

"It's humbling," he corrected.

He rested his back against the rock and spoke out into the gorge. "'In deep, fog-filled gorges, dragons and tigers sleep.'"

She supposed that he was quoting Du Fu, but she wasn't sure, and she was surprised that Quon, a Chinese American, could recite those words as though he'd known them his entire life.

"Can you imagine what this must have been like in the old days?" he asked. "Men stripped down to loincloths with ropes slung over their shoulders and their bodies bent down so far with the effort of pulling boats upriver through the rapids that their noses nearly touched this stone floor. Imagine it, Inspector, the immense human effort." He turned to her and smiled again. "For millennia the people followed Yu the Great's approach to the river. He adhered to nature's laws and had great respect for the inherent aspects of water. Then Mao came along and dynamited. Both understood that controlling floods was central to their success. But the results weren't always for the best, were they?"

"Well . . ."

His laugh floated out into the gorge, and he ran a hand through his straight black hair, ruffling it up from his scalp.

"How do you look at the world, Inspector? I bet you like facts—like how the river has its source in the Tibetan Plateau and how it crashes down through the Himalayas. Or how the river should drain into the Gulf of Tonkin but abruptly changes its course in Yunnan so that it washes through the width of China and empties into the South China Sea. Those are facts, but the legends are so much more romantic."

"I'm not from this area, so I don't know them," she admitted.

"Every child knows the story of Yu the Great—"

"I don't. Tell me."

"At dinner," he said, turning so that their arms touched.

"I have to work."

"You still have to eat," he countered.

"It wouldn't be proper."

"We won't be alone. We'll be in a room with scholars and waitresses. We all know who you are and that you're a married woman."

"I meant it wouldn't be proper for me to have dinner with you while I'm conducting an investigation."

He turned away from her, laughing again. "And I thought you thought I was making a pass."

Why did Americans always have to say everything that crossed their minds?

"You're not afraid, are you?" he asked.

"Of course not."

"Then have dinner with me. I can hardly be one of your suspects, so your integrity will be safe with me."

She knew he was daring her, and the only thing she could think of was to call his bluff. "All right. I'll have dinner with you."

She knew a lot about human nature, but she couldn't read his look except that it wasn't the nervousness she'd hoped for.

"You said you wanted to be gone for only an hour," he reminded her.

She suddenly felt an overwhelming desire to hold her ground. "If you'd told me the story of Da Yu when I first asked, it would already be over."

Quon gave in at last. He turned back to look out into the gorge and lifted a hand to take in the sweep of the river. "There was a time of great flooding. Yu used dragons to sculpt China's hills and valleys and chase away the waters. He worked so hard that the hair fell from his shins."

"That's it?"

"The short form."

"There are no such thing as dragons."

"Then what about dragon bones?"

"Even I know those are just old turtle and ox bones."

"You're very practical, Inspector," Quon decided.

"I don't believe in Chinese ghosts or fox spirits either."

"What if you're wrong? What if Yu's dragons did exist?"

"There's no such thing as a dragon," she insisted.

"How do you know? There are scholars who believe that China may have had dragons once upon a time. Call them dinosaurs if you prefer, but still huge, powerful creatures that lived in the time before the great climatic change. Look at this slice of river, where almost every hill has a pagoda with a dragon locked under it, where every rock or curve has some story related to how Yu came through with a dragon and saved the people. Where do you think those stories came from, and why are they all so similar?"

"They came from the minds of simple village people."

"Hasn't it occurred to you that those simple village people, as you call them, may know more than you?" His disappointment in her was palpable. "Come on, let's go back."

CHAPTER

18

AT SIX, DAVID DRESSED IN HIS NEW SUIT, GRABBED THE CATALOG, and walked the few blocks to the Ritz-Carlton. The storm was about to hit Hong Kong, and the wind was furious, but this hadn't deterred a group of demonstrators from parading outside the Ritz with plastic-wrapped placards in English and Chinese that read, DON'T SELL OUR HERITAGE, OUR HERITAGE BELONGS IN CHINA, and RETURN OUR HERITAGE TO THE MOTHERLAND. David was here to see if he couldn't help some of those slogans come true. As Fitzwilliams had said, there wasn't time today to stop the auction through legal means, but tonight David could watch where the pieces that matched Ma's descriptions went and on Monday begin litigation against their new owners if the Cultural Relics Bureau wanted him to.

He pushed through the revolving doors and into an immense air-conditioned lobby scented by bouquets of lilies and tuberoses. He rode the elevator upstairs with Daisy Ting, a Red Princess from Beijing. David had been at her daughter's wedding last year—a lavish affair at the Palace Hotel. As soon as he got off the elevator, he recognized another couple of people from Beijing, including Nixon Chen, Hulan's old lawyer friend who'd vouched for David's abilities to Director Ho.

"Are you here on business or pleasure?" Nixon asked after they'd shaken hands. "We all know that your dear wife has one of the best art collections in the capital." It was Nixon all over—florid, unctuous, but fully aware of what he was doing. Soon he'd be hauling out the American metaphors that he loved so well but usually mangled.

"Those are Liu family pieces," Daisy Ting corrected, sidling into the conversation. "Everyone knows that Hulan's mother's family had some of the most beautiful artworks in the country."

"*Had* is right. Those things were destroyed or confiscated," David said.

"In the Ting family too."

"And even in my family," added Nixon, "which is why I'm here." He angled in close to David. "If I may ask, what are you bidding on tonight?"

"Nothing," David answered. "I'm here for the Cultural Relics Bureau."

"Of course! Now we'll learn nothing! Attorney-client privilege! Attorney Stark always plays his cards close to his vest, just like you, Daisy. I know you have your eye on those Song Dynasty ceramics."

"And you, dear Nixon, on the snuff bottles," Daisy bandied back. "No one tonight has a chance against you."

"You rank me too high," Nixon said modestly.

"Tell me who here today does not already know the strength of your paddle?"

Nixon burbled happily at the subtle innuendo, then he and Daisy drifted off. A young woman approached and in an efficient though extremely polite succession of questions determined David's needs. Since he already had his catalog, he wouldn't need to check in unless he wanted to bid. If he wanted to bid and didn't already have a Cosgrove's account, he'd need to make financial arrangements based on how much he might spend this evening. That this was Saturday night wouldn't be a problem as long as Mr. Stark could provide his banker's home phone number. None of this was necessary if he wanted to pay in cash. When David said that he didn't think he'd be bidding, the young woman said that he should go into the ballroom then and enjoy the last few minutes of the preview.

Just inside the ballroom, a staff of uniformed men stood at the ready with flutes of champagne on silver trays. The paintings David had seen in the catalog hung on the walls. The other artworks stood on risers around the perimeter of the room. Folding chairs lacquered a glossy deep forest green filled the middle. A center aisle through the chairs led straight to a podium that had been set up on a platform at the front of the room. Two huge screens flanked this. To the right were lined long tables with computers and other electronic equipment, while on the left another elevated platform provided space for a table thirty feet long with fifteen chairs set behind it. On top of the table were telephones, pads of paper, pitchers of water, and glasses, all set just so.

Most of the hundred or so people here mingled around the risers, turning the objects this way and that to admire the detail, check for artist marks, and look for imperfections. None of the pieces was behind glass, and the number of security guards seemed paltry given the value of the objects and the fact that people could handle them so freely.

Once David figured out the numbering system for the lots, he made his way to the display area for the three *ruyi*s. They lay side by side and were as different from each other as could be, although they all followed the same scepterlike design that Ma had drawn in the dirt the day before yesterday. The first was composed of turquoise cloisonné with an interlocking lotus design in red, yellow, and white. The catalog said it was from the sixteenth century and listed the estimated price between fifty thousand and seventy thousand Hong Kong dollars.

The second *ruyi*, dating from the late Qing Dynasty, was far less colorful but no less ornate. An elaborate rendering of the Eight Immortals had been carved into the jadeite shaft and head. Although this *ruyi* came with its own carrying case, the estimate was a meager HK$1,500 to HK$2,000.

The third *ruyi* was completely different, yet immediately recognizable from Ma's description. It looked like a dried mushroom on a stick. The estimated price was HK$22,500 to HK$38,000, or $3,000 to $5,000 U.S. David felt like a bumbling philistine: He didn't know a lot about art, but he knew what he liked. And he just didn't see how any of these *ruyi*s could be so valuable or what anyone would do with them if they owned them.

"David Stark."

David turned at the sound of the familiar voice and saw Stuart Miller dressed in an elegant suit of beige linen. A middle-aged woman in a skintight *cheongsam* hung on his arm.

"I thought you were at the dam," David said.

"I was."

"I thought you were supposed to stay in China."

"In case you haven't heard, Hong Kong was returned to China," Stuart said lightly.

"Does Inspector Liu know?"

Stuart grinned as if his hand had been caught in the proverbial cookie jar. "Your wife . . ." He let out a low whistle. "We had a nice chat this morning, but my hat's off to you, buddy. She's tough."

"Which doesn't answer my question."

"I didn't tell her my plans. There's nothing to worry about, though. I have my project to finish. I'll be back."

"Is everything okay up there? I heard a report on the weather."

"Yeah, it's a bitch. I took back roads down to Wuhan, then took a commercial flight. Same as you, I'll bet." Stuart smiled disarmingly, then gestured to the woman at his side. "Have you met Madame Wang? How would you like to be introduced, dear? Shall I say you're the absentee owner of the Panda Guesthouse?"

"Whatever makes you happy," Madame Wang answered.

A waiter appeared and silently refilled their glasses with Mumm's. As soon as he'd stepped away, Stuart said, "I'm here for a few days. Why don't you come up for breakfast tomorrow morning?" Then he made quite a show of offering his card to David in the Hong Kong manner, cupping it in both hands in presentation and bowing slightly. Stuart then returned to scrutinizing the competition. "David, have you been to an auction like this before?"

"No, I haven't."

"Bidding?" Stuart asked with feigned disinterest.

"You know why I'm here."

"Then you're in for quite an experience. An auction like this is full of drama. Those two men by the bronzes are dealers from New York. Even though each believes himself to be specialized, there's a lot of overlap in what they buy. So right now they're negotiating over who's going to bid on what. They're competitors but they're also businessmen, and there's no need to drive up the price unnecessarily."

"Sounds like price fixing."

"Except that price fixing is against house rules." Though Stuart spoke graciously, his eyes still surveyed the room. "No, we certainly don't want to call it that, especially not after the Sotheby's and Christie's price-fixing fiasco. Of course that was between the houses themselves over sellers' commissions, and not between buyers. But if the auction houses can call it friendly conversation, so can the dealers and collectors. This is high-stakes poker. Right now Cosgrove's is shuffling the deck, and we, the players, are rolling up our sleeves and checking out who our opponents are and how high they'll bid."

This explained Nixon's jocular inquiries, though even David—an absolute neophyte to the proceedings—could see that Hulan's old friend was not a poker player of Stuart's caliber.

David asked, "How many of these people do you know?"

"Tonight, in this room? Almost everyone, including Nixon Chen and Daisy Ting. We saw you talking to them earlier."

"Nixon Chen and his snuff bottles." Madame Wang sniffed dismissively. "But I saw Daisy examining the two Song *dingyao*s. They're both fine pieces, but did you see the chip on the rim of the one with the ducks and lotus pattern?" When David shook his head, the woman appraised him with steely determination. "Which one will she be bidding on?"

"I don't know," David answered honestly.

"Dear, let the poor man alone. Here, why don't you go and take another look? Don't worry about what the others do. You can bid as you please."

"Of course, of course." Madame Wang languidly glided away.

"Once you get up into these prices," Stuart continued, his eyes admiring Madame Wang's figure as she insinuated herself into another knot of Hong Kong's elite, "Asian art is a very small world, made up of collectors, dealers, and executive directors from museums. They all have their own reasons for buying, their own strategies, their own customers. See that woman over there? She's from a museum in Singapore. The museum's endowment is tremendous, and you could say that for her the sky's the limit in terms of bidding, until you consider the new dot-commers out of the Silicon Valley. She's probably trying to figure out if they were hit by the downturn. What she doesn't know—and neither do I—is who's going to phone in bids, who's placed absentee bids, or who has someone in the room that none of us knows who'll be bidding for him or her."

"And the dealers?"

"They're unique creatures unto themselves. For many of them it's not about the art; it's about the end sale. They're buying on margin and hoping to turn over a piece within the ten days before the final funds are due at Cosgrove's, making a quick twenty or so percent. But if a dealer hasn't sold a piece within those ten days, he's fucked." Stuart grinned.

"They can't all buy on margin."

"True, but I love to watch the ones who do, because there's this moment when they get this great look of triumph mingled with that pit of the stomach sick feeling that says, This one could break me for good. I love it. Sit with me and I'll tell you what's going on."

"Won't you be bidding?"

"I have my eye on a few things. Come on, say yes, and join us for the reception and dinner afterward. The banquet's across the hall."

David thought of Fitzwilliams. "I don't think they'll have room for me."

"The auction is a Cosgrove's event, but the dinner is a benefit for the Hong Kong Museum Council. Madame Wang is the chair. A place will be made."

"Then I accept."

At 6:45, a bevy of pretty women circulated through the room, reminding everyone that the auction would start promptly at 7:00. Unlike most social occasions, when the news that dinner was about to be served was virtually ignored until the third or fourth announcement, the people here quickly took seats.

As the crowd thinned along the sides of the room, David spotted Dr. Ma talking to Angus Fitzwilliams by one of the risers about twenty feet from the edge of the phone bank. Even from this distance, he could see Ma's face red with anger. Fitzwilliams's posture was stiff, and he was shaking his head no in the same jerking movements that David had experienced earlier today when the executive director wanted to show just how opposed he was to an unpleasant subject or idea.

"Come along, David, let's get a good position," Stuart said, already striding purposefully away.

But David went in the opposite direction. Reaching Ma and Fitzwilliams, he saw that they were standing before a riser displaying several jade objects.

"You know these are stolen artifacts," Ma seethed.

"I know nothing of the kind, sir," came Fitzwilliams's frustratingly bland response. "We have documents showing provenance for every article you see here."

"And you know that *that* is a lie. When this comes out, Cosgrove's will be very sorry. My government will make sure you are put out of business in Hong Kong."

Fitzwilliams was unmoved. "If there's something here that appeals to you, then I suggest you use your paddle. Your money's as good as anyone else's."

A young woman approached and very gently touched Fitzwilliams's sleeve. "Mr. Fitzwilliams, sir, it's time."

"Yes, of course." Without another word to Dr. Ma or even a glance in David's direction, Fitzwilliams walked with deliberate purpose to the front of the room and up the stairs of the dais to the podium. He brought the gavel down firmly three times. "Ladies and gentlemen." His voice came out warmly over the sophisticated sound system. "Welcome to Cosgrove's auction of fine Chinese ceramics, works of art, and jade carvings. I'll begin with some ground rules . . ."

David turned back to Dr. Ma, who was staring at the jade—

several perforated disks and another object that had been shaved into a long, smooth shape that looked like a cross between a boomerang and an ax head. Lights had been placed in such a way as to catch the subtle carvings on the stones. Well lit and mounted, they made very attractive decorative pieces, although their prices—HK$25,000 to HK$50,000 apiece—seemed steep for a decorative element to add to a living room.

"Are these disks the *bis* you told me about?" David inquired.

"Yes," Ma answered.

"Can you prove they're from Site 518?"

"You know I can't."

Fitzwilliams's voice came over the speakers in a monotone as he outlined the terms of sale: Cosgrove's had the right to reject any bid, a buyer's premium would be added to the successful bid price, Cosgrove's was not responsible for any errors or omissions in the catalog.

Dr. Ma's gaze still hadn't shifted from the jade. "Do you see the markings? They're archaic characters for *mountain, river,* and *door.* We don't know why yet, but we've found these same markings on other objects at Site 518."

Now that Ma had pointed them out, David saw the characters carved into the jade. He noted especially the character for *river,* which he'd seen as a brand on Lily's forehead.

As Fitzwilliams recited the bidding increments, David asked, "What are you doing here?"

"I've been authorized to bid on these on behalf of the Chinese government," Ma replied. Then he said in an accusatory tone, "I see you're here with Miller."

"I was as surprised to see him here as I was to see you."

"You shouldn't have been. Miller wouldn't miss this. He sees himself as a latter-day Schliemann, only instead of discovering Troy and Mycenae, he hopes to discover the great link to China's past. Except if he really wanted to help, he'd spend his money on research and on putting teams in the field. Instead he's just a rich capitalist who wants to hoard things that don't belong to him."

"He's helped, Site 518 in particular."

"It would take about two hundred thirty million dollars U.S. to save all of the artifacts along the Yangzi," Ma said. "We've raised less than one percent of what's needed. You watch what happens tonight. Miller will probably spend more in ten minutes than we've raised in five years."

Fitzwilliams's voice announced the opening of bidding for Lot 1—a yellow-glazed wine cup with an artist mark from the Yongzheng period of the Qing Dynasty.

"Mr. Stark, we don't have much time. I don't know if it's in my power to save the *ruyi* tonight, but we *must* get it back to China."

"Don't worry, Dr. Ma," David assured the archaeologist. "I plan on hiring local counsel first thing Monday morning to begin litigation. It's a good thing you've come out to Hong Kong, because I think you'll make a very credible witness when it comes time to identify your missing artifacts in court. We'll get your relics back, including your *ruyi*."

"Monday may be too late," Ma said.

Ma had been disagreeable and obstreperous since David and Hulan debarked at Bashan. Now he was pressuring David?

"What's so critical all of a sudden?"

Ma's features remained unreadable, but David could see that the archaeologist was struggling with something. Finally, he said, "I'm not employed by the Cultural Relics Bureau. I work for the Ministry of State Security."

That was China's version of the CIA. Hulan had been right that something was strange about Ma. All of his territoriality could now be traced to issues of jurisdiction, clandestine supremacy, and personal safety. A black-world guy like Ma had to think long term. Once his cover was blown, it was blown for good, which meant this had to be very serious.

"That's right," Ma said as if reading David's mind, "even Director Ho doesn't know who I am or why I'm at Site 518."

"Why are you telling me this?"

"I've already told you. We need your help."

David waited. This revelation was coming far too easily after all of Ma's lies and rudeness. Ma would have to prove himself. He seemed to understand this and began to disclose his history with just enough details to show David he was telling the truth.

"The ministry I work for looks very far ahead, and the men I work for in particular are far-ahead thinkers. When I needed an excuse to be in the States for a long time, my superiors ordered me to study archaeology, because no one would ever suspect a graduate student in archaeology of being a spy. My supervisors also anticipated that construction on the dam would come to pass. Everyone knew about the archaeological sites, but few anticipated what the foreign interest would be. My superiors did, and they were right. Stuart Miller, Lily Sinclair, and others all came to me. Miller was a particularly fortuitous prize, for obvious reasons. He had access to things that we'd love to have."

The auction was moving along. Fitzwilliams was already on to Lot 8—a white jade imperial seal from the Qing Dynasty.

"Then Brian McCarthy brought in the *ruyi*," Ma went on. "He never told me where he found it, but once he showed it to me and I recognized its significance, my position at Site 518 took on even greater importance. As you know, the Ministry of State Security's concerns are international in scope."

"Why didn't you say something before? Why didn't you ask for Inspector Liu's help?"

"I am told you are an intelligent man, Attorney Stark, but you're not appreciating the game here. Your wife was sent by her handlers to find the *ruyi*. They're hoping to use it to strengthen their position in the government. And there are other factions who want it too. I'm asking for your help because you're an American. You understand that the wrong power in the wrong hands could be detrimental to world stability. I hope you will put aside personal loyalties and do the right thing."

But David wasn't understanding anything. He'd seen Hulan get her assignment. There was no covert operation that he knew of, or was there? Would Vice Minister Zai have knowingly sent Hulan into danger again after everything she'd been through? And if so, would she have kept it a secret from David? A far more likely scenario was that Ma wasn't telling the full truth. But what could be so important about the *ruyi* that Ma would be tempted to confide in David at any level, bring up global dangers, and suggest that Hulan was working for a secret entity within the government?

"Complete your job, Attorney Stark. Retrieve the *ruyi*. Deliver it to me. Inspector Liu is in over her head," he reiterated. "By helping me, you may be saving her."

David stared at Ma, calculating. "Why me? Why now?"

A grim smile twisted Ma's lips. "I'm giving you an opportunity to help China. Now you'd better get in there and see what you can do." Then, not for the first time, Ma turned his back on David and walked away.

19

HULAN AND MICHAEL GOT BACK TO TOWN ABOUT SIX. HE LEFT HER on a street corner, saying he was going to continue his walk, so she went on alone to the Panda Guesthouse. Michael had been right. She felt refreshed and ready for this interview. She dropped off her umbrella, then went to Angela's room. Hulan said she had a few more questions, and Angela motioned her inside. She plopped down on the bed, tucked her bare feet under her, and regarded Hulan intently.

"Why did you lie to me about when you came to China?" Hulan asked.

"What do you mean?" Angela's eyes were bright with the knowledge that she'd been caught.

"You left Seattle before your brother died. You lied to Captain Hom. In China, lies are considered criminal offenses."

Angela stared at Hulan with that ridiculous naïveté that was such a weak trait of Americans.

"Your brother is dead. The fact that you've deliberately chosen not to be honest doesn't look good."

"You can't believe I hurt him!" Angela's features crumpled, but the routine had worn thin.

"Miss McCarthy, you're far from any consulate or embassy. Either you can tell me the truth *right now* or I can have Captain Hom put you in jail until you decide to be more forthcoming."

"I thought you were nice," Angela said reproachfully.

"Jail or the truth. It's your call and I'm waiting."

Angela picked at the frayed hem of her shorts.

"Get up," Hulan ordered. "Put your hands behind your back." Angela looked at her in disbelief. "Up! Now!"

Angela stretched out her legs and scooted to the edge of the bed. She held out her wrists for a second, then just as suddenly dropped them. "All right," she said. "I'll tell you everything."

It had been a bluff on Hulan's part, but why had she needed to go so far?

"I told you before that my brother and I wrote e-mails to each other," Angela began. "About two weeks before he died, he sent an e-mail saying he'd found something that would change my life. When I wrote back and asked him what it was, he said I had to come here and see it with my own eyes. I thought he was just screwing around with me. He'd wanted me to visit for a long time, but I don't have a lot of money, and hopping on a plane to China, even though I loved him more than anyone in the world, wasn't something I could do just for fun. He wrote back and told me to look at his web-site."

"The one you and Lily talked about the other night."

"Yes, and it was just as Lily described it. He liked to post photos of places he'd been and things he'd seen, not just for me but for his other friends. Here, let me show you."

Angela got up and rummaged through a pile on the floor until she found Brian's laptop. She attached an adapter to the computer, plugged it in, booted it up, and connected to the file he'd used to store the photos for his webpage. He stood in the center of the screen on a muddy bank surrounded by dead shrubs. He wore the typical outfit for foreigners in this place—khaki shorts, heavy boots, a T-shirt, and a cap. His arms were spread out as though he were presenting something to the viewer—*ta-da!* He was beaming.

Who'd taken the photo? The question seemed unimportant to Angela. "Maybe one of the peasants he met when he was hiking."

Hulan watched as Angela clicked on the icon and the screen filled with the image of an arid hillside. She clicked again and got a panorama showing a low valley of desolate red earth. The next image Hulan recognized as the ragged beach and entrance to the cave where the All-Patriotic Society held its meetings.

"These photos weren't like others he'd posted," Angela explained. "Usually he'd put up a pretty landscape or a portrait of a family on whose property he'd camped. But these are just infertile land."

"Are there any of the dig?"

"In a way." Angela clicked several times in succession so that images of Site 518 flitted past. "I would have expected photos of people he worked with, artifacts he'd found, or the configuration of the pits, but most of these are of the surrounding area—just dirt."

"How was this going to change your life?"

"I didn't know. I wrote him and said that he had to spell it out for me and that I couldn't come out here for nothing. I wasn't very nice when it comes down to it."

"But he still wouldn't say—"

"He wrote back that he didn't know who else was looking at the website. After all, it was and still is available for all of his friends back home."

"And anyone here too."

"I suppose so, but I don't know why anyone here would want to look at these pictures. They already know how ugly Site 518 is. The point is he knew the website wasn't secure, because it was never designed to be secure. But he also didn't want to write anything too personal to me by e-mail because he didn't know how safe that was either."

"He wrote that?"

"Uh-huh," Angela confirmed.

"Do you have any idea what he thought was so important?"

"No, only that if I came here my career would be made." Angela hesitated, then added, "You have to understand. He was my brother. I trusted him. So I came, thinking he would explain everything once I got here."

"What do you do?"

"I'm a mycologist. I study mushrooms and fungus. I thought that maybe he'd found a *lingzhi* fungus. Do you know it?"

"That's the one for long life, right?"

Angela nodded. "The *lingzhi* is found in this area. Well, not here exactly. Have you heard of the Lesser Three Gorges? They're not far from here—up the Daning River from the town of Wuxia just below Wushan. The first gorge you hit is called the Dragon Gate Gorge. On the east side is Dragon Gate Spring, and above that is Lingzhi Peak, which is crowned by the Nine-Dragon Pillar. It's up there that the fungus grows and, because of its value, it's protected by nine dragons."

"You've been there?"

"No, this is my first time to China. But before I leave, I'd like to go up the Lesser Three Gorges, maybe hike up in the hills. That would be great . . ."

Angela looked lost for a moment. Then, as Brian's death came back to her, she shifted into something a little more technical.

"Anyway, you're right about the *lingzhi*. It does have a reputation for giving long life, everlasting youth actually. In my opinion the medicinal properties are about as valid as those for those dragon bones the archaeologists keep talking about, but in my profession, as dragon bones are in theirs, the *lingzhi* has incredible value."

"In terms of giving a key to the past?"

"Hardly. The *lingzhi* has great monetary value."

"For traditional Chinese medicine?" Hulan had some experience with the lengths to which people would go to obtain the raw ingredients for traditional medicine.

"Also in jewelry," Angela answered.

"A fungus in jewelry?"

"It was very popular during the Qing Dynasty in hair ornaments and pins."

"And in a *ruyi*?"

"Especially a *ruyi*. Emperors have always prized the *lingzhi*. The largest *lingzhi* in the world is in the Forbidden City's collection. It's about three feet in diameter. It's very beautiful to me—and to the emperor too, I guess—but to many people it just looks like a giant dried mushroom."

"So you think Brian found a special version of this fungus. Maybe a *ruyi*—"

"I don't care about artifacts, only live fungus," Angela said haughtily. Then she shook off her professional pride and added, "I don't know what I thought exactly. Maybe he'd found one even larger than the Forbidden City fungus, maybe it was a new variety, or maybe there was a special growth pattern. No one knows what causes the *lingzhi* to grow or why it's found primarily in the Lesser Three Gorges."

"Did the photos give you any hints that you were going to find anything like what you're describing?"

Angela admitted that they hadn't. "But there has to be something, otherwise he wouldn't have been so persistent."

"And have you found this fungus?"

"Mushrooms are springing up all over now that it's raining, especially around Site 518. But I haven't found the *lingzhi* or anything related to it."

Throughout the conversation, Hulan had been checking out the room. Camping equipment was piled up under the window, dirty clothes were thrown in a corner, and the desk was strewn with papers and tools.

"Was this your brother's room?"

"They let me have it when I got here. I've gone through everything, even his clothes pockets. I didn't find anything."

"May I look?"

"Go ahead."

Typically Hulan would have searched the deceased's belongings without a survivor present, but Angela made no move to leave nor did she feign some other activity. Instead, the young woman just sat on the bed, watching Hulan and commenting on what she was doing.

As Hulan unrolled Brian's sleeping bag, Angela said, "I already checked and there's nothing inside." When Hulan held up a miner's light, Angela said, "My brother was a caver, but I bet you knew that." Brian had owned a good set of kneepads and a hard hat to go with his miner's light. "Caving was a hobby. My brother loved China, because he had so many new places to explore."

You could never tell how grief was going to settle on someone. Some people quickly got rid of all the deceased's belongings; others kept entire rooms as they'd been in the deceased's lifetime. But Angela was peculiar in the sense that she not only hadn't disposed of her brother's things but was living amid them. No wonder she acted so strangely. And yet there seemed to be nothing personal that belonged to the boy. No receipts, no matchbooks, no condoms in a pocket, and nothing related to Site 518.

"Have you thrown out anything—papers, anything like that?"

Angela shook her head, and Hulan believed her, which meant that someone had gone through this room between the time Brian disappeared and the time Angela arrived, taking away anything that might have helped re-create his actions in the days leading up to his death. Hom hadn't mentioned searching the room, but given his laissez-faire attitude, she wouldn't have expected him to. No one had reported that the room had been broken into, but then Lily's room hadn't been broken into either. Her killers had probably just used the room key she was carrying. The same undoubtedly held true for Brian.

Hulan asked to see Brian's daypack, and Angela got it out of the closet. Again, Angela watched intently as Hulan went through Brian's effects. The bottle of water was still there, along with the pencils and cap. Hulan looked up and said, "Captain Hom mentioned a notebook."

"I didn't find one."

"Captain Hom says he returned it to you."

"You're free to look through the room. I don't have it."

Hulan thought for a moment, then said, "I'd like to go back to something you mentioned earlier. You said your brother was worried about who else might be looking at his website and if his e-mails were private."

"Which was why he wouldn't tell me what he'd found."

"Have you found anything in this room or since you've been here that has helped you determine what that was?"

Angela shook her head. Her eyes welled with tears. "Do you think someone saw what he wrote and killed him because of it?"

"It's possible."

Angela bowed her head and began to cry softly.

"Who else have you told about this?"

"Lily," Angela replied quietly.

Hulan remembered on that first night how obliging Lily had been to Angela. Stuart had spoken of Lily as smart and manipulative, hardly the kind of person who would have befriended a bereaved young woman, even if she was the sister of someone Lily had slept with.

"Did you know Lily before you came out here?" Hulan asked.

"No, but when I got here and the desk clerk told me Brian was missing and presumed dead, Lily was very good to me." Angela began to pick up speed as she relieved herself of those early hours and days. "She took me down to the police station. She helped me deal with Dr. Ma, who kept telling me I wasn't allowed at the dig. She went with me to where Brian had fallen in the river. She liked to eat alone, but at night, after dinner, we'd come back here, sit on the bed, and talk. It was sad but like a slumber party too in a way. We talked about places Brian had gone and things he'd seen. I hoped she'd know what he'd found that was going to be so important to me, but she didn't. What I liked best about her though was that she told me stuff about him. You know, how he slept around and things like that. I guess other people wouldn't want to remember someone that way, but my brother . . ." Angela smiled wanly. "He had a way with the ladies. He liked them. He liked making love to them. Lily was willing to share that with me."

Hulan wondered if Angela had any idea of how peculiar she sounded, but in this recounting, another piece of Lily's life—and perhaps her death—fell into place. Lily normally stayed in China for a few days. After Brian died, she had remained here, near Angela. Lily had courted the American and worked her way into this room.

But whatever Lily was hoping to find had eluded her, otherwise she would have moved on.

Who else had Lily told what she'd learned? Who else had Angela confided in? Who else had Brian spoken to about the mysterious discovery that would change his sister's life? Hulan tactfully maneuvered Angela through these questions. The American didn't think Lily had told anyone about their meetings. What about Stuart Miller? Hulan asked. Angela didn't think so, because Lily had been pretty adamant that the two women keep their friendship a secret. (Which didn't mean that Lily hadn't told Stuart, only that Angela didn't know about it.)

"Could your brother have told Catherine Miller what he'd found?" Hulan asked.

"He wouldn't have shared anything important with her."

Maybe, maybe not. If Brian had confided in either Lily or Catherine, one of them could have passed the information on to Stuart. They both would have had their reasons: Lily was always shoring up her relationship with her client, while Catherine was always trying to gain her father's respect.

What Hulan couldn't piece together though was what special thing could change a mycologist's life forever and still be even remotely valuable to Lily. Hulan suspected, but didn't have the heart to break it to Angela, that her brother may indeed have found something that would have helped his sister in some way, but that others had interpreted his cryptic messages to her as meaning that he'd found something of profound archaeological interest. Which brought her back to the missing notebook. Who else knew it existed?

"Everyone, I suppose," Angela answered. "Just about everyone told me he was always writing in it."

"Has anyone asked to see it?"

"Besides Lily?"

"Besides Lily."

Angela's face scrunched in that way of hers and she shook her head.

"But people knew Lily had asked you about it."

"I'd have to think about that," Angela said. "Maybe."

No matter which way Hulan looked at all of this, she had to re-think Lily's death. She'd been tortured, possibly for the purpose of obtaining information. Maybe someone had wanted the notebook, and if not the notebook, then the information contained in its pages. Would Lily have passed on what little she knew? Given the extent of her suffering, probably yes.

"I'd like you to do me a favor," Hulan said at last.

"I'm not leaving here, if that's what you're going to suggest."

If Angela had followed this conversation at all, she would have understood in just how much danger her life had been since she'd arrived, though why she hadn't yet been killed was an unanswered question in Hulan's mind. But if Angela thought, as Hulan knew she did, that her brother's dying wish had been for her to come to China and find something that was going to change her life, then there was no way Hulan was going to get her to leave this place. Hulan could try to have Angela deported or expelled from the country, but the truth was she didn't meet any of the legitimate grounds. Still, there was one way to protect Angela's life . . .

"It would be helpful if tonight at dinner you could tell the group that you've given me your brother's notebook. Or if anyone asks about it, just tell them to come see me."

"But I didn't give it to you."

There was stupid and there was beyond stupid, Hulan thought. "Can you just do as I ask?"

"I'll do whatever you want if you let me stay here."

It was a bargain Hulan could live with.

20

DAVID SCANNED THE ROOM AND SAW THAT STUART MILLER AND Madame Wang had taken seats on the center aisle about eight rows from the front. He made his way to them and sat in the chair they'd saved for him, his mind racing with everything Ma had said. This case had seemed so straightforward when David and Hulan left Beijing, but now he was being asked by a Ministry of State Security agent to retrieve the *ruyi* without waiting until the courts opened on Monday. How exactly was David supposed to do that? *Why* would he do that? What was it about the *ruyi* that was so important to the Ministry of State Security? The ministry's mandate was to ensure the stability and security of the state by preventing foreign-inspired conspiracies, subversion, and sabotage. David simply didn't see how the Site 518 *ruyi* could play a part in any of that.

The catalog had stated that the auction would take place from seven to nine. Though David had thought two hours was an underestimate, it seemed that things would indeed move very quickly. Fitzwilliams was already on Lot 12—a seventeenth-century bronze Lohan seated on a Fu lion. A projection of the figure filled the screen on the left side of the podium. The screen on the right registered the bidding increments in 7.57 Hong Kong dollars to one U.S. dollar, and then the equivalent in pounds, euros, and yen.

Fitzwilliams's rigid posture was completely gone. His body undulated from side to side, his arms moving gracefully through the air as he acknowledged different bids in a sonorous voice. "Fifty thousand, fifty-five thousand, sixty thousand to you, sir. Sixty thousand. Do I have any advance on sixty thousand?"

"Here, sir," a man called out from the phone bank, where now every chair was occupied by a Cosgrove's employee. Some were on phones with customers bidding on this lot, others were dialing and getting ready for the next lot, while a few simply sat and waited for their customers' lots to come up later. Those on the phones cupped hands around their receivers, which meant that not only could no one on the bidding floor hear them but neither could their colleagues next to them. Although Cosgrove's employees, in this moment they worked on behalf of customers at the other end of the line.

"Sixty-five thousand, sixty-five thousand, sixty-five thousand. Anyone else? Are we all through then? Fair warning to you." Fitzwilliams brought the hammer down decisively. "Sold for sixty-five thousand Hong Kong."

The man at the phone bank quickly gave Fitzwilliams the bidder's number, and it was on to Lot 13—a blue-and-white porcelain vase, which sold in less than a minute for just under the published estimated price of HK$1,500.

Stuart leaned over and whispered, "This next one should be interesting."

Lot 14 was also a blue-and-white porcelain, but instead of coming from uncertain origin in the late Qing Dynasty, it had a mark showing it had come from the Chenghua period. This particular piece had been exhibited in London, New York, Washington, D.C., and here in Hong Kong as part of an international tour. It was being sold from the private collection of someone from Salem, Massachusetts, whose great-great-grandfather had been in the China trade. The catalog estimated that the bowl would sell for between HK$1.5 million and HK$2 million, making it the most expensive piece in the auction.

At the front of the room, split-screen photos showed the bowl's silhouette and interior. To David's left, eight employees on the phones waited to bid for people not in attendance. Fitzwilliams also explained that he had several bids on the books—meaning he would be bidding for absentee customers who'd submitted written bids.

The action was lively and fast, with Fitzwilliams handling the crowd like a snake charmer. Paddles lifted here and there about the room. The men and women on the phones raised their hands periodically to indicate that their bidders were going up another increment. In less than thirty seconds the bidding had reached HK$1.5 million.

"Watch Fitzwilliams, David," Stuart whispered. "If you knew the players, you'd know that he's acknowledging bids for longtime Cosgrove's customers before the bidders who are strangers to him or who he doesn't like."

"I'm out and off the book," Fitzwilliams announced. The bidding had now gone above what the absentee bidders had offered. "Any advance on two million two hundred thousand?"

"See how people are no longer holding their paddles up high," Stuart said. "They don't want the others to see they're still in the game. See that! Just a slight nod of the head or a lifted finger. Most people want to hide in the crowd to do their bidding. But some like to make a big show of it, hoping to intimidate others from even trying. As I said before, it's all in how you play the game."

When the blue-and-white languished at HK$2.4 million, Fitzwilliams said, "I want to remind everyone that Christmas is just a few months away." Laughter rippled through the room from all except the two people still locked in the final phase of bidding. One of the men raised his forefinger, and Fitzwilliams said, "Two million five hundred thousand. Thank you, sir." The auctioneer's body oscillated slightly in the direction of the other bidder. "Going on? No? Fair warning then. Sold to paddle 417. Merry Christmas and good show."

After a small but appreciative round of applause, Fitzwilliams moved straight on to Lot 15.

Madame Wang and Daisy Ting had a lively battle for the Song Dynasty *dingyao*, with the former triumphing. Nixon Chen, as predicted, bid repeatedly on the fifteen snuff bottles that came up as separate lots. After the blue-and-white bowl, the snuff bottles seemed like bargains, priced as they were between HK$500 and HK$6,500. Nixon came away with five, though none of his had gone over eighteen hundred. As Stuart Miller put it, "He's a typical lawyer. He's not the sort to get caught up in the moment." David suspected it had more to do with the years Nixon had spent at the Red Soil Farm in the countryside with Hulan. Nixon had a fondness for luxury, but it was always tempered by the fear that it could be taken away again.

Stuart bid on the jadeite *ruyi* with the carvings of the Eight Immortals but dropped out when the piece went over the estimated price. Ma bid on all of the jade pieces, winning all of the *bi*s but falling out early on the one that looked like a boomerang, which went to someone in the front row. The latter, David read in the catalog description, was actually part of a larger musical instrument. Typically these chimes—whether made from stone, bone, or bronze—were hung from a double-tiered support system and hit with a hammer, creating sounds reflective of the size of each piece.

Lot 47 was the cloisonné *ruyi*, which Stuart easily added to his collection. After that, a pair of green-glazed early Tang Dynasty figures sitting astride horses sold for just over their estimated price. Through all of these lots, Fitzwilliams worked the room, enticing people to join the bidding, luring the audience with extra details about a piece, coaxing people to go higher, and praising them when they did. And when the action stalled or when prices soared, the waiters who lingered on the sidelines passed through the audience refilling champagne glasses, keeping bidders merry and purse strings loose. It was the most beautiful act of commerce David had ever seen.

At 8:45, the Site 518 *ruyi* came up as Lot 95. Only one woman was on the phone and at the ready when Fitzwilliams opened the bidding at two thousand, a full thousand below the estimate. The price rose in the required increments of two hundred until it reached three thousand, then by three hundred until it reached five thousand. Fitzwilliams's movements and the sound of his voice were mesmerizing as he quickly shifted between Dr. Ma and the person in the front row who'd won the chime. David could see only the back of the bidder's head but could tell by the haircut that it was a man and by the color and texture of his hair that he was probably Chinese. Chinese American, as it turned out, which David learned when Stuart Miller once again filled him in.

"That's one of those Silicon Valley guys I told you about. Bill Tang is very greedy, very nouveau riche. He even gives the Red Princes a run for their money. Our old friend Dr. Ma doesn't stand a chance."

The bidding passed ten thousand, then twenty thousand, then jumped to one hundred thousand. It had taken less than a minute, and the price was already considerably beyond the estimated value. People who'd gone to stretch their legs came back. Others, who'd become bored with the proceedings or were waiting for the reception and banquet to start, were suddenly intrigued. Feeling that there must be something to this piece they hadn't realized, a few of the dealers Stuart had pointed out earlier joined in, driving the price up faster than the screen with all the foreign denominations could keep up. In the front row, Bill Tang held his paddle steadily aloft, signaling to everyone that he wouldn't drop out.

The bidding hit 250,000, and Stuart Miller had yet to raise his paddle. A brief round of applause at one million caused Fitzwilliams to pause in his melody of numbers just long enough to chastise, "Ladies and gentlemen." Then the bidding resumed, now jumping in increments of 100,000. There was a temporary lull at 1.5 million, with Bill Tang holding that bid, his paddle still held high enough for everyone to see.

"One million five," Fitzwilliams said. "Any advance on a million five? No more bids?" Fitzwilliams addressed Ma directly. "You, sir, staying in?"

Ma shook his head.

"A million five," Fitzwilliams picked up. "Fair warning then."

Stuart lifted his paddle. The crowd murmured quietly. Fitzwilliams scowled like a scolding parent, immediately silencing the audience.

"We have a new bidder," he resumed. "A million six, seven, eight, nine, two million. Two million one, two, three, four, five." Again the bidding halted, only this time it was Stuart who refused to go on. "Are you sure, sir?" Fitzwilliams asked.

"Too rich for my blood, I'm afraid," Stuart conceded.

Fitzwilliams's stern gaze squelched the smattering laughter.

"Two million five Hong Kong dollars. Fair warning." Fitzwilliams's eyes swept the room one more time. "Are we all through then?"

"Sir," the woman at the phone bank called out.

"A new bidder?"

"Yes, Mr. Fitzwilliams, sir."

"Two six it is," the auctioneer announced.

The price for the lowly *ruyi* had just passed that for the blue-and-white Ming Dynasty bowl, which had been billed as the most valuable piece in the auction. There were intakes of breath as the audience absorbed this.

Then the man in the front row said something audible only to Fitzwilliams, who rang out, "Twenty million Hong Kong dollars! Thank you, sir!"

This was nearly ten times the last bid and well over $2 million U.S.

"Twenty million," Fitzwilliams repeated, then gestured casually from the man in the front row over to the woman on the phone, his motions no different than they'd been for the sale of one of Nixon Chen's snuff bottles. The woman on the phone lifted a finger; the man in the front responded with another tip of the head. Back and forth Fitzwilliams went until the price reached 25 million Hong Kong dollars. Whoever the woman had on the phone held the bid. "It's to the gentleman in the front row." Nothing happened. "Want to go once more? You're here. Whoever's on the phone is not. His or her top price might be twenty-five million. Want to go one more shot?"

Bill Tang finally nodded.

"Twenty-six million," Fitzwilliams said triumphantly, but before anyone could applaud, the woman at the phone bank lifted her hand. "Twenty-seven." The audience let out a collective sigh of disappointment. Everyone was caught up in the drama with the man in the front row, even if they didn't know who he was, while the person on the phone remained nameless and faceless. "We're at twenty-seven. Coming in again, sir? Want to make it twenty-eight?"

It seemed to David that Tang's paddle stayed steady, but Fitzwilliams said, "No? Then fair warning to you. Selling . . . Sold for twenty-eight million Hong Kong dollars."

The audience that one moment before had been with Bill Tang in spirit now erupted in wild applause. The *ruyi* had sold for a thousand times its top estimated value, and more than $3 million U.S. But the applause was cut short when Bill Tang jumped to his feet and shouted, "You cheated!"

Fitzwilliams looked down from the podium with an expression of utter contempt. "It is a sad fact of auctions that we can't always win."

"You didn't recognize me!" Tang still hadn't turned around, but his posture was aggressive.

"Of course I recognized you. You were in the front row. You lowered your paddle. I saw it clearly."

"You shouldn't have closed the bidding! I had my paddle up! I want to see the videotape!"

"Sorry, Mr. Tang, but we don't tape our sessions."

Fitzwilliams made a slight motion to one of the security guards, which Bill Tang caught. He turned and quickly pushed his way up the center aisle to the row where Stuart Miller sat. Madame Wang had the presence of mind to stand and edge out of the way. Tang threw her chair into the aisle and shoved his face to just inches from Stuart's.

"You took what's mine!"

"I'm afraid you're wrong there, Bill," Stuart responded good-naturedly. "Everyone in this room saw me bow out."

A pair of guards reached Bill Tang, but when they tried to take his arms he shook them off and grabbed Stuart by the lapels. "You took what's mine, and I'll get it back!"

Stuart stayed relaxed as he said evenly, "I may have driven up the price a bit. I'll happily admit to that." The words and the smile on Stuart's face further infuriated Tang. He shoved the entrepreneur back with such force that his chair toppled over, which caused the two people behind Stuart to fall as well. Then Tang scuffled with the guards and was led to the back of the room. David helped Stuart to his feet. Madame Wang brushed him off and straightened his jacket and tie. After a little flurry of activity as chairs were righted and more champagne poured, the auction resumed for the last lots as though nothing had happened.

But something very significant had happened. David had recognized Bill Tang as soon has he'd come barging up the center aisle. The man whom Stuart Miller knew as Bill Tang, a foreign-born high-tech industrialist from the Silicon Valley, David had seen just last night standing on a ledge in a cave on the banks of the Yangzi River. Bill Tang was the man who called himself Tang Wenting, a lieutenant in the All-Patriotic Society, who just four days ago in Tiananmen Square had labeled Hulan "mother killer," and who last night in the cave had singled out Stuart Miller for special censure.

David had desperately and repeatedly tried to shift Hulan's focus away from the All-Patriotic Society in an effort to unlock her heart, but she'd been right all along. The cult *was* at the center of this, although he still had no idea what *this* was. The questions were startling and confusing. Who was the unnamed bidder on the other end of the telephone line? Who—*what*—was Bill Tang? What exactly was this *ruyi*—which was valued at three thousand dollars but had just sold for more than $3 million? Had last night in the cave been a ruse to push Hulan into investigating Stuart at the dam, thereby delaying or halting entirely the entrepreneur's trip to the auction? Or had it been designed to get Hulan away from Bashan for some as yet unknown reason? David didn't know the answers, but he had to get them, because Hulan was up there in Bashan without a clue that any of this had happened.

He pulled out her cell phone and dialed the Panda Guesthouse just as the hammer came down one last time and people applauded. All he got was an electronic whine, and he tucked the phone back in his pocket. Quickly everyone stood and began heading to the ban-quiet room. David looked around. Bill Tang was still at the back of the room, negotiating with the guards. David had made a terrible mistake in judgment, and he had to act fast. He tried to push his way through the crowd that had suddenly clustered around Stuart to congratulate him on his triumph. It took a few seconds before David realized that Stuart was being congratulated not for the purchase of the cloisonné *ruyi* but for that of the Site 518 *ruyi*. Stuart acted charming, effusively accepting praise one moment, then coyly denying that he knew anything about the *ruyi* the next. "You were in the room," he said to Nixon Chen. "You saw me drop out." This elicited raucous laughter from the other well-wishers. Stuart's show of bidding then dropping out had just been comical pretense for those in the know.

Dr. Ma waited at the end of the aisle. "Mr. Miller, I hope that you'll return what is China's to China."

"If I did that, Dr. Ma, then I wouldn't have anything in my collection." Stuart beamed happily.

"I'm not asking for everything, only the Site 518 *ruyi*."

"I don't know what you're talking about." Stuart turned to Madame Wang and took her by the elbow. "Come along, dear," he said, and they swept into the party.

Ma disappeared into the crowd. David edged forward, then stopped. Ma had told him to get the *ruyi*. Logic told David to stick with Stuart Miller. He might even be able to convince the entrepreneur to give it back of his own free will tonight. David had several persuasive arguments, and Stuart might want to avoid a lengthy— and public—legal battle. But David wanted answers, and instinct told him that the person he needed them from was Bill Tang, who was just now finishing up with the guards, shaking hands, and smiling. David hurried to the elevator, rode it down to the lobby, and found a place to stand where he hoped he wouldn't be noticed. Sure enough, a few minutes later Bill Tang stepped into the lobby, purposefully strode across the marble floor, and left through the revolving doors. David waited just a fraction of a second, then followed Tang out into the night.

HULAN WAS BONE-TIRED, AND SHE WISHED SHE COULD JUST order something simple from the kitchen, but she'd told Michael Quon she'd meet him for dinner. She peeled out of her sweaty clothes and climbed into the shower. She closed her eyes and let the hot water pound the knots in the back of her neck. Then she turned off the hot tap and let the cool water chill the veins that pulsed just under the surface of her skin at her wrists and at the crooks of her elbows. For the first time since she'd gotten here, she dried her hair with the complimentary blow dryer, then put on a little lipstick and a touch of mascara. She slipped into a simple sheath of pale pink silk and strapped on a pair of sandals.

She found Michael Quon waiting for her on the restaurant's veranda. The red light from a hanging lantern shone on his hair. The air was hot and wet, but he managed to look utterly cool, utterly serene. Inside the dining room, the Site 518 group huddled together in their usual spot. They were deep into their meal, and bottles of Tsingtao beer rose like a model city in the middle of the table. A couple of the men waved, Angela gave a message-delivered thumbs-up, but that was it.

Michael and Hulan were seated at a table at the back of the room. A waitress gave them menus, but before Hulan could open hers, Michael began speaking to the young woman in Mandarin, asking what was fresh and what the chef would recommend this evening. He'd been here longer than Hulan and had picked up more of the intricacies of the Sichuan dialect than she had, but this wasn't what surprised her. His Mandarin was quite good. His American English diluted some of the tones, but beneath that she heard something pure, as though he'd spoken Chinese as a child. Still, it wasn't a Taiwanese accent or a northern accent, either of which she might have expected given his age and that he was an American citizen by birth.

He ordered lettuce soup, bitter melon sautéed with beef and black beans, cold soy sauce chicken, and some China pea greens with roasted garlic in chicken broth. It was not an exotic meal, but it sounded perfect after the day she'd had. The lettuce soup would be simple and rejuvenating, the bitter melon would cut through the dust and dirt of the day, the cold chicken would be refreshing and nourishing, and the pea greens—if straight from the vine, which the waitress promised they were—would be bright and new on the taste buds. The waitress picked up Hulan's unopened menu and disappeared.

"I hope you don't mind," Michael said, switching back to English.

It had been a long time since someone else had ordered a meal for her in a restaurant, and she didn't mind at all.

The waitress came back with a bottle of local chardonnay and an ice bucket. Michael made small talk with the young woman as she uncorked the bottle, poured a little for him to taste, then filled both wineglasses. The liquid that slipped down Hulan's throat was crisp and lively. It was the coldest thing she'd experienced since leaving Beijing.

Michael's seeming disappointment in her at the end of their walk had dissipated, and he effortlessly held up his end of the conversation. In fact, he agreeably answered questions even before she asked them, like how he'd come to be so fluent in Chinese. His parents had left Shanghai, he told her between spoonfuls of soup, and moved to San Francisco at the end of the war. His father had been an engineer, his mother a physician.

"My brothers and I ran around all over the place," he recalled as the waitress brought their other dishes. "In the summers, we'd go to a theater that played kung fu movies back-to-back on Monday nights, when all the Chinese chefs were off. My favorites were *The One-Armed Boxer* and *Fist of Fury.* Have you seen them?"

"We didn't have a lot of films here when I was young."

"Then I'm going to have to take you one day, because these are seminal martial arts films." He said this only half in jest. "My brothers and I had some wild times at those programs. There were all these old bachelor chefs, smoking cigarettes and sipping from pints tucked inside brown paper bags, and then all of us kids, screaming, throwing popcorn, and peeing in the aisles. Afterward the boys would square off. American superheroes like Superman and Batman against the One-Armed Boxer and Bruce Lee—staking out territory, righting wrongs, killing the bad guys, and getting into all kinds of stuff we shouldn't have."

"Like what?" Hulan asked, still visualizing little boys wreaking havoc on a movie theater.

"Driving Mrs. Chan, our Chinese-language teacher, crazy." He brushed a shock of hair from his forehead. "We all grew up speaking Chinese at home, but our parents wanted us to be literate. So off to Chinese school we went. But we were bad! We pulled Mrs. Chan's laundry off the line so many times that she couldn't hang it outdoors anymore, which I have to say was a great blessing to all, because her underwear—girdles, I guess you'd have to call them—was scary." He paused, then added, "Of course you couldn't be part of the gang unless you peed on Mrs. Chan's back door. Now, that took real courage."

"I'm sensing a theme here . . ."

He lifted his glass and toasted the air. "To silly memories."

"To bad boys is more like it," she said, tapping his glass lightly.

She liked listening to him. His candor—which had seemed forward during her interview with him in the hotel lobby because no native-born Chinese man would ever have spoken to her, an inspector from the Ministry of Public Security, so directly—now lifted her spirits. Michael didn't know anything about her and wasn't asking questions either. He was harmlessly entertaining, and she imagined how he might relate this evening at some fashionable Bay Area event sometime in the future: a perfect meal with a surprisingly charming and worldly Ministry of Public Security inspector in a picturesque guesthouse on the north shore of the Yangzi during monsoon season.

"So how did you go from being a boy who literally left his mark on what sounds like every street corner in San Francisco to being here at the Panda Guesthouse?" Hulan asked.

"The short answer is I'm a stereotype," he replied. "My parents expected me to get into a good school and I did. I went to Stanford and got my Ph.D. in math. After graduation I got a job at Hewlett-Packard. You can probably guess the rest. I founded my own company in the early nineties. I took VYRUSCAN public before the bubble burst, and I became a very, very rich man."

Which seemed a very un-Chinese thing to say.

"In a sense that was only the beginning," he went on. "When you've made a lot of money, you feel compelled to make more. I started a REIT to buy land and do development deals. I put up venture capital in start-ups and was very lucky. But making money's just a game after a while, so what's the point? I'm not married. I don't have children. I've provided for my brothers, their children, and their future grandchildren, so who was I building it all for? Once I came to that realization, I retired fully from making money."

"That still doesn't explain how you ended up here."

"When you're forty-two, retired, and money's no object, how do you spend your time? Toys? Sure, I got into that. I bought a Boxster. I bought a boat and put it down in Monterey Bay. Oh, and a house, of course. But all that *stuff* requires work. The boat gets barnacles, and the Porsche is temperamental. The house needs constant upkeep. I've got groundskeepers and maids and—I don't know—people in and out of the place all the time. You laugh, but it's true!"

Hulan was laughing, but she was also listening to the subtext. Michael Quon had been serious when he'd said he'd gotten "very, very rich."

"Hobbies are the other thing people in my position are supposed to take up," he continued. "I started buying contemporary art. After that I studied the Song Dynasty poets, even sat in on a couple of classes at Stanford. I give them enough money, so why not?"

He chatted, she listened. They ate and drank until they were full. When he finally set down his chopsticks, the waitress instantly appeared at his side and asked if they were done. He nodded, and she cleared the table. She returned again and asked if they wanted anything else.

"Please bring some watermelon," Michael said in Mandarin. He regarded Hulan questioningly, then asked, "How about another bottle of wine? We don't have to drink the whole thing, but it would be nice, don't you think?"

When Hulan agreed, the waitress slipped away and brought back another icy bottle. She refilled their glasses, then stepped to her spot against the wall. Michael picked up where he'd left off.

"My mother always wanted me to connect to my roots, but it took the IPO for me to begin searching for my place in the world. The old family and district associations are still operational in San Francisco, but they tend to focus on old-timers—Cantonese speakers from the early days who want only a banquet at Chinese New Year. The Organization of Chinese Americans has done a great job lobbying in Washington, but where do you put someone like me?"

"The Committee of 100?" Hulan asked. I. M. Pei and Yo-Yo Ma had founded the group in 1989 after the crackdown in Tiananmen Square. Today it boasted 140 of the self-proclaimed most important Chinese Americans. Michael Quon should have been a member.

"They asked and I turned them down. What can I say? I think the Committee of 100 is too elitist, but I also wasn't going to be comfortable at the annual family association banquet down in Chinatown with the pledge of allegiance, followed by ten courses, karaoke, and an appearance by Miss Chinatown, all for the big-ticket price of fifty dollars."

"It can be hard to find your niche," Hulan sympathized.

But Michael shrugged off the suggestion and hurried on. "What else have I done? Good deeds, naturally. But giving away money isn't what it's cracked up to be. You give a million dollars to a museum and they say, Well, considering Bill Gates's gift, your donation isn't enough to get your name on the wing, let alone the building. *That* would take ten million dollars. So what does that leave? Travel—"

"And women."

"Yes, and women." He laughed good-naturedly. "You can spend a lot of money on women."

"Anyone in particular?"

"Not really."

"So then for travel you came here?"

"Ummm . . ." He mused as he thought about it. "No, first I took a villa in the south of France. Then I played around in Paris. I took about six months where I just skied—Gstaad at Christmas, Aspen in the spring, then down to New Zealand for the first snow in June. But you can do stuff like that for only so long before you start looking for something else. When you're rich beyond your wildest dreams, it's harder than you might expect to find what will make you happy and occupy your mind." He cocked his head and appraised her coolly. "But you know what I'm talking about, don't you? You have money. You've just had it longer than I have."

"How could you tell?"

"It's something about the way you carry yourself."

He took the bottle from the ice bucket. She realized that the others from the Site 518 team had left.

"It's late," she said.

"Yes," he agreed, "but you still haven't found out why or how I got here."

He poured the wine into their glasses and eased back into his chair, wordlessly challenging her to leave.

"You are very *kan ye*," she said.

"You think I like to brag and boast? I suppose so, but I prefer the less severe definition. I like to shoot the breeze."

Which showed that his Chinese was not just fluent but highly nuanced as well.

"So how long do I have to wait until I hear why you're here and why you've stayed?"

No flicker of victory crossed his features. No wonder he had done well in business.

"I've stayed because there's nowhere else I'd rather be and no-where else I have to be. As for your other question, I told you I took a class in Chinese poetry," he said, smoothly transitioning back into his storytelling mode. "I kept with it even after the class was over. One night I read a poem by Meng Jiao called 'The Sadness of the Gorges.' It begins, 'Above the gorges, one thread of sky.' Later in the same poem, he wrote, 'Trees lock their roots in rotted coffins and the twisted skeletons hang tilted upright.' He was talking about the Qutang Gorge and the hanging coffins, though I didn't know it then. But the haunting quality of the words made me want to look deeper at Meng Jiao, the Three Gorges, and especially the Ba, who'd hung those coffins up on the cliffs."

He went on to talk about the poet, a disillusioned government official, who, twelve hundred years ago, had wandered through the beauty of these hills but had lived in brutal poverty. Meng had called the Ba, some of whom had still been around in those days, wild apes. Here was a man who lived so long ago writing about people who'd lived and walked this land so much longer before that. Michael's interest had been piqued. The more he learned about the Ba and their subsequent disappearance, the more he wanted to know. Then, as he'd studied the mythology of the gorges, he'd been increasingly drawn to the character of Da Yu.

"I love to think of Yu combing these wild reaches and incorpo-rating them into an empire that would one day become China. Be-sides," he added, "Yu was a mathematician like myself. That amused me."

"How can you possibly know if he was a mathematician?" Hulan asked. "He may not even have existed."

"I think we should trust the historical accounts found in the *Shu Ching,* don't you?"

"I don't understand what that is, exactly."

"It's one of the world's oldest books, *and* it's still in print."

But that didn't mean she knew its importance, and this realiza-tion surprised him.

"It's a series of historical documents that covers nearly two thousand years of history up to 631 B.C.," he explained. "The Tribute to Yu canon records Yu's nature as a man and a leader. It's here that you first hear about the Nine Tripods and how the bronze work describes each province's resources and riches."

Michael fell silent. The rain, which had let up considerably during the day, now pelted the roof, and thunder sounded in the distance. He put down his wineglass and continued. "One thing I think is extraordinary about Yu was his vision of engineering. *Da Yu chih shui*. 'Yu the Great controlled the waters,'" he translated, although she understood the words. "He who controls the waters of China controls the people. Think about dikes, canals, dams, sluice gates, locks, cofferdams. When these aren't working correctly, then crops are flooded, methods of communication fail, territorial lines are lost—all of which lead to the destruction of empire. Yu was the first to figure that out, and the central government still believes it."

"So he was a leader, a good businessman, a great engineer—"

"And a mathematician, as I said. Yu developed the Luo script, arranging numbers so that whether added vertically, horizontally, or diagonally they all come out to the same aggregate of fifteen."

"I remember doing that puzzle as a child."

"So do I, and so do a lot of kids all over the world. Today we can look at it as a childish puzzle, but Yu figured it out more than four thousand years ago. He also created the Chinese lunar calendar. You *had* to know that."

"No."

"It's called the Xia calendar in honor of the dynasty he founded!"

"But I didn't know he developed it."

He shook his head, truly surprised at her ignorance.

"Wine was created during Yu's reign. Did you know that?"

"I told you I know nothing about him."

"Right, but wine? That's big! Of course a man like Yu would have to be contemptuous of luxury and pleasure. So this great thing is created, he tries it, and decides it's too harmful for his people."

Hulan tapped a finger on the rim of her wineglass. "But I see you haven't exactly followed Yu's advice."

"You'd be surprised," Michael said. "And I'll tell you about that one day too, if you'll let me. But first may I ask you a question?"

"Go ahead."

"I've been telling you things that any child in China should know."

"'If not for Yu, we all would be fishes,'" she recited. "I only heard it for the first time at lunch the other day."

"How can that be? Did it have to do with the Cultural Revolution?"

"My ignorance? In part. I was sent to the countryside when I was twelve. I left China soon after that and didn't return until I was twenty-seven. Whatever I knew as a child I've mostly forgotten. It's a shortcoming, I know."

As she watched him consider this, Hulan realized that tonight she'd spoken more openly with him than she had with her own husband over the last year. When Michael Quon looked at her, he didn't see her dead daughter, her dead father, the dead women in the Knight factory, the dead mother on the square. Hulan knew she was mixing her Americanisms, but to Michael she was a clean slate, with no baggage.

Finally, as though no time had passed, he said, "You could look at it another way. You were given an opportunity, and you learned a whole set of abilities and volumes of expertise that make you very different here. You *are* different. You realize that, don't you?"

She'd lived with that knowledge every day of her life, and it wasn't just because she'd spent her formative years abroad. She was born a Red Princess in a society that was supposed to be classless. She'd kept her individuality in a society where individuality was often singled out for punishment. She was different in her neighborhood, different at work, different from the people she'd known in the countryside, different—as Michael said—from most people in China.

He looked at her now with sudden understanding. "I bet people don't like you very much."

"No one's supposed to like an agent from the Ministry of Public Security."

"Which is why you chose the job?"

That her father had been vice minister when she started was none of Michael's business, so she said, "I'm good at what I do."

"I can see that. What I don't get is why you left the States."

"Maybe I didn't fit in there either."

He searched her face. "I don't think so. I think you fit in very well, and I bet you were happy too. Why did you come back?"

"My mother was ill. I felt I had a duty to her and to my father. But once I came back and saw how China was changing, I thought I should be a part of that."

He studied her again, this time with raw interest. Again he came to his own conclusion. "You're a beautiful woman, Hulan, but your regrets play upon your face as though your heart were open to me. I think you were afraid to stay, afraid and . . . guilty."

"I thought you were a mathematician, not a psychoanalyst," she retorted, trying to keep the remark light but failing miserably.

Michael laughed. "Don't you know that all the secrets of the universe are revealed through math? Or was that another blind spot in your education?" He didn't wait for her to answer. Instead he pushed his chair away from the table and stood. "Thank you for joining me tonight, Inspector. I enjoyed it. Perhaps we can do it again tomorrow."

"David will probably be back by then."

"Then I look forward to the three of us getting together."

He saw her to the end of the second courtyard, then left her to find her own way back to her room.

CHAPTER

22

AN EERIE QUIET ENVELOPED HONG KONG AS THE ISLAND BRACED for the coming typhoon. Wind whipped light drizzle in undulating sheets across Connaught Road. Though it was after nine at night, the air was unbearably hot and humid. David was gooey with sweat. Most people had gone home in anticipation of the storm, so the automobile traffic had died down and only a few stragglers were still on the streets. David kept to the exterior wall of the Ritz-Carlton as he followed at a safe distance behind Bill Tang. When the lieutenant crossed Connaught to the Star Ferry Terminal, David hesitated briefly before he leaned his body into the wind and dashed across the street.

His senses were fully heightened, and adrenaline pumped through his body. Following Tang was a rash and impulsive decision—the kind of thing Hulan would do—yet even in the irrationality of the moment David's mind was in full gear as he went back to the very beginning of his involvement in this case. Director Ho of the Cultural Relics Bureau had talked about the importance of proving the length of Chinese culture and civilization. Vice Minister Zai had spoken of the need to prevent international embarrassment. An hour ago, Dr. Ma had mentioned that there were "factions" that wanted the *ruyi*. *Factions.* To David this meant much more than an aficionado of Asian art wanting an object for his collection. He thought again of Zai and spread his net wider and broader to include large Chinese alliances with great power. Ma's faction would be the Ministry of State Security, which had increasingly close ties to the military. If Ma were to be believed, then Hulan—possibly unwittingly—was working on behalf of another faction within the government. And now David was tailing Bill Tang, who came from a growing cult in China. The *ruyi* had to have some type of iconic meaning—something that, as Ma said, could influence world stability—to each of these groups and still be of interest to someone like Stuart Miller.

Bill Tang stopped before the main entrance to the Star Ferry. David ducked into the opening to the ferry's parking lot. Was Tang thinking of taking the ferry to the Kowloon side? David wasn't sure if the boats were still running, since most ships and ferries had already sought refuge in the typhoon shelter behind the breakwater on the other side of the harbor. He edged out so that he could see up the street. The lieutenant jerked his head around, and David slipped back into his hiding place. His heart pounded in his chest. He listened, hoping to hear Tang move, but the howling wind made that impossible. David deepened his listening and felt something— someone—else besides Tang out there. It had to be Ma, hiding in the shadows. Was Tang aware of him too?

David peeked out again and saw Tang looking back up the hill toward Victoria Peak. David followed his gaze to the Bank of China Building. Shooting up around it were other, much smaller skyscrapers, the names of their owners smearing in bright lights across the tops. To the left and behind the Bank of China tower was another building with only a symbol at the top: a series of concentric squares. David knew he'd seen it somewhere before . . .

Tang was on the move again. He turned right just beyond the Star Ferry building. David sprinted to that corner and looked down a flight of stairs toward the harbor. There were no lights. The air was redolent of diesel fuel, grease, oil, and creosote. Going down the walkway was not a good idea, but Hulan would have done it if she were here.

David took about ten steps down the stairs and stopped. Waves stirred up by the wind breached the seawall below him. Great wooden piers rose up to his right. He couldn't see far into the murkiness behind them. Tang could be anywhere in the darkness. There was no use pretending that David was sneaking up on the lieutenant; clearly he was the one walking into an ambush.

"Tang," he called out. "It's David Stark. Come out. I want to talk."

A wall of rain and grimy seawater splashed against David. He held his footing, then took another couple of steps closer to the harbor.

"I know who you are, so there's no point in hiding—"

Tang emerged from the shadows onto a platform just before the seawall. "It's better if you don't know who I am, Mr. Stark," he said.

David held out his hands, catching the wind in his palms. "This is no place to meet. Let's go inside."

"I don't want to hurt you. I don't want to hurt any of you."

Tang appeared willing to talk. He also seemed to want to help— or confess. David went down another two steps.

Tang went on. "I've done my best to warn you and your wife."

This was exactly the kind of thing David wanted to hear. However, instinct told him to proceed cautiously.

"I thought you might have done that," he said, wanting to build on Tang's admission. He casually strolled the rest of the way down the stairs to the platform until he came face-to-face with Tang. "I understand you're a businessman. Let's use your experience to figure this thing out."

"There's no way to change what has already happened. My future is already set."

Sensing that Tang's resolve was weakening, David forged ahead. "Tell me about—"

"Noooo!" Tang spun around on one leg. David had just enough time to recognize that he was about to be attacked and raised his arms in front of him against the blow, but it didn't come to his face, chest, or abdomen. Tang's leather shoe smashed into David's head above his left ear. David went flying. He landed on his side, and Tang kicked him in the stomach. He curled into a fetal position, but it was no protection against what came next. The blow to his ribs sent pain hurtling throughout his body. Another kick in nearly the same spot proved excruciating. David fought hard against the darkness that threatened to blanket his brain.

Tang hunched over him. The smell of his cologne curdled David's stomach. "You cannot change what will happen. Nothing can change the great river."

Then Tang pulled himself back up to his full height. When he took a step back, David knew what was coming. The blow to his head sent him spiraling into unconsciousness. He had a vague sensation of being dragged, of falling, of being enveloped by cold and wet, and then sinking, sinking, sinking . . .

"Hang in there, David!"

The feeling of being pulled through liquid . . . More pain as someone reached under his arms and yanked . . .

"Breathe! Breathe goddamnit!"

Floating through a dense miasma . . .

"Wake up, David!"

Rising . . .

"Breathe!"

Choking . . .

"I'm going for help. Stay still."

Then slipping again into the comforting blackness.

David felt raindrops stinging his face. He opened his eyes, rolled on his side, and threw up filthy seawater. He hurt all over.

The typhoon had arrived. Waves crashed nearby, wind screeched over him, and the pier groaned against the storm's irrefutable energy.

He pushed himself to a sitting position and tried not to pass out again. He swallowed hard several times. He reached into his pocket and pulled out Hulan's cell phone. He opened it, and water poured out. He tossed it into the harbor, and an impression of sinking came to him. The harbor . . . Tang had dumped David in the water just as Brian's body had been tossed away like a piece of trash. The knowledge of what he must have ingested from the bay sent David's guts into more spasms. He wiped his mouth with the back of his hand and saw his watch. His vision was blurry, and he blinked again and again, trying to get his eyes to focus. It was three in the morning. In his fogginess he tried to calculate how long he'd been out here. Six hours. Six lost hours. But he was alive. Ma had pulled him out of the harbor . . . Didn't he say he was coming back? David thought he remembered that . . . maybe.

He had to get moving. He had to call Hulan. He cupped a hand over his ribs, but that gave little protection from the agony that speared through him as he stood up. He staggered up the stairs, every step an immense effort. He crossed the deserted street to the Mandarin Oriental. There were no taxis queued up under the porte cochere and no doormen to welcome guests. The lobby was empty except for one person, who sat behind the reception desk reading a magazine and didn't look up. The mezzanine bar was closed.

Once David reached his room, he locked the door and called the Panda Guesthouse. He got the same electronic whine he'd gotten after the auction. He called the operator and was patched through to a Mainland operator, who told him that Sichuan, Hubei, and Anhui provinces were reporting downed telephone lines within the Yangzi's flood zone. If he hadn't gotten through already, he probably wouldn't until all service was restored after the waters receded.

He had things he needed to do. If anything Ma had said earlier was true, then calling the police was the absolute wrong thing to do. David did call the U.S. Consulate, however, and left a message that the legate should call him as soon as possible. He also called the Ministry of Public Security and left a message with Vice Minister Zai. But after what Ma had said at the auction about Hulan possibly working for an independent group within the government, David wasn't so sure he could trust her old family friend in the present circumstances. He thought fleetingly of Dr. Ma. He had lied about his identity and, from David's perspective, was working for the wrong side, but he'd also saved David's life. Didn't he now owe Ma the benefit of the doubt? The least he could do was wait here until the spy showed up at his door.

David was still sopping wet, and he smelled of blood and harbor scum. He stripped off his clothes, cramming the entire slimy mess into the hamper. He looked in the mirror and hardly recognized the person who stared back. His face was haggard, his skin a ghoulish green. A dark bruise was coming up on his jaw where the skin had been shredded by Tang's shoe. His forehead and hair were matted with blood and bits of asphalt and dirt. A huge bump had developed on the side of his head, and he had a gash above his left eyebrow. He dabbed at the cut gingerly with a wet washcloth. He needed stitches. But none of this was as bad as his torso. His entire left side was bruised an angry purple. He carefully probed his ribs and figured a couple of them had to be cracked or broken.

The shower hurt like hell, but he felt better once he got out. It was four in the morning. His whole body hurt, and his brain felt like mush. He needed Band-Aids and painkillers to tide him over until Ma got here. He sat on the bed and called down to the front desk to ask for the house doctor to pay a visit, but because of the weather, the doctor, along with most of the hotel's staff, had been told to go home long ago. David checked his Dopp kit and found some Tylenol. He fished around in his suitcase, searching the various pockets, hoping he'd find some leftover bandages from another trip. Nothing. He pulled out his satchel and looked in the center compartment. Again, nothing. Then he unzipped the side pocket and found the papers and notebooks that he'd picked up in Lily's room for Hulan during their meeting with Pathologist Fong. In the chaos of the last two days he'd forgotten he had them. He pulled them out, laid them on the bed, and scrounged around at the bottom of the bag until he came up with two Little Mermaid Band-Aids. They'd been Chaowen's favorites. He went back to the bathroom and taped them over his cut, trying to use them like butterfly bandages by squeezing the pieces of sliced flesh together. Again he stared at himself in the mirror and this time bit back an overwhelming desire to cry.

He returned to the bedroom and picked up Lily's journal. He opened to what seemed like the center and read a quotation that was accompanied by a pen-and-ink drawing of cliffs and water.

"Destructive in their overflow are the waters of inundation. In their vast extent they embrace mountains and overtop hills, threatening the heavens with their floods, so that the inferior people groan and moan."

—Yau (2357–2258 B.C.), as recorded in the *Shu Ching: Book of History,* James Legge translation

David had no idea who Yau was, but he remembered Catherine Miller's mentioning the *Shu Ching* during that first lunch. He flipped through the pages, stopping to glance at entries about the Yangzi River that Lily had culled from local myths as well as other sources. She had liked to take mundane facts and turn them into compelling sagas. The journal showed just how dedicated she was to this pursuit.

David skipped ahead and stopped at a very different entry.

Just got back from an All-Patriotic Society meeting. It's amazing to me how Xiao Da changes his identity so thoroughly from day to night. I believe what he says about spiritual matters, but it is his views on the river that have made me a convert. We must save what is here at all costs. Although I am a foreigner, Xiao Da says I should become a lieutenant. My Chinese is good enough, and with the travel I do for Lily, my movements along the river would not be questioned. But he also says I could be the first American to speak on his behalf when I go back to the States.

This wasn't Lily's diary at all. It had to be Brian's. David turned back to the first page and began to read from the beginning.

THE WILD DOMAIN

(Huan fu)

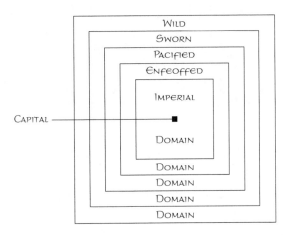

WILD
SWORN
PACIFIED
ENFEOFFED
IMPERIAL
CAPITAL
DOMAIN
DOMAIN
DOMAIN
DOMAIN
DOMAIN

The most remote. The last 500 *li* are allotted to the wild
ones of cultureless savagery and those criminals undergoing
greater banishment.

23

DAVID TURNED THE PAGES, LOOKING FOR ANY INFORMATION THAT would shed light on everything that had happened—from Brian's death seventeen days ago to Dr. Ma's claims early tonight about the *ruyi*'s significance to "other factions." The journal started a year ago in June, just before Brian left Seattle for the first time. David skipped these early entries, which detailed Brian's adventures getting to Bashan.

On June 28, Brian wrote:

> Dr. Strong is old and his mind wanders. Today he got caught up in the love that the Chinese have for numbers, beginning with the ancient Nine Provinces and Five Domains. He also went on about the Five Punishments. These date back to the Canon of Shun, which was the first of the ancient documents in the *Shu Ching*. The Five Punishments are branding on the forehead, cutting off the nose, cutting off the feet, castration, and death.

Branding, cutting off the nose, cutting off the feet—Brian and Lily had both suffered some of the ancient Five Punishments. Anyone who worked at Site 518 would have recognized them, but Hulan had kept those forensic details secret. Even in pain and even with what he felt sure was a concussion, David was a lawyer. He got up and fished around in his satchel until he found some plastic sticky notes so he could mark highlights in the journal. He put his first on the entry about the branding and then every place he saw the first mention of a visitor to the dig. Michael Quon had come through around the Fourth of July. Like Brian, Quon enjoyed caving, and the two of them had explored a couple of caverns away from the site. Stuart Miller stopped in often to meet privately with Dr. Ma.

July 5—The thermometer has hit 42 for the last four days. About 107 degrees, I guess. I'm dying. So is Lily. Although she lives in Hong Kong, she's from England and as susceptible to the heat and humidity as I am.

Three days later, he wrote:

Lily invited me to her table for dinner last night. She's very clever and very funny. (She's clever and funny in bed too! Ha! Ha!) She went back to Hong Kong today. Says she'll be back in a couple of weeks. Says she wants fun but no games. Suits me if it suits her.

Over the next two weeks, Brian listed artifacts he'd uncovered and why they were important. During this time, he went to his first All-Patriotic Society meeting. David thought about how Brian—an orphan, poor, rootless, and still too young to have made many decisions on his own—would have felt great solidarity with the plight of other followers in the gorges. Their desire to save their homes against inundation would have appealed to his desire to save the river, its artifacts and archaeological sites. This seemed innocent enough, but David tried to look at it from the Chinese government's perspective. The Falun Gong's spread to the United States and its demonstrations on street corners in New York and Los Angeles were huge embarrassments to China. Would the Ministry of State Security consider the Society enough of a threat to China's sovereignty to have ordered Brian killed? That would make Ma a prime suspect, but then why would he have murdered Lily? And why the branding and other mutilations?

David skimmed several pages, then stopped when he hit Brian's first encounter with Catherine Miller. They were close in age, but unlike his dealings with Lily, Brian showed restraint toward the daughter of his benefactor. "Catherine's great," he wrote on July 19, "but I want to come back next year." Nevertheless, he gradually found himself being "drawn to Catherine's enthusiasm," although he felt inhibited by his lack of money.

As a result, Brian had been ripe for Lily's offer to help her get artifacts out of the country. His entry about this was blunt and to the point: "If the Chinese aren't going to preserve the past, then someone else should." The fun and games that Lily had predicted earlier had evolved, and David attached another sticky note.

While Dr. Ma tried to keep everyone focused on the Four Mysteries, Brian seemed bewitched by what David knew to be China's more specific goal—making a physical link to history five thousand years old. "Wouldn't it be sweet," he jotted on July 27,

> if we could actually find something that showed that Yu the Great had come through here when he was clearing the floods? His wife was reputedly born in the South Mountains near Chongqing. I'm going this weekend—tomorrow!—to check out her temple.

Loose pieces of the puzzle—those random and seemingly innocuous comments made during the investigation—were starting to come together. One such piece was why the archaeologists had always seemed more interested in Yu than in the Ba people and why Xiao Da had invoked him in the cave. Anxious for Brian to provide an explanation, David read on.

> July 29—Just got back and I feel like I learned more about Yu and his father than I did about Yu's wife. Kun, Yu's father, was hired by Yau—one of China's first three mythical emperors—to

stop the floods. Kun labored for nine years. He stole magical soil—a "swelling mold" called *shi tu* or "living earth"—from the heavens to use to help block the waters.

Here was another piece. The old blind man had called the land around his home "living earth." David didn't know enough about the subtleties of Chinese to know if this was a common phrase, something unique to the region, or something that somehow tied Brian's research and Wu together. However, for the next few pages Brian concentrated on Kun, whose flood efforts failed so badly that the new emperor, Shun, banished him. Later Kun was executed. He decomposed for three years until his belly was cut open and Yu emerged fully formed. Shun then assigned Yu the task of finishing the flood work and gave him a "dark-colored stone" believed to be a *gui* as an emblem to carry during his labors.

This time, with Heaven's blessing, Yu borrowed the swelling mold and used it to build China's great mountains. Then he cut canals to provide outlets for the waters to drain into the sea. He deepened beds, raised embankments, changed the course of rivers, and created the Three Gorges. He taught the people about agriculture and how to breed and eat animals. A feudal system replaced the old nomadic societies, and China's first hereditary dynasty began. "Could the swelling mold exist?" Brian asked. "Is it some type of soil, such as loess or clay? Or is it a purely symbolic fabrication?"

David was getting bogged down and in frustration jumped ahead.

August 2—The vultures heard about my trip to Chongqing and invited me into their cave to tell them about it. The vultures say that the Chinese people have never lost their sense of the ancient past. It is an ocean of religion, philosophy, geography, customs, and literature that envelops them. These things are not just "ago" but have the ability to come full circle to inform the present and give a window into the future. We also talked a lot about the ancient books—and what it meant to contemporary Chinese society and politics to save them.

David knew that the vultures liked to speak in riddles. What were they trying to tell Brian? Was it something to do with current—possibly world—events? Could the vultures have been part of one or more of Ma's so-called factions that were tampering with China's global stability? That seemed wholly unlikely to David. Meanwhile, Brian remained firmly stuck in the past.

Can I prove that the stories of Yu's works are a blueprint of the Chinese mind? For ten years, Yu endured tremendous hardship. His nails were worn from his fingers. His hands and feet became callused and hardened. His face and eyes became black. Many times he passed near his wife's home here on the Yangzi but did not stop. He heard his son, whom he'd not yet met, crying, and still did not stop. These sacrifices for the good of the people allowed him to become emperor.

Last night Xiao Da asked me, if Yu was a real man, what of his story could be real?

This was the first time Brian had mentioned Xiao Da by name. If Brian was actually meeting one-on-one with the religious leader, then he must have already become deeply entwined in the cult.

Was Yu truly helped by a winged dragon that trailed his tail upon the ground, carving channels to the sea? How could one man, even with the help of the masses, have diverted the waters so thoroughly?

The Xia Dynasty went on to have another seventeen emperors, all descendants of Yu. The last, however, was a tyrant of the worst sort, and Heaven showed its displeasure by raining down plagues and disasters of every kind. Xiao Da says this pattern of corruption followed by heavenly condemnation in the form of natural calamities has trumpeted the end of every Chinese dynasty.

Reading the next entry, David learned that Brian's interest in Da Yu and the Xia had also sparked lunch conversation at Site 518 about the Nine Tripods. This, in turn, gave Catherine an idea. She was fed up with Lily's "ridiculous stories" and thought it would be "fun" to trick her into believing that one of the tripods was right near them in a whirlpool in the waters of the Yangzi. Lily fell for the charade "hook, line, and sinker," much to the amusement of the other scholars at the site. Brian added: "Lily's going to ask me to dive in the whirlpool one of these days! Catherine says it would serve me right."

By now Brian and Catherine were more than just friends, but Stuart Miller's pampered only child was way out of Brian's league. Although others at the site had painted him as an outdoorsman, it turned out that his desire for solitude had been born out of the necessity of putting some distance between himself and Catherine. On weekends, he headed into the hills. He wasn't a great artist, but he drew what he saw. During the week he scouted out different places until he settled on the little stretch of beach where his belongings were later found.

August 7—Today I finally met the old blind man and his family whose house I pass to get to my beach. Their land is poor. The son and his wife aren't educated. They're the first people I've met here who aren't curious about me. I guess a foreigner passing by your door isn't worth the energy when you're practically starving to death. Just past their house is the trail I take to get down here. It's so quiet you can hear pebbles rolling along the riverbed. I can see the Unlocked Gates Gorge across the way. Partway up the hill is the Beheading Dragon Platform. On the other side of the gully is the Binding Dragon Pillar. Next Sunday I'll try to get over there.

A couple of days later:

I passed the Wu house again today. The old man is a wild one. The son is no different. The daughter-in-law is very shy. Today she was washing clothes in the river near where I have my lunch. At first she wouldn't answer my questions. I teased her, saying I thought a fox spirit had stolen her tongue. She said my accent was atrocious. Actually she said I was as hard to understand as a river turtle.

As promised, he did go exploring farther east.

Explored the Unlocked Gates Gorge today. On my way back I ran into the Wu daughter-in-law, and she explained some of the stories that relate to the gorge's geography. It seems that the Jade Dragon left his home on the upper reaches of the Bashan Stream to go visiting. The creature got lost, became angry, and in his rage caused mountains to crumble, land to flood, and people and livestock to die. A goddess threw a string of pearls into the air, which turned into a rope that bound the dragon to the pillar. The goddess then ordered Da Yu to behead the dragon on the platform. Wu Taitai pointed out the coiled shape of striated stone where the dragon can be seen. Although she is a Society member, I haven't seen her at a meeting.

Toward the end of summer, Michael Quon returned to the dig for a couple of days and wanted to go caving, but for some reason Brian balked. "Some people think that their money can buy them anything, but I'm not for sale." This comment brought him back to Catherine.

The prank that she had cooked up about the Nine Tripods had backfired. Lily was completely obsessed with the missing tripod. She needed someone to retrieve it from the whirlpool, and that someone was Brian. "As if," he wrote. By this time, Brian had acted as a go-between between Lily and Wu Huadong; her payments would make a huge difference to the Wu family. Notably, from David's perspective, Brian didn't mention what relinquishing his travel up and down the river would do to his aspirations for becoming an All-Patriotic Society lieutenant. In fact, David realized, Brian hadn't written about Xiao Da or the Society since his entry about the Wu girl being a follower.

Brian's last two weekends had been spent literally underground as he explored local caves. Reemerging into the sunlight after one descent, he finally noticed what Hulan had seen on her first day at the dig. The site and the surrounding area were uncommonly barren. On September 9, he wrote that he had an idea about the land and made a note to talk to his sister about it when he got back to Seattle. His last entry before leaving China read:

> No one would believe in a thousand years how I got home today. Lily would love it, because it would be a great embellishment to her stories. Maybe I'll tell her when I come back next year. I could make some real money.

David closed his eyes for a moment as a deep unease settled into him. A blunder had given him the diary. In a way he was glad he had it, because he was sure he had more pieces of the puzzle than Hulan did, but he was worried about her. He'd gotten this far since he'd left her at the Three Gorges Dam yesterday. Where was she now in her investigation?

David took a deep breath and picked up the story with Brian's return to the University of Washington. He devoted himself to his classwork and to applying for a new Miller Fellowship. His journal evolved from being a personal record to being a place where he kept track of his research for his master's thesis and future dissertation. He studied early jade, in particular *bi*s and chimes. These shapes were the same as the objects that had been up for auction at Cosgrove's last night. Brian had been looking at these pieces a year ago!

He then began an examination of the differences between a *gui* and a *ruyi*. David bolted upright as he read that last word. Here again, Brian was interested in an object months ago that had catapulted David into this horrible situation. As usual, Brian stuck with an academic approach as he described the differences. Both objects shared similar inspirations and aspirations; both were considered scepters. But as time passed, *gui*s—usually in the form of carved jade tablets—had ceased being given as "passports" for important assignments and had been used by court officials to hold in front of their mouths to deflect their breath away from the emperor. The *ruyi*, by contrast, was believed to have emerged centuries later from the Buddhist tradition. In its root or fungi form, it was used as a meditative object not unlike scholar's rocks. People then began to make *ruyi*s in other materials for use as scepters. They had also been given as imperial gifts for nuptials and in honor of deeds well done. Today the back scratcher with its fingerlike phalanges was a direct— though plebeian—descendant of the *ruyi*.

Despite what the history books said, Brian had a very different take on the *gui* and *ruyi*. In archaeological terms, it seemed to him that the *gui* had to have developed after the *ruyi*, which had its source in a natural element. Again and again Brian went back to some obscure scholarly debate about Yu's "dark-colored stone." Had it been given at the beginning of Yu's quest? Or was it, as some scholars believed, an object that Yu found in his travels—an artifact so precious and remarkable that it would be worthy of presentation to a sovereign? Was the stone actually a stone? Couldn't it be interpreted as something dark and hard, like a petrified mushroom? "I think this could connect to what I found in the earth around Site 518," Brian wrote. "I need to take this up with Angela but not until I'm absolutely sure. No point in getting her hopes up needlessly."

Again David stopped to reread the passage. This was the second time Brian had mentioned that there was something of interest at the dig to Angela.

In mid-March, Brian had spun back again to Yu with the cryptic question

> Which version of Yu's world is correct? Do we follow what is written in the Tribute of Yu document, which describes the Nine Provinces and Nine Tributes, paving the way for the first tithing system on earth?

Xiao Da had talked about Nine Tributes. Was Brian beginning to question the All-Patriotic Society's policies?

> On the other hand, what are we to make of Yu's map of his domains? Yu ordered two officials to pace off the world from east to west and from north to south. They determined that the

world was perfectly square. Leave it to a mathematician like Yu to come up with a scheme like that!

Next to this was a full-page drawing showing Yu's world with several squares lined up concentrically, each with its own designation. It was a crude version of the symbol David had seen on the top of the building near the Bank of China tower earlier tonight. How did it relate to any of this? Brian continued:

Did Yu mean for the map to be taken literally or as a figurative map of politics and culture? Xiao Da has used it for commercial purposes, but I'm not so sure he understands its true significance. If he does, then he's more dangerous than I thought. More research required.

But by April, Brian had arrived at a conclusion that had nothing to do with Xiao Da.

The pictographic nature of the Chinese language encourages the idea of mapping not only in the practical sense of creating a visual record of the domain but also within the language itself. Characters are not just words in the traditional sense; they are also geographic clues. E-mail Dr. Strong about this. It's in the characters. I know it now!

After bouncing from one interest to another—from Lily to Catherine, from Xiao Da to the vultures, from archaeology to literature—Brian had finally found his intellectual passion. He zeroed in on Yu, his map, and early Chinese language. According to the journal, Brian peppered Strong with e-mails, made charts of early characters found on dragon bones and how those characters had evolved into present-day Chinese, narrowing himself to those that were pictographic rather than phonetic in composition. The archaic character for *below* was a line with a dot below it, *rain* came down as drops falling from the sky, *door* was comparable to the swinging doors in a western saloon. Here was the character for *mountain* (three linked peaks), *field* (four cultivated squares), *cave* (a rounded portal with two boulders hanging in the corners), and *river* (the three squiggly lines David had seen branded into Lily's forehead). Just as David had once been interested in the layering of written Chinese—how two *trees* created the word for "forest"—Brian expanded on certain ancient characters and their meanings. A *river* with a line drawn through it became *misfortune* or *calamity*—both caused by flooding—while a heart beneath a window illustrated the concept of *alarm* or *agitation*—to know with a tremulous heart what was coming.

At the end of May, Brian received news that he'd been awarded a second Miller Fellowship, which would allow him to stay longer at Site 518 and flesh out his myriad ideas. He revisited his initial Miller proposal, added what he'd learned since he'd submitted it, and composed a draft of what he hoped would become his dissertation topic.

> Legend has it that China's Three Gorges were created by a folk hero named Da Yu, who—with the help of dragons—configured China's hills and valleys to drain the land and make it habitable for humans. Dragon bones are the mythical bones of dragons, which are said to have magical powers—the ability to give superhuman strength, the ability to heal, the ability to triumph over adversity, and the ability to lead. But dragon bones were actually oracle bones, which form the earliest recorded Chinese written language. However, the time has come for us to consider that there may be earlier "dragon bones" to be found in nature and that these—and not oracle bones—are the true source of Chinese characters. In these natural dragon bones we will find a skeletal structure, which gives the country its myths, political realities, and even its codes of behavior and emotional resonance. These "bones" (and *longmai*—veins) weave together a geography that holds China in an embrace of meaning, linking the plains and mountains of the physical world with the emotions, thoughts, and culture of the humans who reside upon it.

Brian arrived back in Bashan on June 20. He made no mention of who was at the site other than Dr. Strong, with whom he shared his theories and discoveries. Unfortunately, Strong's mind had slipped even further, and he was of little help. Brian wrote nothing more on his camping trips, what was being unearthed at the dig, or even the All-Patriotic Society. However, he did encounter Lily, and she was most adamant that he bring her new artifacts. He refused.

Then, on June 30, he scribbled:

Our joke on Lily has ended tragically. How much could she have paid Wu Huadong to dive in the whirlpool? Of course she denies any responsibility. In fact, she blames me. If I had brought her new artifacts from my "treasure trove," as she now calls it, this never would have happened. How can she not take responsibility and blame me at the same time? I'll visit the Wus tomorrow and see if there's anything I can do.

The next day he wrote:

Have now learned the truth. Only one way to salvage what I've done. Making one more trip to the cave. Imperative that Xiao Da never know what I've found. Must send photos to Angela in case it's too late. I've been very stupid.

During the last eighteen days of his life, Brian eschewed words, preferring to sketch local landmarks, paralleling them with their ancient Chinese characters: The meandering of the river next to the symbol for *river*, the doors of country houses and how they related to the character for *door*. He'd done the same with the characters for *cliff* and *cave*. On one page he'd attempted unsuccessfully to draw the face of a child but then had scratched it out. Next to it he'd written the character for *good*, which was composed of the pictograms for *mother* and *child*.

The more David looked at these drawings, the more they appeared to be maps, because in one he recognized the perimeter of Site 518, with the various pits where artifacts had been found. Another showed the river, Bashan, the dig, and the Wu house with archaic characters dotted here and there. In the middle of these pages, one sheet had been torn out. Finally, and most important, Brian had become very tense and fearful, which was made even clearer by his final, sad entry written two days before his disappearance.

July 17—Don't know what to do. I can't tell what I know and I can't do the right thing either without putting other people's lives in danger. I hope Angela understands what I sent her. Angela, if you read this and you haven't figured it out yet, look at the photos. Really look! I love you and I'm sorry.

Instead of signing his name, he'd carefully drawn the characters of a window above a trembling heart. He'd seen what was coming, but as the characters suggested, he'd been powerless to stop it.

David closed the journal. Brian and Lily had died because of the *ruyi*. Bill Tang—who had been sent to Hong Kong to buy it—had nearly killed David. Whoever had the artifact now was a target.

David jumped up, fought a wave of dizziness and nausea, then rushed into the bathroom. He pulled his sodden clothes out of the hamper and riffled through them until he found Stuart Miller's card.

DAVID RAN OUT THE BACK DOOR OF THE HOTEL AND JOGGED
through the storm, away from the harbor and the business district
toward Victoria Peak. He saw no cars or taxis plying the streets. A
few minutes later, he'd gone past the entrances to the Peak Tram,
the YMCA, and the Botanical Gardens. The area became increasingly residential, with great apartment towers all around him. The
climb was steep, and his lungs burned with the effort of running up-
hill. The wound on his head throbbed, and his side hurt almost as
much as when Tang had kicked him. David ran every day but not
with this kind of pain. He stopped for a moment, put his hands on
his knees, and tried to regain his breath. Then he pushed off his
back leg and continued on.

Land was at a premium in Hong Kong, and few homes remained
within sight of the main harbor. David began to pass some of them
and knew he was getting close. He turned onto another street and
trotted another few hundred yards to Stuart Miller's property. The
electric gates were open, but all of the windows were shuttered
against the storm. David bounded up the front steps, looked around,
then as quietly as possible tried the doorknob. It turned. David hesitated. He could be wrong about all this. If he was, he'd be breaking
into Stuart's house. If he wasn't and he opened the door, the sound
of the storm might alert whoever was inside.

David entered the house and closed the door behind him. Dr. Ma was sprawled in the middle of the foyer. A bullet had obliterated half his face, and blood had pooled around him on the marble floor. His one eye was open and unseeing. David edged around the body and peered into the living room. The lights were on, but the room was empty. The walls had been painted in muted earth tones, and the furniture blended into the sepulchral gloom. Museum-quality lighting focused attention solely on the art that lined the walls and perched on risers in the living room. Even to David's untrained eye, the value of the art was incalculable. He readily spotted works from the Ming, Han, and Tang Dynasties. Having spent some time with the Cosgrove's catalog, he also recognized bronze pieces from the Shang Dynasty, some of which had to be nearly four thousand years old.

He systematically filtered out the sounds of the storm—the rattling of the shutters, tree branches hitting the sides of the house, the shrieking wind—until he heard voices upstairs. As stealthily as possible he climbed the stairs. A long hallway extended in front of him. To his left was a series of open doorways; to his right, more risers with archaic bronzes and carved pieces of jade. He moved down the hall, stopping before each open door to listen before crossing in front of the opening. He got to the end of the hall and one last open door. He recognized the voices of Stuart Miller and Bill Tang. David edged around the doorjamb. Stuart was tied to a chair. His face was puffy and bruised. Blood ringed his lips and dribbled down his chin. Tang had his back to the door. Another door on the far right of the room was open, but David couldn't see what was inside. He pulled back and glanced around for a weapon. The heaviest thing he could see was a tableau carved in jade. He reached for it and hefted it in his hands. It weighed a few pounds. The tableau was rounded, but the bottom had an abruptly sharp edge. David shifted the piece in his hands. He took a deep breath, rushed into the room, and brought the tableau down on Tang's head. The lieutenant crumpled to the floor, and David dropped the jade.

"Untie me, dammit, before he wakes up." Stuart struggled vainly against the rope.

David untied Stuart, and together they used the rope to bind Tang's feet and hands. The lieutenant didn't budge. David felt for a pulse. Tang was alive, just out cold.

Now that he was out of danger, Stuart collapsed into a chair. His face was pale, and his body shook. David grabbed a blanket off the bed and wrapped it around Stuart's shoulders. Next he found the phone and called the police to report Ma's murder. He was asked if anyone was in immediate jeopardy and answered that he didn't think so. Then the police operator informed him that it might take a while before someone got there. The department was spread thin, dealing with the effects of the typhoon. Someone would come as soon as possible, but the police had an obligation during this disaster to attend to the living first.

David crossed back to Stuart and sank to his haunches. "I take it you didn't give Tang the *ruyi*."

"I wasn't about to give it to that little shit," Stuart said, still staring at the floor.

"He would have killed you."

Stuart lifted his eyes. He looked terrible. The last thing David needed was for Stuart to keel over with a heart attack.

"What happened?"

Stuart began speaking in a monotone. He and Madame Wang had stayed at the banquet until one in the morning. He'd seen Madame Wang to her penthouse, stayed for a nightcap, and left her about three. He drove home and had just put the *ruyi* in the vault when he heard someone knock on the door. He thought a neighbor might be having problems with the storm, but when he unlocked the door Tang accosted him, demanding the *ruyi*.

"I told him I didn't have it, and things went downhill from there." A bit of Stuart's normal jauntiness came back, and he attempted a smile. "I bet I don't look as bad as you do, though." But this was no time for false bravado and Stuart knew it. "You saw Ma?"

When David nodded, Stuart went on. "He must have followed Tang." He shook his head as if to correct himself. "What I mean is, Tang started in on me, and Ma arrived soon after that. He must have come in . . ." He faltered. "I don't know exactly . . ."

"I want you to listen, Stuart. You need to give me the *ruyi*."

"If I didn't give it to Tang—and believe me, he tried to make me—why would I give it to you?"

"Several reasons. First, you need to get rid of the *ruyi* before someone kills you for it." When Stuart didn't seem to buy this, David added, "You've got to realize that someone like Bill Tang doesn't operate alone."

David didn't add that Dr. Ma wasn't acting alone either. If the *ruyi* was what David thought it was, the Ministry of State Security would never give up, which was why he had to get it to Hulan, not Vice Minister Zai, not Director Ho, but his wife, the one person in the world he trusted. She would know where it would be safest and cause the least harm.

"Second," he went on, "even if you don't care about your own life, how would you feel if someone went after Catherine?"

"That wouldn't happen. Tang is just a thug—"

"A thug who tried to kill me and now you." David didn't wait for Stuart to respond. "Third, you *know* the *ruyi* belongs to China. In addition, I'm going to make you a hero. And finally, in giving me the *ruyi* you're going to become even richer than you already are."

"How's that?"

"You give me the *ruyi* before the police get here, then they don't need to know that you're in possession of a stolen artifact. I take the *ruyi* back to China and tell the government that you bought it at auction in order to return it to its homeland. Think of the gratitude. Think of the contracts you'll get—forever."

Stuart considered the logic. As a lawyer, David knew that Stuart really had only one option. Finally Stuart said, "A hero, huh?"

David nodded.

"Not bad for three million dollars." Stuart sounded nonchalant, but it had to have been a huge concession.

"Not bad at all," David agreed, "and it sure beats being tied up in litigation, or worse, ending up in a Chinese jail."

Stuart sighed long and hard. "All right." He stood shakily. "Come with me."

Bill Tang was still out and not going anywhere, so David followed Stuart to the open doorway on the other side of the room. It looked like a closet, but actually it was the antechamber to Stuart's vault. Tang had gotten much closer to his prize than Stuart had wanted to admit. He punched in an electronic code, and they stepped into a room lined floor to ceiling with drawers. He opened one of the drawers. Inside were four *ruyis*. They were horribly ugly and horribly beautiful at the same time—the way the fungus stems twisted, the way the heads unfurled. They were natural yet somehow seemed beyond nature in their otherworldliness. Stuart picked up the Site 518 *ruyi*, wrapped it in linen, and handed it to David.

"I hope you know what you're doing." It was the first time Stuart had acknowledged he might know more about the *ruyi* than its collectibility.

"What do you mean?" David asked, hoping Stuart could confirm what he suspected.

"This is China's Holy Grail. Have you thought about the power it has to unite, control, and rule?" Stuart asked. "I don't mean to be melodramatic, but have you considered what could happen if it fell into the wrong hands? The *ruyi* could be used symbolically to strengthen the Chinese military and in the process destabilize the current government. We, as Americans, may not like everything about the regime that's in power now, but at least we know what we're dealing with. So I hope you know what you're doing and who to trust, because this could change China's future."

"Is it really Da Yu's *ruyi*?" David asked point-blank. "Did Brian actually find Da Yu's scepter?"

"You never met him, but Brian was a brilliant kid," Stuart answered. "The fellowship proposal he sent this spring was amazing. It not only confirmed for me that he'd found a tomb or some other treasure chamber but that he'd made a discovery about Chinese culture through artifacts and language. Think about it, David. Think about how few artifacts there are in the world that have had an impact on how people view culture. The Rosetta stone provided the key to the decipherment of Egyptian hieroglyphics. The discovery of oracle bones did the same for Chinese language and history."

"But the *ruyi* doesn't have anything to do with language."

"That's right. I believe Brian made two separate discoveries. One was theoretical and would be of interest only to scholars; the other was something tangible and of far greater importance."

David tried to mesh what Stuart had said with what he now knew about Brian. The split between language and the *ruyi* as separate entities in Brian's journal entries backed up Stuart's hypothesis.

"So in answer to your question," Stuart went on, "yes, I believe Brian found proof of Yu the Great. But it's shocking that he gave it to Lily."

Drawing conclusions from what he'd read in Brian's journal, David tried to explain. "He didn't realize what it was at first. Once he did, I don't think he had any intention of giving it to Lily or anyone else. He needed money, sure, but he was an archaeologist first. Once he realized that there were people after it, he knew he had to get it out to a safe place at any cost. He must have been very frightened or else he wouldn't have told Lily what it was. He did tell her, right?"

"Yes, and he also told Catherine. What I don't understand is why."

"To save it. You were his last hope."

"To save it from Bill Tang?" Stuart sounded skeptical. "I'll admit that the guy's gone around the bend—"

"He's not who you think he is. He's a high-ranking member of the All-Patriotic Society. Brian wanted to keep the *ruyi* out of Xiao Da's hands."

Stuart snorted in disbelief. "You've got this all wrong. Tang's not some religious wacko. He's just a VYRUSCAN tech head. He's probably lost money in the stock market or . . . I don't know—" He visibly struggled to make sense out of what had just happened to him and what he knew of Tang. When nothing connected, he said in exasperation, "Tang's a computer nerd. Christ, you've met the guy he works for."

"What? Who?"

"Michael Quon. You had lunch with him at Site 518 the other day. Bill Tang's to Michael Quon what Paul Allen is to Bill Gates." Stuart's words caught David off guard, and all of a sudden he noticed how much his head hurt. He didn't want to hear this. "Michael Quon," Stuart repeated. "Don't you know who he is?" When David shook his head, Stuart said, "He's the inventor of VYRUSCAN. You know, the software? Squares within squares and all that."

"Do you mean five concentric squares?" When Stuart nodded, David grabbed him. "Show me!"

They went back through the bedroom, where Tang was awake now and wrestling futilely against his bindings, but David and Stuart just rushed past and hurried downstairs to the library. Stuart turned on his computer and said, "Look, this isn't a big deal. You probably have it on your computer even if you don't know it. Think Norton Utilities, only Quon doesn't have his photo on every product that goes out like Peter Norton does. Come on, David, you've heard of him. Quon's like Larry Ellison—"

"I wouldn't recognize Larry Ellison, or Peter Norton for that matter."

"You've been away from the States too long." It was another ill-advised attempt at humor. "Look," Stuart said, "you'll recognize this." He pointed to the lower right-hand corner of the screen. David had probably seen the symbol a thousand times but had never really noticed it. Just like Da Yu's map of his empire, the VYRUSCAN logo consisted of five concentric squares. The conclusion was horrifying in its implications.

"Michael Quon is Xiao Da," David said.

Stuart's eyes widened as he absorbed this, then whatever color had come back to his face in the last few minutes drained away again. "Catherine—"

"Hulan!"

Then David's mind froze. He couldn't think beyond the terrifying knowledge that Hulan was up in Bashan with Michael Quon. David had told her again and again not to worry about the All-Patriotic Society. She was in extreme danger and, because of his insistence that she abandon her investigation of the cult, she didn't know it.

"David!" Stuart's voice was sharp and commanding. "Here are my keys. Take my car. Do you have your passport? No? Then stop at your hotel and pick it up. Take my car to the airport. I'll call ahead for a plane reservation. David, are you listening to me?"

David nodded, but he barely comprehended what Stuart was saying.

"You've got to go before the police get here. I'll take care of things on this end."

Stuart shoved a huge wad of cash into David's pocket, then pushed him out of the library and toward the front door. The pain in David's ribs jolted him back into some semblance of awareness. They were in the foyer. Ma's body was still on the floor. David looked at the wrapped *ruyi* in his hand, then at Stuart.

"Just go," Stuart said.

David jumped into Stuart's Lexus, careened down the mountain, and skidded under the Mandarin's porte cochere. He ran through the lobby. The desk clerk called his name, but David didn't stop. He threw his things in his bags and was back in the lobby in five minutes to check out. There was no line. No one was going anywhere in this storm.

The desk clerk—a professional at one of the world's greatest hotels—took in the awfulness of David's face but spoke with deliberate calm. "I tried to get your attention before, Mr. Stark. I have a fax for you. It came in about an hour ago marked very urgent."

While the clerk printed out the bill, David opened the envelope. The first page was short but to the point:

Phones and electricity out in Sichuan due to flooding. No word from Hulan and can't reach her. Please give attached information to her if you get to her first. I am on my way to Bashan. Zai.

The next two sheets were in Chinese, but Zai had written short notes at the top of each page. The first was a toxicology report on Lily. The blood on her body was hers but showed traces of mycotoxins, which, Zai explained, derived from fungi. Traces of the same fungus had been found in her mouth. The fungus, however, was not poisonous and had not contributed to her death. Finally, in examining Lily's wounds more fully, Pathologist Fong had found slivers of some sort of stone. This was being analyzed for type and source.

At the top of the next page, Zai had written in his uneven hand:

Transcription of document found on McCarthy's body. These are ancient Chinese characters. Have sent document to Beijing University for translation.

But David already knew what the characters were. He'd read them in Brian's journal: *river, cliff, cave, dragon, below,* and *door.* Below *cave,* Brian had written the one character that made the whole map make sense. It was the ideogram for *good.* David now knew where Brian's secret cave was. He also understood with a kind of deep sadness that the young archaeologist was far smarter than even Stuart had given him credit for.

David folded the papers and put them in his breast pocket. The worst of his worry dissipated to be replaced by deadly focus.

HULAN WAS WRAPPED IN HER SILK ROBE WHEN SHE ANSWERED A soft knock at her door and found Michael Quon asking if she was going to the dining room. She thanked him for stopping by but said no.

"No breakfast?" he asked, stepping inside the room.

"Just tea," she answered.

Once he noticed how sheer her robe was and that she was wearing nothing underneath, his eyes darted around the room uneasily. "Your room's very neat," he said.

"Thank you, Dr. Quon."

"I guess I'll be going then." Then he backed out of the room, his eyes still not meeting hers. "Have a good day."

She closed the door and climbed back on the bed. She decided she wasn't even going to *think* about that encounter, because there was no secret to the fact that women were naked under their clothes all the time and men and women still managed to go on about their business.

Electricity and phone service had been restored during the night, but for how long Hulan had no idea. She got through on her first try to the Mandarin Oriental and learned that David had checked out, then the line went dead and evidently so did the electricity, because the overhead fan slowed and finally stopped. She thought about where David could have gone. Knowing he might not be able to get back to Bashan because of the weather, he'd probably taken an early flight to Beijing. If he'd retrieved the stolen artifacts, then he'd want to get them to Director Ho at the Cultural Relics Bureau as soon as possible. At least that's what she would have done if the situation were reversed.

She still needed to speak with Vice Minister Zai. She figured that Captain Hom was the only person in Bashan who might have access to a method of reaching the capital, but when she got to his office he didn't have any great ideas. He had a cell phone, but the mountainous walls that surrounded Bashan prevented it from working within the town's footprint. He sometimes drove up into the hills to reach a relatively unobstructed spot, but a landslide had closed the road last night and workmen were still trying to clear the mud and debris that kept seeping down the rain-saturated hillside.

"There's always a way to move around in the countryside," Hulan pointed out. "A back road, a special trail—"

"They're either under water or under mud."

"The river—"

"It rose another two meters last night. Even the fishermen are staying ashore."

She had no choice but to wait it out, he told her as he walked her to the door. "I can see you worry too much, Inspector," Hom said, exhaling twin streams of cigarette smoke from his nostrils.

"It's my nature," she admitted.

"Weren't you the one who told me to beware of my nature?"

He had her there.

"Well," Hom went on, "even I can change my ways. I thought about what you said the other day about the All-Patriotic Society. Tonight I will see for myself if what you say is true."

"Be careful," she cautioned. "They don't like the uninitiated."

"I was invited."

Hulan's eyebrows rose in surprise and question.

He nodded complacently. "My brother-in-law and I were invited to go together. I think it's a good opportunity for Zhou to explain what he did to the people."

"Self-criticism? We both know that didn't have good results during the Cultural Revolution. We both know a crowd can turn dangerous very quickly."

He grinned, showing his yellowed teeth. "I don't think we have to worry about that. We were invited by Officer Su, your favorite. He sees an opportunity to make things better in Bashan Village. I'm putting a note of this in his *dangan*."

"He is a Society member?"

"Maybe," Hom answered, his throat rattling with nicotine, "and maybe he's serving as a bridge between our office, Bashan's problems, and the people."

If this were so, then Su had made another smart move. It was through the recommendations of superiors or through political activities that helped maintain the status quo that junior officers earned promotions. Although the All-Patriotic Society was illegal, the purpose for which Hom and his brother-in-law had been invited sounded as though the outcome could lead to restored tranquillity among the masses.

"This invitation shows an open heart," Hom remarked. "Do you want to join us? It would make Officer Su happy."

She shook her head. She walked down two steps, then turned back to Hom. "I still don't think you should go."

"My subordinate invited me, Inspector."

Old customs regarding manners reached deeply, even in the Public Security Bureau. Of course he would go. She waved again and continued down the stairs. She went back to the hotel and asked the desk clerk to find a driver to take her to Site 518.

While in town the dock's concrete steps, which disappeared each day under the Yangzi's swelling volume, seemed the focus, at Site 518 the water itself held center stage. The quiet banks were no longer a cradle against which the river eased on its incessant course to the sea. The current had picked up more earth in its travels, turning the waters murkier and more foreboding as they frothed, billowed, chopped, and lurched. The canyon resounded with the roar of gravel and boulders rolling against the riverbed, of trees grating and shredding, of waves smashing against shoals, rocky shoulders, and massive abutments. Hulan knew that up in the hills peasants still worked the terraces, clearing waterways and opening irrigation channels. Here the archaeologists toiled in pits barely protected from the wind and rain under leaky and quivering tarps.

Hulan walked to the cave shared by the five men from the municipal museums. They were awake but barely. Four of them sat together around their little table, wearing grubby undershirts, smoking Magnificent Sound cigarettes, and drinking tea. The fifth hovered over a hotplate stirring *congee*.

"You look like you just washed down from the Tibetan Plateau," Li Guo, the one she recognized as the most talkative, called out. "Come in out of the rain. We'll give you warmth."

The other men thought this mildly risqué comment hilarious. Hulan gave them a look that should have shriveled their balls to the size of peanuts, but the men were unrepentant.

"Are you looking for your husband? We don't have him in here this time, right, Mr. Hu?"

The man stirring the *congee* made a great play of scanning the dark recesses of the cave. "No *yang guizi* here."

The five chortled, coughed, choked on their tea, spat on the ground. They thought it was all very funny; she thought that in this one regard Ma had been right. These men were vultures.

"Do you know when Dr. Ma will return from Hong Kong?" she inquired as pleasantly as possible.

"No time soon," Li answered. "He said he went to buy back what Brian and Lily stole, but he's probably down on Hollywood Road right now selling precious antiquities that should go to our museums. He calls us vultures. We say he is a shark!"

Hulan left them clucking at the loudmouth's wickedness. She was unsure of what to do next. She wandered down the hill to the pit where Catherine Miller and Annabel Quinby labored. Hulan spent the next three hours scraping at the ground and making small talk as the rain cascaded down around them.

She did as instructed but kept most of her attention on the way

Catherine and Annabel interacted. Annabel was more senior, but when Catherine uncovered a shard of pottery, their conversation seemed to be between equals. The piece turned out to be just a couple of centimeters in diameter, but the ancient artist's design could still be read. Catherine told Hulan that these designs were one of the things that archaeologists and linguists looked for when trying to make the link between artistic patterns and the pictographs that composed the earliest archaic characters of what eventually became the Chinese written language.

This conversation reminded Hulan of something Stuart had said out at the dam site, and she brought it up now. "Your father told me that Brian found some pieces here with motifs that were different from those typically used by the Ba," Hulan said. "What did he mean by that?"

"The Ba had very distinctive works of art," Catherine explained. "They made weapons and common articles like pitchers and bowls that suggest a highly developed artistic, though warlike, culture. The Ba's axes were of particular interest to Brian. They were made from jade or bronze, but they were similar in shape and style to the musical chimes found at Yellow River sites. This made Brian think that the Ba hadn't developed their ax organically. He thought the shape had been transported—and its original use changed—from a musical instrument of the Yellow River peoples to a weapon."

Annabel, who'd been listening to the exchange, looked up and added, "But how did that transformation happen, Inspector? Even today, at the beginning of the twenty-first century, we're secluded within this gorge. So how did the Ba come to interact with the other more established cultures on the Yellow River? Why did the Ba need to be so warlike, and how did their artistry develop?"

"Your Four Mysteries," Hulan said. As on her first day here, Hulan had picked up something sticky on her hands. It had to be some property in the soil. She thrust her hands out into the rain, rinsed them off, and wiped them on her pants.

"Two of them anyway," Annabel responded. "Mystery One: How did the Three Gorges, which actually insulate through their geography, become a cultural watershed? And Mystery Three: What caused certain artistic styles to take hold here and continue for millennia? Brian was profoundly interested in those questions, which is why it's all the more distressing that he chose to take artifacts from the site rather than let us study them in context."

"What context, Annabel?" Catherine asked. "You know Brian's pieces didn't come from here."

"You're right as always, my dear," the older woman admitted.

Hulan was thoroughly confused. "I thought you said that the ax Brian found *was* a Ba artifact."

The two women looked at her as though she were an imbecile.

"Absolutely not! It looked like a Yellow River chime," Catherine explained.

"The jade *bis* weren't Ba artifacts either," Annabel added. "The Ba didn't have an emperor in residence who would have needed to commune with Heaven."

"Most important," Catherine picked up, "this is a subsurface site. Now consider the *ruyi*. How long do you think a dried mushroom would last under the soil before it deteriorated?"

Lunch under the large canopy—which had been moved yet again up the hillside—came as a reprieve. The meal was much the same as on the first day—rice, noodles, and a chicken dish. The conversation also bore a striking resemblance to the one Hulan and David had heard that day. As she had back then, Hulan tried to listen for anything that would help her solve the murders of Brian and Lily. But she didn't see what that could be as the five vultures babbled on to Michael Quon about the patriotic benefits of the dam, a sentiment Catherine tried to shoot down by pointing out that the Chinese already had the Great Wall. Despite his obvious glee at being addressed by the beautiful foreigner, Li Guo felt compelled to correct her: "The Great Wall has always been a bad symbol. Since the days of the evil Qinshihuangdi, it has been a concrete example of our foreign policy—keep outsiders out."

Dr. Quinby agreed, adding, "It has also symbolized China's inability to compromise, its isolation from the outside world, and its assertion of superiority."

"But, Annabel, you can't believe that the dam is a good replacement." This came from old Dr. Strong.

"Ancient China has been my vocation and my avocation," she admitted, "but I would willingly sacrifice a few relics to change world perceptions."

The other archaeologists nearly fell off their benches. "You can't mean it, Doctor," the professor from Heidelberg blustered, reeling from the betrayal of her words.

"I expect more from *you*, Professor Schmidt!" Annabel retorted. "Your treatise on the symbolism of the Great Wall is still the academic standard."

Zai had sent Hulan here in part for her ability to see through political code, and she felt something trying to come together in her mind, but her speculations were disturbed when she sensed Li Guo's dark eyes boring into her. "For the future," he said, "we will have the dam to remind us of the Confucian ideal of a sage emperor who serves the people."

Yes, that helped. She almost had it . . .

"You forget one thing." It was the first time Michael had spoken, and it completely disrupted Hulan's train of thought. "The dam, too, is a false symbol. You mustn't be deceived into thinking that your government isn't using it for its own corrupt ends. You block the river, you destroy your history and your heritage."

"You're a foreigner," the vulture said to the Chinese American. "You don't know our country."

Michael held up his hands in the universal sign of surrender. "I'm only saying that an edifice can't represent a country's soul."

"Matters of soul are a privilege, Dr. Quon," Li Guo retorted, but his eyes still hadn't left Hulan's. "China needs to think about global identity. Brian understood this."

Catherine brought them all back to safer territory by asking if anyone had been able to phone out, which led to a discussion of the weather and how it would affect their work, which led to the Four

Mysteries, which led back to the dam, which would eventually circle back to a discussion of nationalism. No wonder Brian had taken to eating his lunch elsewhere.

As the group slowly broke up and the teams returned to their pits, Hulan decided to retrace Brian's final movements one more time. Just as she reached the upper path, she spotted Angela, protected by a plastic poncho, kneeling in the mud near a cluster of dead bushes with her backpack at her side.

Angela looked up, and Hulan saw something in the young American's face she hadn't seen before. Suspicion or caution, Hulan couldn't tell which. But before either of them could speak, Michael Quon's voice came floating over Hulan's left shoulder. "She's looking for mushrooms," he said. "She's been doing that since she got here. Find anything interesting?"

"These are golden mushrooms," Angela answered, her voice oddly flat. "They popped up last night."

"Are you going to give them to the chef tonight?" Michael inquired lightly. "Maybe he could sauté them with butter and garlic."

"These aren't for eating."

"Poisonous, then?"

Angela didn't bother to respond.

"Aren't mushrooms usually found in shady areas?" Hulan asked.

"This once was a shady area," Angela answered, then gestured to the skeletal remains of the nearby bushes. "Something killed the trees and this shrubbery."

"Too bad those mushrooms aren't *lingzhi*," Michael went on. "You would have struck gold."

Angela's face reddened. To cover the emotion, she bent her head back down to stare at the little cluster that had surfaced near the trunk of one of the dead bushes. When she didn't look up again, Michael looked at Hulan and shrugged.

Hulan headed east along the path. Michael followed, although she hadn't invited him. In fact, she'd wanted time alone to think about what Li Guo had said. She was sure he'd been trying to send her a message. But Michael didn't ask permission to accompany her, and she didn't send him away. As he'd shown yesterday, he wasn't a bad companion. His stride was steady and surefooted. He kept quiet even when they passed the little shack that belonged to the Wu family. The door was closed, but they could hear the baby crying inside.

They crossed over the trail that led down to the cave where the All-Patriotic Society held its meetings. A short way beyond this was another path. Hulan had already explored the main route to Brian's refuge with David and Dr. Ma the other day, so she dipped down onto this new path, hoping it might give her a different perspective. Soon enough she could see the cove where Brian's things had been found, though she wondered how much of the beach would be left there given the rising waters. Still, she wanted a closer look and edged down farther.

Michael was right behind her when she heard the Wu infant's cries again. They sounded as though they came from below her, which meant that there had to be some kind of acoustical anomaly caused by the cliffs around them. She went down another five vertical meters and came to the entrance to a cave. The baby's cries seemed to emanate from deep within. Hulan ducked inside, pulling her umbrella shut.

"Do you hear that?" she asked.

Michael nodded. "The mother must have taken the baby out, then gone into some other part of the cave." He listened, then added, "I can remember my mom and dad piling us in the back of the car when my little brother wouldn't sleep. This woman doesn't have a car. Maybe walking the kid helps."

Hulan took a couple of steps farther into the cave and called hello. The sound disappeared into the blackness. The baby continued to cry.

Michael reached into his knapsack and pulled out a flashlight. "I've been in here before. Want to take a look?"

To know the killer you had to know the victim, and Brian had spent his lunches and his weekends exploring caves.

"I'll follow you," she said.

They hadn't gone far before the temperature began to drop. The umbrella had kept Hulan's top half relatively dry, but her legs and feet were wet, so she chilled quickly. Otherwise, this cave was much like the one that she and David had been in the other night, except that there seemed to be many more side tunnels that led in different directions. Hulan and Michael went another fifteen meters past several turns and bends until they reached a room about four by four meters.

"Here's where you have some choices," he said. "This shaft used to let out down by the river." He pointed the flashlight into a narrow opening that looked more like a well than a tunnel. "But now that the river's risen, it's running through the lower caverns. Hear it?"

She could. That passage could very well have led to the cave where she and David had talked with Ma on that first day. Now that she heard the water, she focused more clearly on the smell, which was not so much the muskiness of damp soil but something deeper and more primitive, as though the cave were alive.

"Caves *are* alive," Michael explained, "and filled with organisms similar to those found on the ocean floor." He swung the flashlight's beam to another area. "This shaft also goes down, but it narrows into a crawl space very quickly. We'd need some other gear to go that way—headlamps, jeans, and maybe kneepads for you." He arced the beam to the back of the room. "Or we can continue on. There are other caverns to explore, none of which are that difficult. There's a hollow ahead with some spectacular formations."

By now Hulan was very cold, and she was feeling the weight of the mountain all around her. The baby's cries still echoed through the cave, and she wondered why his mother hadn't done something to sooth him.

"Did you come here with Brian?" she asked. Her voice reverberated off the walls, and she felt increasingly claustrophobic.

"Once. But Brian preferred to cave alone."

"I would have thought you'd follow the buddy system, just like swimming."

"I do when it's really challenging, but Brian and I didn't consider this cave to be all that rigorous." He scrutinized her, read her discomfort, then said, "I think we should go."

He took a step toward her, and she watched in horrified fascination as he purposely stumbled on a rock and let the flashlight fall from his hand. The flashlight clattered to the floor of the cave and went dead, thrusting them into pitch black.

Hulan stood completely still, waiting for her eyes to adjust. They didn't. There was nothing to adjust to. Cold fear held her in place. Was Michael Quon the killer? If he was, then she had foolishly walked into his trap. She heard nothing. After all the crying, the baby finally went quiet. Hulan held her breath, listening. She could hear Michael breathing nearby.

"Don't move," he ordered. There was absolutely nothing threatening in his tone.

She heard his shoe edge out across the floor. She felt his hand on her arm. He pulled her to him and wrapped his arms around her.

"Don't be frightened," he whispered in her ear. His heart beat steadily against her fluttering one. Her body felt how gentle he was, and her heart began to slow to match his rhythm.

"I'm going to look for the flashlight," he told her. "Stay still." Then, using her body as a guide, he ran his hands down her waist, over her hips, and down her legs. He kept one hand in a proprietary grip around her ankle while he searched the ground with his other hand. A second later the flashlight was back on. He took Hulan's hand and led her out to the cave entrance.

They stood at the mouth of the cave looking down on the roiling river. At last Michael turned to face her. "I'm sorry. That was a boyish and stupid maneuver to get us alone together in the dark. I shouldn't have done that." Then he dropped her hand, stepped out into the rain, and with an assured gait headed up the hill back toward the Site 518 encampment.

She waited a few more minutes, trying to understand her feelings, then she followed the path down to where it disappeared into the rushing current. Brian's little beach had to be three meters or more below the raging waters.

26

THE WEATHER HAD CALMED TEMPORARILY, BUT THAT WAS TO BE expected. The storm would circle back again at least once before blowing itself out. But even with the break, the airport was nearly deserted. No one wanted to fly in this weather. David went to China Southern's ticket counter and checked in for the 11:50 flight to Wuhan. He hadn't eaten in about twenty-four hours, so he got some breakfast while he waited for his departure. A television was tuned to the news, where every fifteen minutes the scroll across the bottom of the screen reported that massive flooding along the Yangzi below the Three Gorges had now claimed twelve hundred lives. At 11:30 he boarded the plane; it taxied out to the runway, and then everyone waited as thunder rumbled and lightning streaked around them. Three hours later, in another momentary calm, the plane took off. Even after reaching cruising altitude, the seat belt sign remained on because of violent turbulence.

David couldn't stop thinking about Michael Quon. He was sophisticated. He'd figured out how to propel his cause through money and charisma. He was masquerading as a religious leader, but he had a rotten and corrupt core. He advocated austerity yet partook of the finer things in life. He was also probably very good with women, if for no other reason than that success and money are great aphrodisiacs. He'd used the Society's tenets as a means to gather a group to him, with the understanding that religion is more powerful than politics. That was why Communism was failing, while groups like the Falun Gong and the All-Patriotic Society were growing.

Xiao Da was all about manipulation and control. He believed himself to be the wind; the inferior people were the grass. He got away with that in China, where the people were, as Hulan said, susceptible to indoctrination. Xiao Da mirrored what others wanted to see. For poor Chinese peasants on the banks of the Yangzi, he was a savior who would protect them from the dam. To someone like Neighborhood Committee Director Zhang, he was a way of catching the newest fad. For someone like Brian McCarthy, he was a way of honoring the past.

David wondered if possession of a mushroom could be enough for the man who called himself Xiao Da to wrest the wind from the current Chinese government. It might be if he had a religious hold on the masses. Beyond that, could a foreign-born person be influential enough within another country to upset global stability? Stranger things had happened in other parts of the world.

This line of reasoning led David back to Vice Minister Zai. How much of this did the old bachelor know? He had made a strong and believable case for David and Hulan's trip to Bashan as a possible last chance for their marriage. At the time, David had been embarrassed but also grateful. But Zai had said other things that day, about David and Hulan reconnecting to the special gifts they each had that made them able to see beyond the petty cases they'd both been working on in recent years. For David, that would mean larger, more sophisticated, global matters; for Hulan, the rekindling of her ability to see into the mind of a killer. Zai had also talked about David's method of using logic to deal with cases, while Hulan put her physical body between herself and evil. Was that why Zai was on his way to Bashan now? Had he truly sent the two of them into danger without telling them what they were about to encounter? Or did he know that something had already happened to Hulan?

All this "logic" was just a way for David to manage his feelings. He couldn't lose Hulan. He couldn't face the world without her.

That night electricity was out in Bashan Village. Candles and a couple of hurricane lamps illuminated the Panda Guesthouse's dining room in a warm glow. The chef managed to put together one of his better meals. Beer was on the house. A sense of camaraderie reigned. There is nothing like a natural disaster to bring people together.

Given the conditions, talk turned once again to the great edifice being built at Sandouping. Without the five men from the municipal museums, the conversation was measured. What if the dam was built to a height of only 150 feet? What if a series of smaller dams was constructed instead? What if China allotted twenty more years for archaeological excavation? What if only half a million people had to move?

Hulan sat next to Michael Quon. He'd come by her room to escort her to the dining room. This time she hadn't objected. How could she, since she was going there anyway? But he'd stood just inside her door as he had this morning, waiting as she finished getting ready, looking around with that same measured appraisal that he used to take in everything. They didn't speak then about what had happened earlier, but as the rain poured down and the candles cast their golden light, Hulan kept going back to that moment when she'd been swallowed by the blackness of the cave.

What if when Michael dropped the flashlight he'd tried to kill her? Hulan would have attempted to fight him—in the pitch-black without a weapon. But even if she'd somehow triumphed, what would she have done then? She would have tried crawling out. She might have fallen down through one of the shafts that led to the river, drowning in the dark. She might have chosen the wrong route and could still have been flailing in the tenebrous gloom even now. No one would have known where she was, and when the lake behind the dam flooded those caverns sometime in the next few years, her bones would have been lost forever, like so much else along the river. But what she couldn't shake from her mind now was that moment of surrender when Michael Quon had held her in his arms and she'd let her heartbeat follow his.

From the international terminal on the outskirts of Wuhan, David grabbed a taxi to drive to the airport for small local flights. The term "buckets of rain" came to him as the taxi inched down the highway. Here the weather was not so much a storm—with winds and lightning—as one huge waterfall cascading from the sky. More than once the taxi floated several yards before the tires found asphalt again. The first bridge they came to was completely submerged. When the driver said he could go no farther, David reached into his pocket and pulled out the money Stuart had given him. He counted out five hundred dollars U.S. and promised the driver more if he would do whatever he had to do to get David to the local airport. The driver made a U-turn and sought out a different—and ultimately successful—route.

The local airport was as different as could be from Wuhan's international airport. David saw no radar and no landing lights flanking what passed for the runway, which sat in the middle of a flooded meadow. The terminal, an old Quonset hut, was packed with stranded passengers, and it had the smell of sweat, home-cooked food beginning to go bad, and stale cigarette smoke. David was the only foreigner.

He went to the desk of a company that gave helicopter tours of the Three Gorges, but the people shook their heads and said flying would be impossible today. He next tried the companies that flew small planes locally. There had to be an airstrip somewhere near Bashan. If he could fly there, he'd get to Bashan, even if he had to go on foot. But the people who sat behind the counters looked at him—with his bruises, the huge lump on his head, his Little Mermaid Band-Aids, and his wild insistence—as though he were insane.

The airport didn't have a bar, but it did have a little stand that passed for a café. David quickly struck up a conversation with a couple of men who flew planes to Yichang near the dam site. They introduced him to a helicopter pilot. None of them wanted to fly. They all said it was crazy. But his cash offer, worth more than two years' salary, was enough for the helicopter pilot. David knew the trip would be bad, however, when the pilot left the money with his friends—just in case.

They left Wuhan at eight. David held the wrapped *ruyi* on his lap. It would take almost two hours to reach Bashan.

After dinner, Hulan went to her room and locked the door. She decided to go through all of the material she'd gathered again. She lit a couple of candles and began to read. David always said that her greatest strength as an investigator lay in the intuitive leaps she made. She thought, however, that her strongest attribute came from what she knew about people—that they nearly always acted out of greed and that they told only one-third of the truth. She always took steps back from a crime scene, but this time she did it differently, by looking only at what people had wanted and what they'd lied about.

She started with Vice Minister Zai. She loved him more than her own father, but she also knew that he didn't always tell her the truth. She didn't believe that the death of a foreigner or the theft of artifacts would matter to the Ministry of Public Security or to the men across the lake. She'd been sent here for a political reason. She'd wondered from the beginning if it had to do with the All-Patriotic Society and, later, a possible threat against the Three Gorges Dam. She'd followed those theories all the way to the dam, but having seen the security measures there and heard Stuart's reasoned explanation of the redundant safety systems, she didn't think that the MPS's interest had to do with the Society, terrorism, or sabotage. Yet Annabel Quinby had been right today when she talked about how the dam presented China's national face. And Hulan was sure that Li Guo, the vulture, was trying to tell her something. His *dangan* said he was a low-level functionary, but he spoke in riddles about the power of symbols for the country. He also said that Brian understood their importance. Why couldn't she?

She thought of David's legal style and focused her mind into a sharp beam. Director Ho: A musty old man dealing with forces beyond his control. Dr. Ma: Spy, probably at the core of this. That he still hadn't returned from Hong Kong was now of great concern. But had he lied? His arrogance suggested he hadn't. Greedy? Yes, but for what? He'd had plenty of opportunity to steal from the site, and one could say it would even have been expected of him, but if Zai had sent Hulan to deal with Ma in some way, she'd failed miserably. Hom: His lies had actually shown him to be honest and honorable. Hom's officers: Not worth considering.

Now to the people on the site. Stuart Miller: His lies had to do with buying stolen artifacts, not murder. Catherine Miller: Stuck in a body that didn't match her brain. Only she had pointed out the most obvious and salient point about the *ruyi*. It couldn't have come from the soil of Site 518. Annabel Quinby, Schmidt, and Strong were useful to Hulan only for what they'd said about Brian and Lily.

Angela McCarthy had lied about how and when she got here. She'd also lied about her brother's website and what those photographs meant, because they'd been strong enough to lure her here even though she didn't have much money. And there was the question of Brian's journal. Captain Hom said he'd turned it over to Angela, who vehemently denied it, but that didn't mean she didn't have it. Hulan would ask Angela again about the journal and other things in a moment, but first she wanted to sort through her thoughts about Lily Sinclair one last time.

Lily had been a natural liar. This ability was central to her character, her successes and her failings. She certainly had lied on the night of her death. Her story about the Panda Guesthouse and the Wang family had been amusing though there'd been very little truth to it. Later she'd lied to David and Hulan when she said she was going to bed, because Catherine had walked with Lily to the outskirts of town. What had Lily done in those hours that she was still in the hotel? What had inspired her to leave town so late at night? And how had her body been brought back without anyone seeing it? Her killers hadn't come through the front door, and no one could have gotten past the old caretaker and her back gate. Only one person had mentioned anything out of the ordinary. Hulan flipped back through her notes to her interview with Dr. Strong, whose room was directly opposite Lily's. He said he'd heard noises in the courtyard.

That easily Hulan understood everything. She jumped up, got

her Luger out of its hiding place, then ran down the hall to Angela's room. Hulan pounded on the door with her fist. Angela opened the door a crack, and Hulan pushed her way in.

"I need your brother's flashlight and some other gear," she said in a rush. She looked around, grabbed Angela's backpack, and dumped the contents on the bed.

"My specimens!" Angela cried.

Hulan ignored the outburst and hurriedly sorted through Brian's things, which still lay in a messy pile under the window. As she stuffed gear into the backpack, she asked, "Where's your brother's journal?" When Angela didn't answer, Hulan dropped the bag, turned, and pushed the girl up against the wall. "More people are going to die unless you tell me right now about your brother's journal!"

"I gave it to Lily."

"On the night she died?"

Angela bent her head and nodded.

That meant David had it with Lily's other papers! Hulan shoved Angela toward the door. "Go to the front desk. Tell the night clerk to run to the Public Security Bureau. He has to tell Captain Hom not to go to the All-Patriotic Society meeting tonight."

Angela stared at her dumbly. Hulan shook the American's arm roughly. "Do you understand?" Angela nodded. "Go!" Hulan pushed Angela toward the lobby, knowing in her gut that the errand would be fruitless. Hom was probably in the cave by now. But Hulan had to prevent his death if she could.

She ran through the corridors back to the third courtyard, with the rooms for Lily and Dr. Strong. When she reached it, she left the colonnade and stepped out into the central courtyard and thrashing rain. A clap of lightning lit the sky for a moment as though it were midday, then it darkened again. She scurried to the scholar's rocks in the middle of the courtyard and circled them twice, looking for an entrance. She circled again, focusing on the ground this time, hoping there might be a trapdoor of some sort. Nothing. She took a couple of steps back and looked at the rocks again, ignoring the fact that the rain had soaked through her clothes. The three rocks appeared to abut each other, but she could see now that there was empty space in the middle.

She circled again slowly, then stepped forward and slipped her hand into an opening between the two largest rocks. Even with the warm, wet wind whistling around her, she could feel cool air. She pulled her arm back out, slipped the backpack off her shoulders, and gripped it in her hand. She took a breath to calm her nerves, turned sideways, then slowly eased through the seam of the twin rocks. Once inside, she reached into the backpack and groped for the flashlight. She stood on what looked to be the edge of a well. She had to be more careful!

She hunched down with her back against the rock, careful not to lose her footing on the rim of the precipice. She aimed the flashlight into the hole and saw footholds carved in the sides. With all of the rain she couldn't test if this was actually a well. She had only two hands, and she was going to need them both. She turned off the flashlight and tucked it into the waistband of her pants. She shimmied around carefully so she could put on the backpack. Then, without a moment's hesitation, she descended into the dark hole.

Five minutes later she'd reached the bottom and had the flashlight back on. Again, she rummaged through her bag until she found the miner's lamp, which she put on. She looked up one last time, felt the rain on her face, then jogged down the dark tunnel. What had made Lily's stories so enticing was the little grain of truth that had lain embedded in them. She had said that Wang had disappeared from the courtyard in plain sight of the liberating soldiers. He'd used this tunnel to escape, just as Lily's killers had used it to bring her body back into the hotel. The monumentally difficult job of getting her up through the hole and back to her room without being discovered must have been outweighed by the knowledge that they were creating a seemingly unsolvable mystery.

As she ran, Hulan could hear conversations waft down from the village through cracks and holes that ran up to the surface. She knew she'd left Bashan behind when the muffled sounds of civilization ceased and she heard only her own footfalls and labored breathing. She had no idea what direction she was going or even where she was, but at least this stretch of pathway was clear and there were no obvious side tunnels or crawl spaces.

After a half hour, new sounds came to her from the darkness—thunder, lightning, the roar of the river somewhere near, and the scrabble of scurrying rats. Up ahead a flash from a lightning bolt lit an exit. Hulan slowed as she neared it, reached for her weapon, and aimed it ahead of her. At the edge of the exit, she peered out. Night had settled fully now, and the storm ravaged what little visibility there might have been. But in the momentary brightness of another streak of lightning, she saw that the tunnel opened onto a small track, which cut into the edge of the cliff less than a foot above the raging river.

She pulled her head back inside the cave and wiped the rain from her face with her forearm. She'd need both her hands free to traverse the rocky ledge, so she put away the gun and flashlight, then stepped out into the rain. With the light from the miner's lamp, she saw the river churning just inches below her. The water crashed on the rocks, sending murky waves over her sandals, threatening to sweep her feet out from under her. The path narrowed even further as it inclined steeply. She put her back against the cliff that towered behind her and edged forward. No one ahead of her or behind her as far as she could see, but then she couldn't see much as the rain lashed her face and obscured anything and everything around her.

Her left foot slipped out from under her, and she clung to a root. She regained her balance. Branches of lightning lit the world for another frightening moment. Water everywhere. Hand over hand she climbed, trying to secure her footing with each step until the path leveled out.

She still wasn't exactly sure where she was going, but when this path dead-ended into another one, her instincts told her to go down. It was hard to tell in the dark, but this path looked unused except by animals. Then she heard chanting coming through the deafening sounds of the storm. After a few more meters, the chanting became very clear, even though she knew she was nowhere near the main entrance to the cave where the local All-Patriotic Society met.

"Subdue the wild tribes in our hearts. Practice the abstinence of alcohol, tobacco, and fornication."

Hulan stepped through a small opening in the cliff and into deeper darkness. Unlike the first set of tunnels, this one had a strange musky smell. She remembered Michael Quon's words to her earlier in the day: "Caves *are* alive." A shudder passed through her body unrelated to the cold of the cave. She knew she was far from the cavern where she and David had first spoken with Dr. Ma, yet she knew from the overpowering odor of earth and mold that this cave had to be part of the larger system that riddled this entire hillside.

Murmured syllables floated to her. "Xiao Da, Xiao Da, Xiao Da." Another piece fell into place. Wu Huadong's father, the old blind man, had said that he'd *heard* Xiao Da, not that he'd seen him. Xiao Da's voice must have traveled up through the cave system to the Wu home, just as the old man's grandson's cries had traveled down not just to the cave where Hulan and Michael had been today but to the cave on the beach where Brian's body had disappeared.

Her eyes would never adjust in this gloom, and the miner's lamp wasn't much help. She shined the flashlight around her. This was a small cave with only one way to go. She shielded the beam of the flashlight so that it lit only the ground before her feet and crept forward.

"It is virtue that moves Heaven." Xiao Da's strange, unearthly voice echoed up to her. "And it is Heaven that punishes the guilty, for Heaven hears and sees as the people hear and see."

"Be reverent," came the response.

It was much cooler in here. Soaked clean through, Hulan shivered, and her teeth chattered.

"The river brings us life, so too does a leader," Xiao Da told his flock. "When a leader gives repose to the people, his kindness is felt and the wild ones cherish him in their hearts."

The roof began to slope down, and Hulan had to bend at the waist to get through. She came around a turn and up a small dip and saw a slight flickering on the walls and ceiling up ahead. She stopped and listened. She could hear people moving about. As quietly as she could, she took off the miner's lamp, set down the backpack, and felt inside for her Luger. She steadied her grip on her weapon with her left hand and walked around the last corner and into the light.

Captain Hom lay naked on a bed of stone. His nose was gone. His bare feet hung off the edge of the platform above twin buckets—waiting. His hands had already been amputated and his arms pulled away from his body so that the blood could drain from his wrists into another set of buckets. His mouth was stuffed with something brown and pulpy. A horrible mess of tissue and blood coagulated where his penis had been. His eyes were open and staring at the stalactites above him. Next to him lay another naked man, presumably Hom's brother-in-law, already dead. His nose, feet, hands, and penis had been cut off.

Michael Quon—the man who had tantalized Hulan with his stories of Da Yu, the man who was a mathematician like Da Yu, the man who had so obviously emulated Da Yu that he had twisted and corrupted his name to become Xiao Da—sat cross-legged on a rocky plinth just inside an alcove to the left of the gruesome tableau. On either side of him were braziers, which emanated both light and heat. A metal poker—probably the brand—nestled in the flames of one of the braziers. To the far right were a cot, camping table, lantern, and portable stove—creature comforts for long, undetected stays.

Quon looked at Hulan and spoke just loud enough for her to hear. "We make sacrifices for the good of others."

So they were going straight into it, Hulan thought. Her fear and resolve were one.

"Da Yu meant personal sacrifice." She slowly moved the Luger in Quon's direction. "He labored so hard that the hair fell from his legs. Isn't that what you told me?"

"Animal sacrifices were made. All of the ancient sites tell us this."

"Animal sacrifices, not human."

"And who says those two are human? The contractor killed his own people. The captain looked the other way while the masses suffered. Punishments are a blessing for the wicked."

The alcove where Quon sat was actually a large opening. She could hear chanting coming from behind and below him. She and

David had been down there just two days ago, and now she was in the inner chamber high on the ledge above the practitioners. They could not see what was happening in here, nor could they hear Quon speaking in his normal voice.

There was a movement behind Quon, and Officer Su entered. His eyes widened for just a fraction of a second upon seeing Hulan, then he covered his surprise with a smirk before addressing Quon. "Xiao Da, they wish to hear you speak."

Without shifting his attention from Hulan, Quon raised his voice, and it corrupted into something beautiful, melodious, and otherworldly as it bounced off the walls. "The waters of inundation are destructive in their overflow. In their vastness they embrace hills and overtop great heights, threatening the heavens with their floods. The lower people groan and murmur."

Listening, Hulan knew the words were not his own, but the people down below recognized the meaning to their lives and responded accordingly.

"Xiao Da, Xiao Da, Xiao Da . . ."

"We embrace Nine Virtues. Tonight you must discuss among yourselves the ninth and most important virtue—boldness with sincerity and valor with righteousness."

A low rumble of conversation rose from the lower cavern. Quon smiled at the sound. Officer Su picked up something that looked like an ocean sponge and used it to smear Hom's brother-in-law with his own blood.

Hulan edged toward the platform where Hom lay. The pulpy matter in his mouth prevented the people below from hearing his suffering. The only way he could breathe was through what was left of his nose. Air bubbled through the bloody muck in the middle of his face. The three wavy lines that composed the ancient character for *river* had already been burned into his forehead. Keeping the gun aimed at Quon, Hulan reached down and touched Hom's shoulder. His eyes moved to her, and she saw something beyond physical pain pass over his face.

"You can't do anything to help him," Quon said. "He's beyond redemption."

To Hom's right, Su kept at his grisly task.

"Michael . . ."

He held up his hands to silence her and said, "Please don't say something like I won't get away with it."

"I—"

He shook his head to stop her from speaking. "And don't say someone will come to rescue you. No one will rescue you. The police, as you see, are already here."

"There are others," she said.

"Who? Your husband? I think not. If anything, he hurts your chances."

Strangely, Hulan felt no fear. She was the one with the gun, didn't they see that?

At David's insistence, the chopper pilot radioed a local airstrip, was patched through to the Panda Guesthouse, and was told that Inspector Liu had left on some sort of emergency. When they tried to get through to Bashan's Public Security Bureau and no one answered, David knew with horrible certainty where Hulan had gone. He frantically ordered the pilot to alter his course. David knew where he wanted to land, but when the pilot saw it he told the American he was out of his mind.

"See that cliff?" the pilot yelled. "With the wind we'll be blown right into it! The rotors—"

But even as tenacious gusts buffeted the craft while it tried to maintain its altitude just below Bashan Village, David could see during the flashes of lightning that he'd made the right deduction. There, towering above the hillsides up ahead, was the geographical character for *door*—the Kuimen Gate—that Brian had used to mark the entrance to the Qutang Gorge on the coded map from his journal. Directly below them was the *river*. Just parallel to the pilot's window were two smaller peaks, each topped with rocks that David knew from Brian's map marked the Beheading Dragon Platform and the Binding Dragon Pillar. From this vantage so high in the air, David could clearly see the curled ancient *dragon* after its death and the places that Brian had marked as *fields,* though there were no fields there now and probably hadn't been for centuries. The geography itself created *cliff*, and the formations buttressing the entrance to the Wu house formed *cave*. And just above *cave* was an outcropping of stone with a single large rock protruding beneath it—the character for *below*.

Lightning streaked around them. The chopper shook violently.

"Bring it down!" David shouted. "Now!"

The pilot fought the weather for control of his machine. They were about ten feet from the ground when a surge of air hurled them back out over the river. The pilot screamed, "I can't do it! If the wind goes the other way, we're dead!"

The weather had the upper hand. The wind pushed the chopper toward the cliff. The limestone face rushed toward the windshield. Then, in one of those quirks of nature, the wind right against the cliff died just long enough for the pilot to land. With the *ruyi* in hand, David jumped out and ran through the mud and rain. He banged on the door of the Wu house. No one answered, but he knew that even with the riotous sounds of the storm the inhabitants had heard the helicopter. He hit the door again as hard as he could.

It opened, and David entered the one room that made up the Wus' home. The old blind man sat on the edge of a *kang* next to a kerosene lamp. His daughter-in-law, who'd answered the door, backed away and stood against the stone wall, clutching her swaddled child protectively.

Now that David was here he wasn't sure how to proceed. His impulse was to shake out of the woman what he needed to know, but her terrified countenance told him she was already in danger of shutting down completely. He took a breath, closed the door, and replaced the bar that protected the Wus from outsiders. As he turned, he heard a distant murmur slink through the room. "Xiao Da, Xiao Da, Xiao Da . . ."

The old man spoke in a quavering voice. "Who is it?"

David kept his eyes on the young widow as he answered, concentrating on his tones like never before. *"Wo shi nimen de pengyou."* I am your friend, he told them, but he addressed his words solely to the woman. He reached into his breast pocket, and she cowered against the rocky wall, frozen by fear. He unfolded Brian's map and slowly stepped toward her.

"We embrace Nine Virtues." The sound rippled through the room as though Xiao Da were there with them.

"We don't want visitors," the old man said.

David didn't bother to respond. He held out the map and pointed to the ancient character for *good*—a mother protecting her child—then to the woman. She looked at it, then up at David. Her eyes were anguished. He reached out his hand. The woman shrank another inch or two down the wall, but she had nowhere to go. His fingers lightly touched the dirty blanket. As gently as possible he pulled the blanket away from the baby's face. The child was awake. He had blue eyes, and his hair was just beginning to come in as light fuzz. The old blind man couldn't know that this infant was not his grandchild.

David pointed to the symbol for *cave* on the map. The woman averted her face and closed her eyes.

"You should go now," the old man said.

Again David spoke to the young woman before him, using the purest tones he could manage. "Show me the way." Then he leaned forward and whispered in her ear, "Brian died protecting you. Now you can save someone else."

"The people will know," she whispered back. She held the child out to him.

"The people will know anyway," he said.

David watched several emotions play over the young woman's features. She covered her baby's face and brought him closer to her chest, then slowly and with great effort stood up. She looked at David, then nodded to the stack of boxes that made up the family's storage area. He crossed to it as the woman went to the door. He timed his movements to hers. As she pulled up the bar, he pulled away the top crate. As soon as she opened the door and the sounds of the storm filled the little room, he yanked away the other boxes, grabbed the lantern and the *ruyi,* and stepped through the dark opening. He didn't look back.

27

HULAN KEPT FLASHING BACK TO THE KNIGHT FACTORY AND THE women who'd died. This was an equally volatile situation. She didn't want anyone to get hurt or die who wasn't already a lost cause. She was willing to be left alone with Michael Quon rather than do something that would risk triggering a mass movement from the followers in the cavern below, which would only add to the tragedy. She would wait for them to go home before she made her move. But the only way to buy time was to engage Michael Quon in the intellectual cat-and-mouse game he'd played with her from the first time they'd spoken in the lobby of the Panda Guesthouse.

"You're no better than the Falun Gong." It was lame, but it was a start.

"We're not as big," Quon responded agreeably. "They have forty million followers worldwide. We have half that—all in China. But give us another year or two and the Communist Party's fifty-five million will seem minuscule by comparison."

"You think you can move so quickly?"

"I already have. The people have been waiting for someone like me. They see the corruption of the state and they embrace magic, *qi gong*, and—"

"And religious quacks like you." She shook her head dismissively. "Your methods have been used by others before, but the people will understand the truth about you soon enough. As Mao said, the one who thinks he's smarter than the masses will be abandoned by the masses."

"The people look at nature and they understand the larger concepts of the universe. They see flooding and they know it is a message from Heaven that all is not right."

"And you think you can help them?" Hulan baited him. "How? By preying on their weaknesses? By stealing their cultural heritage? By preventing them from enjoying the benefits of science and technology? Your motives aren't so pure."

The chanting resumed. Hulan fought her desire to look at her watch. Most of the people below were peasants. They would need to get up early to work their fields. The meeting had to end soon . . .

"You can't stop the river from flowing," Quon said.

"This isn't about the dam or the people who'll be moved from these shores," she countered, trying to break his reliance on his religious platitudes. "This is about the power of a single man. Do you really believe you have the Mandate of Heaven? You've said before that I know nothing of my country's history, but let me tell you what we both know. Every dynasty was brought down by corruption, even that of Yu the Great."

"You're right. Each new Xia emperor was more corrupt than the last. First the amusements of the palace, then drinking and gambling, then women—"

"And you begin your rule with those most corrupt acts! I've seen you drink. I've seen how you are with women. And then there's this . . ." She gestured to Hom and his brother-in-law.

Michael's jaw clenched. She had to be careful.

"You say one thing to the people, but you're just another fat rat stealing from them," she goaded him.

"I'm not afraid of the intoxicating qualities of liquor."

"Because you put yourself above the people! Tell me, Michael, did Yu labor for the good of the black-haired ones, or was he looking to create an empire for his own edification? What of his pride, his pleasure, his ego? During his labors he distressed his body, but he was rewarded by having the people under his control. This is no different than Qinshihuangdi or Mao. And you're no different from them in your lies."

"They destroyed the past. I'm preserving it."

"By stopping the dam?" Hulan scoffed. "Even you can't stop that."

"Nature must be allowed to take its course."

"Why? So people can die? You seem to forget the thousands of years of floods and deaths."

"You look like a modern woman, Hulan, but you're so old-fashioned. Confucian ethics won't work on the river."

With that, the Taoist elements of the All-Patriotic Society's beliefs that had eluded her began to make sense. He'd used them with the people as shorthand to decry the benefits of technology.

"From the earliest days of Yu, two moral schools of thought emerged about hydraulic engineering," Michael said, veering back into the stylized language of Xiao Da. "Do we confine nature or let it run free? Do we let raw sewage pollute the reservoir or let it flow to the sea? Do we build high dams that barricade nature or deepen channels? Do we let the silt gather behind those high walls or do we let it fertilize the fields downstream? It is the classic battle between the male and female, the *yin* and the *yang*. The high walls are masculine, while the excavation of deep concavities is feminine—"

"You are so full of shit!"

"Kun failed to prevent floods because he tried to repress nature. His son guided the waters to the seas."

"Confucian and Taoist practices have no place in a Communist state."

"The state can resist, but the old beliefs run through the body of China like dragon veins—hidden, sometimes suppressed, but always affecting those who live on the surface."

"Stop talking to me like I'm one of your followers!"

"All right then. Let me put it in words you'll understand. You're a good Communist, but can you tell me you haven't lived your life hemmed in by the strictures of Confucian thought? Filial duty—"

Officer Su stepped back through the opening. "They are ready, Xiao Da."

Michael kept his eyes on Hulan as he raised his voice so that it would resonate through the cave system. "Go forth tonight with my message. Do not wallow in pleasure. Subdue the wild tribes in your heart. Remember the Nine Virtues, remember your grade, remember your tribute." He paused to lower his voice for a final blessing. "Be reverent," he said, and below the tithing began.

David put his left hand on the wall to serve as a guide as he maneuvered down the tunnel, but he pulled it away after just a few yards. His hand was covered in something gooey and smelly. Without stopping, he wiped it on his pants leg and continued on. He rounded a corner and entered a small chamber filled with artifacts. His eyes grazed over the jade chimes like the one he'd seen at the Cosgrove's auction and some pots still whole, but now was not the time to stop.

The tunnel began to lead down, breaking off here and there in new directions. Leaning his head into one shaft, he heard water rushing below. Focusing on another small opening, he heard echoing silence. He listened at every shaft, tunnel, alcove, and indentation, trying to home in on the chanting. Even when it stopped, he could still hear voices. Hulan was down there somewhere! Though he couldn't make out the words, he could catch her inflections and cadences floating to him through the darkness. A tumultuous combination of relief and gritty determination pushed him forward.

The tunnel narrowed and shortened until he had to get on his hands and knees to pass through. He pushed the lantern and *ruyi* ahead of him, then edged behind them. His head and side throbbed. Each movement sent searing pain zapping across his nerves. He began to hear the lies Michael Quon told. He heard the mistakes as well. He knew that Hulan had found her way here somehow, but she still didn't know the truth of what had happened. He hoped that ignorance would protect her.

The rocky ceiling lowered even farther. If it got much tighter, he'd have to abandon the lamp and do this blind. If it got much tighter than that, he wouldn't be able to make it through at all.

The people below had gone home, and it was just the four of them now: Hulan, Michael, Su, and Hom. She still had her weapon, and it was loaded, but she could see that Su had his service revolver, and for all she knew Michael had Hom's. But every time she tried to focus on how to disable the two men without getting killed herself, Michael interrupted her thoughts with his persistent and increasingly personal conversation.

"How many times has your husband gotten you into dangerous situations?" he asked.

"I've gotten myself into things that were dangerous."

Michael considered this, then said, "Your husband led you to your father's hiding place. Your father would have killed you."

But David had taken the bullet for her.

She stayed beside Hom and put her hand on his chest. She wanted him to know she wasn't leaving. To Michael she said, "You've researched my life, but so what? Any fool can find my life history. A search on the Internet, a day reading newspaper clippings . . ."

Michael ignored her words. He stood and gracefully stretched his arms above his head, then brought his hands down to the small of his back and stretched again. He crossed over to her and hunkered down so that they were eye to eye. "And what man who loves a woman would let her go into a factory of death?"

Yes, the terrible deaths at the Knight factory, but Michael didn't know the truth of that day either.

"I went in there against his wishes."

"That man has no sensitivity to our culture—"

"It is not *your* culture—"

"If he'd opened his eyes, he would have known you weren't safe. He would have protected you," Michael wheedled.

"I've protected myself—"

"You've protected your heart."

"You're trying to exploit my weaknesses just as you've abused the weaknesses of the people, but it won't work."

But even as she contradicted him, she knew that he'd hit the core truth about her. She didn't deserve happiness. She had never been strong enough to protect the people she loved, whereas the real Liu Hulan had loved so much that she'd been willing to lay her life down to save an entire village.

"Actually," Michael said, as though reading her thoughts, "you would let your body go in a minute. That is why you have always put yourself into positions where you could die."

"I'm not brave. If you knew anything about me, you'd know that." She looked down at Captain Hom and squeezed his shoulder. "But this man is a hero, and he'll be remembered as a martyr when you're revealed as a fraud—a foreign one at that."

Michael's eyes flashed angrily. Could she provoke him into making a mistake? Again he seemed to read her mind, because with the grace and speed of a *qi gong* master he'd grabbed her gun and tucked it into his belt even before she could begin to react. Then he motioned to Officer Su, who set down his sponge, picked up an ax, and in two brutal motions chopped off both of Hom's feet. Hulan heard Hom's muffled screams through his gag. Su looked at Michael, who motioned for his underling to put the ax on the stone platform next to Hulan. She wasn't sure if he was tempting her to pick it up or warning her that her end was inevitable.

Michael resumed his niggling. "You marry this David Stark, but you don't really love him."

"Of course I do."

Michael shook his head knowingly. "The man loves you—anyone can see that—but you don't love him with your whole heart. Your heart is a fortress against happiness."

In spite of herself, Michael's dime-store babble was getting to her. She broke eye contact with him and looked down at Hom. "You can't know what's in my heart."

Hom's eyes were glassy. His skin, which had always looked jaundiced and unhealthy, was even more depleted, wrinkling as the life ran out of him.

"Your husband gave up so much to be with you—his homeland, his career, his happiness. You can't do that to a man."

"I tried to make him happy."

"But you failed. You failed in the one way a woman must never fail."

She turned back to Michael. His smile was beautiful, and his skin glowed in the candlelight. "Yes, Hulan, I'm talking about your daughter."

"How do you know about her?"

"You were after us, Hulan. It was important for me to know everything about you."

Hulan knew what she was dealing with now. Michael Quon was not a psychopath. He'd gotten to this point with the cold and deliberate plotting of a mathematical mind.

"You should have done more," he said. "You should have protected her."

She'd been trained never to be tricked into giving personal revelations, but she couldn't stop herself. "I did everything I could."

"Why didn't you take her to the hospital sooner? Did you not want to make a fuss because no girl child is worth it?" He paused, then recited, "'When a girl, obey your father; when a wife, obey your husband; when a widow, obey your son.'"

Hulan could almost hear her father grinding those words into her as a child. "I never thought that way about Chaowen."

"No, because you'd been too corrupted by the West," he said in a mocking voice. "You probably thought the whole world was open to her."

Why didn't he just kill her and get it over with?

"You're a thoughtful person, analytical in your own way," Michael continued. "Think about that night. Were you embarrassed that your daughter was sick?"

Each word he spoke smashed deeply into Hulan.

"Were you afraid people would think you weren't a good mother?"

Her heart ached and she felt utterly defenseless, yet something strange was happening. She was beginning to relive those last days.

She was seeing them as they were, not as her grief had warped them.

"Did you delay in going to the hospital because you didn't want people to see you fail again?"

"That's not what happened," she said. And it wasn't. Instead of tormenting her, the truth was beginning to feed her strength. "Everything that could have been done for my daughter was done."

"But you *could* have done more," he pressed. "You *could* have taken her to America—"

That thought had been looping in her head for a year. If only they had moved to Los Angeles earlier, Chaowen might never have gotten sick. If she had, she might have had better medical care. But here in this cave, at what Hulan supposed was the end of her life, she finally understood that those were only wishes that could never be known or fulfilled. She had done everything humanly possible to save her daughter.

Hulan noticed that Michael was speaking again.

"When she died, you got what you think you've always deserved—an empty heart." He spoke his conclusion triumphantly, not realizing that he'd failed in his task. His ignorance was an advantage Hulan could exploit. "But it doesn't have to be that way. Open yourself, Hulan, join me. Not as a follower, but as an equal. Think what we could do together."

She almost had to laugh. How could he think that his flirting these last couple of days had meant anything to her? There was a big difference between being flattered by a man's attentions and giving up her moral center to him.

"Some people deserve happiness. Some people earn it. You've earned it, Hulan."

"Maybe living righteously doesn't deserve a reward." She knew the truth now, and it gave her the fortitude to fight for her life.

"But what about those who do wrong?" As he spoke, Hulan realized that, for all of his supposed awareness, Michael Quon was completely blind to the things he didn't want to see. "Don't you think Lily deserved punishment for the things she did?"

"She was not an honest person, but she didn't deserve to die."

"Mankind has come to believe in science and the exactness of math," he offered thoughtfully. "For every action there is a reaction, and all that. But maybe the ancients had it right when they trusted in karma, fate, and getting your just deserts. Certainly you've seen people who deserved the worst but received no punishment."

Hom was dead now. Within arm's reach was the ax that Su had used. The thing was covered with bits of flesh and blood, but she could also see that the blade was made of some type of chiseled stone, which had been strapped to a wooden handle.

Quon answered her question before she asked it, just as he had last night at dinner. "It's a chime," he explained. "White jade is the strongest stone in the world, and it makes a clean cut. Every one that Brian stole and Lily put up for sale I bought and brought back to its rightful place."

"But not for its rightful use," she pointed out. "It was supposed to make music, not be an instrument of torture and death."

He ignored the comment and asked, "Where's the rest of it, Hulan?"

"What?"

"The chimes. I've been looking for the rest of the set." His eyes glittered in anticipation.

"I don't know what you're talking about."

"I choose to believe you," he said mildly. "In that case, give me the journal."

"I don't keep one."

"But Brian did. Once I knew you had it, our path together was clear. You can help me find the rest of—what is it, Hulan?—a tomb or a treasure chamber?"

What had been right in front of her these last years as she'd tracked the activities of the All-Patriotic Society finally dawned on her. "Your travels, Michael, I understand them now," she said. "You went to ancient sites along the Yellow River. Then you came to the Yangzi. The Society's growth mirrored your journey and you used the watershed of the rivers to proselytize."

He stared into her eyes, and she stared back, reading the calculation in his. Should he respond to her? A subtle shift deep within him signaled his decision, and her courage expanded yet again.

"You hear so much about the Yellow River as the birthplace of Chinese civilization," he said at last, "but we know people traveled. We know that Yu came this far south. I first came here because I was following his legend—through poetry and art, then myth, and finally fact."

"To see the nine provinces. To see the places where Yu stopped the floods. And you found more followers."

"So much had to do with planting seeds," he admitted, and Hulan felt another surge of hope. She could draw him out. She could distract him. He traced something that looked like a maze in the dirt between them.

"Do you know what this is?"

She shook her head.

"Ha!"

She looked at him squarely. "I never pretended to be anything other than ignorant."

"I never lied to you, Hulan. You should know that. But I did omit a few things. I told you that I loved puzzles as a boy and that I liked Yu's mathematical game. It was nothing special really, but I got hooked on the man. I even used his map as my company logo. When I came to China four years ago, I began searching in my own way to find my *purpose*. As I told you last night, I wasn't going to fit in with organizations back home, not even the Committee of 100. I am a very rich man, yet I will always be seen as an outsider in America because of my race." He leaned forward and confided, "You understand that. Being an outsider in your homeland is one of the things that binds us." Then he relaxed and resumed his story. "But it's all a process and, as you said, I began following Yu's landmarks of the nine provinces. The next year I began making speeches as Xiao Da."

"You began to believe your own propaganda."

"Xiao Da has been an invigorating experience. He brought me closer to Da Yu."

Quon spoke now of the transition from looking at arbitrary sites to something much more focused. "The most successful emperors understood the power of symbols. I knew that by bringing the past to the present I could consolidate the people, but what would our symbol be?"

He realized that the key to his grip on the multitudes lay in the mythology of the past. Mao Zedong had understood this very well when he'd said, "Make the past serve the present." When Catherine Miller began talking about the missing ninth tripod, Quon was convinced he was following the right course, because even the conniving Lily had been caught up in its mythology, though all historical evidence said it couldn't possibly be in the Yangzi. But Brian had tired of the game and, to avoid Lily's nagging, found solace in caving.

"He invited me along, because I'm, well, I'm Michael Quon—inventor of VYRUSCAN. The first time we entered this cave it was like going back to the mother. You smell it, don't you, how this place is alive?"

To Hulan these caves had always reeked of something moldy and rotting. Now she watched as Quon reached up, sank his fingers into the roof of the cave, and came away with a spongy mass, which he handed to Su. The officer took the blob, dipped it into one of the blood-filled buckets, then began coating Hom's body with his own drained fluids.

"Last summer," Quon went on, as though nothing had happened, "Brian and I explored a lot of caves. I showed him this one." He tilted his head deprecatingly. "I told him who I was. He became a convert, and I have to say he was very helpful. He did extra research on Da Yu, which I incorporated into Xiao Da. Brian gave me entire passages from the *Shu Ching* to use in my sermons, knowing they would speak to the people on an atavistic level. He came up with some of our better chants. 'You can't stop the river from flowing' and 'The river brings us life' were his. Then the kid falls in love. I granted him religious power and he turned it down for a piece of ass."

Hulan wished Xiao Da's followers could hear him now.

"Maybe he had doubts about what you were doing."

Quon shrugged off the idea. "I came back to Bashan this year after I bought my first chime from Cosgrove's, because I knew Brian had hit pay dirt, so to speak. But Brian would no longer talk to me. He had a secret and he wouldn't reveal it no matter what I offered him, not even money. I had to wonder why. So I kept exploring. I found the tunnel into the guesthouse and the life of this cave. While these things have served me well, they were not what I was looking for. Meanwhile, Lily continued to put up for auction some very interesting pieces. She also sold privately through Cathay Antiquities. I bought discreetly. Only I could see what the others didn't—these pieces had all come from the same source, and her primary source within China was Brian."

After Lily had gotten Wu Huadong to jump in the whirlpool, everything had changed. Which was a shame, because Quon had spent a lot of time with the boy, enticing him with spiritual and financial riches if he'd reveal the secrets of the earth. "He was ready to help me."

"'From the fist of the past to my fist to the fist of the future,'" Hulan recited Wu Huadong's promise to his father.

But Lily had meddled and was fully responsible for what happened next. Two days after Wu's drowning, Brian went to her with more of the chimes, the *ruyi*, and some other items, which were then listed in the Cosgrove's catalog. Throughout it all, Quon kept an eye on Brian's website. The photo addressed specifically to Angela—a mycologist—told him it was time to get back here.

"I went back and reread the *Shu Ching* and all of the other sources on Yu. I thought more about the 'living earth'—the 'swelling mold'—which Yu had used to stop the flood. Could this cave be the source of that living earth, and could the *ruyi* be somehow connected to it?"

Hulan understood only half of what Quon was saying, but the other half was transparent. He was trying to sound like a concerned scholar, but his real interest had been the growth of his political power. The dam might be a more monumental statement, but even the Central Committee would be in danger of losing its hold over the masses if Yu's scepter could be found. But why hadn't Quon gone to Hong Kong to buy the *ruyi*? His relaxed confidence told Hulan that he must have sent someone else to bid on it. He had to stay here and find the hidden chamber so that when he won the *ruyi* he could hide it again, then "discover" it in a place of great symbolic significance.

"There came a day when I found Brian coming out of one of the lower caves down by the river," Quon recalled as he paced back and forth in the confines of the cave. "I demanded that he tell me the location of the tomb. We scuffled on the rocks, and Brian died. It was an accident, but how could I explain to the authorities the reasons behind our argument?"

Fortunately, one of the keys to the All-Patriotic Society's success had been the conversion of local law enforcement through religion and/or money. In Bashan, Officer Su—a true religious convert—had been a great help in setting up Society meetings and keeping Captain Hom out of the way. Now Su suggested taking a bad situation and making use of it.

"As you noticed, Hulan, Su is quite clever," Quon went on. "Brian's nose had been broken in the fight, but it gave Su an idea. Cutting off the nose is the second of the ancient Five Punishments. I felt we couldn't have the second punishment without the first, so we added the brand. I know you think this is cruel, but I was hoping to send a message to the other archaeologists: Don't go digging into things that aren't your business. But we didn't imagine that Brian would wash so far away or that you would never mention these details."

As Quon spoke, Hulan wondered why he hadn't searched through Brian's backpack when he killed the boy or why he hadn't taken it later from Lily's room. Had Lily been so avaricious that even as she'd been tortured she hadn't revealed its whereabouts? Or had she gone into shock too quickly and been unable to respond? In both murders, had Quon, in his attention to the details of creating scenes that would send messages to anyone he considered a threat, simply overlooked the obvious?

"And Lily?" Hulan asked.

Lily had been far more forthcoming than Brian, admitting that she'd put together what he'd written in his journal with the stories she'd heard about the Wang compound.

"But she didn't come through the tunnel," Hulan said. "She left Bashan on the main road."

"It turns out Lily was afraid of the dark," Quon responded apologetically. "She was hoping to find another entrance. Imagine her surprise when she ran into my lieutenant on the road." He'd said this as though Hulan would understand, but she had no idea why Lily Sinclair would have known anything about Tang Wenting. "She was even more surprised to see me when he escorted her here."

Later they'd brought Lily's body straight into the compound. Su, who'd appeared so shocked at the sight of Lily's corpse, had played the perfect sycophant, even providing Hulan with a map showing the routes Lily and Catherine had taken through town. Now he went about his chores with methodical determination. She'd seen his kind so many times in her life. She should have known better.

Quon kneeled in front of her again and said softly, "I'd like that journal now."

"I don't have it."

"But I do," came a new voice to the chamber.

David processed the scene quickly. Hom and some other man killed by the Five Punishments. Officer Su aiming a gun at David's torso. Michael Quon, possibly unarmed. The opening behind Quon, another opening on the far side of the chamber, and the opening David had come through. The look of great love and great fear that passed over his wife's face when she realized he was there.

"But I have something more important to you than the journal," David said, holding up the wrapped *ruyi*.

"What is it?" Quon asked, his eyes still resting possessively on Hulan.

When Hulan heard David's voice, she didn't want to believe it. Then she saw him—wet, covered with dirt and slime from crawling through the caves, Chaowen's Band-Aids on his forehead. He'd come all this way for her. He always had.

"The *ruyi*."

Hulan heard in Quon's voice something entirely new—barefaced greed.

"The *ruyi* of Da Yu!"

She watched as David held on to the kerosene lamp with one hand and awkwardly began shaking the linen off the wrapped object with the other. Didn't he understand what was going to happen if he gave Quon what he wanted? Michael motioned to Su to get the *ruyi*. Her husband would be dead as soon as he handed it over.

Hulan had been raised to be a martyr, but she'd denied her destiny at every step of her life. For the last thirty years, the knowledge of the consequences for others of her denial of her duty, obligation, and blood imperative had been almost too horrible to endure. Now in the dankness of this cave she understood what she needed to do. Her heart so long shielded had been battered and cracked by Michael Quon's pernicious attacks. Now it shattered open, releasing wave upon wave of feeling. She would give Quon her life to save David's because she loved him. She loved him in the way that the first Liu Hulan had loved her village.

With Quon and Su focused on David, Hulan reached for the jade ax. She glanced toward her husband one last time, hoping that when she made her move he'd know to get out of there.

"The *ruyi* for my wife!" David grasped the *ruyi* by the handle and held it aloft. Out of the corner of his eye, he saw Hulan leap up, reach for the ax that lay next to Hom's body, and hack it into Su's belly. In that same instant, David threw the *ruyi* and the lantern at Quon. The glass shattered against Quon's chest, sending kerosene in flaming rivulets down his body. He glanced down in surprise and then, as the fire began to eat away at his clothes, he dropped and rolled.

David bounded across the cave, shoving his wife into the tunnel on the wall opposite the one he'd entered. He lurched blindly in the darkness, bashing into the rocky walls, fully aware of the unseen crevasses that might appear as traps beneath his feet but unable to do anything but press on. He hit something soft and giving. He recoiled instinctively.

"It's me," Hulan whispered.

They stood in the absolute midnight of the cave, listening to Su's agonized screams and, below them, footsteps.

"This way," she hissed. She held David's hand, and they edged along the wall.

Behind them, they saw a flashlight beam.

"Are you armed?" David whispered.

"No," she whispered back.

They would be caught by Quon's light in a couple of seconds. Hulan picked up her pace, but without sight they were helpless. They rounded a corner, and the beam disappeared from view. David held Hulan back from going any farther, then he let go of her and clenched his hands into a sturdy interlocked fist.

He watched for the beam, trying to judge from the angle just when Quon would come around the corner. When the beam shone through at waist height, David swung his hands down on Quon's arm, dislodging the flashlight, which clanged to the ground. As the chamber went black again, David brought his clenched hands up and bashed Quon's chin. Quon grunted from the impact and fell away.

David felt Hulan reach for him and pull him deeper into the cave. But before they could get very far, she stumbled, bringing him down with her. In the deathly stillness he heard the three of them panting. He concentrated on slowing and quieting his breaths. Hulan and Quon did the same until there was nothing—no light, no sound.

"Hulan." The syllables sounded intimate—almost loving—in the darkness. "I have it, Hulan." Quon sighed into the ebony vacuum.

Hulan's hand found David's shoulder, felt its way to his face, and clamped down over his mouth. She crept closer to him, and when he felt her hair on his face he knew she was leaning over him.

Her movements seemed impossibly loud, and somewhere nearby Quon moved in response. "Come to me, Hulan," he murmured. "Fulfill your destiny now, with me."

David tried to shake her hand free, but her grip was unnaturally strong. Then she broke away from him and plunged into the inky void. He rolled over, reached out, felt nothing. He heard the two of them wrestling in the blackness, then a long cry cut through the air. As the sound fell away, then abruptly ended, David realized that the person must have plummeted into one of the crevasses. What he couldn't tell was if it had been a man's or a woman's voice or to whom the thready breathing that remained belonged. He felt the ground for a rock or the flashlight—anything he could use as a weapon. He heard the other person move, slithering across the ground toward him.

"David"—his wife's voice came to him strong in the darkness—"stay where you are. I'll come to you."

EPILOGUE

THE RAINS FINALLY SUBSIDED. WHILE NO ONE COULD BELIEVE everything that was written in the *China Daily*—or the *International Herald Tribune,* for that matter—the floods were devastating. Despite everyone's best efforts, the Minzu Yuan dike in Hunan Province collapsed, creating a landslide that took out several hundred homes, then sent downstream a huge wave, which washed away the next two villages. This tragedy served as a reminder to all of past and possible future tidal waves.

Yichang, near the Three Gorges Dam, reported the highest water level to date, with the flood cresting at fifty-two meters. Twenty-two million acres of farmland had been swamped, 2.9 million homes destroyed, and 2,500 deaths reported. Outbreaks of hepatitis A and typhoid had been contained—not bad considering that although only 1.8 million people had actually been evacuated, more than 140 million people had ultimately been affected. However, the economic cost—in terms of crops lost, manufacturing production shut down, and homes and property ruined—was staggering. Although monsoon season was not yet over, the Central Meteorological Station expressed confidence that the worst was past. The cleanup began.

David and Hulan were extremely busy during the week after the events in the cave. Working side by side, they pieced together more of what had happened—both personally and in their respective cases. Hulan interrogated Officer Su, who was recuperating in a local hospital, while in Hong Kong Investigator Lo questioned Bill Tang, who was being held for the murder of Dr. Ma. Both Su and Tang were singing like proverbial canaries, and both were well-aware that if Michael Quon wasn't found, they'd be made the scape-goats. Quon had fallen into one of the tunnels in the cave that led down to the river, but his body had not been recovered. If he'd somehow survived, then he'd disappeared into the black world. As for the *ruyi*, both Hulan and David hoped it had washed out to sea and would never be retrieved, for it had already brought out the worst greed and covetousness in those aware of its existence.

Hulan had been changed by what had happened in the cave. David had heard it in her voice when he was crawling through. He'd seen it in her eyes when he reached her. She was a different woman now, and he was deeply grateful. David had changed too. For the first time in his life, he'd gotten totally out of his head and had operated on a purely physical level. His body had paid a price for that, though. When he saw Bashan's only doctor, he received thirty stitches and was diagnosed with five broken ribs and a concussion. Hulan joked that the concussion may have been what had caused him to act so out of character.

David also spent a lot of time agonizing over what happened to Wu Huadong's wife and baby. After he had gone into the tunnel, the chopper pilot saw the widow dash into the storm and straight out and over the cliff, following, it turned out, the same path her husband had taken a few weeks earlier. That was the official version, but David knew something the others didn't. He'd misread the widow's gesture when she'd held her baby up to him and said, "The people will know." She hadn't been preserving the location of the hidden chamber; she'd been trying to protect her child. Sadly, although the widow had plenty of money stashed in the house—Lily had been generous in her final payments to Brian—she was still an uneducated peasant with a half-Caucasian child. She had no way to know the world of options that awaited her outside the Three Gorges. Perhaps her suicide was inevitable, but David felt his actions had accelerated the process. He'd carry those deaths with him forever. Hulan knew exactly how he felt.

By looking for greed and the inability of people to tell the truth, Hulan had found that even those who'd been altruistic and honest had helped create the cascade of events that had resulted in so many tragedies. Catherine, who had set so much in motion the previous summer with her prank about the Nine Tripods, now proved to be very forthcoming. In Brian's efforts to get away from Lily and her obsession, he'd found his beach on the river's edge, where he met Wu Huadong's young wife. Their romance had started with small gestures—a little money from him, a container of noodles from her. Eventually, their picnics turned into something more. In his journal, Brian wrote that he'd gotten Lily to hire Huadong to help the couple escape their brutal poverty; in fact, it had been a very convenient way to get the husband out of the picture. When Brian returned this year, he'd been surprised to find the peasant girl hugely pregnant. Two weeks later, the baby was born. Huadong had taken one look at the infant and thrown himself over the cliff. When his body was found in the whirlpool, the other archaeologists mistakenly blamed Lily. Why had Brian confided all of this to Catherine? He was smart in so many ways, she said, but he didn't have much experience with the messiness of real life. He wanted her advice, and she gave it.

From the journal, what Hulan learned in the cave from Michael Quon, and further interviews with Catherine, other aspects of Brian's last year unraveled. Last summer Wu's wife had told Brian her greatest secret—her husband's clan had stood guard over this property and its hidden caverns for thousands of years. Brian had begun taking things from the chamber and selling them to Lily, which set in motion a whole other chain of events. Once Quon started making his increasingly threatening demands, Brian understood his fate. He'd fought to the death to protect something or someone. Since he'd already looted the chamber, even the most hard-bitten investigators chose to believe Brian had died for love.

David left Bashan for a day to accompany a team that descended on Cathay Antiquities in Hong Kong, where stolen artifacts from numerous sites, including Site 518, were found. He also paid a visit to Angus Fitzwilliams's apartment. The auctioneer freely admitted that he'd ignored Bill Tang's bid in favor of one by an older and more loyal Cosgrove's customer. This was not a prosecutable crime, but shortly thereafter Fitzwilliams and his wife retired home to England.

David knew that Hulan saw everything in a geopolitical light—the struggle over image between countries, the battles within those countries for the hearts and minds of their citizens. But to him so much came down to familial actions—Catherine's desire to impress her father, Brian's desire to protect his child and its mother—that had resulted in the most deadly reactions. Perhaps none was more insignificant on the surface—but with more lethal results—than the pictorial message Brian had sent to his sister on his website.

In the photograph, Brian stood on a barren hillside with his arms outstretched as though he was presenting the whole panorama. Only Angela saw that his fingers were pointing to tiny golden mushrooms that had sprung up in the crannies around some rocks. Those mushrooms were known to surface after a rain above an *Armillaria ostoyae*, a much larger honey mushroom, which grew under the soil. Three years ago, Angela had been on a team that had discovered a twenty-five-hundred-year-old honey mushroom in Oregon that was three and a half miles in diameter, making it the largest organism ever found on the planet. What was now known as the Bashan Fungus was at least twice the size and perhaps twice as old.

It had grown from a single spore too small to see without a microscope. For thousands of years, black shoestring filaments had radiated underground, strangling roots, killing trees, and leaving behind a sticky substance. The fungus had spread across the surface of the earth, wiping out vegetation from the river's edge to the tops of the hills above Site 518, from the outskirts of Bashan to another half mile past the Wu house. Rhizomorphs stretched down as far as ten feet and had permeated the caves, giving them their peculiar odor. Michael Quon had said the caves were alive; he just hadn't known how alive they were.

In addition to the paleobotanists who'd arrived to study the fungus, archaeologists, cultural anthropologists, biocultural anthropologists, and linguists descended on Bashan. David and Hulan watched their activities with interest. Some were engaged in DNA testing, hoping to prove that the Wus were longtime descendants of the wild ones that Yu the Great had met in his travels. Since no coffin or mummified remains had been found, others researched the purpose of the chamber. Had Yu brought these artifacts with him as gifts of culture—music and art specifically—to the wild ones? Had the Wu clan been left to guard the treasures—the white jade chimes, the *bi* disks, the pottery, the weapons of war, and the *ruyi*? Or had the Wus been left to guard the fungus? Some believed that Yu left the *ruyi* with the Ba as a symbol of the tasks they were to do, just as Emperor Shun gave a symbol to Yu when he went about clearing the land of floods. Others thought that, instead of bringing culture and civilization, Yu's gift had actually sown the seeds of the Ba's destruction by birthing the invasive Bashan Fungus. Others wondered if the fungus could actually be *shi tu*, the "swelling mold" or "living earth" that Yu and his father had used to control the flood. Meanwhile, old Dr. Strong was doing his best to help a team examine Brian's theory that not only had geography informed early Chinese language but this very area might be the birthplace of characters like *dragon, cliff, cave,* and *river,* predating those found on oracle bones by hundreds, if not thousands, of years. The land itself might be that long sought after proof of five thousand years of continuous Chinese culture.

Debates raged about Brian's discoveries. Could one graduate student find both the Rosetta stone of Chinese language and China's Holy Grail? Some felt that he'd just lucked into the *ruyi*, which, since it was lost again, was suspect anyway. Some felt that his theories about the connection between his so-called geographic dragon bones and the thoughts and culture of the people who dwelled in the gorges had limited academic validity. Others found his research truly significant and were thoroughly analyzing and critiquing his journal. All agreed that Brian's premature death was a great loss to the field of archaeology and that further study was required.

Everyone would have to work quickly though. Although this had been a major discovery, the lower caverns would begin flooding in 2003, and by 2009 all of this area would be below the Lake Within the Gorges. This knowledge impelled a group of engineers to examine the impact the inundation might have on the dam. Would flooding the caverns—no one knew just how deep they went—trigger earthquakes? Might Ba Mountain collapse, causing a massive tidal wave? The scientists put a positive spin on these possibilities, but David was glad he wouldn't be living downstream. In the meantime, every day the river saw more luxury cruise ships for tourists who were plying the waters between Chongqing and Wuhan for a last-chance view of the Three Gorges.

On Hulan's last day in Bashan, she met with Vice Minister Zai on the veranda outside the guesthouse's dining room. It was a beautiful day. Sun filtered through the bamboo, and the koi pond glistened. Zai, who'd arrived once the weather cleared, congratulated her on her success. He praised her for upholding virtue and compassion, eliminating those who destroyed order, and stamping out corruption. He reminded her that the excesses of the past could not be repeated or else, like previous dynasties, this one too would collapse.

"Remember that the slogans of Mao and Deng are not so different from those of any ruler," Zai said. "Remember that the first Xia Dynasty collapsed through corruption."

But by now she'd learned something about her nation's history. Powerful slogans and great monuments did transcend time. Mao had understood this very well, but so had Confucius, who'd compiled the *Shu Ching* from many sources, and Qinshihuangdi, who'd built the Great Wall. What Zai and the men who controlled him had forgotten was that corruption comes in many forms. Building a dam—no matter how many patriotic slogans were used—wouldn't divert the masses from the truth forever.

"A monument doesn't make an empire," Hulan told him.

"You're right, Xiao Hulan," Zai agreed, summoning up the diminutive he'd used with her when she was a child. "But it does encourage an atmosphere of political enthusiasm and harnesses it at the same time. This leads to stability. Without stability, nothing can be achieved and successes attained will be lost."

"The problem with nationalist sentiment," Hulan responded, "is that it focuses attention on leadership."

"Again you are right," Zai said, obviously pleased by her understanding. "If we are unable to meet the people's expectations, we may find, to use an old expression, that in promoting nationalism, we have 'mounted a tiger that cannot easily be dismounted.'"

Hulan and Zai quietly considered this as doves cooed and wind blew gently through the stand of bamboo.

"We have entered a new century," Zai went on. "If you go back to the end of the nineteenth century, Britain still thought it ruled the world, but it was on its last legs. Go to the end of the twentieth century and America thought it ruled the world, but I believe it's on its last legs and doesn't realize it. Outsiders once called our country a sleeping dragon. That dragon has awakened. This will be China's century. As the Great Helmsman said, the east wind will prevail over the west wind. You understand all of this, Hulan, because you are Chinese—"

"You've often accused me of not being Chinese enough." She felt her courage waver for an instant, then she said, "I have a facility to understand the frailty of human nature. You sent me out here—"

"Because we have friends abroad and friends at the site who told us a trusted presence was required. Li Guo, the one they call a vulture, is a true patriot. For years he has kept the Ministry of Public Security apprised of Dr. Ma's activities on behalf of State Security."

"Li must also have told you that Brian had found the *ruyi*—"

"And that the boy was somehow involved with the All-Patriotic Society."

"Why didn't you tell me this before you sent me here?"

"Following traditional leads had not helped you bring down the cult," Zai explained. "I thought that letting you use your best gift—your intuition—might get a better result."

"I don't think so," she said. "You didn't send me here to find Xiao

Da. You sent me here because I've always been susceptible to the powerful and to indoctrination. I've always followed the wind, and you gambled that Xiao Da would find me."

Zai had no response for this. How could he when she spoke the truth?

"You know my failings, and you've played upon them very well," she continued sadly.

But the concerns of one individual were of minor interest to Zai when the philosophical conflicts between Zhu Rongji and Li Peng—and the Ministry of State Security and the Ministry of Public Security—were being played out in Beijing, where what mattered were issues such as how the dam would proceed and would a Confucian or Taoist methodology be followed, where consideration had to be given to how China would approach the United States about Michael Quon, his involvement in the All-Patriotic Society, and what he had attempted to do with VYRUSCAN at the Three Gorges Dam. Trying to control the masses was one thing; trying to destroy the dam was quite another.

A deliberately defective version of VYRUSCAN—the program that had made Quon so wealthy—had been located in the Three Gorges Dam's computerized safety system. Michael Quon had broken many of his many tenets, but perhaps this was the most insidious of all. He had used dreaded "Confucian" technology to try to disrupt the dam's systems so that the river might run free again and he could solidify his position as a religious and political leader. *He who controls the waters . . .*

"The bombing of the embassy in Yugoslavia and the downing of the American spy plane pale in comparison to this scandal," Zai said, "but is it worth political chest beating on either side of the Pacific? Is it worth tapping into the U.S.'s worst xenophobic fears about spies and terrorism at a time when our two countries need to work together to fight both of these threats? And what if worming versions of VYRUSCAN have been implanted either narrowly or broadly in the States? China's future hinges on the U.S. staying economically strong for a while longer."

Perhaps even more important, Hulan thought, was it worth riling up the masses to let them know of Michael Quon's demonic acts against China? Was it worth more anti-American demonstrations? Or would this knowledge merely provoke unwanted questions about the dam's vulnerability and the leadership's vincibility?

"But why do we talk about all this?" Zai asked lightly. "What matters is that you and David are happy again. We will all go home to Beijing, and everything will be the same."

"It will never be the same," Hulan said. "I loved you like a father, but you were willing to risk our lives—"

"Nothing happened to you, and we have had a happy result," he said reassuringly, but his features were filled with pain and remorse.

She turned her face away from him. He stood up, and with his fingers he gently lifted her chin. "Whatever decisions you make, know that I will always love you," he said. "Good-bye, daughter." With that he walked away. She was unsure if she would ever see him again.

Hulan got a ride out to Site 518 with Officer Ge Fei, who was now the highest-ranking policeman in Bashan's Public Security Bureau. On the way, she reflected on some other aspects of the case. Stuart Miller didn't get to be a big public hero; however, people in power noted his role in all this and he'd been quietly given a medal in gratitude for his efforts to aid China, while his company was awarded several very lucrative state projects. Captain Hom, by contrast, became a true Chinese hero. Hom had wanted desperately to protect the people of Bashan, but the government now used his death for very different reasons. He was being held up as an exemplar of socialist behavior in the same category as martyrs like Lei Feng and Liu Hulan. Tales of his childhood were being collected for a picture book, while a small volume of his sayings was already being rushed to press by a publisher in Chongqing. Thanks to Captain Hom, all across the country posters for the All-Patriotic Society had been painted out, Internet connections cut, and phrases like "Be reverent" (an admonition first spoken by Emperor Yao forty-three hundred years ago) removed from daily discourse. Fortunately for Hom's extended family, his brother-in-law's life and death had "disappeared." Nothing could be allowed to mar the propaganda value gained by Hom's death.

Hulan arrived at Site 518, found David, and together they passed among clusters of people to say good-bye. Then Hulan and David walked out past the Wu house and down the path until they reached the little beach that had been Brian's refuge. The river had calmed and lowered. The cliffs that soared above the current were now covered with trash at the high-water mark: plastic bags suspended on jagged rocks, bottles jammed into the tangle of roots, clothing twisted, torn, and flapping on inaccessible precipices. All of these things would stay where they were until time wore them out, wind ripped them away, or the next flood washed them to sea. Hulan had great faith in the river's persistence. It might be slowed, but it would never stop.

Hulan let all of her regrets come into her mind. She thought about the way she had denounced her father during the Cultural Revolution and how his time in a labor camp had changed him into a killer. She had been a child then who didn't know any better, and now she took her regrets about everything that had happened as a result of her actions and tossed them into the river. She thought about her mother and let all of Jinli's suffering float away on a little wave. Hulan thought about the women in the Knight factory and understood in a way she couldn't allow herself to before that she had saved more lives than had been lost. She wrapped those mothers and daughters in love and released them into the current. She conjured up the woman she had shot on the square and knew in her heart that she had saved that little girl. They too drifted out of sight. She remembered Hom—his bravery and the terrible pain he'd endured—then let him peacefully swirl and ripple away. Hulan had tried to save all of them, and she forgave herself for the ones she couldn't. Finally, Hulan let her daughter come fully into her heart. The tragedy of Chaowen's death could never be forgotten, but Hulan could honor her by loving her and her father forever.

Hulan looked up into David's eyes. She saw in them unconditional, unending love. During these last few days, David and Hulan had talked about moving back to Los Angeles. They had also discussed trying to get pregnant again—not to replace Chaowen but to create the family they needed, wanted, and deserved. Hulan truly believed they had a chance at happiness. She squeezed David's hand, and wordlessly they began the long journey home.

AUTHOR'S NOTE

CHINA AND THE YANGZI RIVER HAVE BEEN MUCH WRITTEN ABOUT.
I am particularly indebted to the multivolume *Science and Civilization in China* by Joseph Needham and *Shu Ching: Book of History* (a modernized edition by Clae Waltham of the translation by James Legge). For those who are interested in life on the river, I highly recommend *The River at the Center of the World* by Simon Winchester, *River Town* by Peter Hessler, *A Single Pebble* by John Hersey, and *Golden Inches* by Grace Service. For those wishing to visit the Three Gorges, don't forget to pack *The Yangzi River*, a brilliant guide by Judy Bonavia, and *Yangtze River: The Wildest, Wickedest River on the Earth*, an anthology of poetry and other writings compiled and edited by Madeleine Lynn. For those intrigued by the Chinese language, Dr. Léon Wieger's *Chinese Characters* is amazing (if you can find it), Oliver Moore's *Reading the Past* is a lovely introduction to the subject, and Cecilia Lindqvist's *China: Empire of Living Symbols* is both informative and fun. For those who wish to learn more about the impact the Three Gorges Dam will have on the river, the activist Dai Qing has put together a powerful warning in *The River Dragon Has Come*. The International Rivers Network's website also offers a wide range of articles from all over the world on issues surrounding the dam. All of these sources have influenced and informed *Dragon Bones*.

Dragon Bones benefited greatly from the help of several people affiliated with museums. June Li at the Los Angeles County Museum of Art found and translated supplemental information for me on the history of the *ruyi* and *gui,* which Brian McCarthy and other characters in *Dragon Bones* warped for their own purposes. David Kamansky and William Hanbury-Tenison of the Pacific Asia Museum were delightfully knowledgeable about the international trade in stolen artifacts, provenance, and the darker side of auction house business practices. Anne Shih's Forbidden City exhibition with the giant *lingzhi* at the Bowers Museum of Cultural Art made an obvious impression on me, and Anne was most gracious in sharing her expertise. I also had the privilege of working with Michael Duchemin at the Autry Museum of Western Heritage on the "On Gold Mountain" exhibition for six years. He taught me a lot about the ethos and ethics of museums.

Floridia Cheung let me borrow her Chinese name for Chaowen. David Humphrey gave me more information on the *lingzhi,* while the art historian Lydia Thompson made a crucial *bi* correction. Steve Wasserman sent me a wonderful collection of photographs of the Yangzi and the dam site at a moment when I was feeling blue. Andrew Tsao made me laugh with tales of his naughty childhood. Michael Firth of Linklaters offered advice on the Hong Kong legal system. Ge-Qun Wang, an inveterate bachelor, passed on information about marriage procedures in China, while Henry Tang of the Committee of 100 opened many doors for me. Patty Williams took another beautiful author photograph.

I'm very lucky to have people who write to me through my website from all over the world. Special thanks go out to three of them: Terry Hardison, who sent me some lovely lines from Du Fu; Alice Lu, who offered wonderful insights into David's character; and Dave Feagans, whose jokes and anecdotes have given me daily encouragement. In addition to these cyberspace friends, there are others who have been invaluable. Kate Cooney and Andy Wohlwend did a lot of legwork, while Alicia Diaz kept life running smoothly. In China, I offer innumerable thanks to all of the people who got me to the places I needed to see, provided extra translation, and told me their stories in the most openhearted way.

I'm deeply grateful to my agent, Sandra Dijkstra, and all of the wonderful people in her office who work so hard on my behalf. My Random House editor, Bob Loomis, is a true gentleman—smart, kind, an absolute pleasure to work with. At Random House in England, Kate Parkin's enthusiasm for *Dragon Bones* was deep, lasting, and profound.

I'm very lucky to have a family that supports my projects. I'd like to thank my cousin Leslee Leong for her advice on the business of selling Asian antiques and for letting me borrow a $24,000 *ruyi* to use in my author photo. My gratitude also extends to her husband, Joe Schulman, for spending time with me at auctions and for giving me the inside skinny on what goes on at them. Thanks as well to my father, Richard See, for getting "lost" on Bali (and to "our man on Bali" for not finding him). My father and his wife, Anne Jennings, both anthropologists, also offered the expertise of their fields. My grandparents Stella and Eddy See not only instilled in me a love of China and Chinese antiques but also left me their incredible collection of antiquarian books on both subjects. I have quizzed my husband, Richard Kendall, on things such as Chinese law, American legal ethics, and what he'd do if he'd just returned to his hotel room in the middle of a typhoon after being beaten up and left for dead over something that could alter contemporary Chinese history. My sister Clara Sturak is a great editor and a great inspiration to me; my brother-in-law Chris Chandler always saves the day when my computer acts up; my mother, Carolyn See, is a daily example; my sons, Alexander and Christopher, are my best advocates, offering both motivation and enlightenment. Thank you!

A final word on the story: Although there are numerous archaeological sites in the Three Gorges related to the Ba people, Site 518 does not exist. The village of Bashan is a melding of several towns in the gorges. The weather and subsequent flooding in the novel are based on actual events that transpired in the summers of 1996 and 1998. To the best of my knowledge, all statistics on the dam, resettlement, and the great storm of 1975 are accurate. A giant mush-room was found in Oregon in 2000, but so far China has not found a fungus to match it. The All-Patriotic Society does not exist, but the *Shu Ching,* from which Xiao Da liberally developed his tenets and slogans, does. The martyr Liu Hulan was a real person; however, ar-chaeological proof has yet to be found for the existence of Da Yu. All errors—and fabrications—are my own.

ABOUT THE AUTHOR

LISA SEE's first book, *On Gold Mountain*, a memoir/
history of her Chinese American family, was a *New
York Times* Notable Book and national bestseller. The
book became the basis for an opera produced by the
Los Angeles Opera and an exhibition that traveled to
the Smithsonian Institution. *Dragon Bones* is the
third in a series featuring the characters Liu Hulan
and David Stark. Lisa See lives in Los Angeles with
her husband and their two sons. You can find out
more by visiting her website: www.LisaSee.com.

ABOUT THE TYPE

This book was set in Fairfield, the first typeface from the hand of the distinguished American artist and engraver Rudolph Ruzicka (1883–1978). In its structure Fairfield displays the sober and sane qualities of the master craftsman whose talent has long been dedicated to clarity. It is this trait that accounts for the trim grace and vigor, the spirited design and sensitive balance, of this original typeface.

Rudolph Ruzicka was born in Bohemia and came to America in 1894. He set up his own shop, devoted to wood engraving and printing, in New York in 1913 after a varied career working as a wood engraver, in photoengraving and banknote printing plants, and as an art director and freelance artist. He designed and illustrated many books, and was the creator of a considerable list of individual prints—wood engravings, line engravings on copper, and aquatints.